WINDWARD

S. Kaeth

Published by:
Hakea Media
350 W 6th St #932
Dubuque, IA 52004
hakeamedia@gmail.com
www.hakeamedia.com

Paperback ISBN-13: 978-1-955220-02-6
Ebook ISBN-13: 978-1-7333281-1-1

Cover by Dave Brasgalla
Author's website: www.skaeth.com

<u>*Content Warning:*</u>
Includes descriptions of combat, framing, jealousy, gaslighting, death of a loved one, and unequal power dynamics.

To my lovey. You know why.

Chapter One

The sky was theirs.

Palon leaned forward, peering around Windward's line of neck spines as the dragon banked hard. Far below, the series of green valleys surrounded by sheer cliff faces rotated to her side as they turned. This was life as it was meant to be.

Twisting, Palon stole a glance behind.

The four walavaim were still in close pursuit, giant winged felids each nearly five times as big as she was. They were still smaller than Windward, but that didn't matter much since their teeth were almost the same size. As if responding to her thought, the lead walavai wrinkled his broad muzzle in a snarl, revealing curved yellow fangs.

"They're catching up!" she yelled to Windward. She didn't need to talk, but it felt more natural. Information was instantly translated along their bond, so the real trick was keeping things from him.

Windward rumbled, belching fire at their pursuers. His possessiveness beat like a drum in her skull as he clutched his meal tighter to his belly, his shoulders hunching. The freshly killed herdbeast was theirs.

The dragons had confined the large herbivores to the bowl-shaped valleys generations ago, allowing them easy access to prey that had grown fat in havens of dragon design. All the herdbeasts were theirs, no matter what the thieving walavaim thought.

Windward looked back, one golden eye locking on to her. Though expressions were difficult to form with a scaly reptilian face, Palon's years of experience reading every whisper of emotion he showed told her all she needed to know.

She tightened her hold on her harness and he dove again, spinning as he dropped. The wind snatched at her, tearing her hair loose from her braids and whipping tears of cold from her eyes. Ground and sky turned in a dizzying tunnel around her while she struggled to keep an eye on the walavaim. The leather straps cut into her numbed fingers, and her blood roared in her ears as the wind stole away her breath. A familiar elation filled her as she and Windward pit their skills against those of the walavaim. The edges of her vision were beginning to dim when Windward leveled out, flying low in the opposite direction into the nearby canyon.

Palon blinked furiously as her vision returned, now that she could breathe. She twisted, looking back again. "They're still with us! You've got to do better than that."

His indignation flared in her mind, and she grinned at him, teeth bared to the chill wind.

This was far from her first flight; she and Windward made a team of such prowess walavaim should tremble at the very sight of them.

Windward roared his appreciation of her thought, and Palon sent him the current positions of the walavaim. He surged upward, his long curved horns slashing through the air on either side of her as he strained for altitude. Adjusting the herdbeast again in his claws, Windward veered sharply toward the canyon walls.

"Can you handle the food and fly at the same time?" Palon teased.

He bristled in her mind, chiding her to focus on her task while he kept them alive and unharmed.

"Shift now!" Palon said. Before they got too close.

A negative, so emphatic she blinked at its force, was his reply. There was no arguing with a dragon.

Palon patted his body scales, smooth and hard like pebbles beneath her hand, still damp with condensed moisture from flying through a cloud earlier. The contest was what she lived for, the thrill of flight, herself and Windward against the walavaim. Shading her eyes, she focused on the cliffs high above them.

More movement above, as she'd feared. "Another, ready to drop!"

Windward swerved, tail lashing behind him as he shoved off the rock face with his hind feet. Enormous claws ripped through the air by her head, grazing her harness as she laid herself low along Windward's neck spines. Palon checked the hand-thick straps. Her last two flying harnesses had been shredded by walavaim claws, but this thickened one should make it for the flight back, probably, assuming no more near misses.

An enormous red walavai on their right roared, rancid breath choking her. Her ears rang and she swayed with the hammer of noise. The walavai's territoriality washed over her, roiling with Windward's. The telepathic chaos as walavai and dragon shouted at each other sparked rising nausea. Her dragon's side of the conversation thrummed through their bond, along with his reactions to the walavai's accusations. Palon bared her teeth in rage when the walavai had the audacity to name Windward a thief.

Struggling to focus despite the ruckus, she twisted to watch her dragon's exposed side. Sure enough, a smaller tawny walavai shot upward toward them from the left and a black one from behind, all working together to herd them toward where the walavai above was waiting to drop on them.

Steadying herself on the spine before her, Palon tried to look for the last walavai below, but couldn't see around Windward's bulk. It was too dangerous to lean out too far with the walavai pack mobbing them.

She clutched the leather straps of her harness as Windward rolled and belched a plume of fire. One of the walavaim fell away, twisting with superb flexibility to clamp down on Windward's hind leg with his broad jaw. A stab of pain shot through Palon's foot, a shadow of Windward's own, gone almost as soon as it appeared.

Windward bellowed, ducking his head to bite the walavai, and Palon screamed her fury. Dragon and walavai tumbled through the sky, hampering each other's wingbeats in their struggle.

The red one closed in from the side. Palon tore a dagger from her suit and flung it at the walavai. As their enemy dodged, Windward's wing struck him, sending the felid tumbling. A fierce grin spread across Palon's face.

Another walavai slammed into them, sharp claws raking long lines in Windward's scales. The impact sent Palon hurtling over the edge, snatching her hands close to her chest as she fell to avoid tangling. Her teeth slammed shut on each other as she hit the end of the tether, crashing into Windward's scales moments later. She hung there, black and red filling her vision. Her nose burned as she floundered, recovering her bearings, while Windward twisted and turned violently beside her.

Palon reached painfully above her, sparks filling her vision as she moved her head. She couldn't see down here, couldn't help him. Hand over hand, she dragged herself up his side. She had to climb the tether quickly to secure her position so she wasn't distracting Windward, so she wasn't flying loose in the wind. No dragonbonded flew for long if they were dead weight on a rope.

Windward couldn't flame the walavai, not with her in the way, but he did blast a stream of fire toward one of the others.

Finally, Palon reached her usual perch, hastening to tuck her hands in the straps. The moment she was secured, Windward folded his wings, rotating close to the cliff's wall and belching flame at their pursuers as he plummeted. Just before they hit the sandy basin at the cliff's base, Windward snapped open his wings again, streaming along the canyon bottom. The walavaim were more agile, but the dragons were faster, especially Windward. The red and tawny walavaim both dove half-heartedly after them, but the pack soon veered off.

Palon let out a breath, watching them fade to black specks in the distance while her dragon labored to gain more height.

Windward cautioned her to hold on. Now that things were calmer, he could concentrate properly. They were going to Shift.

Palon obeyed instantly, stilling her mind and closing her eyes, her own little habit for these things. It was far too disconcerting to see the land transform into an entirely different place as the dragon jumped from one realm to another.

Fierce winds beat at her, slicking her skin with moisture as they lifted her in the harness. The straps creaked with the strain. Her chest spasmed, unable to draw in any air. Serenity filled her, regardless of the struggles of her body. Windward had her. They took care of each other. They always had.

Abruptly, she could breathe again. No longer caught by the wind, she dropped onto one of Windward's spines. She crawled back to her seat, gulping down air. Windward's wings stretched wide on either side of her as he glided lower. The cliffs and barren sandscape had been replaced by boulder-dotted green meadows and dense tree cluttered mounds: Stonefield, the northwestern region of their island home of Rinara.

Fatigue tinged Palon's mind, a brush from Windward. He dipped his head to grab the herdbeast from his forelegs, and they landed heavily on a hilltop. Windward's gait lurched unevenly as he slowed to a stop, and Palon patted his scales, a concerned frown tightening her lips. He dropped to the lush grass, sides heaving as he curled his long tail around himself and his prey. Palon unhooked herself from the safety straps and slid down, careful of his wounds and of the rocks hidden in the grass.

While Windward regained his breath, Palon walked around him to catalogue his wounds. Several slashes marred his scales, though the tear on his side was only matched in severity by the long gash down his left hind leg. She winced at it, grateful Windward kept his pain mostly private. It was a dragon thing, hiding pain and injuries. Of course, all the bonded knew that if they ever felt the full force of their dragons' pains they'd surely go insane, just as Naros had.

When Palon had been a newly bonded, the dragon Catbane had fallen to the walavaim, though he'd managed to Shift himself and his bonded back to Rinara and land before he died. But afterwards, Catbane's bonded, Naros, had alternated between wandering blindly, standing catatonic, and screaming in psychotic terror and rage. He was a broken man, irreparably damaged from his ordeal, even though he had only been thirty-five. Windward had explained that when Catbane died, his telepathic barriers failed, and Naros for a brief moment had shared the great dragon's torment.

She shivered, though the sun was warm on her skin. Windward watched her, his golden eyes amused as he shared her memory. And then, the lower lid rose and the upper lid drooped, leaving only a crack of gold in the middle, and he laid his head down on the ground, tilting so she could see a scrape on his nose.

Palon shook herself and pulled the container of healing salve from an inner pocket of her riding jacket. The big wounds might scar, but that didn't matter, so long as they healed.

"Did you have to antagonize them so much?" she muttered, rubbing the sticky goop into the scales of his nose.

The thrill of the challenge filled her, the pleasure of catching the walavaim lurking, and the success of drawing them out during their patrol.

She worked through Windward's answer, breathing slowly to control her rage at the damage the walavaim had done as she moved toward his side. "You just ate two days ago."

He sent her a swirl of memory, color, and emotion. Starting a fight with the walavaim allowed him to draw them out of their craggy warrens and injure them.

"It was good we went on patrol today." She nodded, working along one jagged edge of the rip in Windward's side. "The walavaim should stay clear for a time while they lick their wounds. The older dragons won't have to worry about being harassed by the filthy thieves."

There was a bit of chagrin to Windward's next thought. He hadn't expected the pack to be so large.

She wrinkled her nose, fury surging in her as she worked on the other side of the wound. The pack loitering by the dragons' herdbeast pastures was bad enough. Even worse, they'd dared injure Windward.

He flinched, admonishment blasting through her along their bond.

Apologizing, Palon lightened her touch on his damaged scales, carefully tending his leg. She tucked the salve away again and walked around him, inspecting him critically as she stretched the soreness from her back, stiff from hunching against the wind. She flexed and extended her fingers repeatedly, aching from hanging on to the harness so long against such forces. The harness needed mending, but it could wait until they were home. At least they were safe now. Nothing in Rinara could hurt a dragon.

Behind her, Windward pinned the carcass with one huge clawed foot, shearing meat free from the bone in large bites with his crystalline, serrated teeth. The smell of blood filled her nostrils, both real and along their bond, and she felt as well as heard the crunch of the bones.

Palon approached, searching the remnants of the carcass for a suitable piece of meat. The dragon teased her—she, so small and soft, unafraid next to his powerful jaws.

"Well of course," she said. "Even eating, you're not *that* clumsy."

Windward lowered his muzzle to her level and snorted. The salty gust of wind sent her reeling backward. Recovering her balance, she raised her eyebrows and folded her arms. But then Windward bent his neck again, and she couldn't help admiring how his purple-grey scales gleamed in the sunlight.

His amusement, pride, and chiding washed over her, and she snorted. "I should have known better than to feed your vanity."

Haughty agreement came through their bond, and Palon laughed, ripping free a chunk of meat that he hadn't slobbered on too much yet.

"Would you mind?" she asked, tossing it into the air.

He blasted it with a belch of fire, and she let the grass sizzle where it landed while she picked some edible flowers to munch. She slid the meat along the grass to wipe off the sticky remnants of the dragonfire, then picked it up, tossing it from hand to hand to avoid burning her fingers. Tearing into it with relish, she chewed and swallowed as fast as she could. She was ravenous, suddenly.

Suspicious, she raised her eyebrows at Windward; he sometimes sent her hunger just to toy with her. Windward watched her, tearing off another leg and gulping it down, as she ate—he still found it amusing, even after ten years being bonded, that she ate plants "like a herdbeast". She smirked, chewing exaggeratedly, but he only shook out his neck spines and nudged his snout through the remains of their meal.

Finishing her lunch, Palon checked the sun for time of day. After such a meal, Windward would want a nap to sleep it off, even without his wounded leg. He turned away as if on cue and laid down, resting his head on a spongy patch of turf.

Palon poked him hard in the snout, though she would hurt her finger long before she'd hurt his plate-like scales. "Sleep it off at home, lazy."

He lifted his head and tilted it to look down on her. Then he laid his head back down and shut his eyes.

"There's no good basking spots here," Palon said.

Windward continued to shut her out.

Palon scowled at him, tapping her foot. The idea of sitting here waiting while her dragon rested felt onerous. The herdbeast hide needed to be readied for the trip back, but far too much energy thrummed inside of her. She would attend to that task later. Turning away, she set off across the craggy terrain, picking a boulder at random and walking toward it, then another, then another. Windward had once told her that the huge uplifted stones were the remains of a dwarven kingdom, but they belonged to the fae now, who lived under the mounds. Palon's nose wrinkled and she sneered. Another reason for them to leave this place quickly.

Keeping alert for fae—or any other living thing for that matter—she continued to loop a wide circle around her dragon. Windward was fierce and more than a match for any creature in Rinara, but with him tired and injured she still felt the need to check for potential dangers. All she found was a handful of feathers, which she scooped into a pocket for Aturadin; her mate would be delighted to add them to his collection.

As she completed her loop, a glimmer caught her eye—sunlight flashing off a slight uplifting of the lush green land. She swerved toward it, gripped by curiosity. Nestled near the base of a thick patch of moss, a smooth, sharply-angled stone gleamed, as if someone had encased clouds and moonlight in glass. Among the smooth grey and brown stones underneath the moss, it was distinctive and beautiful.

Palon caught her breath, circling around it at a distance. She *had* to have that rock. The need arose in her, an obsession none the weaker for having been so suddenly born. But in fae land, it was always safest to be paranoid. The fae loved their traps, and there was no love lost between them and dragons. A dragonbonded caught unawares in a filthy fae trap would be a disgrace.

She tightened her loops, creeping closer and closer, but found no traps, no hidden watchers, nothing. Palon dropped to her belly and tried to peer beneath it without touching it. Still nothing. She sat back into a kneeling position, then rose to a crouch. Snatching it, she took off at a sprint.

Nothing happened, and Palon smiled, slowing to a jog. It was hard to believe it'd been that easy, but she wasn't going to complain. Caution was good if it kept you alive, and finding no danger was better than finding any, even if you were prepared.

Raising it to the sunlight, she examined the crystal that filled her hand. So smooth, so brilliant, it had a pleasing weight to it. It would make a wonderful addition to her collection. Glee rose in her until she practically vibrated with it, struggling to contain herself. She'd found a beautiful rose quartz earlier this morning too. It was rare luck to find two such extraordinary additions to her collection in the same day. Pausing before cresting the small ridge separating her from Windward, she slipped her new find into an inner pocket of her jacket.

The dragon shifted, opening one eye as she neared. With a tilt of his head, he sent her an inquiry about what she found.

Palon bared her teeth. "It's mine."

It was useless to deny that she'd found something, but dragons loved shiny things, an instinct that spilled through the telepathic bond to their dragonbonded. Exactly how the compulsion manifested varied from one to another, but all bonded collected something, and each was as intensely territorial of their collection as the dragons were about theirs. She understood his drive, his curiosity, but if she showed Windward the stone, he might take it from her. He collected rocks too.

Windward raised his head, and her mind was filled with his laughter.

Relaxing her shoulders, she approached to put another coat of salve on his wounds, then pester him to go home. She reached into her riding jacket for the container, careful not to inadvertently show her find. The hair on the back of her neck prickled, and she turned to find him peering over her shoulder. Glaring at him, she jabbed her elbow into his snout. She tugged her jacket straight and shoved his nose away.

He raised his head, opening his jaws slightly to display his teeth, and she squared her shoulders and returned his open-mouth display with one of her own.

His laughter resounded in her mind as he withdrew from her minuscule threat. Hooking her jacket closed again, she held the small container of salve in one hand as she folded her arms.

He showed her his view: how ridiculous her threat display was with her feeble and tiny teeth. Her light blue eyes gleamed like jewels, hair like the prairie grasses in autumn sticking up from her braids, her face scraped up and reddened on one side, even through the deep brown of her skin. She didn't even reach to the top of his head, tiny thing, but pride reverberated from him.

Palon pushed him away mentally, though it was a bit like a gnat pushing at a boulder. "I'm your bonded. You won't hurt me."

The dragon focused on the bruise blooming on her face. Regret hummed in him as she gingerly prodded her cheekbone, brow, and chin, aided by his image of her. She would probably have a nasty black eye, and that side of her face was tender and bruised, but she didn't think anything was broken. She'd be fine in a few days.

She smiled. "Alright, you insufferable, overgrown lizard. You won't hurt me on purpose."

Windward rested his head on the ground, so near her that the soft scales of his chin touched her boot. Reaching up high, she stroked the smaller scales around his eye, and he turned his head, angling sideways so she could reach higher. The dragon sent her affirmation, along with a brief thread of affection and his thought of her as a prize among dragonbonded, fearless and loyal.

She slapped the broad, hard scales of his snout. "You're melting, you great sap. Are you finished napping?"

She had a prize, too, and she was eager to see it safe in her collection. For answer, he snorted, blowing her backward again.

Her thoughts filled with her new find, she checked his injuries, then hastily scraped the large sections of herdbeast hide clean so they could bring it home.

Once the hide was bundled, Windward trudged to the top of a hill. Palon scrambled up to her usual perch between two of his large neck spines and snapped on the safety hooks. He stretched his wings, flaring the thin leathery membrane, and took a deep breath, his sides expanding. Exhaling, he lumbered into a gallop down the hill. Palon leaned low over his shoulders, minimizing her drag and matching the contract-relax cycle of his muscles.

The dragon leaped into the air, his back arching and tail lashing as he strained to become airborne. He landed, limping and lurching with his injured leg, and Palon rubbed his scales in sympathy and encouragement, the only help she could offer him at the moment. Lumbering up to speed once more, he crested another hill, this one too small, but he galloped down it, his neck outstretched, his wings straining for lift. Palon wrinkled her nose, wincing at his uneven, wounded stride.

He'd chosen his resting spot well. Wide open areas abounded along with hills to help a dragon become airborne, even a young dragon like Windward. Older dragons needed high drop-offs to gain flight and therefore rarely flew. The very thought of not being able to fly anymore sent shivers down her spine. She enjoyed the wind in her face and the new sights far too much to have to be home all the time.

Windward leaped, hit ground, and leaped again. On the third launch, he gained lift, flapping laboriously until he found a thermal where he circled, relief and exhaustion tingeing the bond. They rose until the land looked small beneath them, lighter green areas spotted with the darker green of forests and decorated with the spindly blue of rivers. Just above them rushed the Airstream, where the winds blasted across the land, too strong for anything—even a dragon—to fly in.

Tilting his wings, Windward left the thermal, gliding for the range of jagged grey peaks capped with snow and glistening like jewels in the afternoon sun. The ledges and huge caverns there were home to the dragons. Other species also lived in the mountains, but dragons cared little about them, so long as they didn't trespass and bother the dragon nests. The little races lived only a brief time in the sun, too brief to get invested in for the most part.

Of course, the dragonbonded were the exception to this rule.

The massive slab of granite that served as the entrance to their dragon nest appeared before them among the other peaks, jutting out as a ledge perfect for landing. Jagged stone spires rose up around the edges of their nest where young dragons climbed to catch the sun. The mountain's slope formed a wall that shielded the bonded as a windbreak, as well as forming the entrance to a system of caves. And on the larger slabs of stone, adult dragons basked. All efforts made by vegetation to colonize the area were promptly eradicated by dragons moving around, stomping the green growths out.

Other nests dotted the mountains too, but dragons from other nests rarely intermingled—dragons were fiercely territorial.

Windward's wings flared, catching the wind to slow them, his tail helping to counter-balance as he tried not to limp on his injured leg. He landed, and Palon unclipped herself and slid down Windward's side as he walked between the natural pillars of stone into a wide, shallow basin ringed by numerous basking platforms. She landed in a deep crouch without him ever having to break his stride.

From one of the ledges, a dragon whistled, welcoming them home. Another dragon trumpeted, picking up the call, and another, with Windward blasting a call of his own in answer. It was good to be home. Palon smiled, listening to the voices as she walked further into the nest. That call was from Skyward, that one from Dusks Dive... Her smile grew. That one was Scorch Frost, which meant...

Aturadin burst out of one of the tunnels that opened onto the basking platform, greeting Windward as he passed by. With a grin, Palon embraced her mate. His slender arms encircled her, pressing her against him briefly with the strength concealed in his lithe frame. His face held a broad smile, his deep brown eyes alight, and he'd braided his shoulder-length black hair up into a dragon-like crest.

Scorch Frost must have passed along the message of their arrival to Aturadin. While by and large the dragons ignored friendships, enmities, and other relationships among the bonded, they couldn't help but take an interest in the relationships that were meaningful to their own.

"How was the patrol?" Aturadin asked.

"Caught a walavai pack of five. They injured Windward some, and I need to check my harness."

"Nothing so exciting here, although High Flight is gone."

Palon groaned. "I hope he doesn't do anything stupid."

Windward's chiding blasted through her, and she lowered her head, submitting to the correction. Dragon doings were dragon doings, as bonded business was bonded business.

Aturadin grinned at her, leaning in to whisper, "I feel the same way."

Laughter escaped her at the look of chagrin that passed his face shortly after.

"Your bonded looks a little battered, Windward!" Standing high above them on one of the ledges bordering the basking area, Laetiran gave a wide grin, his white teeth flashing. Tall for a bonded, with strong features, he seemed to always be smiling.

Palon narrowed her eyes at Laetiran, dizzy with the rage boiling off her dragon. Resentment filled him at the implication he hadn't adequately cared for her. She cut off her retort, seeing Tsían approaching. He was the leader of the bonded now, since the highest ranking dragon was currently unbonded. Tsían frowned, sweeping the dust from his leather riding jacket as he looked them over, and she lowered her gaze, as suited her place in the hierarchy.

"Palon, you must tend your dragon and then yourself. How did you come to be injured?"

Annoyance pricked at her. "We were attacked by a pack of walavaim. I slipped. The harness held." She smiled at that victory, puffing up with pride. She'd been working for months to improve her harness.

Glancing upward, her smile vanished. Tsían had bared his teeth. "I have told you to keep the straps shorter."

Lowering her head again, Palon gathered her harness as Windward wiggled out of it. "I like to be able to move around. It's a risk we knowingly take."

Tsían hissed. "Take better care of yourself."

Palon stepped back, fingers twitching. She couldn't react to the threat. Tsían was only reflecting the dragons' agitation; Silver Spine, the oldest, was dying, and it made all the dragons snappish, flowing through to the bonded. So she and Windward had taken to flying every chance they got.

"Tend your dragon," Tsían said, his speech even more crisp than usual.

Aturadin squeezed her shoulder as Tsían stalked off, and he grabbed the hide from where it had fallen to the ground. "Here, I'll help you."

Palon nodded and they walked toward Windward's private cave, where he kept his collection. Through the years and occasional injuries, Windward had never allowed her to bandage him in the open —dragons hated showing weakness. The dragon's back swished back and forth as he crawled over the basking places and under a magnificent natural arch of red stone. It was weathered to a polished sheen and served as a transition to the more private areas of the nest.

As they cleared the arch, Windward sent her an abrupt warning. She grabbed Aturadin's arm, shoving him back and away as Windward reared back, wings flared. Fired Sand, Laetiran's dragon, lunged into the path with a hiss. Gaping a threat at him, Windward limped and hopped on his injured hindfoot.

Fired Sand's display put Windward's to shame, his wings and body steady as he held himself upright, russet scales gleaming, set off by his tan markings. He exuded power and strength, and humiliation burned in Palon.

She followed Aturadin as he dashed for the viewing ledges: large open-sided stone slabs specially cut for bonded to be out of the way for dragon business. Ignoring the steps on the side, they scrambled up the coarse rope netting that draped the grey stone's front face. When riding dragons, one never knew when one might have to unexpectedly bail.

Windward roared, the vibrations causing her teeth to chatter. His claws scraped on the stone as he lashed his tail. Fired Sand trumpeted, puffing up even larger.

Filled with Windward's annoyance, Palon almost hoped Windward would challenge Fired Sand—he deserved it. Blocking archway access was the least of his rude behaviors, and the two dragons had been nursing their grudges for a long time. Both were about the same age and size and of similar rank. But dragons rarely actually fought. When dragons fought, mountains wept. She had no desire to witness such an event, particularly not so close, and certainly not with Windward already injured.

When Palon and Aturadin made it to the top of the ledge, Laetiran was already there, watching the dragons with his back against the wall. Palon glared at him and dropped to a crouch, well back from the edge in case he knew something she didn't. Aturadin mimicked her just as Fired Sand beat his wings, the sudden wind gusts nearly toppling them. Palon grabbed Aturadin's arm, bracing herself against the wind while Laetiran laughed.

Palon grumbled under her breath. "I just want to push him off that ledge."

Aturadin nodded. "Everyone does. Don't worry; Scorch Frost says Stone Eyes is on his way."

The cacophony of two male dragons screaming at each other drowned out everything else. Palon huddled up, pressing her hands tightly to her ears.

From all directions, dragons approached to view the face off. Black Cloud, ebony scales gleaming in the sun, came roaring from her cache site and barreled into the two males from the side. The screaming began again as the three faced off in a furious triangle. Long necks snaked from side to side as mouths opened wide in roars that shook the ground. Being female and older, Black Cloud was the largest of the three, nearly half again as big as either male. Windward backed up, his awkward retreat so hasty he nearly tripped over his tail several times, head lowering to the ground as he went. Fired Sand scrambled in the opposite direction, neck spines flaring in irritation though he kept his head low.

Palon bit her lip. Why was Black Cloud overreacting so? Typically, the female dragons stayed out of dominance scuffles.

The hairs on the back of her neck rose as Stone Eyes bellowed, galloping into the basin. Black Cloud nipped at Fired Sand for moving and lashed her tail, catching Windward across the snout. Stone Eyes roared and Black Cloud bellowed in return, facing the most dominant dragon of their nest eye to eye.

First Black Cloud, then Stone Eyes intervening in what should be a minor scrap? Something was terribly wrong.

Palon stared at Windward, demanding to know what was going on. A commotion spread among the dragons like wind through tall grass. Denial and outrage filled her, coming from Windward. Aturadin squeezed her hand.

Someone had stolen from Black Cloud.

Chapter Two

Stolen.

Whispers rose to fill the air like startled birds as dragonbonded emerged from the tunnels, eyes darting about and hands fluttering with the unease that spread through the nest. Black Cloud stood tall in a furious display, her wings outstretched, matched by Stone Eyes. Already his gold and copper scales looked somewhat duller since his bonded had died several months ago. They'd been linked for eighty years, and that absence still haunted the caves, making Stone Eyes snappish. Rather than let Black Cloud bellow her fury as was normal, Stone Eyes confronted her, hissing and nipping at her.

Palon shuddered, denial strangling any words she might speak. It couldn't be. Theft from a dragon was impossible. She'd more easily believe the sun had turned blue.

Windward had shuffled backward to hunker down low with the other younger, smaller dragons, watching well out of the way of the two massive beasts in all their glory. He rolled a great golden eye her way, and she dropped to the ground. Around her, most of the other bonded were also crouching low, mirroring the stances of their dragons. Only those bonded to very high ranking dragons remained standing, their dragons balancing on hind legs, wings outstretched, watching the face off.

Black Cloud's curved teeth gleamed as she bugled, lashing her tail behind her. Facing her, Stone Eyes took a deep breath, his sides heaving, and rumbled low and steady. Palon frowned, the back of her neck prickling. Was the soothing rumble for Black Cloud, or for Stone Eyes himself?

She sighed in relief as Cave Song lumbered into the circle of watching dragons, her tail waving behind her, wings relaxed. As the oldest dragon in their nest next to Silver Spine, Cave Song generally kept the peace. Silver Spine no longer took part in the affairs of the nest anymore—not for the last couple months.

Black Cloud lowered her head and dropped to all fours, her mouth closing and wings folding. Stone Eyes nodded, wings and neck spines relaxing. The risk of a dragon fight faded, and Windward's mental tension eased. Rolling her shoulders, Palon began to rise, the others around her rustling as they, too, found their feet.

But tall, blond-haired Eltavae leaped to her feet, baring her teeth. Palon dropped to the ground instinctively in response to the wild look in her eyes as the higher-ranked bonded shouted, "The polished wood! Her favorite pieces are gone!"

Eltavae's dragon, Shadow Soars, roared into the open space from the private caves that lay beyond the basking platforms. Mouth gaping, she extended her sleek, dark green spines and wings in a full threat display. Black Cloud and Stone Eyes leapt up to match her display, and Cave Song trumpeted, flaring her wings.

The air rang with whistles and roars as the other dragons scrambled for their caves, leaving Black Cloud, Shadow Soars, Stone Eyes, and Cave Song in the middle of the basin. Palon shivered, the hair on the back of her neck rising. Windward's need to check his collection pressed on her chest, though she stared unseeing at the basin. One dragon was bad enough, but two? She reached in a wild surge for Windward, wishing they could go flying again. Out there, even in a dive or spinning in combat, the world made sense. They could handle anything together.

"We need to check our cache," Aturadin whispered urgently.

Palon drew a haggard breath, cold creeping up her spine. Were her things safe? Had someone stolen from her, too? Such a thing was impossible, and yet... She was now living in a time where someone stole from dragons. The meaning of impossible had changed.

She grabbed her harness and bolted into the nearest tunnel. The need to check her collection coursed through her, driving her on, on, on. Around them, others stampeded through the rounded tunnels that had been carved long ago by bonded like them. They clogged the passageways in their headlong rush, pushing and shoving and squeezing in three at a time as the ceiling arched above them, bouncing their panicked breaths along the stone.

In all the chaos, Aturadin kept pace right next to her, steady as

Windward, always dependable without suffocating her. They were the only bonded in the nest to share a cache site, for the territorial instinct was unrelenting. The only person Palon could possibly allow so close to her collection was Aturadin, in part because his was nothing like hers.

Their shared cache was a small cave between Windward's and Scorch Frost's, their dragons' instincts helping to keep their collections safe when they weren't there. If anyone disturbed the cache, the dragons would smell them.

If anyone had stolen from her, they were going to pay.

The pressure of compulsion and the panic squeezing her heart made her skin crawl and her fingers twitch. Even as a child, Palon had collected rocks. After bonding with Windward, any shiny stone was something she simply had to have. It was the same way they all became territorial, that aspect of their dragons passing through the bond. They even stashed their collections in a similar manner—Windward jealously guarded the cave where he collected his treasures, rarely allowing even Palon inside. Occasionally, bonded were sent below to the Monks for healing after especially bad fights over collections or cache sites.

Aturadin liked to say they were no longer wholly Rinaryn, which always made Palon roll her eyes. Of course they weren't. They were more. They were bonded.

The leather straps of her harness slapped against her legs as they raced, shadows dancing in the light of the lanterns hanging from crudely carved hooks.

Who would steal from a dragon? The question ran through her mind over and over. No dragonbonded could even think such a thing, and none of the dragons would risk stealing from each other. None of them were that stupid. She shook her head. No one and nothing was allowed in the nest that wasn't dragon or bonded.

Taking a sharp turn, they bolted through an intersection. The crowd thinned, the tunnel no longer filled with the vibrations of over forty feet pounding against the stone. Palon adjusted the loops of the harness as they passed the Equipping Cave without slowing. Two months ago, Aturadin's harness had failed during a flight. He'd barely gotten home alive, clinging to Scorch Frost's neck spine. Only after he was safe had Palon remembered seeing Laetiran hanging out near the Equipping Cave, smiling as always.

They couldn't prove it, not enough to carry with the dragons. The cut marks on the harness weren't enough either, as anyone could have taken that harness and everyone had knives. So Palon and Aturadin had taken to storing their things in their cache to prevent possible sabotage.

Of course, this had given them a reputation for snobbery and led to snubbing by some of the others, but Palon wasn't about to back down. The fact that Laetiran knew she knew, and knew she couldn't do anything about it, only angered her further.

She darted into a crack in the rock, following its blind zigzagging and negotiating the traps she and Aturadin had devised before finally squeezing through the last narrow gap. Their cache opened up in front of her.

It was a small space, littered about with Aturadin's glossy feathers on one side and Palon's rocks on the other, a rainbow of colors with a spread of textures and sizes. The mind-numbing tension continued until she had checked over every piece in her collection, then again, then one last time just to be sure. Everything rested in its place, just as she had left it.

A knot loosened inside of her and she could breathe again, think again. Windward's rustling filtered through the slits in the top of the cave walls as he rooted around in his cache, and somehow it was unbearably funny.

Giggles erupted from her throat, turning into full-fledged laughter at the giddy relief on Aturadin's face. Grasping at a tenuous control of her emotions, she set the harness in its alcove and shrugged out of her riding jacket. It dipped to the side, the pocket with her treasures weighing it down. Aturadin's surprise was in there too, she remembered. Smiling in anticipation, she reached into the inner pocket and gently drew forth the handful of feathers.

"Look what I found," she said, stretching out her hand.

His nails scraped her palm as he snatched them up, eyes gleaming in the lantern light. She grinned as he inspected each one intently, watching the possessiveness and joy rise in his face. Laughter burst from her as he dropped them on the stone shelf beside him and squeezed her with glee until she had to beat on his arms breathlessly to get him to stop.

And then he snatched up the new feathers again, holding them in his hands with his fingers curled tightly around so she could barely see them. "Ooh, this black one here is a secondary feather from an eilir. Looks like a juvenile, see the bands? And that's interesting because they usually live in forested areas—did you and Windward go into a forest?"

Laughing, Palon shook her head, but he was already on to the next feather, which was apparently from a waterfowl of some sort. She had never understood his fascination with feathers, beyond the beauty of shiny things and the compulsion to collect, but she smiled at his joy, nodding while she forgot all the information he spouted at her as soon as she heard it.

As Aturadin began reorganizing his collection to try to find the optimal arrangement that included his new feathers, Palon turned her back on him, taking out the new stones she'd found: the rose quartz and the white gem that seemed to gleam all on its own, the likes of which she'd never seen. It was quickly becoming her favorite.

She turned the new stone, staring at it. It was hers, only hers. That fierce possessive instinct rose in her like the wind in a dive.

"What's that?" Aturadin asked, hovering close to her shoulder. "Can I see?"

She slapped her hand over the gem, rounding on Aturadin with teeth bared. "Mine."

Aturadin backed up to the wall and crouched, head low. "Yours. I don't want it."

His distance and posture relieved some of the aggression that had surged in her, but not all of it. Her blood still pounded in her ears, urging her to protect her collection, to keep it safe. If someone would dare steal from dragons, they wouldn't hesitate to destroy the selection of rocks she'd spent years gathering. She couldn't let that happen.

Palon glared at him a moment longer, lips still curled back from her teeth, but Aturadin's stance remained loose, holding submissive posture. Finally, she was able to relax and Aturadin immediately looked up.

"Can I see it? It seems familiar."

Palon couldn't help herself—she bared her teeth at him again.

Aturadin clasped his hands behind his back. "See? I won't touch it."

Her hand trembled as she reluctantly opened her fingers. Moving with care, he leaned forward, holding his hands faithfully behind his back. He frowned, and Palon fought off the urge to hide the stone and guard it. Her trembling fingers closed over it.

"Can you turn it over?"

Narrowing her eyes at him, she turned the stone slowly so that he could see all sides of it. When he retreated, she clasped the stone to her chest, the tight knot of anxiety loosening in her stomach.

"Isn't it beautiful?" She smiled.

"It is beautiful," Aturadin agreed, but he was still frowning.

Scowling at him, Palon tucked her stone carefully away among her collection, arranging the pieces among the alcoves in the stone wall. When she turned back to face him, she stood between him and her treasures. She decided to stay there.

Aturadin stood by the opposite wall, brows knitted. She glared at him. That was not how he was supposed to react to her stone.

"Where did you find it?" he asked.

Possessiveness raged in her and she stared him down, her upper lip rising despite herself.

He turned so he was shoulder to shoulder with her, about a pace away. "Palon, don't let the dragon in you take over. I honestly don't want your rock."

"You don't even like it," she shot back at him, though the urge to defend her collection was starting to subside.

"Nope. I like feathers." He smiled, his expression as relaxed as his posture.

She sighed. He was unflappable in this sort of mood.

"I found it in Stonefield," she managed, trying to force the tension away. "Let's get out of here, back to the main basin. I'll be able to relax more there."

He didn't move. "I've seen that sort of design before. Did Windward see it?" Aturadin's voice was low and tense.

"No," she growled, leaning against the cave wall. "I wasn't going to let him take it."

"I think it's dangerous, Palon. You should show the dragons."

"No! They'll take it!" Suddenly she was glad her dragon was so preoccupied with the safety of his own cache. Even so, she tried to lower her voice.

"They probably will," he said. "Once, when I was at the Monks of Annularei, I spent the afternoon in their library."

"Why?" Every bonded knew about the Monks' library. Why anyone would want to be cooped up in there with nothing but books was beyond her.

"The dragons don't tell us everything." He grinned. "But the Monks, they write down everything a dragonbonded tells them. Everything."

"Well of course, that's why we keep former bonded—"

"*Everything*, Palon."

Palon rolled her eyes. "Nothing exciting, nothing you can't wheedle your dragon into eventually telling you."

"Did you know there's a ritual for when a bonded is wronged by a dragon? The pairs duel. Tsían didn't even know until I told him about it."

She frowned at him. "Well, that would never happen, so why would anyone care to know? It's useless. What does that have to do with my crystal?"

"In one of the books, I saw a drawing that looked like that stone. The writing was scrawled around it, like the person holding the brush was upset. I didn't get a chance to read much, but I think it's dangerous, Palon."

"What did it say?"

He shook his head. "It was a long time ago. I'm not sure... I remember... enemy of dragons..." He sighed, rubbing his forehead. "I can't remember. But it was a warning."

"Enemy of dragons? Do you think it could, I don't know, call walavaim? Or control them? No, that just sounds stupid." She chewed the corner of her bottom lip in thought. Maybe the fae? What would a rock have to do with either, though?

Aturadin shrugged. "If anyone knows anything about an enemy of dragons, I'd bet it'd be the dragons."

Palon scowled at him. He made sense, but it would mean giving up her stone and it was so beautiful, so precious. She couldn't do that. She was holding it in her hand again and she didn't remember picking it up. But staring into it, the light filtering in from the air vents glimmered inside the crystal. And this thing was supposed to be dangerous? It was only a gemstone. And it was hers.

Her hand swept up, pressing it to her heart. Her decision was made, as powerful as dragon rumblings shuddering in stone. She shook her head, muscles tight as she fought against the surging need to protect her things, breathing deeply to remain calm in expression and tone. "No. I'll figure it out myself. Don't tell, Aturadin."

"Palon..."

She growled, clutching the stone until her fingers went white. "Don't tell them!"

He nodded, stepping away with his empty hands raised, though his dark eyes were wells of disappointment she pretended not to see as she turned her back to him. "It's your crystal, Palon."

Ignoring the pangs of her heart, she placed the stone prominently on a natural shelf. Palon took one last look around, though her gaze shied away from Aturadin's while she checked one last time that everything was as it should be. She nodded, then turned to go. "Come on. It's been a long day, and I need to check on Windward."

"I'll see you later," he said, grabbing a container of polish and picking up her harness. "This probably needs to be looked at after your adventure."

Palon forced a smile, trying to push her gratitude to the surface through the sudden dread in her heart. Still, her feet dragged traitorously as she left him behind, heading out to the main tunnel. She shouldn't have this reaction to leaving Aturadin in the cache. In fact, now that someone would dare to steal from dragons, it was probably even smart to leave someone guarding her collection.

She shook herself, feeding the fire of anger burning deep within her as she dropped off the hide in the Processing Cave on the way to the basin. If she could trust anyone, she could trust Aturadin. But how could she trust anyone or anything now? She shifted, fingers twitching. She needed to fly. Flying always put things in perspective. Everything was small and insignificant when you soared among the clouds.

Her chest ached with tension until she stepped into Windward's cave and drew in a deep breath of his reptile musk. As his scent filled her lungs and she went to work, her nerves were soothed and her muscles relaxed. She bandaged Windward's foot and then climbed over and around him, inspecting his scales for damage from the harness rubbing against them. Windward seemed to take as much solace in her company as she did in his, pointing her to an itch to scratch for him, and then there was a spine growing crooked for her to see to. She grinned at him. He just wanted attention.

Most of the other dragons were still curled up in their personal caves, guarding their treasures, Windward told her. Another wave of his paranoia washed over her, and she fought to keep from shuddering or running back to check on her own collection again. Even so, her eye twitched, worries swirling through her mind. He retreated mentally, leaving her floundering until he buoyed her with a powerful soothing, humming to both of them that all would be well.

Reaching up to stroke his nose, Palon went over Windward one last time, checking for any other needs, assuring him and herself at the same time that whatever came next, they could handle it together. And if by chance they couldn't, there was always the freedom of the skies.

Whistles erupted from outside, shattering the fragile calm she and Windward had built. She capped the salve and herbal rubs she'd been using, throwing them back on their shelf and dashing into the evening air. The sun was setting fire to the foothills westward, and High Flight's winds made gusts of the crisp air as he set down in the middle of the Basking Basin rather than using the landing platform as was normal.

It made his landing awkward, even more so as he stumbled, flapping his wings and lashing his tail for balance while he kept one foot curled underneath him, raised up from the ground, holding something in his claws. The young dragon looked about him, eyes round with surprise. The basking sites were eerily empty, especially as Stone Eyes, Shadow Soars, and Black Cloud bugled a welcome in dismal tones.

High Flight's spines stiffened. He rumbled a questioning note, and Stone Eyes rumbled in response. Palon peered at High Flight's forefoot, which still hadn't touched the ground. Brown hair poked out from between his toes, and she groaned. Just what they needed right now.

"Have respect." Tsían had appeared behind her, a frown sharpening the lines of his face. Palon stilled her expression to avoid more trouble —Tsían always took his responsibility for the whole of the bonded very seriously.

She ducked her head in submission. "Yes, Tsían. But do you see?"

"I see." Tsían sighed. "Forest Blaze counseled High Flight against such whims."

"As did Dusks Dive," said Salann as she emerged from the tunnel, flicking two of her braids back behind her shoulder. Tall and sleek, the only bonded in the nest with more poise than her was Tsían. "And she is not in a good mood. Some of her collection is missing as well."

Palon's stomach twisted and her skin prickled. She kept her head low, watching them with the deference due their stations. That made three dragons now who had been stolen from, all females. She wouldn't have believed it had she heard the story without witnessing it. And one was Dusks Dive? That would make Salann part victim of the theft. Someone would dare target Salann? Salann, who was highly ranked among the bonded, keeping the nest running smoothly, always fair amidst squabbles? She'd shown Palon around when Palon was new, helping her adjust before Miros took over teaching her the ways of dragonbonded.

Salann had taught her to fly; Miros had set her on the walavaim. She'd forever be grateful for that.

Her heart leaped as Aturadin emerged from the tunnel, his eyes lighting at the sight of her. She wanted to embrace him, to cling to him for a moment amid the storm of their nest's troubles, but she resisted the urge. She refused to let the weakness in her be visible. But her heart settled ever so slightly as Aturadin stood next to her, his features calm but for the tightness around the corners of his mouth and eyes.

Tsían glanced at Salann. "What do you suggest? We cannot take on a newly bonded, not now. All this change and upset while Silver Spine deteriorates. Miros hasn't moved from his side in days."

Salann nodded. "When he passes, even a stable cave would be rocked by enormous grief. With all this turmoil, with someone daring to steal from dragons, and now with a new bond to worry about, such grief will be..."

"Difficult," Tsían said.

Salann inclined her head. "This is possibly the worst time to take on such a delicate process, especially with the dragon's seasonal torpor looming."

"High Flight will be dealt with. What to do about the newly bonded?"

"Could the Monks take this one?"

"They will be taking Miros once Silver Spine passes! Do we ask them to take on a newly bonded and break that bond as well?"

"Could the dragons take such a strain? Can a bond solidify before torpor?" Salann's voice cracked with anxiety.

Palon exchanged a glance with Aturadin and his hand brushed hers. A chill ran down her spine. The dragons would settle in for torpor in a few months, and the bond would have to be strong enough to survive that. Normally, newlings had several months of calm in which to grow their bond. This one would have a few short months of chaos eroding the bond even as it formed. Dragons didn't deal well with change.

Tension thrummed in the air around them, given voice by the dragons bellowing and trumpeting as they emerged reluctantly to welcome High Flight back and see the newly bonded. Down in the basin, High Flight opened his talons, letting a small figure tumble out.

The newling looked unconscious, which did not bode well for the smoothness of the bond. Palon and Windward's bond was hailed as a strong and easy thing. She had arrived riding in his foot, clinging to his

24

toes with his talons curved around her. She'd been annoyed with him at the time for not allowing her to ride on his back. A smile pulled at her mouth, for she knew now how insane that would have been without a harness.

Tsían sighed, pinching the bridge of his nose. "Forest Blaze says to try. If we can do this, we'll have a new pair to replace Silver Spine and Miros."

Palon winced. No one could replace Silver Spine and Miros, especially not what they meant to her. But the nest would need more bonded to continue on, to share the work.

"Stone Eyes says we can't allow it to fail," Tsían continued. "The bonding must go smoothly."

Salann looked as skeptical as Palon felt. That was a lot of demand on a process that was often tumultuous while the newling adjusted.

Tsían went to the stairs and paused. "I'll have Maea watch her overnight. Tomorrow we'll sort everything else out." Tsían rubbed his forehead, looking pained, then shook his head and straightened his shoulders. His eyes fell on Palon and she ducked her head.

"Palon, Aturadin," Tsían said, his voice sharp as dragon teeth. "You are in charge of the newly bonded. Teach her what she needs to know, and be careful to protect her bond with High Flight, ill-advised though it is. You are responsible for that bond. We will deal with the thief."

Palon nodded, hiding a grimace. This was going to be trouble, but there was nothing she could do about it. The bonding was difficult, there was no getting around that, but this one's experience would be even more so. Could a newly formed bond stand against the current telepathic stresses of the cave?

Tsían's tone became stern. "Be sure not to allow the newling to attach too much to you. I do not agree with the timing, but neither will I allow this bonding to fail, particularly not now."

Palon swallowed hard, but nodded again. She waited a moment, watching Tsían and Salann make their way down the stairs and across to High Flight, crouching by the unmoving figure. The young dragon whistled and dipped his head, backing away with cautious steps to give them room while eyeing Stone Eyes, who stood like a bronze statue.

High Flight. She narrowed her eyes. He never should have taken the risk of ignoring a more dominant dragon, especially when Stone Eyes was already cranky. Even disregarding the turmoil of the thefts, it had been a stupid move.

Windward's worry about his own stash crashed along the bond, exposing the calm they had built to be as false as her serene expression. The outrage and worries of the dragons filled the air, so strong they were almost physical. How could the newly formed bond stand against the mental stresses of sixty furious dragons?

Aturadin's arm draped over her shoulders as they descended the stairs to the basin and he tugged her close. "Come on," he said. "Time for bed first. We'll figure out the newling tomorrow."

She nodded, leaning into him. Past the edge of the landing slab, the horizon blazed red and orange as the stars peeked through the twilight sky. Bonded were just beginning to gather near the center of the basin, and the dragons formed their ring around the outside of the basin. Young dragons, those unable to fly yet, scampered further into the caves, to the Nesting Cave, while those just flight-sized curled up in the inner ring, though they left a ring of open space around the bonded. No dragon would dare purposely injure any bonded, but when walking with creatures of such enormous size it made sense to be prudent. All the remorse in the world wouldn't save a bonded after a dragon inadvertently stepped on them.

Palon took a deep breath, sighing it out slowly as if she could breathe out the tension of the day. She had always loved the night, especially once her bond with Windward had solidified. There was something comforting about the bedding down of your family, about relinquishing the worries of the day and reliving the adventures. The effect was usually even more pronounced when the weather was fair as it was tonight and they could sleep under the open sky. This evening, however, the day's concerns clung to her with a tension in her shoulders she found hard to shed.

High Flight had bonded, and what would happen would happen. They would just have to make the best of the situation. Taking another deep breath, she nestled into the pile of bonded between Eltavae and Aturadin, letting their closeness ease the tension from her shoulders like the stored warmth released from the stone beneath them.

Chapter Three

Palon whooped as Windward breezed past a stone pillar, so close she swore she might be able to touch it. Everything was better out here with just the wind and the sky, rather than in the stuffy dragon nest with the onerous task that awaited her on their return.

Smug amusement leaked from Windward as he surged upward with great flaps of his wings, the leathery membranes glossy in the sun. He wouldn't have a newly bonded to check on, nor Tsían looming at him, pressuring him that nothing go wrong. He circled, using the warm air of a thermal to rise high above the land once more.

Snorting, Palon muttered, "It's not my fault she's slept a whole day."

It wasn't just the newling weighing on her. She pushed away the memory of Silver Spine's tail hanging off the ledge of the Sequestering Cave as they left that morning, the absence of Miros's raised hand in farewell. Would the pair still be alive tomorrow?

Windward gave her a mental nudge, suggesting she let the stresses of the nest stay there, rather than carry them with her. The only nagging worry he had was for his cache, though the rewards of flying with her were worth the risk.

Palon patted his scales, reminding him that Scorch Frost was watching for him.

And her own cache was protected by traps, Windward responded as her thoughts touched on it. He folded his wings for another dive.

He was right. She was wasting a perfectly good day. Tossing aside her worries and frustrations, Palon leaned forward, crouching behind the meager shield of the spine in front of her, her braids lashing behind her in the wind of their passage. A wild glee filled her. They were heading back toward the same natural tower from a different direction so that three other jagged columns of stone stretched upward behind their target like fingers reaching for the sun. Windward flared his wings, catching an unexpected gust of wind. Palon clutched the flying harness, leaning with him as he corrected with a sweep of his tail.

He was too close to the target pillar. They weren't going to be able to replicate the earlier flyby. Disappointment stabbed at her, but she shrugged it away. After all, if they missed, they'd just have to come around for another try, which meant more time spent in practice. More time doing what she loved.

Oozing confidence, Windward breezed past the stone spire then flapped hard, reaching ahead with all four legs for the second one. As his body curved forward, Palon pulled herself closer with the harness to avoid drifting back to where his neck spine sharpened.

Windward hit the stone finger and leaped off it, his neck curving upward and ivory horns sweeping through the air on either side of her as he reversed direction. A sharp crack split the air as the pillar gave way.

"You broke it!"

He suggested she look up, but she already was as he turned sideways, wings outstretched in a great vertical line. The target column was rushing toward her, and she yelped and ducked low along the base of the spine in front of her. Dragon laughter echoed through her head.

Then it was past, and she dissolved into breathless giggles while he chided her for not touching the pillar when she had the chance.

"I'm not stupid—I'd lose a finger."

Still laughing at her, Windward straightened out and Palon released her white-knuckled hold on the harness, flexing and straightening fingers that were hot from gripping so hard. She shifted her legs too, easing their pressure against his scales.

"That's a good move to try on the walavaim," she said. "We should be able to adapt it to the cliffs surrounding the herdbeast pastures. Maybe we'll even get lucky and catch a walavai with the falling rock."

She glanced down as the rocky ground sped past, rising and falling in minor peaks, while around them stood the solid, major summits of the mountains. Great grey slabs of granite jutted out, impenetrable to the roots of the various trees and other plants which clung stubbornly to the surrounding land. Far in the distance, another dragon wheeled, likely belonging to another nest. It didn't matter. They soared effortlessly above the clutter, untouched, unaffected by it. Higher than all the chaos, just where Palon liked to be.

"We should go back and try again," she blurted. She wasn't ready yet to go back to the nest, where the grief and anger and fear would weigh on her. Where she'd have to sit and wait through the boredom until the newly bonded woke up.

Windward laughed at her, for she was only delaying the inevitable. Besides, he wanted to keep an eye on his cache.

She shook her head. The maneuver was a good one, but it wasn't enough. "Last time we fought the walavaim, they thought of me as only a vulnerability for you—I heard them, saw how they dismissed me. I refuse to be a burden."

Angling his wings, Windward caught an updraft and threw them into the clear blue autumn sky. She was not a burden, he sent her with a finality that made her wince. No bonded flew better than she.

His fondness warmed her heart and she smiled. "Maybe next time, if I unhook my straps, I can jump on them. Do more than just distract them for you."

Windward rumbled. She did more than distract them, and she knew it.

Palon dropped her gaze to his polished scales, mostly grey with a hint of shimmering purple. Tracing them with her fingers, she murmured, "I don't know how we would practice such a stunt anyway."

Unease roiled in Windward as he angled toward home, and he pressed on her not to try it. He'd be afraid for her throughout the fight, unable to focus. The walavaim were far more agile than dragons and could likely throw her off.

"You'd catch me," Palon said, pressing her hand against his scales as if she could press into him the warmth of her belief.

Whistling, he turned to eye her, his worries hammering against her.

She patted his side. "Fine. I won't do it. Stop worrying."

Her spirits drifted downward as Windward descended, for the fun would soon be over and all that would be left was chores.

With sweeping beats of his wings raising up a cloud of dust, Windward landed, running forward a few paces until he could overcome his momentum. Palon focused on the feel of his gait. Though he hid it, there was a slight unevenness as he favored his foot. Unclipping her safety straps, she slid down, landing on his elbow just as he raised it and then flipped to the ground, her movements perfectly synced with his.

As she jogged out of the way of his hind foot, she grinned, pride filling her chest, especially when an appreciative whistle rose from the one of the ledges. There should have been more whistles, but considering the strength of the fears and fury and grief of the dragons stifling her through her bond with Windward, she was grateful for any alleviation of the dark mood of the nest. Her dismounts were a spectacle, as they should be; her flights with Windward were a spectacle as well. It was one reason they were one of the favored teams to patrol the herds and battle the walavaim packs.

Which is what they should be doing, instead of boring watch-the-newly-bonded-sleep duty.

The newling had arrived sleeping, of all things, and then stayed sleeping. The girl was old enough she should have been preparing for her yah. How could she expect to survive a month in the wild alone if she was so weak? How would she survive being bonded? A dragon nest was no place for the weak. The thought of seeing a newling hurt because of High Flight's impatience turned her stomach, and anger flared in her anew.

Windward crushed that anger. Rebuking a dragon was not the place of a bonded, just as dragons did not interfere with bonded. Stone Eyes would deal with High Flight. The hierarchy kept everyone safe.

"Palon!" Salann's shout echoed across the basin.

"What is it?" Palon asked, pulling the jar of salve from her riding jacket as Windward crawled up onto a free basking ledge.

"Tsían gave you a task, did he not?"

She held back a groan. She'd just gotten home, and already Salann and Tsían were hovering over her. "Yes, the newly bonded. Windward and I—"

"The newly bonded is a priority, Palon," Salann said. "We can't afford a damaged bonding."

"I know. Aturadin is with her," Palon said, unsuccessfully trying to keep the edge from her voice as she pulled Windward's foot around to rub more salve into it. She ignored his grumbles that this was too public a place for such things. Clearly, she wasn't the only one whose spirits had been boosted by their flight, for he let her tend him despite his mild protests.

"She's awake, and Tsían's concerned. Don't let him think you're ignoring the task," Salann said, her tone softening a bit.

"Windward and I had something we wanted to try out." She

rankled against the implication that she might be shirking her duties, even if she *had* jumped at the chance to leave Aturadin with the girl and go for a quick flight. Flight practice was also important, and she had to juggle the responsibilities.

Windward's amusement lighted along their bond, teasing her with thoughts of basking while she was burdened with chores.

Salann rose up on tiptoe, peeking at Windward's foot over Palon's shoulder as Palon capped the salve. "Something that reopened that wound?"

Windward rumbled low and shifted, awkwardly curling his foot under him, and she turned to face Salann. The older bonded was no danger, but still Palon stood between her and Windward, the need to protect her dragon fierce while he felt vulnerable. Windward was *hers*.

"Well, it worked, and that's what matters," Palon said. "Windward and I have a new technique for next time we see walavaim."

"They're fast." Salann's brow furrowed with skepticism.

"We're faster." Palon tied off the bandage and patted Windward's leg, grinning.

"Well, go help Aturadin," Salann said. "I'll tell Tsían I sent you off to the newly bonded."

Palon suppressed another groan and nodded as Salann left them, though she could feel Windward's agreement. He would much rather bask with her alongside him. Narrowing her eyes as if to focus them on her duties, she stripped off Windward's harness and smoothed out his scales until he warned her she might be flirting a little too close with trouble from the higher-ranked dragonbonded.

As she left Windward to bask, she glanced up at the ledge of the Sequestering Cave. No sign of Miros or Silver Spine. Her shoulders wanted to droop, weighed down by more than simply the flying harness she carried, but Palon held her head high. She jogged to her cache, checking that the tunnel was empty before squeezing through the gap and navigating the traps. A smile touched her lips and her hand reached out almost of its own accord to touch her crystal, even as she stashed her harness. More than anything, she wanted to hold the newest piece of her collection, to see the sunlight fracture inside the gem. What could such a brilliant thing have to do with an enemy of dragons?

She shook herself and pulled away. She had a duty to perform; she couldn't linger. She bolted from her stash, some irrational fear filling her that she'd stay indefinitely if she didn't break free. A longing filled her to bring it with her, but that was silly too. Without the pockets of her riding jacket, she'd have nowhere secure to stash it, and if she kept the fur-lined jacket on, she'd surely draw comment. It was just a stone. She was being silly.

The sound of her footfalls bounced off the rounded walls as she followed the tunnels toward the Wounds Cave. The newling was uninjured, but they hadn't been able to think of a better place to keep her while waiting for her to wake, since the Sequestering Cave was occupied by Silver Spine and Miros.

Normally placid Maea hurried toward her, and Palon winced at the shock and dismay on the brown-eyed woman's face. Before leaving that morning, she'd asked Maea to look in on Aturadin in case he needed anything. They didn't want the newling waking up in a strange place all alone.

"The newling alright?" Palon asked. "She still in the Wounds Cave?"

"She's horrible! She woke up and just... erupted. Aturadin had to hold her down so I could get some calming herbs in her. She bit me, see?"

"I'm going," Palon groaned, quickening her pace.

This newling was going to be one of the interesting ones, wasn't she... Often they spent a few days overcome by their decision, sometimes in fear or dismay, and sometimes arrogant and aggressive, in need of lessons in humility. Everyone needed to know the new shape of their social world and their place in the scheme of things before they were fully incorporated in the hierarchy. The dragons couldn't tell them—until the bond solidified, communication was crippled.

Aturadin and the girl were exiting the cave as Palon reached it. The newling was a slip of a thing, with tangled brown hair, skinny little limbs, and brown eyes that held the promise of retribution. Her clothes of woven and dyed cloth stood out—with the hunting skills of the dragons, leather was easy to come by, while cloth was scarce and quickly worn through. Dragons tended to be hard on cloth.

"I heard it was exciting for a while." Palon brushed her fingertips down Aturadin's arm, watching the newling for signs of further trouble.

Squeezing her hand in greeting, he grinned and shrugged. He kept one arm extended behind the girl as if to keep her moving forward. The girl didn't respond, trudging forward with her head down except for brief pauses to glare around her.

Palon raised her eyebrows. "Keeping things entertaining along with your dragon, newling?"

The girl scowled at the floor.

Well. Teasing hadn't worked. Palon twisted her lips and tried again. "You going to tell us your name?"

When the newling ignored her, Palon clicked her tongue, struggling to suppress her impatience. It was just a name, and she was only trying to be nice. "I'll just have to call you Girl then. Girl—"

"It's Tebah." The girl drew in a deep breath, clenching her fists. "I'm Tebah, from Faralir in Dragonmoor."

Exchanging a look with Aturadin, Palon sighed. Some newlings clung to who they were rather than accepting their choice. She'd chosen to bond, or High Flight wouldn't have brought her here. Honesty would cut through whatever stories the girl was telling herself.

Palon tried for a smile, though the stresses of the cave made every muscle tight. "No one cares what village or region you came from. Such things are meaningless among dragons. We'll get you settled in, never fear."

The girl's eyes pierced her with fury like dragonfire. She stumbled toward her, but recoiled before reaching Palon. A flicker of disgust lit in her, that this girl couldn't even commit to a show of violence. But watching the girl shrink away from the tunnel walls, her breath coming in little hitches even as she glared at them, Palon sighed. She'd forgotten—again—that Rinaryns were naturally claustrophobic. It would be a while before the bond strengthened to the point where High Flight's instincts carried over to the girl, allowing her to suppress that reaction.

"It's alright, Tebah. Palon and I are here to help you." Aturadin grimaced in sympathy, but he didn't touch her.

Had the girl's reaction been so bad that even Aturadin would think twice about offering comfort? Maea had said the girl bit her—had she hurt Aturadin as well? Palon stomped down the anger that thought sparked; this was just a newling, ignorant of their ways.

Falling in on the other side of the girl, Palon accompanied them back through the tunnels to the basking platforms. Once they got out under the open sky, the girl relaxed some, though her expression remained tight and rebellious.

Unsure how to reach the girl, Palon fell back on duty. She pointed to

High Flight's cave, tucked away in a corner which was now half in shadow. "Here's where you'll stay. You'll have your own room, if you behave, next to High Flight's."

The girl stopped, pressing her lips together, her eyes fixed on the cave. Palon gestured to her to move along, but the girl looked past her.

Wrapping one hand around the girl's skinny little wrist, Palon hauled her forward. "Aturadin and I will teach you what you need to know until your bond progresses to where High Flight himself can teach you. Do as we tell you and you'll be fine. Don't go being stupid. The cave is already stressed with Silver Spine dying. If you were to be injured, well, that'd be bad."

Aturadin shook his head at Palon, gesturing as he explained further. "Any time the nest loses a dragon or a dragonbonded, it destabilizes us all. Since we'll soon be losing Miros and Silver Spine, one way or another, we're all on edge, which puts a telepathic strain on all the bonds. No one is supposed to go get themselves a new bonded while the cave is under stress—such as at the end of a dragon's life—but you're here, and Palon and I will help you settle in as much as we can. It'll be rough winds though, for you."

"I do not understand." Tebah's gaze was fixed on her feet, her words coming out in a sulky mutter.

It was going to be more than "rough winds". The dragons mourned with a ferocity matching the greatness of their hearts, and Palon could already feel it building inside her, like water pushing against a dam, ready to break loose and wash away a mountainside in grief. It made it hard to think in terms the newling would understand, hard to be patient.

This bond was a mistake, but they had to somehow make it work. Could they manage to force an understanding of dragon ways into the girl before the dragons bedded down for torpor in the winter? If not, the bond would weaken, sicken, even die.

She wouldn't let that happen.

Palon sighed, struggling to condense dragon society to a few sentences for the girl. "We're bonded to our dragons for life. They are fiercely possessive of us, especially once the bond solidifies. If the bond is broken or if the bonded is injured, it hurts our dragons, which bleeds out to the other dragons."

The girl's shoulders stiffened. "I will not be trapped, bound to a dragon all my days."

Aturadin sighed, and Palon ground her teeth, letting him explain lest she lose her temper. "If you were to jump off a cliff, you can't take that decision back. No more can you change the decision you made, but it's not bondage, it's bonding. Your dragon will change just as much as you will. That's part of why it only works if you're willing—because the bond is the foundation on which you and your dragon can build a partnership."

"Because they're telepaths," Tebah said.

Palon nodded. "As are you. A weak telepath, because otherwise High Flight wouldn't have chosen you."

"I could be a strong one." The girl raised her head, a stubborn fire in her eyes.

Aturadin shook his head. "Strong telepaths might wrestle the dragon for control, which weakens the bond. A weak bond is dangerous—you wouldn't have the trust and clear communication of a strong bond. The bond is all important."

There was one leader of the nest, and that hierarchy went all the way down, protecting everyone, keeping the nest stable. Everyone was answerable to someone.

Tebah narrowed her eyes. "You're a fool if you believe them. Everyone wants to be stronger than someone."

Palon bristled. Who was this girl, to come here and insult her mate? "It's not about who's stronger. That's exactly why strong telepaths aren't chosen, though—that very sentiment. That and the dragons discovered that the weaker the bonded, the stronger the bond, just as a waterfall gains power in the fall from high to low."

Calm as ever, Aturadin broke in. "But they must have some telepathic ability, or the bond doesn't work. The difference is too great."

"Why should I care?" The girl's eyes glittered, and she pressed her lips together. "I will not be here forever."

There was no time for going slow and gentle. Palon had a duty to perform and a tight deadline to keep. "You need to know this because you're bonded now. Eventually we dragonbonded get sick or we get old. We can't do our duties anymore. So our dragons dissolve the bond with us, slowly so as to minimize the harm to us and to them. But it causes great grief in the dragon, which again, affects the rest of the nest. You will feel this sooner or later."

"And that's happening now?"

Her heart squeezed like a vice. But Miros wasn't gone yet. What use was there in grieving for him before he was even gone?

She shrugged. "Sort of. When Silver Spine dies, his bond with Miros will snap; he's too old and tired to slowly dissolve the bond. We'll lose both dragon and bonded, one way or another."

"Miros will stay here for a while after, to be sure he won't give away any secrets, and then we'll send him on to the Monks of Annularei," Aturadin said.

"Those who knew him best will send him on." Palon couldn't resist correcting Aturadin. She was determined to be one of those who took Miros to the Monks. She owed it to him to give him that last honor. Drawing a deep breath, she forced down the surge of grief. He nodded at her, resting a hand on her shoulder.

"Wait, what? Give away what secrets?" Tebah asked.

Exasperated, Palon exchanged a glance with Aturadin. "High Flight really needs to get better at this." She turned to Tebah. "Didn't he tell you anything?"

The girl shook her head slowly.

Wrinkling her nose, Palon asked, "Why in your right mind did you go with him, then?"

Tebah stared at the floor, stone-faced. "I'm not staying here forever."

"Have you ever known any stories in which a dragonbonded returned home for more than a brief visit or to deliver a warning in times of danger?" Aturadin's voice was gentle.

"But—"

"You're not Rinaryn anymore, Tebah. You're bonded." Palon tried to mimic Aturadin's soothing tone. "The people you left behind are no longer yours."

"No!" There was fear in Tebah's eyes. Palon looked around for a reason but saw none. Surely the girl knew the stories of dragonbonded. She'd have been familiar with the concept and would have had to make a decision to bond with High Flight. Such a thing could not be forced on someone.

Sympathy filled Aturadin's voice. "It's hard, I know, but it's the truth. It's best to accept it."

"I'm going home!" Tebah started toward the landing platform, but Palon took one arm and Aturadin took the other.

She took a breath, forcing softness into her voice. "You are home."

Chapter Four

Rage whipped through the bond, and Palon dropped the rake on the sand in the Nesting Chamber and ran. Never mind the prickly newling, never mind the endless arguing of the past three days. Windward was in trouble. Footsteps behind her told her Tebah was following, but she didn't spare the girl a backward glance as she burst out into the Basking Basin.

Fired Sand stood on his hind legs, his mouth gaping in a threat display, and Palon's heart sank as Windward immediately matched his stance. Yet another scuffle. The grief and rage of the dragons kept spilling over. With his injuries, Windward had little chance of winning. Scorch Frost lay nearby, submitting to Fired Sand's display, and along the side, Aturadin mimicked his dragon, head lowered.

True dragon fights were rare—most were just displays and bluster —but Windward's rage roiled in her, combining with her own. He was not going to back down.

In a flash of bronze, Stone Eyes rammed into both of the younger males, his tail lashing behind him. Windward stumbled and fell, shaking small stones loose as his bulk slammed into the basin floor. Palon dropped to a crouch beside Aturadin, draping one arm over his shoulders. With a gasp, Tebah huddled beside her. Even the second-ranked male, Forest Blaze, looked surprised and confused. Why was Stone Eyes getting involved? This was the second time in a handful of days.

Shielding the newling with her free arm, Palon gritted her teeth, worry churning through her despite the weight of her dragon on her mind. Dominance squabbles were private affairs, and uninvolved dragons typically did no more than watch, unless there was risk to the nest as a whole. Before the last few days, the last time a dragon had intervened had been a few months ago, shortly after Stone Eyes's bonded Kepaeros had died. Fired Sand had bulled Skyward off his perch and Stone Eyes had come roaring in the moment Skyward hit the basin, smashing into Fired Sand and driving him clear across the open space, almost off the ledge of the mountain.

Fired Sand had dropped lower in rank than Windward—lower than most of the dragons, in fact. He and Laetiran considered this unfair and let everyone know it.

Drawing in a deep breath, Palon shook her head at herself. Dragons took care of their own, with all possible meanings of the phrase.

Stone Eyes's roar filled the basin, forcing Palon to drop to her knees, her hands pressed over her ears as his noise echoed around her like the battering winds of the Airstream, beating the two dragons into submission. She gathered his message through Windward: no dominance battles would be allowed, not until the cave returned to stability.

It still felt like an over-reaction to Palon, but it was not her place to say. She huddled low, her gaze locked on Windward, skin prickling with the residual sense of danger.

Windward rolled to his belly, claws scraping on the stone, but he kept his long neck and his head resting on the ground. His nictitating membrane flickered across his eyes, dimming them and protecting them from the dust being thrown up. Palon scowled, realizing Laetiran was standing nearby, smiling at the scene below.

Stone Eyes lowered his head to scream a hands-breadth from Windward's face, and the dragon closed his eyes in response.

"Watch," Palon breathed, distracting herself from Laetiran by nudging the newling, who was watching with huge eyes. "Submissive posture. When you anger High Flight or any bonded, take submissive posture."

"Why should he hurt me?" Tebah asked, her voice filled with bitterness.

"They won't," Palon said. "Dragons try very hard not to hurt bonded."

Aturadin jutted his chin at the dragons. "Watch and learn how to act around other bonded. Dragon habits and body language pass over onto us. Windward is showing complete submission there. It'll keep you safe if you get into trouble."

The girl scoffed.

As Fired Sand retreated, Stone Eyes lunged forward, his horns hooking Fired Sand's and pulling him forward. The bronze dragon stepped on Fired Sand's head and roared at every dragon and bonded cowering around the rim of the basin. Every head bowed low until the basin was surrounded by a ring of dragon horns sweeping toward the sky. Palon winced at the display of fury. She'd never seen such temper from the dragons.

Swallowing visibly, Tebah shrank back from the scene. Even so, some fire remained, glimmering in her eyes. "But why should posture help when the dragons are telepathic?"

Palon wrinkled her nose. "Once your bond solidifies, talking telepathically with another dragon will feel…"

Aturadin shuddered. "Gross."

Palon nodded. "And you can't communicate with another bonded telepathically; the bond takes up all of your telepathy. Knowing proper body language will help you avoid misunderstandings because words can be clumsy things."

"Why do we care? We aren't dragons, we're Rinaryn."

Why was the girl so stuck in the past, so stuck in her own limitations? "You're not Rinaryn anymore, Tebah. You're bonded. You have a new family and new customs to learn about now, and Aturadin and I are trying to teach you."

"Dragons see the world as an extension of themselves, like anyone else, I assume—" Aturadin began.

Palon cut him off, getting straight to the point. "Dragons have a hierarchy. Bonded have one too, reflecting that of the dragons—the higher your dragon's place, the higher yours is. That's the way it is. Respect it and you'll be fine. Ignore it and you're asking for a fight."

Laetiran grinned at them as he passed by, dropping over the side to the netting.

Palon frowned, watching him go. His ambition had known no bounds, ever since he felt he and his dragon had been wronged. Climbing back up in rank would not be enough for him—he clearly ached for revenge.

She turned to Tebah. "You'll have to watch him eventually. He'll pick a fight with you if he thinks it'll help his dragon gain rank. You're safe for now though—scuffling with a newling serves no one."

Tebah's brow knit, her lip trembling.

Hoping to distract the girl, Palon jutted her chin at the dragons. "Windward, Scorch Frost, Fired Sand, and High Flight are all approximately the same rank. Fired Sand wants to climb back up."

Aturadin pointed with his chin too. "Stone Eyes is the dominant dragon. He can win any fight. Do not cross him."

"Don't cross any dragon," Palon said. "Or Tsían, the leader of the bonded."

"And Cave Song is the oldest you'll encounter. She's so old, she no longer takes bonded and can't fly," Aturadin continued.

"Dragons honor their elders," Palon added. Unlike the girl, who seemed eager to paint everyone Palon loved as a monster.

While they spoke, Stone Eyes had stared each dragon in the eye until each in turn lowered their heads and averted their gaze, even Cave Song. He flared his wings, the scales glinting gold and red and copper in the light of the afternoon sun, and turned his bright eyes on the bonded on the ledge. Palon shrank back with the others, huddling in a ball with Tebah pressed against the wall where she couldn't cause trouble, just in case. She cringed to think of the tongue lashing he must have given the other dragons, thankful she hadn't been subjected to it.

"What are you talking about... ranks?" Tebah asked, her voice shaking as Stone Eyes lashed his tail and stomped away to a basking platform.

Frowning, Palon tried to think of how to apply it to what the girl would know, but soon gave up. "Once you're no longer a newling, your rank among bonded will reflect your dragon's rank. The only way a bonded can affect that rank is to pick a dragon fight on your account, and then only if your dragon wins."

Aturadin nodded. "You can easily become a humiliation or a pride for your dragon, though. So you must try to learn."

Tsían cleared his throat. He stood in the tunnel entrance behind them, every braid in its place as he fixed a stern gaze on the three of them. "Take Tebah to High Flight."

Bowing his head, Aturadin rose, tracing his fingers along Palon's shoulder before towing Tebah down the stairs.

Palon paused. "How's the hunt for the thief coming?"

Tsían shook his head. "We're still looking. It seems to be a bonded—we found some scuffed tracks. The dragons do not smell other dragons in their caches, which is fortunate, or things would be worse. Are you missing anything, you or Aturadin or your dragons?"

Palon shook her head.

"We'll get the thief. You keep your focus on Tebah."

* * *

Palon ducked, wincing as the metal tray clanged against the wall. It was going to be like this today, then. The girl's temper tantrums were grating, but Aturadin and Windward had at least found amusement in the situation. Behind her, Aturadin began to laugh, and she tossed him a glare. He covered his mouth, shoulders shaking.

In the middle of the room, Tebah stood on the grass mats they'd given her to ease her transition. The girl spent far too much time moping on them, but her expression was anything but mopey now. Kicking away the leather straps that coiled by her feet—where had those come from?—Tebah charged Palon.

It was ridiculous, and Aturadin dissolved helplessly into full-fledged laughter.

Mirth from Windward filled her mind as he pointed out that this was the second time the newling had attacked her. One more would be a record.

Palon rolled her eyes at them both as she caught the newling. Their amusement was contagious, but Windward teaming up with Aturadin was just wrong.

Windward quieted, but not before observing that newlings attacked her far more often than they attacked anyone else. Shaking her head, she pushed him away.

The girl was clearly untrained in fighting beyond the basics necessary for Rinaryn life, but she made up for what she didn't know with exuberance. One of her flailing kicks caught Palon's upper arm. Spinning her around, Palon pinned the girl's arms behind her back. Shouting and stumbling, the newling struggled. If she'd been able to reach, Palon wouldn't have doubted for a moment that the girl would have bitten her.

"Stop," Palon bit out, trying to keep the girl from wrenching her arms with her antics. "Stop now."

"Palon..." Aturadin was no longer laughing.

With a grunt, Tebah leaped and kicked backward with both feet. She missed Palon's knees, and Palon let her fall on her face rather than rip her arms out of their sockets. The girl hit the ground hard enough to stun the breath out of her. Dropping on top of her, Palon grabbed her arms, securing them behind her back once more. She glanced up at the vents at the top of the cave. At least High Flight was away for a moment. She wasn't sure how much of the girl's anger would translate through the forming bond.

Tebah refused to talk to High Flight and avoided him to the point where Aturadin and Palon had to supervise her to make sure she spent any time at all with him. They'd settled her in beside High Flight; simply being close to her dragon would strengthen the bond, regardless of the stone walls between them. Every time Palon checked on the girl, her skin crawled with a sense of wrong, walking into someone else's cave, and her irritation was only compounded by the girl's foul attitude.

"Get off me!" The girl squirmed and spat.

Of course she was going to be trouble. The more obstinate she was, the longer it would be until Palon could go flying again without checking in with Aturadin. She hated the restrictions, small though they were. Aturadin didn't deserve to be stuck with the girl all the time, and Palon wasn't going to shirk her duties. The girl could throw the entire nest into chaos.

Aturadin crouched in front of them while Palon sat on Tebah. Red faced and grunting with effort and outrage, the newling kicked and fought, even though she had to realize she wasn't going to win. She had to know she needed to submit. Why all the defiance?

"Tebah." Aturadin's voice was calm and not even all that loud, but he had a trick of speaking where he captured your attention and briefly held it hostage. It worked even on the recalcitrant girl, and she paused in her fit.

"Something you should know before you continue. As a newling, you're at the bottom of the hierarchy. Anyone can punish you."

Bonded hierarchy was as strict as the dragon hierarchy it ran parallel to. Just as Tsían held Palon and Aturadin responsible for Tebah's well-being, any higher ranking bonded was allowed to correct the newly bonded for perceived slights or challenges.

"What?" Tebah gasped. Her brown hair was a tangled mess. Palon would need to dunk the girl and pin her down to get the snarls out of her hair if she wasn't going to take care of herself. Yet another chore.

The girl gasped again, and Palon shook her head, refusing to fall for the 'I can't breathe' trick. Aturadin looked at her with raised eyebrows and then put on his pleading face.

Palon scowled at him. Prepared for the sudden lunge for freedom, Palon scooted back, kneeling on Tebah's legs instead. The girl squirmed, but not as much as Palon had expected, instead panting on the stone floor.

Aturadin raised his eyebrows, his smug expression sparking Palon to twist her lips at him in annoyance. She turned her concern on Tebah as the girl's breathing finally calmed. What had Aturadin seen that she missed? How had he known the girl wasn't faking?

"Tebah." It was that voice again. "You talk back, you make faces, you disrespect those higher ranked than you—which is everyone—or you attack someone, and they'll take it as a challenge."

Tebah shook her head, and Palon scooted off her legs. She kept herself in a ready stance between Tebah and the entrance, but the girl didn't bolt for the tunnels. Instead, she scrambled to the far corner and curled up tightly.

Palon gave Aturadin a worried look. He shrugged minutely, moving forward and crouching in front of the newling. Behind them, Palon kicked the scraps of leather with her boot again, then squatted to inspect them further. Aturadin was far better with the newling than she was—she'd let him deal with her for a bit.

Aturadin's tone remained mild. "You need to know these things. Your world has changed. It has dragons in it now."

"This is not my world, not my home," Tebah mumbled through her tangles.

How could the newling be so attached to her old life? Dragons picked people like Palon for bonding, those unattached to families and villages, who longed for more than their old lives could give them. It was strange enough, Palon remembered vaguely, going from village life where your identity was tied up with other people, to living as a dragonbonded, where your identity was mainly linked with your dragon. She'd never regretted her decision to leave, not even during the rocky adjustment period.

Aturadin tilted his head. "That life died when you accepted the dragon's offer."

"I didn't know it would be like this!"

"None of us knew exactly what to expect, and how could we?" Aturadin replied. "But you knew the stories—enough to know what you were accepting, at least. Strength and knowledge as well as responsibilities."

Distaste filled her, and Palon struggled not to let it show. The power and freedom of a dragon could only be shared through the bond—by becoming dragonbonded with all that went with it—and every Rinaryn child knew that. Still, some newlings railed against the decision they'd made, at least during the adjustment period, and Palon had never understood it. Why go back on a decision made? Selfish, fickle, and childish they were, and she was stuck with one of that lot, of course. She took a deep breath, trying to find her patience. There was still a chance the girl wouldn't be so bad once she settled in. She just wished she had time.

Aturadin smiled. "Think back to when High Flight called you. If he had said that to earn the freedom of the skies forever, you had to spend a few awkward months acclimating in a strange place, would you have refused?"

"Yes."

Palon scowled at the girl. That was impossible. If she really would have refused, High Flight never would have chosen her, because the bond would never take. Windward's promise of freedom and adventure had lifted Palon through the confusion of her own first days, and he had fulfilled that promise. It made the times when she was temporarily grounded especially irritating. Like now, while the newling threw her temper tantrum. Stuck here in the nest, it was almost like she never left her village, but for Windward's companionship.

How could anyone reject a life with dragons, especially after first accepting that deal? The girl was lying.

The words burst from Tebah as she trembled, though fire lit in her eyes. "High Flight said I would learn how to cure my great-mother. But I have learned nothing that matters!"

Palon and Aturadin hissed. To gain a newling when a higher ranking bonded forbade it was bad enough. To do so through misleading—no, through lying to—that newling was even worse. It should have been unthinkable, just the way the thefts should have been unthinkable. What was the nest coming to? All around Silver Spine's last days, too, as if the world was conspiring to send him out with turmoil rather than peace, as was good and decent.

She met Aturadin's outraged eyes, but he spoke first. "You need to tell Tsían."

"No! You tell him!" Tsían's wrath would be fierce, and Palon tried to keep from angering him as much as possible.

"Not a chance."

"Just tell me," Tebah shouted, her hands curled into tight fists.

"Your bond won't be able to carry enough information for High Flight to teach you things for a long time." Fury roared in her at High Flight. The newling wouldn't be able to learn anything beyond the basics from him for a year, until her connection to High Flight fully stabilized. Even then, she wouldn't be able to simply demand his knowledge.

"High Flight isn't a bad dragon, just... not really a thinker."

Palon elbowed Aturadin, but he skipped to the side. The girl was clearly not a thinker either. How could she assume she'd have access to the dragon's knowledge right away? Rinaryn life was hard, and chances were her great-mother would die before the girl's bond was complete.

"Then I might as well leave now," the girl said.

"Why do you cling to this idea of leaving?" Aturadin asked.

The girl's eyes glinted with stubborn fury. "I only wanted this one answer. Now I'm just going home sooner than I otherwise would."

Palon rocked back on her heels. The audacity of this girl! "What were you prepared to give up to gain that knowledge, if not stay with a dragon? It's only been a few days and you already plan to cut on your end of the deal."

Tebah glowered at her, but Palon was carried on a wave of fury. "I have no sympathy for people who want to go back on their word."

The girl's mouth opened and closed, but nothing came out. She had bonded and promised to partner with a dragon, all the while planning a betrayal. Palon was glad the newling didn't give any excuses—she wasn't sure her temper could handle it.

Aturadin bumped her lightly with his shoulder, his way of telling her he thought she was going too far.

She drew a deep breath. Maybe a different angle would help. "Did you know High Flight chose you out of all those people? Not only in your village, but in your region? He saw you, the real you, and decided you were something special. And you are. He asked you, and you said yes, though many would have rejected him. You're dragonbonded now, whatever your misgivings, regardless of your faithlessness. You can accept that and explore all the amazing world that has opened up to you, or you can be a child and scream and cry."

Aturadin sighed, giving her an exasperated look. "Palon's right. Dragons don't choose lightly, and you accepted this when you accepted the bond. Even if you're nervous and afraid and homesick right now. Even though he lied. The bond cannot be undone."

Palon's gaze snapped to Aturadin, but he just shrugged and continued, unfazed by the unspoken warning. He'd never cared much about the hierarchy, but he didn't usually rustle any wings, either. High Flight's youth and foolishness made it easier somehow to disrespect him. If that passed on to the newling, though, the girl would surely make things even more difficult.

"He should have told me how it would be!"

Scoffing, Palon shook her head. "To him, not much has changed. He's old, older than you can imagine. Your lifetime is a drop of water in an ocean, an exhalation in a gale of wind. He can't possibly be expected to understand what you're going through, not until your bond solidifies and you can show him yourself. He'll understand because you will change him through the bond, just as he changes you."

Aturadin nodded. "That's why we're here to help you in the transition. Palon's among the most dragon of us. She understands them the best."

"And you'll probably grow to like him." Palon jabbed a thumb in Aturadin's direction. "Most people do."

"Undo the bond, or I will refuse to cooperate until you can no longer stand me."

Palon's patience snapped. "You'd die, you brat, or go insane. If you made it back to your village, you could hurt your family—your loved ones—because you'd be out of your mind. High Flight could go insane. The bonds of others in the nest could be damaged because of the telepathic strain. Your bond, at this very time, is precarious, but also extremely important. You need to forget this selfishness." Palon clenched her teeth, seeing the disappointment on Aturadin's face.

Tebah stared at them, fire in her eyes once again. "I will never stop trying to run, and if you try to stop me, I will keep trying to escape. And I will succeed, eventually."

"Then we'll have to lock you up." Palon said. "Or High Flight will find you and bring you back."

Aturadin shot her another look, and she shrugged at him. Those were the terms. She'd already said too much in her outburst, possibly scarred the girl emotionally.

"You already bound me once. How much worse can it get?"

Aturadin heaved a sigh of exasperation and turned on Palon, his mouth opening to scold. She cut him off. "I didn't do it." She raised her eyebrows at Tebah. "Who tied you up?"

Tebah glared at her, jaw clenched tight.

Dragonfire, the girl was tiresome! Crouching beside Aturadin, Palon leaned forward, trapping Tebah in the corner. "Who. Did. It? Describe them!"

"A man." Tebah shrank back, avoiding her gaze. Palon leaned back to give her space. That ruled out half the bonded.

Tebah continued, talking to the rocks beneath her feet. "He had black hair in a braid, cut short on the one side. He was watching the fight, before."

"Laetiran." Anger roughened Aturadin's voice.

Palon nodded. Laetiran's distinctive hairstyle resulted from trying to jump another bonded in the tunnels a couple months ago. Yiyin had pulled a knife and nearly scalped him in retaliation.

Realization struck her. Yiyin and Laetiran's dragons had fought severely because of the incident. Stone Eyes hadn't mediated, too preoccupied with the death of his bonded just that morning. To avoid further injury and give Stone Eyes the telepathic space to grieve, Cave Song, Black Cloud, and Dusks Dive had separated the males.

Those dragons had been stolen from.

"Did he do anything else?" Palon asked.

"What, tying me up and leaving me helpless isn't enough?" Tebah shrieked. Palon winced. She hadn't meant that. Lying helpless like that would be a nightmare, and she wished she knew how to comfort the girl. She'd have to confront Laetiran and make certain he knew how badly he'd misstepped to mess with the newling.

"If Laetiran comes near you again, you let us know," Aturadin said, patting the girl's shoulder.

"He'd better not," Palon growled.

Tebah flinched, but Aturadin chuckled. "Don't worry. Palon likes you."

Shaking her head, Palon stalked back to the leather strips. She scooped up the pile and shoved it in her pocket.

"How did Laetiran tie you up? High Flight should have stopped it," Aturadin asked.

The girl turned away. "High Flight was gone." She cleared her throat, her voice rising to a screech, "And he can stay gone. I do *not* need him!"

Aturadin's expression was troubled as he looked over at Palon. High Flight must have needed to hunt, drink, bask briefly, or perform some other necessity—like he was now—and Laetiran had taken advantage of the opportunity for mischief. They needed to protect the newling. As if things weren't troubling enough.

She nodded at him. "Windward will help watch. And you and I can watch the tunnels."

Flashing her a brief, tight smile, Aturadin turned back to Tebah.

"Now then, did you eat any of the food before you chucked the tray at Palon? Mind you, I wouldn't try such a thing twice."

"You won't get away with it a second time," Palon said.

Tebah's voice was cautious. "I ate first. I didn't know when you would feed me again."

"You're not a prisoner, Tebah," Aturadin said, sounding grieved. "If you need anything, just ask."

"Except you can't leave," Palon said, cutting Tebah off.

"You're a liar," the girl spat at Aturadin, and then fixed her fury on Palon. "And you're just mean!"

Lashing out at Aturadin went too far.

Palon lunged forward, moving so fast Aturadin scrambled to grab her arm. She shook her finger in the brat's face as the girl drew back in fear. Her voice came out as a hiss between her bared teeth. "Don't you ever—*ever*—call him names again, do you hear me? You don't want him not to be here for you. Think about it—just stop and shut your mouth and think for a moment! He's trying to be nice to you. He's trying to help you. Don't you dare throw that in his face. And yes, I'm mean. Meaner than you know. So don't test me."

"Palon." Aturadin's voice was calm as he rested his hand on her arm.

She shook him off and stalked away, pausing in the tunnel opening as she struggled to battle the offended dragon in her back down. Tebah had gone back to the corner, huddled in a tiny ball. Hopefully it was a good sign she'd chosen the corner to curl up in, that the bonding was strong enough already to suppress the natural Rinaryn claustrophobia. Palon rested her head against the stone, breathing deeply. This bonding process was not going well, and it seemed destined to only become more rocky.

Aturadin looked back at Tebah. "Listen, stay here for now. We'll be back to go for a walk in a little while. Don't try to leave, or Palon's right, we'd have to put you on lock down. We don't want to do that, and we won't so long as you can keep from trying to run away. You wouldn't get far anyway."

If Tebah answered, Palon didn't hear it. She waited for Aturadin, tense with the anger roiling in her. Aturadin threw an arm around her shoulders as they left. "She's just scared, Palon."

"Well, she can be scared without attacking the people trying to help her."

Aturadin laughed. "Can she?"

Palon narrowed her eyes at him.

Aturadin shook his head, lightly squeezing her shoulders. "You're thinking like a dragon, Palon. Think like a Rinaryn—that's how Tebah is thinking. She can't think like a dragon yet. Even the idea would be terrifying to her."

"She'll have to get used to it sooner or later. And she intended to betray High Flight, to steal his knowledge and run!"

"This isn't about that. It's about helping her through the transition. Come on, Palon, can't you remember how you felt when you were newling? You were twelve, right?"

Palon nodded, shifting with sudden unease. She didn't like talking about the past. It wasn't bad, there was just no reason to talk about it. It had no effect on her. She couldn't change it. There was no use sitting around reminiscing, as far as she was concerned. She'd had parents and siblings and a village, just like every other Rinaryn, and then she'd left all those things behind for wings, just like every other dragonbonded.

Belatedly, she realized Aturadin was still talking, gesturing with his hands as they walked down the curving corridor. "...So she'll figure it out faster, ok? And then, her link will be stronger with High Flight, and the dragons will shower you with jewels and shiny stones."

Palon gave him a look, and he grinned. "Just checking to see if you were listening."

She shook her head. "Ok, fine. I'll try to be easier on her. I'll try."

Somehow, they needed to make sure the bond succeeded, for both Tebah and High Flight, as well as for the good of the nest. Every fledging bond was fragile. Tebah's seemed almost certainly doomed.

Chapter Five

When Palon went to get Tebah on the morning of the girl's sixth day, the newling stood ready, waiting in the middle of her room. Edging inside, Palon approached the girl as cautiously as if she were a lãwe, one of the large carnivorous beasts that dwelled in the mountains. Windward thought of them as a delicacy, but they were dangerous to take down, with their sharp claws and teeth.

"Ready for breakfast?" Palon asked, carrying a tray of bread and tea.

"Yes." Tebah gave a small smile, her tone pleasant.

She checked with Windward, but he said no one had come by since she left to grab the food. High Flight peered at her through the slits by the ceiling, his breathing echoing on the stone.

Palon tilted her head, but Tebah stood still, far too placid. On impulse, Palon checked the girl for a head wound, but though the newling eyed her with distaste, she appeared undamaged. Still suspicious, Palon pointed at the door and Tebah obeyed meekly. The hair rose on the back of Palon's neck and she fought off the urge to shudder.

Palon walked beside the girl, watching her out of the corner of her eye. The newling remained passive, giving nothing solid for Palon's suspicions to latch on to.

"We're going to the Sequestering Cave this morning. Do you remember how Aturadin and I told you about Silver Spine and Miros? We'll be eating breakfast with them, and you will be on your best behavior."

"Why?" Tebah's passive demeanor cracked as she growled the question, and Palon quirked a smile at the proof that her suspicions were founded.

"It's good for you to see your path all the way to the end. The dragons care for their bonded. Silver Spine is old and has a very limited time left with Miros; they are spending what remains to them together."

Tebah's shoulders slumped. "Do I have to?"

"You're going."

"Make me." The girl's jaw took on a stubborn set, her eyes rebellious.

Palon seized Tebah by the arm and brought her to an abrupt halt, sloshing some of the tea. She gestured to her face, where the bruises from her fall were fading but still lent her a fierce appearance. "Look at me. This is not a game. Do not challenge me, newling."

Tebah scowled up at her through dark eyebrows. Palon pushed her along through the tunnels. Tsían had been furious when Palon had told him of Tebah's accusations. Dragons were not supposed to lie to bonded, nor were bonded supposed to trick dragons. But the bond had formed, and it was too risky to break it now. High Flight had lied and Tebah had planned to trick him, and now both of them had to live with their choices. Palon clung to the frayed remnants of her patience—ever since the girl admitted to planning to go back on her word, it had been hard to be gentle with her, and the girl's attitude certainly wasn't helping.

There was silence for a while, until Tebah sassed again. "Aren't I supposed to only attach to my dragon?"

Palon shook her head, gathering her patience. "Silver Spine isn't going to bond you. He's focused on Miros. You will get to see the relationship between them. What you can have with High Flight."

Tebah scrunched her face up, but quickly looked down, so Palon let it go. "When we're there, keep your mind calm. Strong emotions spill out, picked up by others like waves in a pond reaching the opposite shore. Do not bother Silver Spine and Miros—they deserve all your respect, especially at this stage in their lives."

The newling was her responsibility and she'd walk through dragonfire before she allowed the girl to be disrespectful. The older dragons were full of the knowledge and wisdom of their long lives, and gratitude filled Palon that she was able to live alongside them, though none could compare to Windward.

The girl glared at her without speaking. The silence between them stretched out, and Palon sighed. She fought the bond with everything in her. She was a mistake, through and through, but Palon was stuck with her. There had to be a way to get through her attitude.

She and Aturadin had even taken to sleeping outside her room to protect her from further visits from Laetiran, though other bonded whispered at the unusual arrangements. And still the girl remained prickly, while the days went by and Palon couldn't find the time to fly —not without leaving the girl unguarded. Dragonfire blast through her if she didn't try everything to reach the girl.

"Do you collect anything?" Palon tried.

The girl's gaze narrowed and she pressed her lips together.

"We all collect something. Shells, beads, rocks, feathers, gems, even sticks. You let me or Aturadin or Tsían know when you start feeling the need to collect. We'll help you set traps to get started."

"I will *not* be asking you for help." Tebah bit off her words.

Palon took a deep, slow breath. "Then ask Tsían or Aturadin."

They turned a corner and walked several paces before Tebah glanced up at her. "Everyone has a collection?"

She nodded. "It's one effect of the bond."

"What will happen to the old one's collection?"

"Whoever dismantles the traps first will either keep it, distribute it, or throw it out."

"Traps?"

Palon nodded, relieved that Tebah's curiosity had returned. "We all trap our caches so that other bonded don't get into them. Most of us keep our collections near our dragons' for further protection. Bonded are very territorial about their caches, just like dragons, so don't let anyone catch you poking around their stash. It won't end well for you."

"Why not just share the same space as your dragons?" Tebah asked, as if it was the most obvious solution in the world.

She had promised Aturadin she'd be patient. Palon waited a breath so her tone would be level, beating down the exasperation. "There's that territoriality. For instance, I collect rocks. Windward also collects rocks. I love him and trust him, but I wouldn't be able to rest knowing my collection and his shared a cache, and neither would he. Aturadin and Scorch Frost collect different things, but Scorch Frost is fiercely possessive of his space. So it's just easier and less stressful to keep our collections separate from those of our dragons."

"Care to show the newling how to get into your stash, Palon?" Laetiran jogged up from behind them.

Palon suppressed a scowl, baring her teeth in a smile instead. She should have noticed Laetiran following them, eavesdropping. "Oh, I'm sorry to hear that," she said in honeyed tones, "I thought maybe you'd learned your lesson last time." She dropped the sweetness for a glare, growling, "Next time, I'll just have to punch you harder."

Grinning in the face of her threat, Laetiran dipped his shoulder. It was all part of their familiar dance: Laetiran eternally trying to get into her cache, Palon forever attempting to persuade him to give up. Normally it was obnoxious, but now, the threat caused her heart to hammer against her ribs. Tsían still hadn't found the thief, though to be fair it had only been a handful of days. It was difficult to be patient, when she couldn't shake the worry that she or Windward were next. Why couldn't Laetiran realize now was not the time for his silly antics?

Probably the same reason Fired Sand continued to jostle for rank. Like his ambition, Laetiran's smile was eternal, regardless of how he actually felt. The distrust between them only made their rivalry more volatile.

She braced against his "accidental" body slam, juggling the tray to avoid losing all of the tea. She sneered, kicking his calf in retaliation, but he just hopped ahead, smiling as if the whole exchange hadn't happened. He tousled Tebah's hair, whispered something in her ear, and then continued on ahead, far too merrily for Palon's taste.

"What is he up to now?" she grumbled. She'd warned Laetiran to leave the newling alone, but it didn't look like he was taking the hint. A peculiar expression lighted on Tebah's face, but she said nothing. The girl was no help at all.

"Whatever he told you, ignore it." Her back stiff, Palon refused the growing urge to check on her stash. The thief was still out there, but there was no way she was letting the newling near her collection. Even if she longed to hold her crystal again, though she'd just seen it last night.

If she could just go flying, the tensions would fade and everything would be right again, she knew it. But Windward was supposed to be resting his foot, and she was stuck with the newling instead of making sure he was getting better.

Pushing it out of her mind, Palon climbed the steps to the Sequestering Cave.

"Hello, Miros." Palon smiled as she paused in the entrance, blocking Tebah.

The bonded lay cradled between Silver Spine's head and his left foreleg, the dragon's long neck curled to the side to almost envelop him. Miros made a sharp contrast to the last bonded who had occupied this cave, in the spring of the year. Kepaeros had been over one hundred, white haired, his eyes beginning to cloud over. Miros was only in his fifties, with sandy hair and a lean figure.

The cave was clean and sparse, with no decorations, only lanterns on the near wall, freshly filled with oil by the look of them. Past the bonded pair, a flat ledge jutted out into the open air, a convenient place for the dragons who used the Sequestering Cave to land and take off. Beyond the ledge, the whole of the Basking Basin was visible, including the enormous granite slab that served as a main entrance to the nest. Everything looked softer in the morning light.

Miros's gaze wandered blankly over them several times, his head wavering on his neck. Some days he was almost his old self, while other days he was so deep in his dragon that nothing else mattered. Palon's stomach turned as Miros seemed not to recognize them, or even that they were separate from the cave walls around them. Her old mentor laid his head back against Silver Spine once more, apparently dismissing them.

She swallowed hard, her voice thick. "May we enter?"

Miros looked up again, his lips quivering as if he couldn't decide whether or not to speak. On the fourth pass, his gaze stopped on Palon, and after several moments, lit up with recognition. He struggled to sit up, his mouth working soundlessly.

Then he demanded with such familiar grumpiness that Palon's heart ached, "Palon! Get over here. Is that my breakfast? Took you long enough, girl! Be prompt next time, will you? Who's the mouse with you?"

Palon smiled, guiding the newling in. "Never, ever, ever enter this chamber without asking permission first, understand? Even if you were sent."

The girl nodded, though her wide eyes were fixed on Miros and Silver Spine, and she walked as if slogging through mud.

Palon set the tray on a flat-topped rock, then brought Miros his tea and three thick slabs of bread drizzled with honey. "This is Tebah, newling of High Flight."

Miros leaned back on one of Silver Spine's enormous claws, which the dragon propped up for that purpose. "Ah, the newly bonded who is causing such trouble, eh?" He snatched the food from Palon's hand, spilling some of the tea as he did so. Palon winced, even as Miros hissed at her, "Mind your clumsiness!"

She offered him a napkin, but he ignored her, his gaze losing focus, so she dabbed up the spilled tea. His harsh words rolled harmlessly off her, for he was with his dragon, and his reality was not quite the same as theirs. Kepaeros had been like this too, in the end. He'd been a natural leader of the bonded, until he and Stone Eyes took to the Sequestering Cave last spring. She'd brought him food like this too, until the last few days, when the only one he would see was Tsían, to "pass the dragonfire", as he put it.

She hadn't guessed Miros and Silver Spine would be using the Sequestering Cave so soon after Kepaeros's passing. She swallowed hard, focusing herself on what she could control.

Sitting beside Tebah a few paces away, Palon gestured at the girl permission to eat, and took a bite of bread herself.

Miros ate slowly, dribbling crumbs down into his beard. His hand shook as he drank his tea, sloshing the liquid. Silver Spine kept his head close to Miros, who in turn maintained physical contact with the dragon at all times, as if the dragon were a lifeline. And in a way he was, she supposed.

Palon had to force herself to chew and swallow. The food was tasteless and stuck in her throat, even the dark, rich bread, Eltavae's specialty. She washed it down with tea, her appetite vanished in the presence of Miros's deterioration.

Keeping her voice low, Palon focused on the reason she'd brought Tebah here. "Note how close Miros stays with Silver Spine, and Silver Spine's protective coiling around him. This is why we all have been so on edge lately. It is hard on a dragon to release the bond."

"They're squashed together." Tebah's voice was appallingly loud in the somber cave, and Palon winced. She glanced at Miros, ready for a tirade on manners, but he simply stared into the distance, drool beginning a track toward his chin.

Palon glared a rebuke at Tebah, partly to avoid looking at Miros. "When you're with High Flight, stop shutting him out. Try connecting with him. I don't care if you scream and yell at him, Tebah, but you need to start talking to him."

Tebah stared at Miros and Silver Spine, silent except for the sound of her chewing. Suddenly disgusted, Palon put her breakfast down and finished her tea. She instantly regretted it because it left her nothing else to do except sit in the heavy atmosphere.

"Why isn't the oldest one the leader?"

"Why should they be?" Palon's brow furrowed. "Tsían leads the bonded, since the most dominant dragon is unbonded. Tsían was only second in command, most of the time. It's a bit awkward, I'm sure, as instead of a bonded team leading us, it's an unbalanced trio—Stone Eyes, Forest Blaze, and Tsían working together. But he's doing the best he can, with the thefts and with you. It'd help if people were more cooperative."

Still staring, Tebah didn't react to Palon's barbed comment, and she had time to regret it. Most of her annoyances weren't the girl's fault, after all. She opened her mouth to apologize, but Tebah whispered, "The dragon seems so... almost tender."

Palon smiled, trying to relax, to make up for earlier. She leaped on the girl's curiosity, eager to move past the rebelliousness and show her the wonders of dragon life. "Tender's the right word. See, a dragon might live eight hundred years. A Rinaryn, only a hundred. So a dragon may have perhaps five bonded in their lifetime, and each one is a carefully cultivated, fiercely protected relationship. Little is more important to a dragon in his prime."

"Why?"

"Dragons can Shift, or realmwalk—they travel to whole other realms. But they can only safely do it with an anchor, until they are old and experienced enough to hold pieces of each realm in their heart. We are their anchor."

She smiled as Windward interrupted, reminding her of when the two of them had had this same conversation. Her eyes half closed as the words he had used echoed in her memory and she shared them with Tebah. "Our people are connected to home. The land runs in our blood. So the dragons take us away with them, and as a magnet, we bonded pull them back home."

Palon grinned abruptly. "When Windward told me this, when I was young like you, I asked, 'The land runs in our blood more than in yours?'

"And Windward confirmed. The dragons are multiplanar creatures, while Rinaryns have only ever had one home. For generations and generations, we pull them home."

Tebah looked down, kicking her heels on the rock she sat atop. "Seeing other places might be nice. High Flight talked about grooming, how a bonded will help keep him cleaner than he can keep himself, and help with injuries, and tending herds and gathering materials. I could do all that at home. I do not want to just clean up after a dragon." The girl's eyes flicked to Silver Spine and her expression went from uneasy to defiant in the blink of an eye.

Palon closed her eyes for a moment, irritation with High Flight drowning her. She gritted her teeth, breathing in deeply. "High Flight bonded too soon. He only lost his last bonded some ten years ago. Most dragons wait fifteen or twenty between bondings, giving themselves time to recenter and clear their thoughts from the cloudiness of grief."

"So why did he decide not to wait?" Tebah asked.

"Dragons are typically very logical, but inside they are highly emotive. The opposite of Rinaryns, really. We complement our dragons, and we become more like each other, working together in harmony once the bond is strong—that's the power of the partnership with your dragon. High Flight... he's—" She stopped herself abruptly, her gaze going to Miros and Silver Spine. It wasn't her place to correct dragons. How many times had Miros drilled that into her head? She refused to do him the disrespect of forgetting his lessons in his presence.

She took a deep breath and reframed her words. "High Flight is right, that's part of our responsibilities. I'm sure he had good reasons for failing to mention the more exciting sides of being bonded to you. When the dragons go into torpor, you'll also be entrusted with guarding his cache for him. He'll depend on you to keep his collection safe."

A light glittered in the girl's eyes, and there was an edge to her voice. "And when is that?"

Looking out into the open sky, Palon grimaced. "Far too soon. Your bond is not ready. The dragons will sleep the winter away, and all weak bonds will degrade." Torpor was her least favorite season. The loneliness and boredom and confinement from the sky were only made tolerable by Aturadin's presence and the games the bonded would play. This coming season felt dangerous. If Tebah's bond wasn't strong enough to survive, both she and High Flight would go insane at best.

Tebah shrugged, picking at her boot laces. "He said bonding would help him communicate with other Rinaryns if needed."

Palon smiled. What a glamorous thing to tell a potential newly bonded. "And that didn't enthuse you either? Well, dragons almost never communicate with anyone besides their bonded and other dragons."

"In my years, I've only been spoken to twice by other dragons, and mind you it was not a pleasant experience," Miros interrupted, his eyes sharp once more, pinning them to the rocks. "Once during the Fire, and another time during the Walavai War."

Miros's stories always brought a smile to her face. He dove straight to the point, somehow understanding exactly what information you needed to know. He'd always been better at this than her, and it was humbling that he was still better than her, even now. But of course, she'd known he would be. Hopefully the girl would take Miros's words to heart, since she refused to listen to anyone else.

Palon nodded to Tebah, fixing her sharp gaze on her. "High Flight is important in your life now. Even though you're angry, you two need each other now."

"You cannot ignore your dragon, little trouble girl," Miros said, his head bobbing on his neck. "The bond must be healthy, for both your sakes. And then, once it's established, you will be welcomed among your fellow bonded."

"It's not fair!" shouted Tebah.

"Who said it should be?" Miros raised his eyebrows. "The rain isn't fair. The sun isn't fair. This is life. This is what is required of you. The bond is all important."

"The bond is everything," Palon chimed in with him, remembering her own drills.

Miros looked at her sharply. "Well, you at last learned your lessons, yes. You'll do alright, Palon. You'll do alright."

Palon blinked rapidly, tears stinging her eyes as unexpected as the rare compliment.

Chapter Six

Palon scowled, watching the ledge below. Tebah stood with her arms folded, her back turned to High Flight while the dragon groveled with his head on the ground, huffing and whistling. Palon stepped back into Windward's embrace as he tucked his wing around her, humming low. Instantly, the press of her worries and annoyances lessened, just like the bite of the day's cold wind.

They had to work it out on their own. Each entered into this bargain of their own free will, regardless of the deception.

"On either's part," Palon grumbled, narrowing her eyes. High Flight should never have dared lie to Tebah, and Tebah should never have dared think to enter into a contract with dragons while intending to run the moment things became difficult.

Windward rumbled his agreement, the vibrations of his enormous voice rocking her to her core, shooing the tension away. She smiled, leaning against him as she let her body relax, from her shoulders all the way to her toes. Aturadin was off hunting with Scorch Frost, leaving her on newling-duty, but at least she had the company of Windward.

Forest Blaze whistled and Windward's head came up, his rumbles ending. Palon rested her hand on his shoulder, inquiring what it was while keeping her eye on Tebah. High Flight hadn't reacted to whatever had grabbed Windward's attention. He crawled forward on his belly, pushing himself with awkward motions of his wings. Still Tebah ignored him, and he stopped a few feet from her, whistling plaintively.

A sharing of information from Windward grabbed her attention, and she looked up. Stone Eyes was coming back and had told Forest Blaze to watch for dragons from other nests. Apparently he'd seen one, far too close to their nest for comfort.

"Remember the one we saw coming back from practice? The day the girl woke up?" Palon asked.

The sun glinted off Windward's horns as he dipped his head, sending her an affirmative. It was possible the uproar in their nest had attracted attention from other nests. They'd be able to feel the tension like jiggles on the web of a spider, though they had hoped such telepathic vibrations wouldn't travel so far.

"If other dragons come looking for trouble, we'll deal with them," Palon said. This nest, these caves, were *theirs*.

Windward roared, and he must have shared the thought, for several other dragons also roared, a great wave of sound welcoming Stone Eyes back to the nest. He added his voice to theirs, stomping on the ground with his clawed feet and spitting a belch of flame.

Smiling, Palon turned back to Tebah. The newling had sunk down to a crouch, but still held her back toward High Flight, who tossed his head, slicing his horns through the air. Stone Eyes turned toward him and puffed up, exuding power and strength. Palon found it hard to breathe, he was so glorious, and she rested her hand on Windward's claw to steady herself.

With a whisper of a whistle, Windward dipped his head to her level, explaining that Stone Eyes was calling High Flight forward for judgement.

She sucked in a breath. Drooping, High Flight slithered off the ledge, carefully avoiding Tebah as he went. His light copper wings picked up dust as they dragged along the ground. The girl raised her head abruptly as he passed by, her eyes full of suspicion.

Without a functioning bond, she wouldn't know what was going on.

Palon patted Windward's claw and scampered down the rock wall separating the ledges. It was an easy step for the dragons, but bonded had to climb. Tebah was so engrossed in watching, she didn't turn as Palon came up behind her, though she jumped with a gasp when Palon tapped her on the shoulder.

"Come on. Stone Eyes called High Flight forward."

The girl glared at her. "No."

Palon raised her eyes to the sky and caught sight of Windward staring down at her in amusement, his two backward-curved horns creating a partition of the cloudy autumn sky. She found herself smiling.

"Come on, so I can tell you what's happening. Aturadin is gone, so you'll have to put up with me."

The girl's stare only increased in intensity. "Why should I care what happens?"

Palon glared at her in return. The same old anger she always found when dealing with the girl begged for release. She should be out there, in the sky, but instead she was stuck here while Windward's foot healed, guarding the girl from Laetiran's pranks and teaching her, and still the girl refused to cooperate.

It'd be easier to deal with all the little annoyances if the girl would at least try.

"You won't understand then. So be it." Palon turned, stalking back to the wall, and began to climb.

"Wait!"

A sigh broke from her. Would the girl ever learn to make a decision and stand by it? Now she wanted to change her mind and make Palon wait instead of just being rational in the first place? It wasn't a huge problem, but it was irritating. That was all the girl seemed to be: irritating.

"Catch up," she said, glancing below her. She couldn't help but smile, seeing the newling's mouth drop open in shock and dismay.

"I cannot climb this!"

"Yes you can," Palon returned. "It's easy. Find a handhold, find a foothold, pull yourself up. Repeat."

"You're crazy!"

"You're lazy!" The words slipped out before she could help it.

"I hate you."

"Tell that to my face." Palon stopped climbing and hung there, waiting. Maybe anger would spur the girl to action where reason failed.

Grumbling threats that Palon pretended not to hear, the newling finally started to climb, scaling the wall quickly until she reached Palon's ankle.

Stone Eyes was waiting, Windward sent her. The dragon also wondered idly if the newling would hit Palon once she reached her.

"She'd have to get to me first," Palon muttered. The ledge wasn't that tall—only one and a half times as tall as she was.

"What?" asked the girl.

"Nothing. Get a move on; Stone Eyes is going to start soon."

The girl kept going, still muttering under her breath, and Palon resumed climbing as soon as the newling reached her waist. If the girl hit her while Stone Eyes was handing down judgement that would be awkward and embarrassing. She wouldn't put it past her, either. Reaching the top, she swung herself over and extended a hand to Tebah, but the girl refused to take it.

"Why hasn't he started yet?" the newling asked, panting, as she pulled herself onto the ledge.

"Dragons move more slowly than we do. Also, he's waiting for you, because he has something called manners." Palon dusted herself off and went to Windward. The girl hugged herself a few feet away, her eyes on the scene below.

It was quite a scene, too. High Flight huddled, wings drooping on the stone floor, a line behind him showing he'd slithered on his belly the whole way, while Stone Eyes towered over him. Windward coiled his neck to lay his head by her, and Palon stood on one of his claws, holding onto the base of his horn. She wanted to be close to him for this.

Stone Eyes looked around, rumbling, and Windward sent her the message. Palon translated for the newling. "High Flight has erred gravely. Not only has he bonded only months before torpor, throwing out the advice of myself and Forest Blaze and Dusks Dive—"

"—As if he needed any extra advice!—" Palon interrupted herself, rolling her eyes at High Flight's folly.

"—but he also misled she who would bond him. The trust between a dragon and a dragonbonded is of utmost importance. The bond is started, the decisions made. It will not be undone. However, this can never be allowed to happen again."

"You believed me?" The newling's voice was barely a whisper, though she didn't look up.

"What do you think we are? Stone Eyes investigated and High Flight admitted to it. This is the consequence of an action we know to be true, not just an accusation."

With a gasp, the girl stiffened, and Palon looked at her, skin prickling. What had happened? Surely no one would mess with the girl during such a grave occasion. Surely she hadn't missed some threat to the newling.

Windward sent her that Stone Eyes had ordered High Flight to dampen his bond.

No danger then. Palon relaxed against Windward's head. The girl must have felt that, hence the gasp—which meant her bond was progressing at least a little. It'd go better if she'd only let it.

Palon glared at her. "You felt him dampen the bond. He feels that when you shut him out too."

"Why did he... what? Dampen?"

With a wince, Palon turned back to the scene below. "Dragon Law."

Stone Eyes roared, the sound of his voice bouncing from one side of the nest to the other, and dragons and bonded alike cringed at the sound. Drawing back one forefoot, Stone Eyes slammed his talons into High Flight's muzzle. The younger dragon screeched, wings flaring and then drooping once more as the dragon submitted to his punishment. Again Stone Eyes raised his claws and slapped High Flight. The younger dragon scooted backward a few feet, whistling a long, drawn out note.

Stone Eyes turned and stared directly at them, and Palon clutched Windward's horn more tightly. Windward jerked a bit, surprise jostling him and therefore her. When Windward relayed Stone Eye's instructions, she nearly fell off his talons.

"What?" Palon stared at Windward.

She shivered as her dragon assured her it was so. Such things were unheard of, but then, so were dragons lying to gain a bonded. So was stealing from dragons.

Glancing at Stone Eyes, Palon turned to Tebah. "Stone Eyes says you decide when High Flight has had enough. You decide when your wrong has been avenged."

"What?" the girl squeaked.

Another screech rose from High Flight as Stone Eyes hit him again. And again. And again. High Flight sneezed, blood spattering the stone, but remained huddled on the ground. Bile burned in Palon's throat.

"Tebah, you say when!" Didn't she understand? She clenched her fists. "The more High Flight is injured, the longer he'll have to suppress the bond to keep from sharing that pain with you!"

"The bond shares pain?" Tebah's eyes glinted.

"Of course it does!"

"Then let him feel mine!" the girl lunged for the knife at Palon's belt.

"You stupid girl, what are you doing?" Palon grabbed her arm. "He won't feel your pain right now anyway because he's suppressing the bond, you idiot!"

The girl froze, a sneer contorting her face. "Then let him be beaten all night, for all I care! He never should have lied to me!"

"And this is to ensure no dragon ever does the same, ever again!"

"Good!"

A desperation similar to panic made her tremble, especially as High Flight gave another plaintive whistle, staring at Tebah. How could Tebah let this continue? She understood Stone Eyes's point—placing dragons at the mercy of the bonded they tricked should deter any who weren't deterred by common decency.

But the girl turned her back, refused to see.

Windward passed on a message, that High Flight was calling Tebah's name, begging for her forgiveness. He'd been so close to his last bonded, and sympathy washed over her in the face of the dragon's grief and guilt. It was wrong that the same sympathy should not sway his bonded.

Snarling, Palon grabbed the newling by the shoulder and whipped her around. She jabbed a finger at the scene. "You say when, Tebah. If you're going to let someone suffer, have the decency to look them in the eye while they do so!"

The girl cringed, crumpling to her knees. That was not the reaction she was expecting. Where had all the tears come from? Palon crouched beside her, one hand resting gently on the girl's shoulder. So she did care after all. The viciousness was all just an act?

Below them, Stone Eyes doled out High Flight's punishment in measured doses, while around them, whistles of concern rose from the watching dragons. No one would forget this scene, not for generations of bonded. Their dragons would show the next generation, and the next.

"Stop!" The girl's sob broke into the open air.

Stone Eyes drew back, staring at them with such ferocity that Palon recoiled. Tebah shook like the last leaf in autumn, huddling against Palon, and Palon put her arm around the girl, holding her close. With a dip of his head, Stone Eyes stepped back, draping a wing over High Flight as the younger dragon shambled to his feet.

"It's going to hurt him to eat for a while," Palon said. She looked down at the girl. "But it's over now, finally. Why did you wait so long?"

Tears streamed down the girl's face, and her hands were clenched into trembling fists at her sides. She opened her mouth, then shut it, staring down at the Basin. Palon tightened her arm around the girl, unsure what to do with all the girl's brokenness.

"The dragons won't stand for a dragon hurting a bonded, see?" Palon said. "And if you feel High Flight's pain, you only need to say.

You are not powerless here."

"How do I know... will he lie again?"

"If you let the bond actually develop, you'll know when he's hiding things from you. You'll feel it. But you have to accept your place here for that to happen."

The girl drew back, away from Palon's arm, as if realizing she was taking comfort from Palon. "You should not have done this."

"This, all of this? This is to protect you and all of the bonded, now and in the future."

"Just leave me alone!" she shouted, and dashed into the tunnels.

Palon kept her movements slow and nonthreatening as she stepped into Tebah's room the next morning. The night had been quiet as usual, and Palon was beginning to think maybe they could stop watching so cautiously. But not only did their vigilance prevent anyone from messing with the newling, it also kept the girl from having a chance to fulfill her threats of running. High Flight's green eyes watched her through the slits near the ceiling, and Palon suppressed a shiver at the intensity of his gaze. The soft bedmats still lay in the middle of the room, but they were empty.

A weight hit her, knocking her off balance. Grasping Tebah's wrist, Palon turned, tossing the girl to the ground. Tebah hurled herself at Palon once more, but Palon was ready for her. She grabbed the girl's wrist again and slammed her into the wall, pinning her there while the newling screamed and struggled. The hairs on her neck prickled as High Flight rumbled, but she took comfort in Windward's mental assurance that he, too, was nearby.

"Are we done?" Palon asked when the girl's struggling subsided. She stepped back carefully.

Tebah crumpled to the ground, hands over her face. Palon sighed and crouched beside her, just inside arm's reach. The girl's abrupt transitions from violence to tears and back were exhausting, and she never knew how the girl would react. When Tebah only kept sobbing, Palon shuffled a step closer, patting the girl on the shoulder, though the movement felt awkward.

"It gets better," she offered, knowing just how little that would seem right now.

"I hate you all," Tebah sobbed.

Palon grinned. "That's fine."

Tebah looked up. Her nose was running, her cheeks were tear-stained, and her eyes were red. She'd been crying all night, clearly.

"Being angry, hating us... I'd worry about you if you didn't, considering your circumstances," Palon said, tilting her head to the side. Tebah had had an audacious plan, both brave and stupid, and it had failed. It made sense that it'd take her a while to adjust to her failure. High Flight likely had adjusting to do as well, facing his own consequences.

The girl's face scrunched. "It's not as if you even care."

"No, I care," Palon said. "Just not for the reasons you do."

The bond had to work out, for Tebah's sake, for High Flight's sake, and for the sake of all of the dragons and bonded in the cave. There was no time to coddle her—the girl needed to get over her anger and accept her decision.

Palon nudged the girl. "Want to go for a walk? You haven't seen the Meal Cave yet. Are you ready to behave yourself enough to eat with the rest of us?"

After a scathing glare, the girl's shoulders slumped with a sigh. She nodded.

Palon rose, rolling her stiff shoulder, and walked to the opening. She watched the girl, ready for her to take off like she sometimes did, but Tebah remained subdued, trudging beside her. They took the long way to the Meal Cave, for Palon didn't want to be overcome by the desire to check on her cache again. The thief was still lurking, and she'd already lost too much time in there in the early hours of the morning.

Head down, the newling didn't comment on their path. She didn't comment at all, and Palon suppressed the urge to shake her head at the girl. The girl was weak and a danger to their entire nest. High Flight never should have bonded her. It baffled Palon that the girl had even considered herself nearly ready for her yah. There was no way this headstrong, angry little girl would ever have survived. And now, she was living with dragons. It was ridiculous.

Voices raised in jest and conversation poured over them as the large space opened up before them, lit by lanterns along the walls. The stone floor was polished smooth by generations of bonded eating, cleaning, celebrating, and just gathering in general. A massive oven dominated the space, with a sloping chute for loading wood into the fire on one side, and a door for the food on the front face of it. A large wooden plank, dark with age, lay across stone supports, forming a flat surface for preparing and serving the food. The sound of the waterfall around the corner always relaxed Palon, and the cold spray it kicked into the air was a pleasant contrast to the heat of the ovens.

The rest of the open area was taken up by four large tables, each able to seat ten bonded. It was more than enough room for their cave these days. It seemed most of the bonded had already gathered for lunch, scattered around the tables according to current friendships and rivalries. Laetiran smiled and gave them a wave, sitting at one of the more crowded tables, and Tebah tugged Palon's shirt sleeve as she jumped behind her. Laros sat with Maea, talking earnestly, and Yiyin shot those two a venomous look as he removed a tray of bread from the oven. Palon wrinkled her nose at the rivalry between Laros and Yiyin. Maea would likely choose one or the other before the mating season.

She missed the normal sense of community she felt. A distance had grown the last few days. Not just with the newling taking up much of her time, but also with the looming threat of the thief. Could it possibly be a bonded, since Tsían hadn't found any evidence of outside interference? Her fingers twitched, a crawling sensation moving up her spine, her every nerve alight for the threat. For the thief. Compounding that were the whispers born of she and Aturadin sleeping outside Tebah's room to protect her, rather than sleeping in the pile, as was proper. She couldn't blame them; it was unusual.

Taking a deep breath, she tried not to allow the fires of resentment in her to grow. Tebah didn't deserve to be the target of her wrath, not for that, anyway. She gave Palon plenty of reason to be angry all on her own.

It wasn't surprising that Yiyin was cooking. He enjoyed it as much as everyone else looked forward to his cooking. The food was merely edible when anyone else cooked—Yiyin made mealtimes a delight. The short, wiry man worked in silence, his knife flashing in the light of the lanterns as he chopped more vegetables and swept them into a pot. Though the smallest of them, he was no less fierce.

As Palon and Tebah joined the end of the line, Yiyin gave them a sidelong look. He silently slid the polished wood trays toward them when their turns came. Glancing at Tebah, he grabbed a hand towel, dunked it in the hot water barrel and then snatched it out with his calloused brown hands. He wrung it out quickly, then tossed it at Tebah, who stood there stunned, the wet towel sticking to her face.

Palon smiled and thanked Yiyin, grabbing the warm cloth and instructing the girl to wipe her face before eating. She picked up her tray and Tebah deflated, obediently washing her face and following behind. As Palon grabbed a cup from the stack and filled it from the waterfall, Tebah gaped.

"Did you make this?" The newling copied her tentatively.

Palon laughed. "No."

"The dragons made it," Yiyin explained. "Not ours—a previous generation. They found a spring and diverted the flow here."

Tebah ducked her head, stepping away with tension lining her small form. "I never knew they could *make* things," she murmured. She stared around wide-eyed as she followed Palon to a mostly empty table.

Palon nodded at the couple of bonded sitting on the other side of the table and chuckled at Tebah. "Why should you? Dragons don't make things for pride or to show off. They make things because they have a good use. Having us requires them to make sure we eat and drink well."

"Did they make the latrine holes too?" Tebah asked.

Palon nodded.

A petulant expression crossed the girl's face. "I suppose we have to clean them out occasionally, then. It's not like they can just dig a new latrine. The rock would be littered with holes."

Palon laughed. "No, the dragons flush the waste out with a different waterfall."

Tebah's brows knitted in confusion, and Palon explained. "Up the mountain from here, there's a river. Beside it sits a giant boulder none of us could have a chance of moving. When the pits get too rank, a couple of dragons fly up the slope and move the boulder. The river rushes down and cleans the latrines, sending all the waste down the slope. After the initial rush has done its work, they shift the boulder back."

Aturadin arrived, dropping into the seat beside Tebah. "Talking about the waterfall?"

Palon nodded, giving him a quick smile.

The girl shifted, looking around. "There's a lot less of you than there are dragons. Unless this isn't everyone?"

"It's most of us," Aturadin said, picking up his spoon. "Not every dragon has a bonded; many of the older dragons don't. The oldest dragons are too big to fly, anyway. Dragons grow throughout their lives, see. They just Shift to the hunting grounds when they're hungry and back. And if they can't for some reason, other dragons bring them food."

"We're not the monsters you think we are." Palon smiled at the girl's dark look.

"But the oldest dragon had a bonded," Tebah said, suspicion in her tone.

Palon nodded. "It's very unusual. Some say that Silver Spine walked himself down the mountains to one of the villages nestled in the foothills, called for a companion, and Miros answered, climbing up to sit on his back, and Silver Spine carried him back home."

Aturadin cut in. "Others say that Miros himself left the village and walked up the mountain, answering Silver Spine's longing with his own, without Silver Spine ever having to leave the cave."

Tebah frowned. "The dragons must know."

"Sure, but it doesn't matter." Palon shrugged. "Dragons don't share everything they know—we'd go mad if they tried to fill our little minds with all the wisdom in their heads."

"Besides," Aturadin grinned, raising his cup. "We bonded have far more fun speculating."

Palon waved a hand as if gesturing his words away. "Either way, their bond is a model for everyone else to aspire to. You saw them. They are so tightly entwined that they are like one creature in two bodies, rather than two working together."

Tebah ate in thoughtful silence. Palon devoured her food, washing it down with the water, and then sat and waited for the girl, relaxing in the lack of conflict. Maybe the girl was finally coming around.

"Why do I have to sleep in a cave? Where's your house?" Tebah asked.

Palon laughed. "This is my house. And yours. As I've told you." She leaned forward, elbows on the table, her tone more serious. "You'll sleep alone in your room or with High Flight for your first year. Once your bond is established, you'll sleep in the Basin when the weather's warm, or the Nesting Cave when it's colder or raining, like all the rest of us, with the dragons curled around."

Tebah's shoulders hunched and she stared at her half-eaten roll, eyes glimmering. "I want to go home."

"It's ok, newling. You are home," Aturadin said, wrapping one arm around Tebah's shoulders.

"Home, where you hate everyone," Palon teased.

Tebah glowered at her, anger replacing tears. It was an improvement.

"Come on. We'll walk you to the basking ledge. High Flight's probably waiting for you," Aturadin said.

Tebah hunched further under his arm. "No."

How many times would they go over the same arguments? Had she learned nothing? Palon gritted her teeth. "Tebah, can you hear High Flight calling you? Are you ignoring him?" She could feel Windward's restlessness in her own mind. If she didn't meet him soon, he was going to go bask without her.

Tebah glared at her, pressing her lips together. Palon matched her stare for stare. "Get up," she ordered, pointing. "Take the dishes to the bucket."

The girl crossed her arms and hunched closer to Aturadin, but he simply finished the rest of his tea and set the cup next to hers. Finally, she stood, slamming her hands down on the table. "You're all mean!"

"Wonderful. Put the dishes away."

Huffing and rattling the dishes, Tebah marched away and dumped them in the bucket of warm soapy water sitting at the side of the cave.

Palon shook her head, watching her. "She doesn't even realize the marvels she's seeing."

"Go easy on her, Palon. She's having it harder than we ever did."

"She'll never bond to High Flight if attaching to us is an option."

Aturadin scowled. "I'm not going to push her away."

Fury simmered in her, and she narrowed her eyes. Aturadin was wrong but didn't want to see it. Going easy on the girl wasn't going to work. "You need to. Just like every other newling."

"She's not any other newling. What High Flight did was wrong."

"So you're going to tear up the nest as a result? High Flight has been dealt with." Palon scowled at him. He was aware of the impending torpor; he just didn't feel it in his bones the way she did. Normally he was right about these things, but talking with Miros had reminded her that Tebah needed to work this out with High Flight, rather than with their help. She had to grow up and face her decision and hold High Flight accountable for his.

"Palon, you're overreacting." Aturadin placed his hand on hers.

She shook her head, removing her hand from his grasp. Aturadin's hold on his Rinaryn side was important for helping newlings, but sometimes he forgot about the dragon side and the importance of the rules. It was normal for newlings to have moments of hatred for other bonded at first while they adjusted to the different lifestyle. That reaction helped solidify the bond with the dragon, who could explain even better than other bonded could. The structure ensured health and safety for everyone in the nest. If the bond failed, the resulting chaos, compounded with Silver Spine's death and the stress of the thefts, could tear the nest apart.

"No, you are not thinking, Aturadin. Stop coddling that girl. She will bond to High Flight and we'll get this whole mess sorted out eventually. You're further upsetting an already tenuous situation."

Aturadin stood and she rose to face him. "You know," he sighed. "You're making it too easy for her to direct her anger at you."

"I don't care how she feels about me. I care that High Flight didn't disrupt this nest for nothing, that our nest will survive, and that means making sure the bond succeeds."

"No." Tebah held her arms crossed over her chest, lower lip sticking out slightly. "I will not bond High Flight any further, no matter how much he begs."

"You will." Palon steered her toward the tunnel entrance.

"It'll get better," Aturadin said to the girl, falling in beside Palon.

Why did he have to be so gentle with her? The girl would only lean on him, use him to avoid High Flight. She was a mistake that needed to be corrected, but they couldn't do that themselves. Only Tebah could, and she was proving to be the singularly most uncooperative newling Palon had ever seen. They were stuck, as surely as if Palon had no wings.

Turning on him, Palon erupted. "She needs to walk this road. Alone. Yes, it's hard. She'll get through it."

"I would rather die," Tebah spat.

"Now who's overreacting?" The others around them were beginning to glance over, some bemused, some annoyed. Windward rumbled in her mind. Excellent. As if they needed to be set apart further from the others. Humiliation burned in her, and she muscled the girl out of the view of the other bonded.

"Let me go," Tebah cried, struggling as Palon pushed her onward. "You're all as bad as that dragon!"

"Yeah, we're regular villains, and you've no responsibility in this at all. Your plan to fool a dragon should have worked, and it's our fault you failed," Palon growled, glaring at Aturadin, who was unusually quiet. He didn't even notice, his expression pensive and troubled, and she picked up the pace.

She'd lashed out at him, and he didn't deserve that. Annoyance rose in her that she was furious with him at all. Guilt twisted in her gut. He was just trying to help.

The newling yanked her arm out of Palon's grip and ran ahead of them down the tunnel. It only led to the Basking Basin, though, so she let her go, scowling.

Tebah was becoming a huge pain in her backside.

The girl was going to run. It was the way of bonding sometimes, but she still didn't like it. She dreaded the thought of having to scour the rocks for Tebah or locking her up. Even worse was the knowledge that the girl was right to be so angry, even if Palon wished she weren't. Anger wasn't fixing things for her.

Anger wasn't fixing things for Palon, either.

Aturadin left her as they entered the Basin, heading toward Tebah with the quick-paced, stiff gait he used when he was angry. Guilt twisted further, sending pains through her stomach, and she tried to push it away, to focus on her own duties. They would keep the girl out of trouble, keep her from hurting those Palon loved, those she only wanted to protect. Palon would perform her tasks to the best of her ability and leave the rest to those responsible for them.

And just as High Flight had been disciplined, Tsían would find the thief and discipline him, and the nest would return to stability. If everyone only did their jobs—including Aturadin—everything should calm down and they would enter the season of torpor without dangerous tension.

All she had to do was persuade Tebah to accept her choice, even if the girl blasted High Flight with her own fire for lying to her.

Chapter Seven

Windward rumbled, drawing her out of her reverie. They were sprawled on a large slab of granite, soaking up the heat of the late afternoon sun. Windward's tail dangled off the edge of the ledge alongside Palon, whose head also hung over the drop-off as she relished the cool breeze that swept past. It wouldn't be long before the warm days were gone.

But when Windward spoke, Palon looked up sharply, wincing at the sun in her eyes. He shifted, golden eye fixing on her, and with a swirl of thoughts and colors asked why she was so troubled.

"It's bonded drama, don't worry. Nothing you need to concern yourself with."

Windward huffed, a cloud of dust rising to twirl in the air. He hated drama, was never overly concerned with status, neither did he worry about the nest as a whole—Palon did that for both of them. Windward reserved his excitement for seeing new lands and fighting walavaim.

It was one of the things she loved about him.

Palon smiled, losing herself in memory with him. She'd grown up in the shadow of her family. Especially her mother, much beloved, easily carrying the expectations of the village, always with a kind word and a smile. Something Palon could never aspire to imitate, despite being her very image. There was a wildness in her that her mother apparently never had.

Then of course there was the hero worship the people had for her brother, for whom physical feats came so easily. She could possibly have been his match, except that she'd never tried for fear of immediately being confined to his shadow the way her appearance confined her to her mother's. She didn't want to just be the Hero's sister. She was more than that—even if she had only weak telepathic abilities—but all they'd seen was cute little Palon, following in her older sibling's footsteps. How adorable.

It was enough to make her gag.

She had wanted to be herself, making her own path, her own mistakes. The freedom to follow her curiosity, to explore without the trappings of the village.

Windward had cultivated that curiosity, showing her what he'd seen that day—only glimpses, she knew now, but back then, it had been like a fresh spring in a drought. He'd told her of living with people from all over Rinara, as well as other dragons who knew far more than he did. He hadn't mentioned that the other dragons wouldn't talk to her, but that had only been a minor point of contention in their early days. The fact remained that when he asked her to come fly away with him, she had accepted, eager to shed her old life like an old coat. And though the bonding process was always a difficult adjustment, she'd quickly grown to love Windward and the adventure that came with bonding with a dragon.

Windward snorted. She must be upset to be reminiscing so. Even so, his enjoyment thrummed through her and Palon slumped against his scales, a large smile spreading across her face. Belatedly, she thought to ask, "Do you need more salve for your foot?"

Shifting his head, Windward look at her with one eye. He had no pain currently; the wound would heal in its own time. He shut his eyes and prodded her to tell of her troubles anyway, lest she continue to dwell on it and ruin his basking.

Palon stared him down. "You hate drama," she repeated.

The rebuff swirled into her mind that she did as well, yet here she was wasting energy on a perfectly good day, worrying at it. He turned, twisting his neck around and suggested that while she was wasting time, she could scratch an itch on his neck scales for him. Obliging, her dragon's pleased hum filling her mind, she tried to decide where to begin. So much was weighing on her, but dragons didn't take part in bonded affairs. Not unless someone died.

"Miros is going to die once Silver Spine dies. He's going to go mad or die." The words burst from her, but when she heard them, she realized how much it was bothering her.

His scent filled her lungs, comforting her, as he reminded her that this was the way of nature. Rinaryns knew all too well of death, especially in the villages. Normal Rinaryn life was dangerous and sometimes short.

She studied the purplish-gray membrane of his wing while tears pricked at her eyes. "Miros would have all our hides, the way we're going."

Windward mentally nudged her when she went quiet, and she sighed, her thoughts tumbling around in her head like a rockfall. "It's everything. Salann being so meek and absent, Eltavae spending all her time out of the cave with Shadow Soars, Aturadin doting on Tebah, Yiyin and Laros squabbling over Maea... Tsían is the only one acting sane and normal. Well, him and Laetiran. The man has no respect. He tried to follow me to my stash the other morning, you know. I kicked him hard enough that he should think twice next time."

Approval caressed her mind.

Narrowing her eyes, she continued, "And we're stuck here while your foot heals. I want to be out there patrolling."

Windward washed her mind with his agreement, thinking fondly of the solitude in flight, just her and him and the wind.

Palon let out a shaky sigh, staring across the ledges to where Tebah stood, her arms crossed, back turned to High Flight. She'd been standing like that all afternoon. "And I don't know what to do about Tebah. She's fighting this bond with everything in her, and I'm supposed to miraculously make her submit to it. I'm not sure it's in her. She's too Rinaryn."

A memory came to her mind of the others she'd mentored.

Palon shook her head, rejecting Windward's point. "They weren't so angry. Even when the changes were hard, they acknowledged that they chose this, or at least decided they were safer with dragons than in the villages. She does neither. I'm afraid to be gentle with her or she'll never attach to her dragon, and we have to spend far too much time with her anyway, to protect her. Anyway, any time I want to explain things better, there never seems to be time, or the words don't come."

She sat up and looked up at Windward. "What's going to happen to the cave when Tebah's bonding fails, right around the time we give Miros to the care of the Monks of Annularei?"

Windward eased open his lower lid, golden eyes staring at her through the crack, and then reached forward with his good hind foot, knocking her over, away from the edge, with one hooked claw. She rolled easily, twisting to face him as she stopped her momentum.

She was a tiny thing, only twice as big as his claw. She put too much pressure on herself and would snuff out her own dragonfire. Tumult came and went. Silly, young dragons caused chaos when they shouldn't. The partnership between dragons and Rinaryns meant they could overcome such things, together. Besides, the entire nest had heard the tongue-lashing Tebah had given High Flight that morning. It was at least a step in the right direction.

Palon pressed the good side of her face against Windward's thick facial scales, rubbing the smaller scales around his eye. He relaxed, letting his lower lid raise to meet the upper lid, his breaths slow and steady while she leaned against him, surrounded by his reptilian musk.

"Do you think it's possible Laetiran stole from the dragons? Those three were the ones who broke up Fired Sand and Night Hunter when Laetiran and Yiyin had their scrap a couple months back," she said.

His rumble reverberated through her whole body, comforting. That job was for Tsían, and she should put it out of her head. Resurrecting the past for worries was silly.

"What about Stone Eyes?" she whispered against his scales. "I think he's been over-reacting. And Fired Sand is more obnoxious than usual, and it feels like everyone is going insane."

He snorted at her. Of course the nest was on edge. The bonds all felt the strain of the nest, and stressed out dragons and bonded both became snappish. But dragon business was dragon business, and bonded needed to stay out of it, just as dragons stayed out of theirs. It was how the nest must work, for the good of all.

"I can't stay out of it when it might get you hurt."

He lifted his head, easily breaking her hold on him, and flared his neck spines. He didn't need her to protect him.

She crossed her arms, unconvinced, and he nudged her to his side, steering her with his enormous snout. Once she settled by him again, he tucked his wing over her on that side, then curled up to fully encircle her. The sun would rise again in the morning and their problems would wait. And then, with rest, they would each face them.

Tucked in tightly between scales and wing, she finally relaxed and fell asleep.

"Don't smile like that," Palon said, ignoring the irritated look Tebah shot at her. They were in the Meal Cave eating lunch while Palon tried to give the girl another lesson in etiquette.

Tebah stabbed a chunk of meat with her knife, as if she were imagining more violent thoughts. "What's wrong with my smile?"

"Your teeth are showing. You smile like that, with open mouth or showing teeth, and it's a challenge or a threat display. You do that routinely, you'll end up in a fight."

"Why can't you people do anything normal?"

"We're bonded to dragons, Tebah. It changes you."

Tebah muttered under her breath. "Not me."

Palon frowned. Doing things the normal way with Tebah only made her lash out, rather than helping her understand. Aturadin was confident that being gentle with her was the best way.

Palon remained skeptical. "The changes happen little by little, often as a natural extension of who you already are."

"Palon!" Yiyin hurried toward their table with a loaded tray.

"Yiyin?" Beside her, Tebah jumped a little at his arrival. Palon resisted the urge to shake her head. What was the girl doing in a dragon nest?

"Hey, newling," Yiyin said. He turned back to Palon, almost immediately dismissing Tebah, and Palon smiled at the way the girl's nostrils flared. It clearly grated on her not to be the center of attention. Maybe that contributed to all her tantrums.

Yiyin set the tray in front of Palon. "Can you send this up to Miros? I'm behind on... everything."

Palon nodded. It wasn't really a matter of him being behind—Yiyin hated seeing the older pair. "Yeah, I'll take it." Miros was infinitely better company than Tebah.

Yiyin hesitated, then nodded and left.

"Do I have to come too?" Tebah asked as Palon gulped down the rest of her food.

Palon gave her a hard look. "No, you may not come."

Tebah scowled. "He's just an old man with an old dragon."

Setting down her bowl, Palon glared at her. "Miros knows more than ten of you combined and never had half your foolishness. And an ancient dragon like Silver Spine? If ever there was a time to pull your head out from your own self-pity, it would be to see that a dragon like Silver Spine has experienced much and learned much in his lifetime. More than our two dragons combined. You want to learn? You could, if you would only stop throwing fits. So no, you will not go near him again until you learn some respect."

"Good," the girl spat.

Palon's tone sharpened like lightning slashing through the sky. "The best thing for you to do is talk to High Flight."

Tebah's glare was a model for all future glares. "No."

"Relationships take work, Tebah. Especially partnerships with dragons."

"I'm not going to work with *him*."

Palon sighed, trying to remain patient. She really wanted to haul the girl into High Flight's cave and lock them both in there until they could come to terms with their decisions. Rubbing her forehead, she resolved to ask Miros if he had any advice.

"Tebah, you chose this when you went with the dragon. You chose to leave your village, or the bond never would have happened. He called, you answered. Now you both need to finish this. Once you're fully bonded, you can—"

"I do not care!"

"Tebah, stop. You're making a scene."

"Oh, well, I wouldn't want that!" Tebah's screeching filled the room. Others were beginning to turn and stare, with expressions ranging from appalled to amused. Palon resisted the urge to hide her face, to completely dissociate herself from this tiresome girl.

"Listen, Tebah. I know—"

"Yes, you know everything. You know something else? I *am* going to go home. You cannot stop me. High Flight's a liar. I hate him. I hate you too. I hate all of you!"

Palon was standing before she knew it, gripping Tebah firmly by the arm. She towed the girl out of the room, ignoring her continuing tirade, trying to ignore the stares as they passed by. She felt for Tebah, but the girl's expectations were far too high. The newling refused to accept that her village would never take her back—her thinking was already changing, becoming more dragon, just as High Flight's thinking was becoming more Tebah, as evidenced in his increasing posturing and snapping. She continued to ignore her own part in the conflict, her own choice to go with a dragon. Dragonfire! Had she ever been this tiresome when she had been new?

Windward's fond amusement washed over her, calming the storm of her humiliation. She challenged him, but her heart wasn't in it. The fact was, dragons were amazing, and she couldn't fathom how Tebah didn't see it. The breadth of knowledge they had, the strength, their long lives, the adventure. She couldn't even imagine living without the dragons, without Windward. Where the girl saw only lies, Palon saw the opportunity for adventure.

Tebah dug in her heels, but Palon muscled her forward, gritting her teeth.

"Where are we going?" Tebah's voice was filled with suspicion.

"I'm going to drop you off with Aturadin while I take Miros his meal. You can throw your tantrum with him."

"I'm not a child!"

Palon spun around, stooping so she was nose to nose with the girl. "Not a child, hmm? When did you go on your yah?"

Shoulders slumping, Tebah kicked at the floor. "I was going to go soon."

"Then even among them, you're still a child."

"I was almost ready! And then High Flight..."

Of course she would try to blame High Flight again instead of taking responsibility for her own actions. "Listen. You stop acting like a child and I will stop treating you like one."

Tebah glowered at her, folding her arms awkwardly, since Palon was still holding her by the arm.

Turning, Palon dragged her along, down the corridors in search of Aturadin. Hopefully he wasn't grooming Scorch Frost—she wouldn't want to interrupt such important bonding activity. Windward sent her a negative—Scorch Frost was basking near him, and Aturadin was not in sight. He, however, had a few scales for her to look at when she came to bask with him, which he hoped would be soon.

Palon promised him she'd come right away, after dropping off Tebah and taking Miros his food. Suddenly it seemed like a lot to do before getting to spend time with her dragon.

Windward distracted her from her impatience, relaying information from Scorch Frost on Aturadin's approximate whereabouts. She jogged as fast as she could with Tebah resisting her.

"Why are you smiling?" Tebah grumbled.

"It's... Windward."

Tebah sighed, rolling her eyes. "And what's so... happy... about your dragon?"

"You'll find out when you complete your bond with High Flight."

"Just tell me already!"

Palon shot her a warning look. "I was just thinking... it's nice that my dragon and my mate's dragon are also friendly. Windward told me where Aturadin was, since he and Scorch Frost are basking together."

"Why not ask Scorch Frost?"

"Don't you remember what Miros told you? It's just... no. How could you even want to?"

Tebah heaved a sigh. "I wish Windward was my dragon."

Palon had her pinned against the side of the tunnel before she realized it. Tebah stared at her, wide eyed as Palon struggled to loosen her grip against the instinctive reaction, the intense possessiveness roaring back and forth along her bond, a flood of mine, Mine, *Mine.*

A dragon trumpeted, the sound echoing through the mountain caverns. High Flight, calling out in panic. His emotion had to have come along their bond, for the newling's expression went from terror to chagrin, and she drooped. Palon was able to take a breath and step back. It wasn't just the girl's posture which communicated a lack of threat to her bond; the girl's reaction meant her bond was still growing despite everything. High Flight was able to communicate with her, at least a little, and she responded to his fear of losing her. The progress was slow and clumsy, but still, Palon would take what she could get.

She released Tebah. "I'm sorry. Just... don't say that sort of thing. Ever."

Tebah glowered at her, rubbing her shoulder. "You're half animal."

"Half dragon," Palon said absently.

Tebah snorted.

Palon looked back at her, raising her eyebrows. "It happens. The longer you're bonded, the tighter the bond, the more dragon your thoughts become."

Tebah stopped short, pulling back.

"I guess you could also say the more Rinaryn the dragon becomes too," Palon mused. She shrugged. "It's just the nature of the bond. Your old way of living won't work for you anymore. They won't understand. They can't. We can, and do."

Tebah grumbled something under her breath, but quieted when she caught Palon's stern look.

They walked in silence for some time before Tebah ventured, "You said something about... your mate?"

Palon nodded. "Aturadin. I love him." She shrugged again. Feelings were awkward things to talk about.

"So... really you're just married, like at home."

Palon shook her head. "No ceremony. Dragons don't care about that sort of thing. You'll probably stop caring about that too by the time you pair off with someone, if you do."

The girl kicked a stray stone. "Will I be forced into that too?"

"Tebah, you'll always have a choice. It's completely up to you, and only when you're ready. The dragons are not abominations."

"Well, they certainly aren't reasonable either."

"You should think before accepting offers then, Tebah. No one forced you to bond a dragon."

The girl sneered at her, and Palon gritted her teeth. It was like she was being purposefully obtuse, seeing traps everywhere. Without her dragon, Palon would have no real freedom. She'd be cut off from the sky forever, tethered to the ground while her spirit withered and died. The partnership involved compromise, as all partnerships did. But the benefits were far greater than the disadvantages.

With a tenuous hold on her patience and a great amount of relief, Palon handed her off to Aturadin, who was happy for help refilling lanterns. The upkeep of the tunnels took up a lot of their time, but it was safer than traveling the caverns with the dragons.

Her thoughts were filled with Tebah as she went all the way back to the Meal Cave to pick up Miros's tray, then headed through the corridors toward the Sequestering Cave. It was one thing on top of another, and she wanted it all to go away so she could fly free, teeth bared to the wind.

Palon carried the tray up the ancient steps cut generations ago into the stone and down the corridor blazing with torches. As the tunnel curved, she paused, glimpsing a figure darting out of sight. What had Laetiran been doing near her and Aturadin's cache? A chill went down her spine, and in her mind, Windward rumbled with territoriality. She glimpsed him in her mind's eye, grumpily standing from his basking area, with his back arched and tail curled around the rocks. He flared his wings and bugled, adding a belch of fire for good measure, and she felt herself puff up too, annoyed and spoiling for a fight.

Her steps paused at the entrance to her cache. He couldn't have gotten in, right? He couldn't have! Was he watching? He could still be spying on her.

Her spine crawling, she stalked down the corridor, forcing herself not to look back. Windward grumbled in her mind, his basking interrupted by her worries. She tried to calm herself, but every fiber of her being wanted to run to her cache and check on everything. Was her shiny crystalline rock still in its place of honor? Had anything been moved? Had anything been taken?

Windward rumbled teasing laughter in her mind, imagining her new rock in his cache. She bristled at him, imagining his current favorite—an agate—sitting in the corner of her cache, tipped over and dusty for good measure. He laughed, though an uneasiness thrummed between them. Windward wouldn't take anything that was in her cache, just as she wouldn't take pieces from his. That was strictly off limits between the two of them.

And yet, since someone had actually stolen from dragons, the old joke didn't seem as funny anymore.

Palon couldn't stand it. She put down the tray, looking around. No one was there. With nerves strung tight, she fled back to the entrance of her cache, slipping through the tight spaces and hastily disabling the traps. Her stomach tightened in knots as Windward launched himself from the basking area to glide back to his cache next door, echoing her own need.

She closed her eyes and breathed, trying to calm herself and Windward. They didn't need the compulsion spreading through the already on-edge dragons.

Everything seemed to be in the right place. Her hand trembled as she reached out, touching each rock in her cache, all beautifully undisturbed. Taking deep breaths, she checked Aturadin's feathers as well, trying to remember the correct positions of all his things. Of course, he would know immediately, just as she did with hers, but she needed to check for him anyway.

The knots loosened in her stomach and the vice around her lungs faded away. Calm settled on her like a blanket, and she took one last look around, then forced herself to leave the cache. She'd made Miros wait too long for his lunch already. She paused at the entrance into the tunnel, poking her head out and checking up and down the corridor before finally dashing out. Hopefully no one had seen her—catching Laetiran so near the entrance to her stash had unnerved her. Picking up the tray, she used that anxiety to fuel a quick walk, pouring her fears and nerves into boots clipping on the stone.

Struggling to settle herself, she checked with Windward to make sure his cache was alright. His calm soothed her. Eyes half closed, she took a deep breath, her shoulders slowly relaxing. She'd hate to disturb Silver Spine and Miros with her own silly, unfounded worries.

Silver Spine occupied most of his ledge of the cave, basking in a loose ball with his neck outstretched, his head resting on the floor, soaking up the midday sun. Miros sat cradled in the crook of Silver Spine's foreleg, his hands on the large scales of the dragon's leg, his temple resting against the smaller, softer scales of the dragon's body.

Palon paused at the entrance, staring in awe and reverence.

Miros smiled without moving, eyes still closed. "Is it stew again?"

Eyes fixed on the dragon, Palon barely heard, waiting for the next breath. She stood entranced, unable to answer until she knew, dreading that the final day had come.

"He still lives," Miros said, opening his eyes and looking in her direction. His gaze was vacant and unfocused, his mind with his dragon. Silver Spine's ribcage expanded in one long slow motion as the giant reptile drew in another great breath.

She sagged in relief and hurried forward with the stew. "Yiyin made it, so who knows what's in it. It was good though. I grabbed an extra portion of the fruit for you too."

Miros nodded, taking the bowl. He ate mechanically, sometimes dribbling stew down through his beard when he forgot to close his mouth quickly enough. Palon stood awkwardly, a heavy anticipation weighing on her, embarrassed to be acting like a newling.

Snagging a cloth, Miros smiled and wiped his face. His face went slack for a moment, his eyes unfocusing, and then the smile returned. His eyes found Palon. "Silver Spine says he'll lick my face if I keep dribbling meat juices on it."

Palon smiled as Miros laughed breathily, his gaze going far away again. She sat down nearby and waited as she was used to doing, the nearness of the ancient pressing against her very being. The words came as if from far away, Miros's eyes still remaining distant. "He says it feels strange, so many people waiting for you to die."

Heart aching, Palon fought to breathe through a desperate surge for her own dragon through the bond. He clutched at her mentally as well, both clinging to each other in the face of eminent mortality. Miros and Silver Spine remained serene and untroubled, and Palon's eyes stung with tears. He was so far dragon that it didn't bother him—or he'd forgotten—what would happen when Silver Spine died. The caves would lose two of their wisest, and she longed to delay it.

"How is he?" she croaked.

"Dying."

Palon floundered. Miros often threw her like that. Sometimes next to him she felt very, very Rinaryn, and very, very small. "Does Silver Spine know about... what's... been happening? In the caves? With the others?"

"The thefts? The increased agitation of everyone? Of course. He's dying, not blind and deaf."

"What should we do?"

"Live."

"But... what should be done about the thefts? Does Silver Spine have any ideas? Do you?"

"We are too tired to care. We are beyond possessions now. No hoard could comfort us, not with the call of the beyond on our soul. What good are these shiny trinkets when we cannot take them with us?"

Palon hardly dared breathe, wondering if she was hearing Silver Spine directly through Miros's voice, or if he had just temporarily forgotten again that he was a separate being.

"Hold to Dragon Law, as always. Hold to Dragon Law."

Palon nodded. "We will. We will, Silver Spine. Miros."

Miros smiled, and Silver Spine breathed.

"Tebah, the newling, is having a hard time bonding with High Flight. She mistrusts him, and she's angry at everyone."

Miros's shoulders shook, though he forgot to make the actual sound of a laugh. His eyes crinkled with mirth at the edges, and she found herself memorizing his face, his expressions. She shook herself. It was like a vigil. It was a bit morbid.

"It's hard, coming to a new home. It's double hard when no one wants you."

"We don't care!"

For a moment, Miros looked at her, fully lucid, his gaze piercing to her soul. "Exactly."

She shivered as his gaze relaxed and went through her, his head leaning back against Silver Spine's scales again. Again, the dragon breathed.

Palon struggled to pick up thoughts like dishes fallen to a floor. "No one wanted her. We thought she was a mistake, the timing all wrong."

Miros's eyelids moved.

Nodding to herself, she continued. "So Tebah went from a loving village, albeit wanting more, else she wouldn't have answered the dragon's call, to a place full of strife, where no one wanted her. All she has here is betrayal, strangeness, and loneliness." She frowned, appalled. "That's horrible!"

Miros grinned in her direction, though he didn't bother to open his eyes. "Now you can see."

"But how do I fix it? She *is* a mistake!"

"Is she?"

Palon's mouth moved of its own accord. Of course Tebah was a mistake. Wasn't she? She sat there in the presence of the ancient dragon for some time, the shadows moving around her according to the sun's travel overhead. Miros spoke no more—he probably forgot she was there. Around them, the dragon musk laden air moved in the regular wisshhh, husssshhh of the dragon's breathing. It was soothing, like the heartbeat of the world itself, something one could imagine was beyond even time's reach.

Finally, she shook herself and rose, taking the spoon and bowl from Miros's limp hands. She checked the latrine to be sure it hadn't clogged, and left a pitcher of wine and a clean cup. She couldn't help but pause at the cavern opening for one last look back at Silver Spine and Miros, curled together in shadow, now that the sun had moved on without them. The dragon breathed.

Her mind whirled with thoughts as she carried the tray back toward the Meal Cave. She was so busy turning over the few words Miros had spoken to her that she didn't hear the buzz of angry conversation in the Meal Cave until she set the tray down by the washing barrel. Then she noticed Yiyin staring at her.

The hairs on the back of her neck prickled. She looked around. The other two dragonbonded in the cave were also staring at her. She took a step back, instinctually seeking open space, and Windward rumbled in her mind. At first, she thought that he was responding to her, but it continued, growing and becoming a bellow. She could feel him puffing up in a threat display. She swallowed hard, trying to figure out what was going on.

Aturadin burst into the room, looked around, and then bolted for Palon. Her fingers curled unconsciously into fists and her heartbeat quickened at the look on his face. Then Tebah followed him in, her expression belligerent, and Palon relaxed a fraction. Nothing had changed Tebah's mood, so it couldn't be too bad, whatever it was, could it?

"We have to get to the dragons, now!" Aturadin said, his voice harsh. "Tsían found the missing items."

He turned and ran, and Palon bolted after him through the corridors. "Where were they? Who stole them?"

Aturadin stopped, his lips thin as he turned to her.

Palon's stomach clenched at the anxiety in his face, and the sudden surge of anger and defensiveness in Windward coming through their bond.

"Palon, they were in our cache. All of it."

"What?"

Chapter Eight

Her crystal was gone.

She barely even noticed the other things littered around, the things that didn't belong. Trembling, rage dimming her vision to red, Palon stared at the empty place where her crystal should have been. That fury rebounded between her and Windward, his bellowing echoing in her mind.

Someone was shaking her. She lashed out blindly. It didn't matter who it was. Not with her crystal gone. That was all that mattered.

"Where is it?" She snagged the next person who touched her, fingers curved like claws. It was just a figure to her, a target for her wrath. She couldn't have recognized them if she tried, her mind drowning under her territorial rage.

"Palon, ow!" Someone shoved her away. She recognized the voice, but couldn't think, couldn't hear for the roaring in her head, Windward voicing her anger. Someone shoved her hard. Her back hit the wall, sharp rocks digging into her shoulder blades before she bounced away from them automatically.

"Palon, come back to us. You're letting your dragon take over."

"Slap her out of it. Here, I'll do it."

"You aren't touching her."

Someone moved in front of her. She blinked, no longer able to see the empty place where her crystal should have been. Desperation filled her. That empty place was the last connection she had to her crystal and she shifted to see it, but the figure moved with her, blocking her view. She bared her teeth, crouching.

"Look, see? She's defensive. She stole them."

"That's ridiculous. Palon didn't steal anything."

"You have to admit, it looks pretty bad. Laetiran has a point."

"No one's saying you're an accomplice, Aturadin. Yet."

"I don't care about that, tell me where my crystal is!" Palon growled.

The roar clawed its way up the back of her throat, choking her. She leaped forward. Her fingers raked across skin. She and her target went down, but Laetiran was wiry, and twisted under her.

She twisted too, using his momentum to drive him into the wall. "Give it back! You stole it, I know you did!"

"Get off!"

"I will hunt you down! Where's my crystal!"

"Stop this!"

Strong hands dragged her back, forced her to stop from beating the confession out of him. She bared her teeth, ragged breaths rasping from her throat as he smiled at her from across the empty space between them. Windward was tearing across the Basking Basin, claws throwing up a spray of rock behind him, flame belching. But the only thing she could see here was Laetiran's smile. An overwhelming need filled her to pound her fists into his face, drive her knee into his belly…

"Palon, you have to stop!"

She curled her fists inward, hissing her breath in and out. Aturadin was holding her, she realized, the deepest parts of her heart recognizing the feel of him, her back pressed against his chest, his arms around her. And just like that, the flames of her fury were doused by worry and regret. Had she hurt him while struggling against him? How could she forgive herself if she had hurt her mate? Laetiran, however, was a different story, especially with that smug grin on his face. She squeezed her fists even harder, but Aturadin's arms tightened around her.

"Palon, don't," he whispered in her ear.

She froze, stomping down her wrath, even as Laetiran's smile grew broader. The dragon in her roared for release, the instincts of centuries crying out for retribution against the worst wrong one could commit against another. Her body trembled in the struggle as she wrestled her emotions back down so she could think. It helped that Windward's fury no longer echoed in her head, his head lowered as Cave Song towered over him, rumbling a soothing that went into his very bones, leaking across the bond into her. She took a slow, deep breath.

They'd been set up, the stolen items from the dragons planted in their cache.

She and Aturadin had sent Tebah to High Flight, shouting at her when she argued, and then ran to check their cache. They'd arrived to find Tsían and Laetiran entering the space. The rage she felt at the intrusion was nothing compared to discovering all the stolen items clustered in their cache. And Palon's crystal missing.

"Aturadin, Palon, do you have an explanation for these things?" That was Tsían. She winced at the tear in his shirt sleeve, wilting under his level gaze. He must have been the one she'd grabbed earlier.

"No. They weren't here before." A muscle in Aturadin's jaw pulsed, his eyes blazing with fire. The tension radiating off him further dampened Palon's fury, allowing her to think, to see.

"Palon said she didn't care," Laetiran said with another easy grin. He was always smiling.

Her stomach turned as she looked around the cache. Feathers had floated to the ground, crumpled in her scuffle with Laetiran. She clenched her jaw on the cry of remorse that demanded escape. What had she done? Aturadin should be furious with her. Maybe he was. She didn't dare glance at him—seeing pain on his face, pain she'd caused, would destroy her.

Her faults went even further than that. She winced again, glancing at Tsían's stern face. She hadn't done anything to make them look more innocent. Tightness squeezed her throat shut, and swallowing was an effort.

"Palon?" Tsían asked, an edge to his voice that indicated his patience was wearing thin.

"I didn't take them. I didn't even see them until just now."

"Of course that's what she'd say." Laetiran simpered at her.

"Shut it, Laetiran!" She stepped forward on impulse, pausing when Aturadin's arms around her waist called her back to sanity.

"I do not need your help, Laetiran. Silence will suffice," Tsían snapped. He sighed, looking at the mess around them. "Well, if there were any footprints here, they're very well obliterated now. So it's not like we can look at tracks and tell if anyone else was in here."

Palon's eyes widened, her gaze snapping to Laetiran's ever-smiling face. The three dragons who had been stolen from. Fired Sand's and Laetiran's ambitions. She'd played right into his hands.

Of course she had, because she'd been an idiot. Windward rumbled in her head, and she pulled in another deep breath. She had to stay calm. Reacting blindly had only made everything worse.

"I'm sorry—"

"Of course you are, Palon. Regardless of what really happened." Tsían grimaced. "I'm going to block the two of you from your cache until we can figure this out."

"They're the thieves!" Laetiran objected. "Clearly, at least Palon is!"

Tsían turned his coldest look on Laetiran. "Your rivalry has not escaped my notice. Do not think it has. Since the thief will be the subject of much rage and indignation, I will not rush blindly into this. I will be sure before I speak a judgement, and you, Laetiran, will have to be content with that."

A sneer twisted Laetiran's face as he looked down, and Palon resisted the urge to smirk at him. He glared at her anyway as he stalked out, past the remains of their dismantled traps and down the hall. She shuddered, leaning against Aturadin's arms as he continued to hold her, though there was no longer a need. She wasn't going to attack Laetiran again. At least, not anytime in the immediate future.

"I understand the need for this," Aturadin was saying. "But is it..."

Palon winced, the sight of Aturadin's damaged and scuffed feathers drawing her gaze again, guilt welling in her. She'd done that to him. She'd hurt him terribly, but he hadn't lashed out like a dragon would. But then, he had always been the least dragon of them, somehow. It wasn't like he fought it; he just somehow retained whoever he'd been before. Maybe that's what drew her, that difference.

She pulled away from him, though his fingers curled around her arms as if reluctant to let her go. Kneeling, she picked up each feather, handling them gingerly, as if they were precious—which they were, to him. And she'd damaged them. Her eyes stung, her chest tight. She had to make it right.

Tsían stepped away from her and she noticed that he made sure to step only on the bare stone, avoiding the feathers and rocks that had hit the ground. The ginger motions were akin to the careful touch of one working around an open wound, and gratitude surged in her through the depths of her guilt. Her skin crawled and her eyes twitched at the sight of her collection all toppled and askew, but she worked her way around them, wrinkling her nose at the foreign smell of pine. She swallowed, though the lump in her throat refused to go. She would tidy her own collection, and soon, but first she had to fix Aturadin's. She owed that to him.

"It is necessary," Tsían said. "By watching the cache, I can..."

Tsían trailed off as the scuffing of boots echoed at the entrance to their cache. More intrusions? It was unbearable! Palon's hands clenched, and she struggled to avoid crushing the feathers she held. What good was it to rescue these for Aturadin if she was only going to thoughtlessly destroy them?

Laetiran poked his head in, and Palon glared at him, especially when she caught the dismay on Aturadin's face. Others appeared, squeezing their way into the cache one by one: Eltavae, Yiyin, Salann, Maea, and more. In moments, the small space was full to the brim. Outraged voices echoed off the walls. Boots scuffed feathers and kicked stones, and shirt sleeves and jackets pulled more of their treasures down to the ground to be trod on and broken.

Wrapping her arms around Aturadin, Palon held him tightly, nausea filling her as the room wobbled around her. She laid the feathers she had collected gingerly in his trembling hands. He spared her a quick glance, though his expression didn't change. His eyes were dark with grief as their sanctuary was invaded and destroyed, their collections, their pride and joys, disturbed and broken and mishandled. She squeezed him again, holding him tightly against their horror.

Part of her screamed, for she hadn't saved any of her own collection. All she had rescued were some dirty, broken, worthless feathers. But they meant the world to Aturadin. And holding his trembling form, pressing her head against his, her cheek on his shoulder, she was grateful that she'd been able to save some small part of his treasures for him. If only she'd been able to do the same for herself.

Windward sent soothing consolation to her, rumbling as he poked his head up at the slits near the ceiling that connected the caves. It echoed oddly, and Palon looked to the other side to see another set of dragon nostrils—Scorch Frost, likely responding to Aturadin's grief and rage. They had put their cache here, between their two dragons, so their collections would be safer. Much good that had done them. Windward reached for her along their bond, though she was too numb with shock and horror to reach back out to him. The intruder's scent was covered up by all the bonded in the cache. All he knew was that the pine stunk.

"Alright, that's enough!" Tsían's voice broke over the uproar. His face was red, as if he'd been shouting for some time. "Get out, all of you. Everyone out! Do not take anything with you. The stolen items will be returned to their owners, but if you take anything out of here, I will take that as proof that you are a thief, and treat you accordingly."

"But those are ours!"

Salann's protest, and Eltavae's open mouth ready to object, were interrupted by Tsían's bellow, cutting through the chaos like a dragon's roar. "That is what will happen, I promise you. Now get out!"

Palon focused on her mate, ignoring the glares others tossed them as they filed past. They were going to be even more unpopular now. Not that she cared, but once again, she'd hurt Aturadin. She squeezed him tighter, a breath of relief breaking from her like a sob when he put his arms around her as well.

"I am so sorry." Her voice broke on the words.

He forced a smile—she could always tell because he crinkled his eyes up too much when he was faking it—and rested his cheek against her head. Gesturing with his handful of feathers, he spoke in a thick whisper. "Thank you for saving these."

Words failed her. He'd had an extensive collection, all meticulously cleaned and cared for, each with its own spot, and he knew the stories of each feather and what kind of bird it came from, and could go on about them for hours at a time. She knew. She'd heard him, and seen him care for them while she'd cleaned and polished her rocks to a brilliant shine. Now all he had was a single handful of grubby, broken feathers, and for that he thanked her. It seemed a cruelty.

Palon turned her gaze to Tsían. She and Aturadin remained the only suspects for an unthinkable crime.

And neither of them had alibis.

She'd been hidden away with Miros in the Sequestering Cave. And Aturadin had been alone but for the newling, whose word meant nothing. No one would trust that they hadn't encouraged her to support Aturadin's innocence. Windward's scales hissed in the air vents as they brushed past the stone when he left his cave, his bad-temper surrounding her as he paced back out to the Basin.

Tsían cleared his throat, turning to them. "I am sorry."

Taking a deep breath and tightly containing her emotions, Palon looked around at the garbage pit that had once been her treasure trove. Nothing was in its spot, and so much had been destroyed by carelessness. By the mob. Many of them would feel remorse later when they realized what they'd done. But that didn't fix anything. That didn't undo the damage. She clenched her jaw, arms tightening around Aturadin as if to hold him together.

"We did not do this thing," she told Tsían. "Fix it. Find the real thief."

Tsían's look could have frozen even dragonfire. "I intend to. I do not need others to tell me what to do."

Aturadin swallowed so hard she could hear his gulp. "What about Tebah?"

Palon winced. The newling was trouble even on her best days. If she was given into the care of someone new to teach her the rules of dragonbonded society, she would surely descend into one of her raging temper tantrums. Who would have the patience to deal with that?

Tsían pinched the bridge of his nose. "I do not want to risk the bond. She must develop a strong connection with High Flight for the good of the cave as a whole, and you two are still the best choice, I think, regardless of whether or not you are the thieves."

"We aren't!" The rage clawed its way back up her throat.

Tsían pinned her with another look, sending shivers crawling up her spine. "This is still my task, to find the thief. Whoever they might be. Now, out, both of you."

Palon pressed her lips together, her hands fisting. The injustice of it all affronted her, but she battled down her emotions. Dragonbonded she was, and the bonding increased the visibility of emotions, but she was still in control. She'd wait and find her crystal and make Laetiran pay.

"Come on," Aturadin said, pulling on her arm. She followed him out of the winding path to the main corridor. Tsían followed them out, stalking past them as they paused in the corridor.

"Thank you for saving these," Aturadin's breath was hot on her ear as he pulled her close. "We'll recover your collection too, I promise."

She forced a flicker of a smile. It was too hard to speak. All she wanted in the world was to curl up in the crook of her dragon's arm and nurse her loss.

Roars from the basking platforms made it clear that would be impossible. Her spirits sank, even though it made sense. Of course the dragons would be spoiling for fights too.

Outrage blasted through her mind, and then Windward dampened the bond. Her blood ran cold, panic squeezing her throat shut.

"Windward!" She sprinted through the tunnels, Aturadin close on her heels.

They emerged into a rainy autumn evening—and into an ocean of sound. Palon stopped short, gaping. The setting sun blazed orange and red beneath slate gray clouds. The eerie light painted the stones and made the basin glow, where dragons trampled with lashing tails, necks outstretched as they bellowed. Bonded fled for cover, climbing the nets to the viewing platforms. The ground shook, stones breaking loose and tumbling down slopes into the basin, where they were kicked aside. One such rock ricocheted off a charging dragon and sped toward them. Palon grabbed Aturadin and hauled him to the side as the rock smashed into the mountain just above the tunnel, covering them with debris and blocking the tunnel's entrance.

Palon peeked back out. High Flight crouched in a corner, head down. Silver Spine and Miros watched from the basking ledge of the Sequestering Cave. She clapped her hands over her mouth and squeezed her eyes shut as Dusks Dive dove past them, only feet away from the oblivious Miros. Aturadin squeezed her shoulder, and she peeked out, relief rushing in when she saw Miros unharmed. Dusks Dive landed with a thump that rose up a cloud of dust. Fired Sand and Scorch Frost were screaming at each other, wings spread wide as they nipped and slashed, their voices and displays drowned out by those of the other dragons.

A dragon bugled next to them, and Palon dropped to her knees, hands clapped over her ears. The basin swam before her, washed away by the cacophony. Fired Sand abruptly gave way before Scorch Frost, careening in their direction.

Palon scrambled to her feet. They had to get to the viewing platform. And yet, the dragons were consumed by their chaos, careening toward them. She shoved Aturadin toward the platform, terror strangling her.

Purple grey scales blocked her view of the oncoming dragons. Her breath gusted out of her with relief. Windward had thrown himself in front of them, forming a passage for them between the wall of the mountain and Windward's side.

The world felt far away and slightly unreal as Palon scrambled to check on Aturadin. He rose to a crouch, muscles taut, his dark brown eyes flickering across the basin in shock. They could have been trampled, with Fired Sand retreating so fast toward them. Backing up was hard, and dragons hated it, but that hadn't stopped Fired Sand. It would have been a terrible accident, a consequence naturally applied to the two bonded stupid enough to be caught on the ground during a dragon fight.

But Windward was *furious*.

The ground shook and bounced as Windward lashed out at something they couldn't see—probably Fired Sand. Her dragon was hampered by their presence. The viewing ledges were safety, impossibly far away. She dragged Aturadin to his feet. He staggered, and she adjusted her grip on him to account for his unsteady balance. Teeth clenched, she hauled him forward, holding him up as they ran.

Windward roared, the sound reverberating deep in her chest until her teeth ached, and then stumbled into her. She lurched into the ground, tumbling until she found her feet. Scrambling up, she ran to Aturadin's side where he was just regaining his feet, one hand held to his head. The shock and fear in his eyes tore at her heart. Wings above them flapped as Windward recovered his balance, creating a safe way through for them again.

Everything seemed far away. Her head swam and her ears rang. Her heart pounded against her ribs and her breath rasped in her throat. Palon grimaced. They had to make it to the ledge. She gripped Aturadin's hand hard.

Tsían, standing on the viewing ledge, caught her eye and waved his arm in a big motion. He seemed to be shouting something, but Palon shook her head, gesturing. She couldn't hear. Aturadin staggered again, too imbalanced to run.

If another dragon slammed into Windward, they could be crushed between her dragon and the wall. Their only chance was to race through the chaos and hope Windward could hold out long enough.

Windward was buffeted back again, his scales just brushing her before he dug in his claws and rebounded. Aturadin couldn't run... but Windward could.

Palon looked at Aturadin and grinned.

"No. No, no, no!" She read Aturadin's lips and her grin broadened.

She sent her plan to Windward. "Can you bend down a moment so we can grab your spines and then carry us toward the ledge? Just give me warning when you're ready."

Assent rang through her. He'd carry them to the ledge if they could grab his neck spines. Palon squeezed Aturadin's hand, grinning at the resignation on his face. The thrill of attempting the impossible, Windward and her working together to beat a tight spot, filled her, drowning out the panic and worry.

Windward sent her warning, and Palon gave Aturadin a nod. Hands locked together, she pulled him toward Windward's foreleg as the dragon slammed one shoulder down to the ground. He swung his neck back and Palon let go of Aturadin to wrap her arms around Windward's spine, gripping with desperate strength as his whole body rumbled with the roar he unleashed. Clinging side by side, they rose into the air, an exhilaration filling Palon despite her worries and Aturadin's tight grimace. She craned her neck to see over Windward's crest.

It was a nightmare. Fired Sand screamed at Windward, tossing his sharp horns. Scorch Frost buffeted Fired Sand's side, but Forest Blaze backed Scorch Frost away with a scream. Several female dragons paced around the edges, lashing out with bad-tempered bites at any combatant that got close enough. Stone Eyes was nowhere to be seen.

Fired Sand's tail lashed against Scorch Frost's leg with an audible crack, knocking him off balance. Awkward, especially with his passengers, Windward reeled backward to avoid Fired Sand's nip. Fired Sand overextended, and Windward galloped past, his neck held awkwardly high. Palon met Fired Sand's gaze. Terror welled up deep within her at the fire in his eyes.

Pushing away her fear, she broke the stare, checking on Aturadin. He clung to Windward's neck spine, his cheek pressed against the dragon's scales. She winced at the tight expression on his face. It would be so uncomfortable to be touching the wrong dragon. She'd have to give him some alone time, away from herself and Windward, once they got out of this. Away from Tebah, too, to let him rest. She embraced her dragon's neck spine fully, holding her body close to avoid any cumbersome dangling.

Searing pain shot through her arm. Windward's neck shook with an impact. Numb, she lost her grip and a shout broke from her. All she could see was Fired Sand's muzzle, far too close, and then Windward's scales as she dropped. Wind rushed around her. She hit a wing, arm blazing with agony, rolling with her momentum as her dragon reared back on hind legs. Air whirled by as Windward's wing carried her upward. Aturadin dangled above her. The ledge rushed closer.

And then Windward dumped them on the ledge. Palon fought to find her feet, though it still felt like she was rolling. She stumbled and someone grabbed her elbow. Agony lanced through her arm and black covered her sight. Blinking rapidly, she sucked in slow draughts of air, willing the dizziness back, willing her eyes to see. Aturadin held onto her, his face ashen, and Tsían was holding onto him, keeping Aturadin from falling over the edge. With a grunt, Tsían dragged them both away from the drop off. Palon fought the urge to drop to her knees, though her legs felt watery and her arm blazed with pain. She and Aturadin had made it. They were safely on the ledge, surrounded by others whose expressions ran from worried to angry, terrified, and amazed.

Windward! Palon spun with a gasp, looking for him.

The ground jolted as Windward bore Fired Sand to the ground, jaws latched on his throat. But Fired Sand curled, his claws raking Windward's back legs and belly. Windward left spots of blood behind him with his footsteps. Forest Blaze slammed into them, driving Windward to the edge of the ring, where Dusks Dive, Black Cloud, and Cave Song all screamed and bit at him.

Palon cried out, surging forward. Her balance failed again, and she fell, red consuming her vision as she caught herself with her bad arm. Aturadin crouched beside her, arms around her as she wept tears of pain, fury, and impotence. It wasn't fair, wasn't right, but the dragons were reacting to the upset just as the bonded must feel it. She was powerless and weak. She couldn't help Windward, but at least she could share her dragon's pain.

Tsían stared down at them, and Palon turned with a glare to shriek at him. "Well? Why don't you beat me, as your dragon is doing to Windward?"

Sighing, Tsían rubbed his forehead with one hand and said something, but Forest Blaze drowned it out with a bugle that shook her to her bones. Forest Blaze rose up on hind legs, wings flapping, tearing the air from the bonded's mouths even high up on the ledge as they were.

The fighting continued despite him, and Forest Blaze fell to all fours. The mountain continued to shake, and Stone Eyes galloped in, blasting flame before him. All around, dragons scattered, dropping to the ground and averting their gaze.

Windward rolled to a crouch, and Palon stared at him, shaking with emotion. He easily gained his feet and joy lifted her. But so many injuries scored his scales that sorrow and wrath buried the short-lived joy. Two of his neck spines were bent at ugly angles, and Palon's heart lurched. He'd taken those wounds protecting her and Aturadin.

Tsían said something, but the words sounded like they were coming from far away. She shook her head helplessly, gesturing to her ears. "I can't hear. We can't hear. Fired Sand's roar hurt our ears."

Laetiran appeared out of nowhere, standing on the ledge with a look of scorn on his face, and Palon had to fight down an abrupt urge to pummel him. She wanted desperately to remove the smugness from his eyes. Just moving her arm however, caused her vision to dim. She looked out over the dragons, fury building in her, no doubt fed by Windward. Certainly fed by Windward, she decided, as her pain faded until she no longer risked vomiting or passing out. With her agony taken by Windward, her mind was free to obsess over Fired Sand's face looming, the smashing impact, falling.

Windward confirmed her whirling thoughts even as denial clouded her mind. It couldn't be. She wouldn't have believed it if it hadn't happened to her. Fired Sand had attacked her. He'd seen they were getting out of harm's way and that Windward was vulnerable while transporting them. Windward was very clear on the memory of Fired Sand's muzzle punching into his neck spine, right by Palon's arm. Windward hadn't been able to dodge fast enough for fear of shaking them completely off; he'd barely managed to bounce them to safety with his wing.

Fired Sand had targeted another dragon's bonded. He'd targeted her. He was going to regret this.

She didn't even realize she was snarling, struggling to her feet, until Aturadin grabbed her, holding her back and holding her up and simply holding her. "Palon, you cannot fight a dragon. Calm down. Calm down!" His words came from far away, from reverberations through his bones to hers, locked in that tight embrace as they were.

He was right. Still, rage pent up in her, and she longed to show Fired Sand a threat display, that she was not a weakness for Windward, that she was not to be toyed with. Windward hissed, like a release for her fury. Breathing slowly, she forced herself to stare at Laetiran, a wiser choice for her ire than his dragon was.

Standing tall and trumpeting, Stone Eyes glared around himself as the dragons limped away, forming a wide circle around him. Heads and wings drooped in the face of his wrath.

"Go to your dragons," Tsían ordered them, looking tired.

"I thought you were smarter than this," hissed Eltavae as she passed by them.

It was difficult to climb back down, but Palon did it, grateful Windward was taking her pain. She could have taken the stairs, but the need to prove her strength filled her. She didn't want anyone to guess that her arm had been injured. His expression filled with worry, Aturadin took her hand once they were on the ground. Allowing herself a moment of weakness, she sagged against him, overwhelmed with relief that he was okay. She sent her gratitude to Windward, finding him standing next to Scorch Frost, which would allow her to stay near Aturadin. It was a little thing, but it meant the world right now.

Her mate's pale face and tight expression worried her. They'd lost so much. They'd nearly lost their lives. She wanted to do something to ease his pain, but there was so much to attend to, not least her arm. If Windward was taking her pain, she needed medical attention. She looked up at his golden eyes, and he hummed low at her, his head hovering mere feet from the ground.

"We did not steal anything. You know it." Palon stared at Windward as she spoke, for speaking to the accusing masses of dragons and bonded was too much. Her courage deserted her just thinking about it.

"We were in our cache just before the thefts were discovered and saw nothing amiss. No stolen items were there," Aturadin added, his hand pressed against Scorch Frost's neck.

Windward transmitted the words to her, for her hearing was still muddied, and she pressed her forehead against his snout. She could always depend on him, no matter what, even for the little things. This was what the bond gave, someone who knew your needs without you ever having to speak of them. Someone who could take your pain, strengthen you, raise you up, and have your back in a way not even Aturadin could match, brilliant though he was.

"Of course, there is no proof of this," Laetiran called back.

"You did it, didn't you," Palon said, turning on him with eyes narrowed. Laetiran's ambitions were nothing new.

"There is no proof of that, either." Laetiran smiled, his pose relaxed.

"Did you take my crystal? I swear by Windward—" She stopped, realizing belatedly that if Aturadin's worries over her crystal were founded, she should not admit to having it. But it had been stolen from her, and the rage burned like fire in her gut.

"You'll what, you thief? You and your dragons are the lowest of the low. Who would think to trust what you say, you who steal from dragons?"

Windward hissed, drawing himself up with neck spines extended, facing Fired Sand even despite Stone Eyes in the center of the basin. His gold eyes had hardened with the anger and challenge Palon could feel coursing through her. "You won't get away with this!" she shouted. "Just you wait, you and your dragon. Fired Sand tried to kill me! Targeting a bonded is a very serious crime!"

"And that is a serious accusation, Palon. Think before your tongue gets you in trouble," Laetiran shot back.

Tsían pinched the bridge of his nose. "Quiet, all of you!"

Stone Eyes and Forest Blaze rose up, bristling at the other dragons, and Windward crouched beside Palon, lowering his head submissively.

Tsían continued. "Scorch Frost and Windward are both grounded. You are not to leave the nest without appropriate escort, nor are your bonded allowed to leave, for any reason. Palon and Aturadin are still Tebah's keepers. The dragons will be sorting through this mess."

Forcing her outrage down, Palon bowed her head. She hated this, the accusations, Windward and the other dragons' turmoil, and she especially hated Laetiran and Fired Sand's smugness. It wasn't strictly proper to have such feelings toward a dragon—any dragon—and yet, she did. Of course, she'd have to be careful not to let on, or she'd be in deeper trouble.

Windward's affirmation prodded her, and she struggled not to flush in embarrassment, even though it was only her dragon who'd found her out. She pressed her hand against his platelike nose scales, her rage and frustration echoing Windward's.

She searched out Tebah, crouched in a ball with her back to her dragon, arms wrapped around her knees. This telepathic chaos would be pressing against Tebah and High Flight's bond, not to mention disturbing Silver Spine and Miros in their last days. How dare Laetiran? It was a tragedy, abhorrent. She wouldn't let it stand.

Chapter Nine

Everything hurt. Mostly her arm, but also the loss of her ability to walk through the caves with her head held high. She hissed as Aturadin fastened the bandage, for even that careful movement caused her arm to blaze with pain. Maea was the best of them with wounds and illnesses, but Palon hadn't been able to let her do more than a cursory examination of her arm. She felt like she was going to jump out of her skin just with that.

Palon and Aturadin had been escorted to the Wounds Cave. Beyond a sneer wrinkling Salann's face, she'd been distant, simply performing her duty. Even so, Tsían had lingered at the door, making sure Salann left before he did. That careful action meant the danger wasn't merely her imagination. The air was filled with wrath seeking a target, and Laetiran had laid that target on Aturadin and Palon.

Everything had gone wrong all at once, and Palon didn't know how to fix it. She wanted to fly until she came up with the answer, but that wasn't possible now. Anger filled her, seeing the sorrow and pain in Aturadin's eyes, the way his fine-fingered hands trembled. It ate at her that their cache had been destroyed, taken from them. She resented that their honor was in question. Laetiran would pay for that.

But he'd set them up well. She hated it, but he'd done a good job.

Eyes glittering with an odd excitement, Maea offered Aturadin a wineskin and Palon a jar of salve. "I'm guessing he won't let me fix his hands."

For answer, Aturadin took a quick step back, though embarrassment flickered across his features at the largely unconscious move.

Palon took the salve, moving carefully. Windward was no longer taking her pain and her arm throbbed dully, but she dreaded anyone—even Maea—knowing how badly she was hurt. Her heart and soul screamed danger that anyone else might know, regardless of logic. Aturadin knowing was bad enough.

She took Aturadin's hands, inspecting the scrapes and cuts left by Windward's scales and his fall to the viewing ledge. Ignoring his hisses of pain, she rubbed the salve thoroughly into his wounds. He stood still for her, just as she had done for him. Between the two of them there was no need for defenses. They could be weak.

With a tight smile, as if struggling to contain herself, Maea took the tin of salve back and put it away. She clasped her hands in front of her when she returned, as if to refrain from reaching out and inspecting their work. Palon's bruised pride appreciated the sentiment.

Words gushed from Maea with nervous excitement. "That was amazing, how you rode without a harness up to the ledge! You could have been killed!"

Palon shrugged a little. "There were no good choices."

Maea's awe felt wrong now, when much of the nest vilified them. Even the dragons were furious with them, Windward had told them, to the point that he and Scorch Frost were coiled in their caches, hoping to avoid retribution from the larger dragons. She glanced at Aturadin, but his gaze was faraway. He was probably checking in with Scorch Frost.

"But the way you grabbed Windward's neck spines, how he scooped you up whisked you out of danger—and Aturadin not even his bonded! I've never seen the like."

Shaking her head, Palon waved away Maea's admiration. "It was just like fighting walavaim."

"But you had no harness!"

Her mouth tightened. Maea's obliviousness to the state of the nest grated. "Well what would you have done? Died?"

"Probably," Maea admitted, shrugging and looking down. Her dragon Lake Bolt hadn't taken part during the fight, Palon remembered.

"That's not an option."

"It's not a good one…"

Palon shook her head. "Are we confined here?"

Maea frowned. Not so oblivious after all, then. "Where would you go? It isn't safe out there, with everyone so angry with you. I can't believe you would steal from dragons." She sounded almost as if she were prodding for truth, but there was an underlying tone of accusation that made Palon bristle.

"Neither can I," Palon said. How could anyone believe it?

"We didn't do it, Maea," Aturadin said. "We're being set up."

"Well, I still wouldn't leave here until Dragon Law comes down. Just in case," Maea said.

Miros had said to hold to Dragon Law, back when she had asked him about what to do about the thefts. Of course, that was before she and Aturadin had been implicated. But she knew he wouldn't change his advice, should she ask him. Miros believed whole-heartedly in Dragon Law—he always had.

"Where's Tebah?" Aturadin asked.

Tebah! Cold shot through her. The girl had stayed in the Basin while they'd been taken to the Wounds Cave. "Someone should check on her," she said.

"I'll send someone next time I see them," Maea said.

"You can check on her, can't you? She's going to be a handful," Palon said.

"I can't leave you two here alone! What if someone came by who *does* think you stole from the dragons? What if they were bonded to one of the wronged dragons?"

Aturadin crossed his arms. "We aren't stupid. Of course Eltavae, Salann, and Laros might wish us harm."

"And Laetiran, of course," Palon added.

Leaning against the wall, Aturadin continued, his eyes on the tunnel entrance. "But what are you going to do if they come looking for us? Confront them? We both know you aren't up for that, Maea."

"What if one of the dragons who you stole from sees you?" Maea shifted her weight, eyes full of unease.

Palon exchanged a look with Aturadin. "We follow Dragon Law. Dragons also need to follow Dragon Law."

Aturadin nodded. "If dragons start injuring or killing other dragons' bonded, then none of us are safe. It would be the end of our entire way of life. Any incident between dragons could shortly turn into murder of the dragons' bonded instead of facing the dragon."

"And the dragons won't stand for that. Besides, it's cowardly." Palon folded her arms, careful of her injury.

"You have a lot of faith in Dragon Law," Maea said, looking skeptical.

"If it breaks down, what else is there to have faith in?" Aturadin asked.

Palon said nothing, but her stomach twisted. That should have been her who said that. She had always had faith in Dragon Law. But every time she closed her eyes, she saw the look in Fired Sand's eyes. He had specifically come for her. Accidents were one thing. An outright attack on a bonded...

A longing rose up in her to go to her cache to calm herself, to relax in the presence of her collection, to be where everything made sense. Her chest ached for the need of it. But she couldn't even do that. It was gone, all with Tsían, and she didn't know where her precious clear stone was. She scratched her fingernails on her pants, trying to find her calm.

Palon glanced at Aturadin, but he was still reasoning with Maea. Boots scuffed in the entrance, and the hair on the back of her neck prickled. She suppressed a shudder as the other two went silent, heads swiveling to stare at the tunnel. Her breath halted, her heart pounding. She was trapped and injured and tired, and the adrenaline rushing uselessly through her body made her head swim.

It was only Tebah. She glared at them, letting the tray she carried drop with a clatter onto a table. "Yiyin said I needed to bring this to you even though you're thieves."

Palon glared back at her.

"Why are they keeping me under the influence of thieves?" A sneer twisted Tebah's features.

"We aren't thieves," Aturadin said, standing beside Palon. She focused on breathing, on chasing down some calm, drawing support from his presence.

Shrugging, Tebah came closer. "The stolen items were all found in your cache. Are you saying they're all lying?"

A frustrated hiss escaped Palon. "You aren't getting new teachers because frankly, we're the only ones who could put up with you."

Aturadin shook his head. "Tsían charged us with your care, and that has not changed. High Flight won't challenge Forest Blaze over Tsían's orders."

"But Tsían's not here," Tebah said, glaring at them.

Was the girl being purposely obtuse? Palon gripped her patience tightly. "If High Flight interferes with us carrying out Tsían's orders, that's the same as him challenging Forest Blaze. Use your brain, Tebah."

Tebah wrinkled her nose. "You're not trying to say you two are the nicest people here."

Palon jabbed a thumb in Aturadin's direction. "He's nice. I'm not. Want some?" She held out some of the bread toward the girl.

"Trust me, you wouldn't want to pull stunts like that with anyone else," Aturadin said.

Her words poured out of her like dragonfire. "Maybe she should."

"Palon…" Aturadin gave her a warning look, but she shrugged, too grumpy to take it back. The girl was a never ending headache.

"Maybe you're liars, and everyone else is nicer," Tebah replied.

"Everyone is plenty nice," Aturadin said. "But you are not respectful."

Palon folded her arms. "If you were stupid enough to make an accusation against the character of a higher ranking bonded, they'd take it personally. Dragons don't hold with flinging around silly accusations, and neither do we."

Tebah grumbled under her breath. "Maybe I will be free of you when they pummel you in the tunnels."

Palon glared at her. Was she in league with Laetiran? She couldn't be—Laetiran had tied her up, hadn't he? But they only had the girl's word on that. Her life had gotten worse and worse since the girl arrived, her flight time slipping away from her little by little, replaced by the thankless task of arguing with a venomous child. And now the others had turned against them, and they were grounded, and all the girl could think about was herself!

"Who?" With a worried look, Maea went to the tunnel's opening.

"They're waiting," Tebah said. "Three of them, going to teach you a lesson." She turned back, yelling, "I told them, alright?"

Part of her longed for a fight to release her pent-up rage, but that would risk more harm to Aturadin. How dare the girl side with the others? Palon's temper erupted. "Get out! Get out, you and your threats and your rebellion! Out!"

The girl jumped, her eyes glimmering with tears, fists clenching. Aturadin held out a hand to Tebah, but the newling turned and ran out.

Aturadin turned to face Palon, his mouth set in a firm line. "You shouldn't be so hard on her."

She barely kept from baring her teeth at him. "She's useless."

"She's young."

"She could be in league with that sorry excuse for a bonded," she hissed.

"Palon."

She winced at the wordless rebuke in his tone, hating that he was right. She'd taken her own troubles out on the girl. Granted, they were big troubles, but she shouldn't have jumped on Tebah about them. She was only a newling.

No more movement came from the tunnels, and Maea shook her head, still standing at the front of the cave.

Palon's eyes went to the entrance, the hairs prickling on the back of her neck. Was there movement there in the shadows? Was someone there, waiting? Laetiran, maybe? Pranks and even fights between bonded were normal, even expected. But would they escalate to lying in wait to do real damage?

Windward uncoiled in her mind, alert and on edge. Palon breathed slowly, calming herself and Windward. She was just upset. Tebah might be making something of nothing, especially since she still didn't know much.

Even so, it might be smart to await the judgment of Dragon Law in the presence of an ally. Someone who regarded Dragon Law with sanctity.

Windward gave her a negative. He couldn't ask Silver Spine—he would be mobbed by the other dragons if he attempted to go to the Sequestering Cave. As it should be. Asking the aging dragon and Miros to shelter them at such a time was far too much.

Palon shook her head. It was their best bet. So much was happening that should be unthinkable. But of course, she soothed Windward, if Miros sent them away, she would not argue. Yes, that meant potentially two mad dashes through the tunnels, and her with an injured arm, but she was willing to risk it.

When she looked around next, Maea was gone, and Aturadin was looking at her oddly. "You have some outrageous plan, don't you."

She told him, and he shook his head. "Windward's right. It's a bad idea. How could we? They are dying, Palon—we can't hide behind them!"

"Do you have a better plan? Find a defensible spot and take turns sleeping, always on edge, until we're exhausted and someone makes a mistake, or they come in force for us?"

Aturadin shook his head, his black braids flicking out from side to side with the motion. "It won't get that bad."

"It's already that bad. Dragons were stolen from! A dragon targeted me! We are literally standing here discussing the possibility of our friends, our family, hurting us in revenge."

"Ok." Aturadin sighed. "Ok, you have a point." He rubbed his forehead with one hand.

"Aturadin, we have to think of the hard things now. The things that we'd rather not consider. Fired Sand tried to kill me. You saw it."

"He tried to injure you, sure—"

"He *did* injure me, Aturadin. And if he had shattered my arm as he intended, I would have fallen. If the fall didn't kill me, I would have been trampled. I would have died. How can you not see that?"

"Stop yelling at me, Palon."

It was her turn to rub her face with her hands. "I'm sorry, Aturadin."

"I know. These are hard times. As you said."

She struggled to keep her voice even. Lashing out wasn't helping. She was better than that. She'd have to make it up somehow to Tebah, later. "I know it's a crazy idea. I know it's a hard thing to ask."

"And I will do this with you."

Palon paused in mid-excuse. "Are you sure?"

"Of course I am. You're not so easily rid of me." He grinned and it was like dawn breaking.

Palon threw her arms around his neck, gasping as pain shot through her arm. She clung to him a little extra until the light headedness wore off, then took a deep breath and let go. "Maea's going to check on Tebah?"

"I wished her luck. She thought I was joking."

She smiled. Gratitude washed over her like a waterfall. Aturadin could bring light into any situation. Even this one. Dragonflight, she loved that man.

Aturadin grinned. "Scorch Frost says Windward says you're getting all mushy."

"Oh, let's go!" Her cheeks felt like they were on fire.

Still grinning, Aturadin held out his hand. She took it, and together they crept to the cave entrance. They went carefully, eyes always open, ears straining for any sign of the others.

The tunnels were a twisting warren, but they knew them by heart. Only a few times did they have to dodge out of sight, but they heard the others much more often than that—boots scuffing, leathers brushing on stone, whispers abruptly ending. Her nerves were strung tight by the time they made it to the stairs leading up to the Sequestering Cave and began to climb. As they neared the top, a figure obscured the tunnel entrance.

Miros raised a lantern high. "Hello Palon, Aturadin. Come on. The others thought you would have more tact than to show up here."

Aturadin scoffed. "Have they met Palon?"

"Are you sure this is alright? We don't want to intrude, especially at this time." Palon watched their surroundings with a sharp eye, her heart beating in her ears as beside her, Aturadin shifted from one foot to the other.

"Don't dither," Miros said. "You made a decision. Now own it." He gestured them into the cave, backlit by the deepening colors of dusk.

Bowing her head to the rebuke, Palon crept forward, reluctance in every motion. She had bet their lives on this, that others would have more decency than she did. She'd been so aghast at other unthinkable actions, and here she was committing one of her own. She was no better than they were.

Trying to quiet her guilt, Palon peered over the edge of the open side of the cave. There was a growing cluster of dragonbonded in the basin below. The dragons were watching them too, with venomous looks. She turned back to Miros and opened her mouth, only for him to cut her off.

"Don't make me repeat myself, not at this time." Miros's harsh tone softened at the edges. "I expect you don't want to be murdered by silly bonded looking for revenge."

Palon wrapped her arms around herself, watching the others, who she thought of as family, set apart from them by mistrust and false accusations. Anger simmered in her that she'd been forced to this, the only way she could think to keep herself and her mate safe. Tebah would be fine—no one would dare hurt a newling. At some point, Aturadin came up behind her and wrapped his arms around her, and she leaned into his embrace, but didn't stop her vigil. Only decency was keeping them from coming over.

It was a fragile thing.

Only when her legs began to buckle with fatigue did she back away to huddle with Aturadin at the far edge of the ledge. Hopefully that would lessen the impact of their presence on the aging duo. Silver Spine put a stop to that, though, stretching one wing out over them.

"Silver Spine says you'd better come closer. No sense being cold or doing all this only to be easy targets for the now-thoroughly-enraged dragons and bonded."

Slowly, Palon shifted a couple feet closer. Miros sighed, rolled his eyes, and pointed at Silver Spine's side. "Sit."

Palon gasped, lurching away.

"We can't do that!" Aturadin objected.

"Why not? Have your legs suddenly broken?" Miros asked.

Palon shook her head, appalled. "Won't our presence disrupt things?"

"That's why you're out here in the first place," Aturadin pointed out. "So the other bonds don't press on yours for these last…"

"Yes, yes, until Silver Spine dies and I go with him or go crazy, of course," Miros said, waving his hand impatiently.

Palon exchanged a glance with Aturadin. She was going to miss Miros's bluntness.

"Oh, come on, we're not dead yet!" Miros flared up. "Don't do all this and then lose your nerve at the last moment, making it all for naught. Silver Spine insists. You will stay here until the dragons decide according to Dragon Law. You will certainly not leave the cave system until such a decision is reached, and there's no use you wandering the tunnels like bait for retribution."

Moving as if the ground would give way under her at any moment, Palon settled near Silver Spine's side, just behind his elbow. Aturadin sat shoulder to shoulder with her, while Miros reclaimed his place in the crook of Silver Spine's foreleg, shutting his eyes and seeming to forget about them completely.

Unsettled silence blanketed Palon. It was warmer here, protected from the wind by Silver Spine. The powerful musk of dragon filled her nose, but it was the wrong smell. She shied away from actually touching Silver Spine, and longed to be sitting next to Windward instead.

Their minds touched, a gentle nudge. He sent her approval for the success of her decision, and she got a distinct feeling of gratitude from him.

Silver Spine helping them like this was amazing, she agreed.

There was a pause, and then Windward inquired about the crystal she'd spoken of.

Pushing him away, Palon carefully guarded her thoughts of it. It was just part of her collection that was stolen, she told him.

The dragon hovered, suspicion swirling in him, but it was soon replaced by a reluctance to pester the older dragon, especially after his unexpected hospitality. Windward damped down their bond.

But Palon reached after him, her brow knitting in concern when he shut her out with the most totality he'd ever done. It left her feeling lost and disoriented, though she knew the bond had to still be there, for her arm didn't hurt as much as she suspected it should.

She still hated feeling cut off from him.

Aturadin nudged her. "You're the craziest woman I know, you know that Palon?"

"It's not over yet."

He shrugged.

"Windward ate four days ago, so that's not an issue. Heat is though."

Aturadin's expression became grave. "That's right. They'll have to come out to bask."

"If they have to stay in there longer than a day, they'll become cramped and cold. They'll be slow and stiff and practically helpless when they crawl out of there, until they have the chance to bask properly. They can't last."

"They can last," Aturadin argued. "They're dragons. They can go into torpor until this is over."

"It's autumn, Aturadin. They aren't supposed to be going into torpor till winter."

Aturadin didn't reply, his face troubled. Palon prodded him. "Is Scorch Frost keeping you out?"

He grimaced and nodded. Palon settled back against him. "Windward too."

"What can we do but wait though?" Aturadin asked.

"You can sleep!" Miros snapped.

Palon smiled, doing as she was bid.

Chapter Ten

Pain blazed up her arm. She awoke with a hiss, blinking until the intensity faded to something she could think through, rather than a white haze. Aturadin was crouching over her, mouth open in a threat display. His gaze was directed toward Laetiran, who scrambled to his feet a pace away. Dragon voices filled the Basin with alarm and questioning notes, while Miros reclined on Silver Spine's leg, both untouched by the chaos outside. A tray lay on the ground, its contents strewn over the rock.

Slowly, Laetiran picked up the bowl, spoon, and tray and turned an almost-believable expression of contrition on Miros. "I apologize—I've ruined your breakfast."

He glanced at Palon. "I hope I did not accidentally hurt you."

"It's nothing."

"You stepped on her arm!" Aturadin growled, still crouched over her, his hand resting on her good arm.

"I did not expect you up here, or I would've been more careful." Laetiran's grin was far too innocent. "No one is supposed to be here but Miros."

"I didn't realize I was imprisoned," Miros drawled. "Am I not allowed visitors?"

"The company you keep is... inconvenient." Tsían appeared in the tunnel entrance, carrying a bundle. He gestured at Laetiran. "Go bring Miros a new tray."

Laetiran hesitated, then smiled, his gaze sweeping past Palon and Aturadin. "Yes, of course. I will bring Miros a new tray right away."

Palon resisted the urge to rub her throbbing arm. The pain had receded enough to allow her to think. To realize that Tsían was

111

holding precisely to protocol, leaving Laetiran free to not feed them. No doubt he hoped to starve them out. But the dragons would figure everything out by then, wouldn't they?

"You two made a bold move," Tsían said, watching Palon and Aturadin with hooded eyes. "Even those who might have been your friends are aghast at your actions. Have you no shame?"

"I despise repeating myself. Am I a prisoner, allowed no visitors?" Miros snapped.

"We hold to Dragon Law." Palon lifted her chin, holding Tsían's gaze. Miros's approval radiated from him like a physical thing.

"We are subject to the decision of the dragons, as ever. We only sought refuge until such a decision could be reached," Aturadin explained. "Clearer heads were not prevailing."

Palon shivered, feeling eyes on her. She twisted to look out the opening of the cave, across the basin, meeting Fired Sand's gaze. The dragon stared at her for a few heartbeats, then blinked slowly, turning away. The message was clear—she was no threat.

Fired Sand had targeted her in view of everyone, though admittedly most of the bonded had been distracted by all the fighting. Anyone could have seen though. And they were getting away with it.

She drew a deep breath, turning back to Tsían. That didn't mean they *would* get away with it. She had to wait for Dragon Law.

"I understand, but I strongly disagree with your actions," Tsían said. "I didn't think anyone would stoop so low."

"I'm a pariah now?" Miros interrupted. Palon suppressed a smile at her old mentor's barbed comments.

Exasperation spilled from Tsían. "You know what you are."

"Well then, as 'what I am,' I wonder why no one thinks I have a say in this. I am not dead yet!" Behind Miros, Silver Spine lifted his head and stretched his wings upward.

Palon crouched low, touching the ground with her good hand, bowing her head against the possibility of wind from dragon wings. Beside her, Aturadin did the same. Miros was forgetting who he was again, speaking as Silver Spine.

"I apologize, Silver Spine," Tsían said, his tone now heavy with respect. Palon glanced up to see him kneeling as well, head bowed.

"Well then," Miros said, yawning as Silver Spine did, the dragon's crystalline teeth glinting in the sunlight, impressive even though age had dulled them. "I say these two are welcome here. Dragon Law is to be respected and preserved. What are we, animals, to attack each other indiscriminately in the warrens? No, we are dragons! Keeping each other fit and aware is one thing. Murder and maiming is something else entirely. Remember that, you who are bonded!"

Silver Spine's roar was shrill and breathy, not the impressive blast it once had been in his prime, but tears pricked at Palon's eyes that he would exert such effort on their behalf. Or perhaps Miros's pride really had rankled and the "prisoner" comments hadn't been entirely an act.

"I apologize," Tsían repeated. He looked at Palon and Aturadin, and then glanced apprehensively at Miros, but Silver Spine was curling up around him once again, bonded and dragon clinging to each other in motions perfectly synchronized.

Tsían returned his gaze to Palon and Aturadin, his composure returning with impressive speed. "What have you done with Tebah?"

Palon's brow furrowed. "We sent Maea to check on her."

"Maea couldn't find her. I thought perhaps you had used her as a diversion, to attempt this ill-fated endeavor."

"No." Palon bristled at the implication. If Maea couldn't find her... "She was having a hard time adjusting, though we tried to help her."

"You were not to try, you were to do. High Flight needs her."

"Tebah is not a normal bonding case," Aturadin said.

"Where is she?"

Miros's voice rose in a grumble from where he reclined against Silver Spine. "If you are all going to yell, I'm going to withdraw my invitation to allow you to stay."

Palon folded her arms, surprised at the depth of the concern filling her. "She kept saying she was going to run away." She shook her head, looking at Aturadin. Guilt stabbed her. "You don't think she actually did it, do you? I shouldn't have yelled at her."

"We were suddenly no longer able to be there for her," Aturadin said, his voice turning harder as he looked at Tsían. "Not by choice, but by necessity."

Tsían shook his head. "And High Flight flew off without telling anyone anything. This has all gone too far. I haven't finished my investigation of the thefts, and you two are making it very difficult to continue. I never would have thought it of either of you."

"But then, we know how far they'll stoop now, don't we?" Laetiran's voice was smooth as syrup. He placed the fresh tray gently on Miros's lap, though the older bonded made no move, his gaze distant once again.

Palon watched him, though her thoughts spun in worried circles, always coming back to Tebah. Someone needed to talk some sense into her. Would she put up a fight, being brought back to the caves? Probably. No, almost certainly. And High Flight would have gone to get her, which would further damage their already contentious relationship. She sighed, rubbing her forehead. High Flight's rushed bonding could hamper the entire cave for decades.

So could all this drama.

How far would it spread, if Tebah's bond broke? Would the stress break the nest apart? Would her own bond with Windward be weakened or strained? No, never. She pushed that horrible thought away, along with the sudden panic clawing at her chest. Her bond with Windward was strong. He rumbled at her, a soothing washing over her for a moment before he shut the bond down again.

It left her gasping, tears clogging her throat, threatening to fall from her eyes. Aturadin was there, and she leaned against his arm, grateful for the meager relief from her grief. Even though he wasn't who she really wanted. She reached for Windward, but he was still shutting her out. The pain was worse than that of her arm.

Tsían shifted, leaning against the rock framing the entrance, his eyes flickering with indecision. She rubbed her arm, stopping when Laetiran grinned at her as he fed Miros.

Miros had gone catatonic again. Palon usually waited him out to spare him his pride and dignity, but she didn't want Laetiran hanging around any longer than strictly necessary. With a glare, she circled around to where she could watch pointedly while not crowding them. Tsían had the best vantage point, of course, and he raised an eyebrow at her in stern warning as she approached the tunnel. She ignored him, leaning against the rocks on the other side, far enough away from the entrance to alleviate his evident concerns.

They stood there in silence for some time, watching Laetiran spoon feeding Miros with care. He was nothing if not respectful, but Palon's mistrust only grew. Tsían shifted, grabbing her attention instantly with the motion. He nodded to her arm when she glanced at him. "Maea said your arm was in bad shape."

Palon shrugged. "It'll heal."

"I didn't see you fall."

"I didn't fall." Her tone was as hard as the mountains surrounding them, though she managed to keep from snapping at him.

Tsían raised his eyebrows again, a silent warning for her. "How did you injure yourself, then?"

Frustration surged in her, but she couldn't vent it at him. That would only worsen their position. Palon glared at him, firmly pressing her lips together and drew in a deep breath through her nose. She'd already told everyone what happened, but he apparently didn't want to believe her. "Decide if you want to assume I'm a thief and gain retribution, or act as leader of the bonded. The duality is too much for me right now."

"Interesting, considering duality is clearly something you're far better at than we'd have assumed." Laetiran grinned, walking over.

Palon sneered at him. She couldn't help it, especially when he only smiled in return.

Tsían jerked his head at him. "Leave."

There was silence as Tsían watched Laetiran swagger down the stairs. Then, he returned his gaze to Palon. "I am the leader of the bonded. My responsibilities include bringing retribution on wrongdoers, as you know well, Palon."

"He's still listening."

His brows furrowed and he paused, a rare moment when she'd caught him off balance. "How do you know?"

She shrugged, glancing at Aturadin as he joined them. "He's scum. Of course he's listening. Especially since you obviously don't want him to hear."

Tsían shook his head. "You two—you three—" he corrected himself, including Aturadin in his gaze, "are taking this rivalry too far. The nest cannot handle such stresses. You must make amends once Dragon Law comes down."

Palon raised her gaze to the large basking platforms where most of the dragons were sprawled according to their ranks. Rumbles and whistles came from the gathered dragons, heads swaying on sinuous necks, tails lashing, and wings furling and unfurling. They would be turning over the recent events, especially the most recent fight, and her and Aturadin's flight here. And her accusation against Fired Sand. She clenched her fists. She should have some insight into what they were saying, but she was deaf to the conversation. Not only was Windward not among the basking dragons, but even if he was, she wouldn't know anything with him shutting her out. Even so, she could feel the unease from here.

Which meant Silver Spine and Miros could as well. Sorrow stung her for her part in that.

Tsían was speaking again. "You think Tebah has run off? I can send a bonded or two after her, maybe take some of the pressure off you, and make sure High Flight can bring her back home alright. But whoever I send might take the opportunity to plot against the two of you."

"We didn't do anything, Tsían. We're being framed," Aturadin said.

"Could be," Tsían said. "But everyone saw the missing items in your cache."

"They'll have raided our cache," Palon said dully. It was another blow. "There'll be nothing left."

Tsían shook his head. "I took everything. After Dragon Law comes down, your collections will be returned to you." He hefted the bundle. "These are your harnesses and riding jackets. I assume you'll want these in your dragons' caches for now, but you'll have to put them away."

Palon blinked at the bundle as he cast it on the floor. "You did? You'd do that for us?" She tore it open, a wild hope fluttering in her heart, but there were just two harnesses and two riding jackets. No crystal. Which made sense, but she still couldn't help but feel disappointed.

"Palon, I'm not for you, but I'm not against you, either. I have to think of the long term stability of the cave, as I have always done."

"It's not stable at all. It's all going wrong," Aturadin said. "With Laetiran's antics—and his dragon's—plus Tebah, it'll be a miracle if the dragons can still function. They don't do well with change."

"There's an understatement," Palon said. Still, it felt like a weight had lifted from her shoulders. Her collection was safe—as safe as it could be. Perhaps Tsían had found her crystal, even. She could only hope that she'd missed it earlier.

"Which is why you must make a truce with Laetiran!" Tsían said, rubbing his forehead with his hand. "Dragons above! Now you're accusing Fired Sand of something too? Not just Laetiran?"

The goodwill Tsían had earned evaporated. His doubt made Palon fume. Fired Sand had crossed the line, but no one would believe them. Not even Tsían. They were trapped. She couldn't speak for the wrath filling her, especially not without further angering Tsían.

Miros snorted, his eyes closed. "What, you were under the impression somehow that your job would be easy?"

Tsían glared at him. "My trouble is not with the difficulty, Miros. It's with this... fiction being treated like reality!"

Aturadin folded his arms. "I know what happened. Palon knows what happened. If you were watching during Windward's apparently extremely dramatic rescue of us, you should have also seen what happened. The question is whether you care to believe your eyes or not."

"Now you're calling me blind? Honestly, do you two want no friends?" Tsían shook his head.

"He's probably still listening," Palon murmured to Aturadin, glancing at the stairwell.

Still shaking his head, Tsían threw his hands in the air. "So be it. If you want to alienate every potential ally, do so. Be exiled from the nest, and good luck trying to find another to take you in. I can't continue to care if you're only going to blame others."

"Tsían, think about it!" Aturadin shouted. "When have you ever known us to point fingers?"

"Apparently, I've never known you! Dragons don't harm bonded!" Tsían shot back, stomping down the stairs and out of sight. "Stay there —don't leave the caves, or I will hunt you down like vermin."

Palon opened and closed her mouth several times, trying to find the right words. Finally, she shook her head. "That could have gone better."

Aturadin smirked at her understatement, but it wasn't enough to lighten her mood.

She buried her head in her hands. "I hope they find Tebah soon, and that High Flight doesn't do anything else rash."

"Dragons help them when they do," Aturadin said, grinning.

Slipping her jacket on, Palon sat down, leaning against Aturadin when he came to join her. She rubbed her arm idly. She hadn't been able to talk to Tsían about Windward and Scorch Frost, about granting them safety to bask. How were they supposed to defend themselves, to come before the other dragons?

Everything was going wrong. How could Tsían not see what Laetiran and Fired Sand were doing? Laetiran wasn't even hiding his glee at their plight, especially their injuries. But if she kept pushing, Tsían was likely to take Laetiran's side, viewing him as the wronged party, victim of Palon's continued and baseless assaults.

And Tebah. The newling should know better than to run off alone in the mountains. Palon still remembered how the dangers of the mountains were stressed over and over to her when she grew up. She'd been delighted when Windward had opened them up as a possibility to be explored by her, though soon enough she had stopped caring. After all, what were the mountains compared to the sky?

And now she was trapped here. In her desperate bid to reach safety for herself and Aturadin, she had further alienated and offended her family, turning the others more fully against them. Laetiran would be a fool not to use that to his advantage, and unfortunately, he was not a fool.

Chapter Eleven

The sound of boot soles scraping on the stone steps woke Palon, and she jumped to her feet. Had Laetiran or another bonded come to drag them out of the Sequestering Cave? Her heart pounded, but she refused to let her fears show. Twisting, she glanced back to where Miros and Silver Spine were still sleeping. They couldn't help, but then she shouldn't need their help, either. Regardless, some of the tension in her muscles faded as Aturadin rose to stand beside her.

Salann came racing up the stairs. She was panting for breath, and there were lines of stress around her eyes and mouth. "Palon! Aturadin! It's Tebah!"

A blast of worry hit her like a fist in the gut. "What's wrong?" Palon asked, surprised at the depth of her anxiety for the prickly newling. Of course she'd worry over her charge, but this felt like she couldn't breathe. Windward shifted, opening the bond just enough to check on her, then shut her out again, leaving her with only the disorienting shadows of pain and cold.

Stopping in the entrance, Salann leaned a hand against the wall. "How do you make her do as you tell her? She's not listening!"

Palon exchanged a glance with Aturadin, who began chuckling. "We don't know," he said. "but if you figure it out, I'd consider it a favor if you tell me."

"Where is she?" Palon folded her arms. Pain lanced through her at the movement, and she barely stopped herself from wincing as she adjusted her position as nonchalantly as possible.

Even so, Salann paused, eyes flickering to her arm, then back to her face. The older bonded's expression was unreadable, though her tone was exasperated. "She's found herself a cave—a crack in the rock,

119

really—and has pressed herself inside. She's wedged tight and was completely unhelpful when I tried to unstick her. High Flight is losing his mind. He swooped down to try to get her out, but the rocks looked like they'd collapse on her. She's *laughing* at him. Laughing!"

"I believe it," Palon said. The girl wholly lacked a healthy respect for dragons, instead wielding her anger like a weapon.

"Is she safe?" Aturadin asked.

"For now. But High Flight can't get her out without risking injury to her, and the space is too small even for Yiyin to get in. She won't even reach out for us. She's not nearly as claustrophobic as I'd have hoped she'd still be. We can't get her unless she helps us."

Palon shrugged. "You'll have to talk her out of there, then." Knowing the girl was physically safe, the tension receded, and she pressed her lips together to keep from smiling. It'd be interesting hearing what the others thought of dealing with the tiresome girl.

"Maybe it's best to just leave her, if she wants out so much. Or let the dragons try to get her," Salann muttered.

"Dragons can't manage that kind of detail work!" Palon's voice trembled as horror filled her.

"What if they cause a landslide or dislodge a boulder on her head? And even if she was only injured, that injury could ground her the rest of her days. We can't risk it. A crippled dragonbonded is little better than a dead one," Aturadin said.

"I don't know what else to do," Salann said. "She isn't giving us better options."

Tebah never gave good options. After all the time they'd spent trying to protect her, trying to help her, and now she was in even more danger. If High Flight succumbed to the panic he was surely feeling, he could hurt her accidentally while trying to rescue her. Her stomach turned, and a sour taste crept into her mouth.

Aturadin's hands slashed through the air. "If she's injured or dies, do you really think the dragons can handle that sort of stress right now?"

Salann gestured sharply with one hand, frustration lining her movements. "She's the most recalcitrant, obstinate, most set in her ways newling we've had here in years! She won't *listen*!"

"Welcome to our trouble," Palon said. Hearing Salann utter the familiar complaints somehow lifted the strength of her anxiety just a little. There was something ever so slightly amusing about it that helped force the bile back down, helped her think. Tebah was safe for now.

"Care for some framing and accusations to go with the rebellion?" Aturadin added.

Palon shot him a cautious look, though a grin tugged at her. Let the others get a taste of what she and Aturadin had been through. Maybe they'd think twice about condemning them.

Salann eyed them. "Well, it's Laetiran's turn to try. Maybe he can—"

"Don't let him near her!" Palon growled.

"No!" Aturadin shouted at the same time.

Salann raised her eyebrows at them, and Palon hurried to explain. "Laetiran tied her up and gagged her during her early days here. Don't you dare let him anywhere near that girl. She was defensive and on edge for days after meeting him. It was all we've been able to do to convince her that we aren't all monsters!"

Salann frowned. "Tsían mentioned your rivalry is becoming an unhealthy obsession. I thought perhaps you'd overlook it to help us, but I guess we see where your priorities lie."

Palon dropped her hands to her side, clenching her fists. The pain was nothing compared to the outrage burning through her. She took a moment, breathing heavily through flared nostrils. The accusation hurt worse than even her arm, and she longed for air as if the wind had been knocked out of her.

"This hasn't been about any rivalry for a long time!" Palon managed as she found her bearings. "He set us up! He—"

"Silence!" Salann hissed, her face inches from Palon's, with a gaze so intense Palon stepped back. "You'll wake Silver Spine! Have you no shame at all, no decency? Well no, I guess you showed that, hiding up here. I don't know why Tsían allows this."

Palon wilted inside, faced with Salann's ire. There she stood in front of them, with her glossy black hair in its impeccable braids, her eyes so dark they were pools of night, and she thought them shameless. Palon felt more stable climbing around on Windward during a fight—indeed, she'd rather be doing that than facing Salann's cold, harsh judgement.

"We were invited." Palon's tone was stiff as she clutched at her self control.

"Right." Salann's tone made it very clear she did not believe her.

Her chest tightened, a sudden need for Salann to understand growing, clogging her throat. "Salann, we've known each other my whole time here! You showed me around on my first day! How could you..." She ran out of words, the betrayal too large to be spoken.

Salann was shaking her head slowly. "No, I guess I never knew you at all. I knew you were rash, Palon. I knew you were the one to take the risks any sane person would never do. One of our best teams to keep the walavaim back, yes. But the evidence..."

Palon bit her lip, the physical pain beating back the emotional. Beating back the tears pricking at her eyes. Swaying backward, her arm brushed Aturadin's, his fingers twining in hers. She squeezed them. "I would never steal from a dragon, Salann. You know that. And Aturadin is far too awe-inspired himself. He'd stand there drooling in the majesty of the dragon and forget what he came there for!"

"Hey!" Aturadin said.

"How could you think we would steal?" Palon pressed.

"The items were in your cache."

"How did you get in to check?" Palon demanded.

Salann opened her mouth, and then stopped, her brow furrowing. She gave a quick shake of the head. "Well, if you were innocent, why would you run here and disturb the final moments of a dragon? It's a desecration!"

"That was an easy choice," Palon said, earning herself a ferocious glare from Salann. But she wasn't alone—she had Aturadin next to her, and Aturadin's honor was just as much in danger as hers. She hurried onward, as if to bury her ill-chosen words. "I wanted to live. I wanted Aturadin and I to live and be uninjured, and I knew several bonded who would be too riled up, too whipped into a frenzy of rage to think straight. We needed somewhere to hide out until the rule of Dragon Law, somewhere we would not need to fight should we be discovered."

Salann glanced at Palon's arm again. "How bad is it?"

Stupid, stupid! Palon hid a wince, trying to wiggle out of the spotlight she'd put on her own injury. "Not as bad as our social situation. Let me go get Tebah."

"Absolutely not. Tsían would never allow it."

"Don't let Laetiran anywhere near her, Salann. Please! For her sake, and therefore for all of ours," Aturadin pleaded.

Palon nodded.

"I'll tell Tsían." Salann turned away, her gaze thoughtful.

Palon watched her hurry down the stairs, then rested her head on Aturadin's shoulder, her fingers still twined in his.

"Drool?" Good-natured prodding filled his voice.

Her cheeks heated. "Sorry."

He grinned. "It's alright. I'll find a way to make it up to you."

She rubbed the bridge of her nose. "What are we going to do? Ugh, Tebah."

"I don't know. We can't leave." Aturadin brushed her braids back over her shoulder. "Palon, don't go thinking anything crazy. If you do something else, everyone might turn against us permanently. Don't do Laetiran's work for him. Make it a little challenging, will you?"

"I don't care about Laetiran," Palon spat. "I care about the dragons. I care about Windward not shutting me out. I care about Tebah coming back safe."

Aturadin smirked. "It's funny how that girl can be so much trouble and yet she got under your skin."

"Yeah, well, you're not completely parasite free yourself." She found herself smiling at Aturadin's chuckles, even though her worries ran deep.

They sat there and waited, while the near constant rumbling of the dragons below them marked the discussion of their fates, the dragons mulling over the evidence in their slow, thorough way. Eventually, Yiyin brought Miros's food, his glances at them many and furtive as he set the tray down and left. Palon handed the tray to the bonded at his next lucid moment, her own stomach growling. Miros raised his eyebrows at her, gesturing with the spoon, but she shook her head. She couldn't take his food. Even if they weren't being watched, to eat food meant for him would be incredibly disrespectful.

As the day wore on, Palon found the confinement more and more oppressive. She paced, gnawing on her fingernails and reaching endlessly for Windward. The bond felt frayed, brittle. She wanted to drag her dragon out of his hiding, but was terrified any more stress would break their bond.

She needed to do something. Almost anything would do, so long as it wasn't nothing. Her normal tasks weighed on her mind. She needed to clean Windward's wounds, to check the scales just behind his elbow where they had been damaged during his last shed. He'd need a good cleaning and polish, too, and his teeth could probably be picked at. His injuries could likely do with more salve, and she wanted to check on how they were healing, especially the one on his foot. And she needed to look at the neck spines he'd broken while helping her and Aturadin.

She narrowed her eyes and tried thinking these thoughts directly at her dragon. He didn't respond, though she got a faint impression of him curling up with his back to her. Pressing her lips together, she stalked along the very edge of the ledge, where the wind buffeted her as it passed by. Her dragon shutting her out was the worst feeling in the world, worse even than the terrible boredom.

She raised up on her tiptoes when she spotted Laetiran returning to the nest. He mingled with the others as the sun went down, and though Palon looked, she saw no signs of Tebah.

"Where is she?" Guiltily, she glanced at Silver Spine, hoping her turmoil wasn't spreading to them, ruining their rest.

She sighed, flopping down on the stone, still warm from the light of the sun. Aturadin gave her a glum look. "We can't leave, Palon."

"I know!" She kept from shouting, but just barely. She glanced again at Silver Spine and Miros and sighed, lowering her face into her hands.

"Is Windward still shutting you out?"

Palon nodded, peeking up at him. "Scorch Frost?"

He nodded. "I hate it. It's like…"

"Like they're dead. Or we're dead."

Aturadin let out his breath in a giant gust. She looked gloomily past him, to the sleeping dragon and his catatonic bonded. It was not good form to discuss such things near them.

When Tsían and Maea brought Miros's evening meal, it was all Palon could do not to tackle him and shake answers out of him. She was surprised to find her hands were trembling. Maea gave them a wary look as she began to help Miros with his meal.

"Did you get to her?" Aturadin spoke first. "Did you bring her back?"

"We can't reach her," Tsían sighed. "She'll have to spend the night out in the cold. Hopefully, she'll come to her senses and we can bring her home in the morning."

A night in the mountains would be dangerous. Even more dangerous if she moved during the night. Fear chilled her, and Palon turned away from it to focus on other worries—things she might actually be able to do something about. "Windward and Scorch Frost need to be allowed to bask."

Tsían shook his head. "I'm not getting between dragons."

"I'm not asking you to get between them. Ask Forest Blaze to—or for him to involve Stone Eyes."

"And where does it end? Dragons don't micromanage each other."

"So you're just going to let them pick on Windward and Scorch

Frost even though they haven't done anything?"

"They can handle it. You know dragons are not fragile."

"Even a mountain erodes with time."

Tsían waved away Aturadin's remark. "The dragons take care of themselves. They don't welcome outside interference. Even from us. Even from each other. You both know this."

This was ridiculous. Tsían couldn't return the nest to peace by pretending everything was normal. Things were only getting worse and worse. She shook her head at him fiercely enough to send her braids lashing. "We do, but what you're not seeing is we can't go on as before. Things have changed. Have you ever known anyone to steal from dragons? Multiple dragons?"

Tsían frowned at her, fierce as a thunderstorm breaking over the mountain peaks. The spoon clattered in the bowl of soup, and Maea ducked her head, as if hoping they'd ignore her.

Palon rushed onward. "Aturadin and I didn't do it. But it's such a shocking crime, so unexpected, impossible to plan for. Of course people are mad. I get it."

"And yet you want me to interfere."

"Yes!"

"I won't. Some things, Palon, a person simply must not do."

Palon folded her arms and scowled, but he was invulnerable to her frustration. "They're shutting us out, Tsían." Her voice cracked as she tried one last ditch effort to reach him.

"The dragons? Well I'm not talking to your dragons for you. Maybe they're angry at you for coming here and disturbing Silver Spine. That's something else no one would think of. You want me to believe more than one person would be so disregarding of the tenets of dragonbonded life? No. It's too much to ask. Much more likely, you went too far and are trying to blame it on Laetiran. A clumsy job, sure, but it makes more sense than your story."

Palon put her hands on her hips, gritting her teeth as pain shot up her injured arm. "You really think I'm capable of this? You think I'd reach so far? That I'd do this to get at Laetiran? If I wanted to get at Laetiran, I would just do it."

"Not now, because the dragons would get involved and right now Windward wouldn't be able to beat Fired Sand. Everyone can see that."

"So who got into our cache? How did anyone get inside to see that the stolen items were there?"

"I'm not telling you and then having you go off for revenge against yet another bonded, Palon. Enough is enough."

Why did this keep coming back to Laetiran? She didn't understand it. Yes, they'd had a rivalry for quite some time, but she'd never put the nest at risk because of it. It baffled her that any of the others would even think she would. "No, that's not—Tsían when did you start thinking so little of me? Don't tell me who it is—it doesn't matter. Just think. Someone besides Aturadin and I knew how to get past the traps, and when Windward and Scorch Frost were distracted. That means that there's another suspect. See?"

"What are you talking about?" Tsían glanced at Maea as she hovered near the doorway and gestured her out.

Palon stared at the tunnel opening as Maea fled down the stairs, then brought her attention back to Tsían. "The person who told you could have moved the stolen items there before telling you."

"Not possible."

Her mouth dropped open. "Why—how can you say that? What would keep the finder from having meddled before going to you? The finder could be the thief!"

"I found the cache."

"You?" Aturadin looked as shocked as Palon felt.

"Yes, me. Now if you're going to attack me, let's get it over with. I have other tasks to attend to as well."

Palon stared at him with her mouth still agape. Attack Tsían? Where was this coming from?

"We aren't going to attack you, Tsían." Aturadin sounded tired.

"Finally, a little bit of common sense from you two."

Aturadin folded his arms. "How did you get in? It was well trapped."

"No, it really wasn't. I was surprised at your carelessness."

Palon exchanged a glance with Aturadin. "You think we would be careless? With our cache? Our things?"

"Listen. You're not going to spin this around on Laetiran. He's become your favorite scapegoat, and it's getting old. You two have made some surprising mistakes, and also some appalling judgement lapses. I'm not going around looking for conspiracies for you, or helping you to pin it on another. Your rivalry needs to be set aside for now. Are you capable of that?"

"But just think—"

"I said, are you capable of that?"

126

Palon subsided. Clearly Tsían wasn't going to listen. "Yes."

"Aturadin?"

"Yes, of course. J—"

Tsían held up his hand, a look of warning on his face, and Autradin stopped. He nodded, lowering his head a few degrees.

Tsían stared at them with eyes full of icy disappointment for several more heartbeats, then turned and walked out.

"You two are entertaining, let's get that right."

Palon turned to see Miros watching them, smiling. Shame filled her, heating her cheeks. They'd been fighting in the Sequestering Cave, right in front of Miros and Silver Spine. This was supposed to be a serene place, not somewhere to shout and argue.

"We apologize for disturbing you," Aturadin said.

"What disturbs me is how terrible you two are at defending yourselves or gaining any allies to your side of things," Miros replied.

Brow furrowing, Palon folded her arms, but Aturadin surprised her, walking forward to sit at Silver Spine's clawed feet. "What would you do in our position?"

Miros laughed. "I wouldn't be in your position. But if I were, I wouldn't alienate everyone around me."

Aturadin was right. They might as well ask Miros for his advice while they were stuck here. It was the smartest course of action, regardless, especially since right now their choices were greatly limited. Palon followed Aturadin, crouching down beside him. "It's not our fault. We're only trying to defend ourselves. Trying to survive."

"And the nest?" Miros asked.

"And the nest. We want it to survive too."

"Then you don't come at it with tremors and quakes." Miros smiled sagely at the ceiling.

Palon paused, glancing at Aturadin. Miros didn't always make sense, but it always proved worth it when she did figure it out.

Aturadin nodded, seeming to understand. "We're pushing too hard, you say."

"Yes. Exactly."

"But we can't just let them win," Palon burst out.

"And who is them?"

She faltered. "The… the other dragonbonded."

Miros cracked open an eye, looking at her with his eyebrows raised. "Do you see the problem?"

Palon frowned. Aturadin drew a deep breath, nodding. "I see why Palon thinks you're wise."

Now if only she could see. Annoyance rose in her. "Of course he's wise—look at all the wrinkles. And no one can understand a word he says," Palon shot back.

Miros laughed. "I'm only fifty-two!"

"Ok, ok. So we can't split the nest by thinking of us and them," Aturadin said. "So how do we survive?"

They hadn't split the nest. Her annoyance turned to anger at the injustice of it all. They shouldn't be stuck here, and wouldn't be if they hadn't been targeted and framed. "But it is us and them! Them is who wants to hurt us!"

"They are our family, Palon. We have to remember that. We are one nest."

She scowled. "Yeah, and some family members need to be punched in the face."

"But they are still family," Miros said. "And they are treated as family, not as other. Not as them."

"Ok." She shook her head, ready to move on, to stop arguing with those she loved and move on to something she could *do*.

"No." Miros's tone took on a hard edge. "It goes beyond that. You treat Tsían, Yiyin, Maea, all of them, as if they are against you. You're afraid of being hurt so you close up your scales and lash out with teeth and tail at those who come too close to you, as a wounded dragon."

"I'm not afraid," Palon grated.

"It pushes them away."

Aturadin nodded. "It makes them other. It makes them 'them.'"

Miros nodded.

Palon sighed, shoulders slumping. "Can I at least lash out at Laetiran? He deserves a thrashing."

"Think of what that thrashing costs you," Miros said. "Dragons shake the mountains when they fight, yes, and they do not flee from fear. But they weigh the cost before they fight. Windward is doing that. This is something you must learn to do."

Her brow furrowed. "What cost? Maybe my hand will hurt if I hit him wrong."

"There's social cost too," Aturadin said. "Tsían thinks we're picking on Laetiran."

"Tsían's blind," Palon said, bitterness filling her voice.

"So are you." Miros raised his eyebrows.

Palon sighed again, nodding. She leaned forward, impulsively putting her forehead against Miros's knee. "Don't leave us."

Miros patted her head, and she could feel his hand slow and stop, resting on her disheveled braids. She held her breath, listening, but Silver Spine breathed, and she began to breathe again too. She sat back, leaning against Aturadin and staring at Miros's slack face and distant gaze.

"It's good advice," Aturadin said, wrapping his arms around her.

Palon nodded. "Sometimes he comes back for a bit. Sometimes he stays far away. Well, with his dragon. So not far."

"Far enough." Aturadin's arms tightened for a bit.

She didn't need to nod. He just knew. She grimaced. "I hate Windward shutting me out. I'm not *me* when he's not there."

He nodded. She scowled at her hands. Dealing with their predicament would be easier if she at least had her stone. Aturadin had a handful of his feathers, but she had lost everything. She sighed, trying to distract herself from her misery and longing.

Her thoughts turned to Tebah, never too far from her worries these days. "I don't want to follow Dragon Law. I want to go get Tebah and bring her back. She's riling up all the dragons."

Aturadin chuckled. "I think you're riling them up more."

It was more than that. She struggled for the words. "She's our responsibility, Aturadin. And then with this mess… she's not helping things settle."

"You don't really expect her to."

"No. But we can't talk sense into her, either." Not stuck here, where she was useless. She stood by her decision, but her fingers twitched, every nerve in her body screaming for something to do.

Sarcasm coated his tone. "Talking sense into the others is working so well."

She rolled her eyes at him and continued on. "Because we have to wait here for Dragon Law."

"We don't have to wait. We can leave whenever we want to, so long as we accept the possibility of vigilante justice."

Palon sighed. She wasn't willing to risk Aturadin for Tebah.

Aturadin's tone was thoughtful. "It'd be worth it, if we could find evidence that we're being framed. But they've had a long time to look around. They probably picked up everything."

Palon shifted so she could look at him. "So do we go, then?"

He shifted to meet her gaze. "How's your arm? We came here for a reason. Leaving sort of negates it."

"No, it doesn't. We've had time to think. And someone needs to go get Tebah."

"Well, you can't go out there. The others will think you're running too."

"Follow Dragon Law!"

Aturadin and Palon spun to look at Miros. The roar had come from him, had been his voice, Palon was sure of it. And yet he lay there, looking completely relaxed, not at all like someone who had just shouted.

"Miros?"

He said nothing.

She couldn't stand it if Miros turned on her too. Not with the rest of the nest thinking they were awful. "We're trying to follow Dragon Law, Miros. But we have to wait for the decision to come down from the dragons. That can take some time. You know that."

Miros's mouth moved, though his expression remained slack, his eyes distant. "The Line of Responsibility. It's part of Dragon Law."

Aturadin blinked, and Palon waited, turning to him. He had his thinking face on, and Palon had to nudge him with her elbow. "What?"

"The Line of Responsibility," Aturadin said. He blinked, explaining, "So, we normally think of the hierarchy as it stands at a glance. We can't leave because Tsían told us not to and Tsían outranks us."

"Shouldn't, not can't," Palon corrected him rebelliously.

He rolled his eyes and continued. "However, the Line of Responsibility doesn't always coincide with the hierarchy. We have responsibility for Tebah, because Tsían gave us responsibility for her. He passed it to us. We hold that now. We never passed her on. We didn't have time."

Palon frowned, thinking through it. Aturadin's love of digging into books gave him insight into the more obscure parts of Dragon Law; Palon only understood it instinctively. "So we're still responsible for her antics. Her running off, her hiding and not coming out. All of that."

"Right."

"But Tsían is responsible too."

Aturadin shook his head. "Only by proxy, through being responsible for us. Remember, he's not the one who holds the responsibility for Tebah, not directly. Which means he can't actually interfere between her and us. He holds responsibility for us, weighed against the nest, but not Tebah, because he gave that away."

"So we can leave. He can't tell us not to."

"Not only that," Aturadin said, looking a bit nervously at Miros. "I think we have to. Or should, anyway."

Palon nodded. It was a loophole, but it was entirely legal. "We'll have to go now, then, if we have a chance of finding her. She's going to move during the night."

"You think she'd do that?"

Palon rolled her eyes. "She's trying to run away, Aturadin."

He nodded thoughtfully. "Ok, we go now. We'll have the cover of darkness and the others will be sleeping."

"Good enough for me." Palon leapt to her feet.

"It took you long enough to figure all that out." Miros smiled faintly. His gaze was still distant, his voice weak.

She paused, looking back at him. "You didn't need to give us riddles."

"Too long to explain. Too much fighting."

Grinning, Aturadin nudged her. "Yeah, he sure knows you."

Palon rolled her eyes. "Come on. We have a newling to find and drag home."

She leaped down the stairs. At the bottom of the steps, she turned around and bounded back up, passing a bemused Aturadin.

She knelt by Miros, kissing his forehead. "Thank you."

Then a quick kiss for Aturadin as she caught up once more, heading through the tunnels. She wished she could feel Windward as more than a shadow in the corner of her mind. She reached for him, but he still shut her out. Narrowing her eyes, she yelled at him anyway, telling him to go bask, telling him to trust in Dragon Law, despite everything. She couldn't tell if he heard her or not.

It was a shame he couldn't join her. She desperately wanted to see him—being separated even for this long was agony, like a persistent itch she was unable to scratch. She poked at Windward one last time through the bond, telling him of the adventure he was missing out on, the chance to fly. Still, he didn't respond, and she gritted her teeth. She couldn't go to him, not without jeopardizing her new mission. She had to leave him.

"Ready?" Palon asked Aturadin, slipping into her riding jacket. She'd missed it.

"Actually, I think I'll stay here," Aturadin said. "I want to poke around and see if I can find out how Laetiran did it. See if I can prove it."

"We're disregarding Tsían's orders," she said. "He'll be mad if he sees you, even though we're following Dragon Law."

"I know. It'll help Tebah, though, and that's worth it, even if I can't find anything to help us."

"Be careful."

"Only as careful as you ever are," he said.

Chapter Twelve

Palon rubbed her hands together briskly, pulling her fur lined jacket closer. It was cold out in the wind. Her arm ached, but she ignored the pain. She was dragonbonded, and dragonbonded were tough—they had to be. If she weren't, she never would have made it this far. Still, she longed for the nest, for a slacking of the thirst that swelled her tongue and the hunger pangs that stabbed her stomach. Her limbs trembled with exhaustion, timed to the pulsing in her arm.

But she kept going. She had to find Tebah.

A glint of a fire lit between the rocks, getting ever larger as she neared the tiny camp. It had to be Tebah. She snuck carefully across the rocky terrain, fearing to cause the newling to run farther. Aturadin was in the nest without back up, trying to find the truth, and she longed to get back to him, to keep him safe from any possible retribution.

But lashing out at Tebah had caused this problem in the first place, so Palon tried to find her patience. The wind whipped and howled around the rocks, and she smiled. It'd been a few days now since she'd last flown. She had missed the wind in her face, the power, the challenges of flight. Being grounded was thoroughly boring, so much so that this little adventure was more enticing than it should be.

Palon crept closer. The flames of the small fire leaped, wood crackling, lighting the entrance of a small cave. Tebah's head was lowered, her hand pale with cold as she poked up the fire. Palon smiled, thankful for Tebah's rashness for once. A fire while on the run was a terrible idea, but then, so was navigating the mountains without intimate knowledge of them. She stepped into the light thrown by the fire and Tebah looked up. The girl gasped, backing into the cave.

"Don't," Palon said. "I really don't want to chase you any farther."

Tebah paused, then crouched further in the cave, hastily throwing supplies into a pack.

Palon scowled. "You know I'll just find you again. And if it's not me, it'll be High Flight, or another bonded or dragon from our nest, likely angry."

The newling looked back, fear in her eyes. "Angry?"

Palon chuckled, stepping closer. "You think we like tracking little girls who run off through the mountains, especially when they really need to be at home?"

Tebah looked briefly abashed, then frowned. "You can't keep me prisoner." But she didn't move, watching Palon warily as she stepped closer.

She needed to make amends, somehow. "You really frustrated them, you know, hiding in that crack in the rock. Especially High Flight. It was smart, waiting for High Flight to fly off to sleep before leaving."

"I wasn't sure he ever would."

"He must have been exhausted, or he wouldn't have left. I'm glad you're not still in that crack."

"I was safe there. They couldn't reach me."

Palon scoffed, continuing forward, blocking the entrance. How little she knew! "You know their next idea? To let the dragons try to get you out."

Tebah's expression darkened, and she skittered away from Palon with the pack, her gaze darting to the cave walls around her with the realization that she was trapped now. "You people are terrible."

With a groan, Palon leaned against the cave wall. The heat of the fire felt good on her cold hands and feet. "They're not awful. Their idea is, but they are furious and frustrated and have no patience for your antics. They're looking for the easy solution, not the best one."

Tebah looked at her, then away. For a moment, Palon thought the foolhardy girl would try to get past her, or jump over the flames, but she shivered instead, crouching closer to the little fire.

Palon spread her hands to the flames. "Where do you think you're going to go?"

"Home." Tebah lifted her chin.

Palon suppressed a sigh. She'd known that answer was coming, but she was tired of this argument. Trying to seem casual, she raised her eyebrows and pointed back toward the nest. "Home's that way. We can go and get you warmed up."

For a moment, concern crossed Tebah's face, as if she was wondering if she was going the wrong way. Then she stared at Palon with fire in her eyes. "I'm going home to my village. To my family. It's clear I won't learn what I need to know, so I'm leaving."

It was difficult not to glare at the girl. How dare she? "You would go back on the promise you made to a dragon?" she asked, glad there was only a touch of knives to her tone.

The newling glared at her. "He lied to me."

"And you lied to him. You never intended to stay."

Tebah's gaze dropped, her fingers entwining in her lap. She scowled. "You hate me."

Guilt stabbed her through the heart. "I shouldn't have lashed out at you. I was upset and angry, and it really doesn't matter." She wasn't here to make excuses. She was here to make amends. "I'm here to take you home. To your real home, your only home."

When Tebah didn't respond, Palon said, "You have courage, though. Or you're just foolhardy. I can't decide which. To dare to back out on a deal with a dragon—to trick him in your own way—and then to run out into the mountains, regardless of the dangers. Not what I would have done, but yeah, you have courage."

The newling's look was venomous. "Of course it's not what you'd have done. You've never done anything wrong in your whole life with the dragons."

Palon rocked backward, tilting her head. That was interesting. Did Tebah resent her, the way Palon had resented the never-ending comparison to her family?

"I came out here to get you, to make sure you're safe. To keep you from getting hurt," Palon said, not taking her eyes off the girl. She felt a bit surprised, seeing a flicker in the eyes of the newling. Had that been a flash of happiness? Well, but Miros had told her about that too, how it would feel to be unwanted. "How did you get away, anyway?"

Crouching closer to the fire, Tebah watched the flames. "It was easy. No one cared that I was going. I just took a pack I found laying on a table in the Meal Cave and left." She shifted. "How can you think this is ok? I want to at least be with my great-mother while she dies."

"I disobeyed an order not to leave the nest. I did that to fulfill my duty to you."

The girl's expression only darkened, and Palon winced. She was making a mess of things again. Rubbing her aching arm with stiff fingers, Palon stared at the fire. She needed to come up with the right words to reach this newling, to make her understand. But still the right words evaded her.

Sitting on the rocks by the fire, Tebah looked small and lost and very young.

"You look awful, though. You should have grabbed a coat."

Tebah glared at her, wrapping her arms around herself as she shivered. "I didn't know where they were. Not that you care."

Palon sighed. Exhaustion and hunger were wearing at her, and her voice was becoming hoarse from thirst. She nudged Tebah's pack.

"Did you bring food and water with you?"

Tebah scowled. "I'm not stupid, of course I did. Didn't you?"

Her stomach rumbled. Palon reached down and opened the bag. She needed food. Mostly, she needed a drink. "I was a little distracted."

The newling preened, rather like a dragon. "So I was actually more prepared than you. You brought nothing."

Palon smiled. "I guess you were." She pulled a water pouch out of the girl's pack, eager to quench her thirst.

"Hey!" Tebah cried out as Palon drank. Her stomach cramped with hunger, and she dug around some more until she found a hunk of meat and crammed it into her mouth.

"What, now I'm not a burden, so you can steal from me?" Tebah growled.

"I'll make it up to you, I promise. I haven't eaten in a while."

The girl crept closer, but only to grab a roll and a piece of fruit and guard them jealously. The possessive look in her eyes made Palon's heart lighten. The dragon in the newling was shining through.

Tebah watched her as she ate a roll. "Why haven't you eaten?"

Palon raised her eyebrows, surprised by the question. She chewed, buying time to think how to respond. No good excuse came to her by the time she swallowed, so she went with simple truth. "Aturadin and I are in trouble."

"Good. For me?"

"What? No, of course not!"

Silence answered her. Palon held out a chunk of meat, but Tebah didn't grab it. She shrugged, and tore off a bite with her teeth.

"You should have got in trouble. You were responsible for me."

"We've been a bit busy," Palon said. Ah, the conceit in this girl!

Bitterness filled the newling's voice. "You don't even care about me."

Palon shook her head. "Girl, you are not the center of anyone's world, except High Flight's, who you ran away from. That doesn't mean we don't care. Aturadin and I have been worrying about you since we heard you ran off."

"You sent me away like I was nothing!"

"We sent you away so you'd be safe. Dragons were fighting, do you understand? It was dangerous."

"Not too dangerous for you."

"I've been living with dragons for ten years, Tebah. I'm not some bratty newling railing against my dragon and everyone trying help me!"

"When I came back to see you, to ask you why, to warn you, you yelled at me."

"I was angry and in pain. I... I wasn't thinking straight."

"No, you're just mean."

Pausing, Palon set down the water pouch. She took a deep breath to calm herself. She'd made such a mess of things, and it might be beyond her to fix them. "Yeah, I am that."

Tebah snatched the water pouch and drank. "Why are you so mean?"

"I don't mean to be," Palon said. A gust of wind made her shiver, though it also brought a small smile to her lips. She'd missed being outside. As soon as they went back, she'd be confined until the dragons got everything under control again. Until Dragon Law came down, and that could take a while.

Everything had been taken from her—patrolling, her cache, flying, her relationship with the others. She was even starting to question their lifestyle, with all the chaos, with being targeted by other bonded. There had to be a way to protect the potential bonded from being tricked. The dragons could take care of themselves, but the bonded were at a disadvantage, especially when new.

She shied away from the thought, but remained unsettled. Bonded life was fantastic with a dragon like Windward. For others, though, with other relationships, it could be harder. She sighed. All she had left was Aturadin and Windward.

Tebah snatched another piece of fruit, glaring at her as she bit into it, and a smile pulled at Palon's lips. She really could be a fool sometimes. But things were starting to make sense.

Everything had been taken from Tebah too. Everything. Palon had driven her off when she'd lashed out in the Wounds Cave. The girl's bonding to High Flight was still rough, and Palon had shouted at her when Tebah had few other sources of comfort or advice. No wonder the girl ran.

"You still need that water pouch?" Palon asked.

It made a thud and a small puff of dust as it landed at her feet. Palon grabbed it, tearing the cap off and drinking deeply before capping it and handing it back.

"I came out here for you, Tebah. I can't really use my arm. I haven't eaten for days, hardly drunk anything. I'm so tired I could have done with a nap, not a hike down here to deal with a recalcitrant youngster who's upset that I don't show my caring in the ways she thinks I should."

"So you're hungry and thirsty and tired and hurt. So what? So am I."

Palon laughed. "Now you're being mean. Learned from the best, huh?"

Silence greeted her. Palon let it sit for a while before filling it. "Imagine you can't use one arm. Imagine your legs feel like water, and the ground sometimes wavers like your own personal earthquake. Now imagine that people who are really, really angry at you are watching you. They are bonded, like you are. You're bonded enough to feel it by now, that drive not to show weakness, even to those you know."

Of course! A realization struck her, so intense she slapped her forehead with her good hand. Her stomach turned at her own callousness. She sighed. "So, of course, you come out here. Away from eyes that would see your weakness. And hid in a crack and refused to come out when they kept watching you, and acted all prickly to make them go away."

Silence.

"Well, I'm on to you. I'm slow, but I'm on to you now. And I'm gonna have to sit here for a bit before I can make the climb back up, so what's a little longer? Bet I can outlast you, girl. You might as well talk or come back home with me."

Tebah's voice was tired and small. "You said the others would be my family. Family doesn't make you scared. Family, you can trust."

That stung a tender part in her soul. The bounds of decency were proving far too fragile. Too many were willing to break them: Fired Sand, Laetiran. Her. She shoved the discomfort away with a growl.

"We're talking dragonbonded here, newling."

"My name is Tebah."

"I know your name."

"You don't know anything."

"Yeah," Palon said. "Not much, anyway. But here's what I do know. I know that if you tried to stay in your village, your family would reject you. If you left, it could destroy the nest, destroy High Flight. You're dragonbonded, Tebah, however much you rebel against it. You're even starting to speak like us."

Tebah hunched lower, hugging her knees. Palon winced, continuing, hoping she wasn't scarring the girl, but unsure what else to do but lay it all out for her.

"I know that the dragon in you doesn't want to show weakness. That will never change, for you or for any of us. But no one else will understand all that goes on between you and your dragon. The connection. The bond. Everything that goes along with it. I know things aren't easy right now. The dragons are upset."

"What, and this is supposed to convince me to come back?" Tebah asked, her voice trembling. "I wish I knew you cared about me for *me*, not just caring about High Flight."

Palon sighed. She was still doing this all wrong, no matter how much she tried. "Tebah, if you talk to High Flight, let the bond develop, you can probably figure out a clue. And though you might not be able to go back, we can get a message to the Monks of Annularei. They might be able to get it to your village."

"Really?" The rocks scraped as Tebah came closer. "Why would you keep this from me?"

"Tebah, there are no guarantees here, only a whole lot of 'if's. I don't want to raise your hopes and hurt you more if they don't pan out. The chances of things going your way are slim, and you may never know the outcome. It might be too late, anyway."

Tebah frowned, wariness crossing her features. "You're lying."

Palon poked again at the fire. Tebah's bond had been wrong from the start, on both sides. And the girl was stronger than Palon had initially thought, to be so obstinate. "Tebah, I can't guarantee that everything's going to be better. This nonsense of running away annoys me. I hate that your bond seems doomed, that both you and High Flight began this relationship dishonestly. But if anyone has half a chance of making it work, it's you. You're stubborn, and you're strong, and once you have an idea in your head, you don't let it go. But I can't decide for you—no one can. You're the only one who can save your bond, if you choose."

She shivered in a cold gust of wind and pulled her collar up. It was easier to talk to the fire, rather than Tebah's eyes, blazing with accusation and challenge. "I love my nest, my family. The family I chose. Even if there's chaos and even violence right now, with bonds strained by grief, I still love them. Even though I'm injured and Windward is hiding from the anger of the others, I'd still choose them. Because when reason prevails again, and it will, they understand me better than anyone. When I get mad and that anger makes me stupid, they understand. So I understand them in return. And Windward—no one could ever understand me so completely, love me so unconditionally, and the same's true for him. If he could never fly again, even then I wouldn't leave him, and I know with the same certainty that I know the sun will rise tomorrow that Windward feels the same about me. If it came to it, we would give up everything for each other."

Her heart warmed, love surging along her muted bond. It was true, every word. She'd give up her freedom for Windward, would give up flight. If he needed her to, she'd live in a hole locked away from the sun, not because he would ever ask her to, but simply to make his life more bearable. And even if she were crippled and couldn't fly, she knew he'd stand by her, day after day, because he'd give up flight for her too, even though she'd never ask it of him.

"But I don't trust High Flight!" Tebah said. "He wouldn't give up everything for me."

Palon nodded. It made sense suddenly. The girl was terrified, and no wonder. To be asked to give up one life for another with a dragon she didn't love and couldn't trust, on top of all the other changes. "No dragon should ever lie to a bonded."

She bit her lip. Tebah's relationship with High Flight shone a light on the stark difference in power between dragon and bonded. They would never be on truly equal footing—the differences in species could never allow it—which is why the laws were so important. But the rules had been broken for Tebah just as Fired Sand had broken them attacking Palon, and everyone was pretending that the age old protections still worked. It angered Palon. It would petrify a newling.

"I'm sorry, Tebah. I'm not sure I'm doing a good job of helping you succeed, but I don't know what else to do. I love Windward. But love can't be asked for, nor can it be demanded. It can only be given freely, or it's not real. You and High Flight have made a mess of your relationship so far, and it'll take a lot of work to build a trust upon which love can grow. No one should ask it of you. I won't."

She didn't realize she'd made a decision until the words were out. Staring up at the stars, Palon tried to think of the right words, but came up empty, as usual. She sighed. "Well, you've grown on Aturadin and I. Like an infestation of scale fleas."

The girl glanced at her, a quick flash of the eyes, and twisted her lips.

"You don't trust High Flight right now," Palon said, "And dragons know I've given you no reason to trust me." Her trust in their lifestyle, in the other bonded, in the dragons, had been shaken, and she understood and loved the dragons. How much more terrified would the girl be?

Tebah poked at the fire. "I didn't actually think anyone would come for me. No one seems to like me."

"If you leave now, I won't chase you. But if you come back with me, and if you need me, I'll always be there for you, Tebah. And if you can teach me to be better, I'll teach you dragons. If you want."

"And if I don't?"

She sighed. "If you don't, your bond is doomed anyway. So maybe I never found you."

Tebah scowled at her, but then nodded hesitantly. Her voice was a whisper. "Ok." She shivered as another gust of wind swept past.

"Come here and get warm," Palon said, opening her jacket toward the girl. "It's too dark to head back now. We'll have to wait until morning."

Palon slung her good arm over Tebah's shoulder as they trudged along a ridge. She pointed out the cluster of figures made small by distance. "They're coming down to look for you, see? We do care. They'll be following High Flight."

The girl craned her neck, staring at the sky, but the dragon circling over them could have been anyone. Hopefully Tebah knew—hopefully it was High Flight and her bond told her that, just the same way Palon knew Windward was still curled up, hiding. Cold. He curled up tighter and pushed her away.

Tebah pointed, her finger wavering. "That's where I was hiding, those rocks there that rise up."

At least the newling was talking. Maybe all was not yet lost. If only

Palon had realized before what Miros had seen in an instant, how Tebah would feel being unwanted, unwelcomed. And Aturadin had seen it too, but she'd been too busy fighting him, too busy being afraid to let the girl attach to her at all. All she'd done was push her away.

Well that was done now. No more pushing her away, though hopefully it wouldn't sabotage the forming bond. Nothing could hurt it worse than another runaway attempt. "Thought so. It was a good hiding place. I'm glad I didn't have to drag you out of there. And moving in the night was a good idea too. Just don't ever do it again."

Tebah snorted, but then shrank against Palon. She followed the girl's gaze. Two dragons were speeding toward them out of the deep blue sky. Palon grimaced, tightening her arm around the newling. They'd be in trouble on their return, for sneaking away, but it didn't matter. Tebah was coming home.

High Flight led Night Hunter, wheeling in their direction. Palon glanced up at the dragon circling above them—that wasn't High Flight, then. Who was it?

High Flight whistled, a long shrill note and turned a tight circle above them, whipping the dust into their eyes. Gleaming like ebony, Night Hunter followed, and Palon waved in greeting to Yiyin, who rode above Night Hunter's shoulders, his expression unreadable. Tebah hesitated, and Palon pulled her forward. Eagerness filled her to get home, to check on Windward, to check on Aturadin. To clear her name.

Yiyin raised a hand as his dragon turned, and a net deployed, hanging over the dragon's side.

Palon took Tebah's elbow, pushing her closer to the edge of the ridge. "Get ready to jump."

"Jump?" Tebah shrieked, struggling in Palon's grasp.

"This is our ride. What, you thought they'd stop and let us climb on?"

"That's madness!"

"So's running from dragons." Palon grinned at the girl. She'd shown she had some mettle to her after all—she only had to not lose it.

Yiyin swirled his arm, signaling that he'd securely attached the net. Arm aching with a sudden ferocity, Palon struggled to breathe and hold on to the panicking younger bonded. Night Hunter would have to come in at an angle and swoop out in a curve to reach them—the walls of the cliff behind them were too close for Night Hunter's wings to fully extend. Over and around him, High Flight flew, sometimes dangerously close to the larger dragon. Night Hunter roared at him, neck spines flaring, but High Flight continued, whistling shrilly. The black dragon had to spout a burst of flame at him before he slowed his manic flight, giving some space.

Palon focused on Tebah, trying to keep the grin from her face. This was better than no flying at all, and this maneuver was always fun. Too bad it was the wrong dragon. "Listen. This is how it's done. When I say, you jump. You grab the net and you hold on tight. That's it. We'll get a ride to the nest and be back in no time."

"What if I miss?" Tebah squeaked.

"Night Hunter's going to be flying as close to us as she can. The netting will swing out a little on the curve. It won't be far, but jumping helps keep you from hesitating. Now, ready, ready, ready... go!" She shoved her hard and leaped forward herself, hitting the net just after the shrieking newling did.

The girl stuck like honey to bread, but Palon's bad arm screamed agony at her, unable to handle the stunt. Palon slid down the net half her length before she finally managed to get a grip on it. Heart pounding, she quickly tucked her good arm through the ropes, sucking in breaths until the hot throbbing pain dimmed to a reasonable level. She looked up at Tebah, who clung to the net with claw-like hands. Palon tapped the newling's boot with one hand to get her attention, then pointed to her own elbow, looped into the netting. The girl hesitated, then carefully mimicked her, hugging the netting tight and holding her arms close to her body. When Tebah looked back, her rictus of terror slowly softened into a tentative smile. Palon gave her a broad grin and closed her eyes for a moment, reveling in the feeling of the wind whipping past her.

Their ride was short. As Night Hunter's back legs touched down, Palon leaped from the netting, pulling Tebah with her. High Flight alighted, slowing his momentum with powerful gusts that blew them off balance, and they hit the ground harder than Palon intended. She stumbled, wrenching her arm, and gasped for breath as the pain made black dots swim in front of her. Windward whistled, the shrill notes splitting the air.

She glimpsed him on one of the lower, less desirable basking ledges, but the bond stayed firmly damped down. Only a short message came through: he was fine, but couldn't take her pain, not with him carrying greater wounds. He was glad that she was home safe. Then, nothing. Even so, she was overcome with giddiness at having that small contact, until the pain retreated marginally.

Night Hunter stalked away from them all, tail swishing behind her, with Yiyin patting and murmuring to her.

High Flight's head bobbed up and down, his feet dancing and a near constant whistle coming from his mouth as he bent to Tebah's level, then raised his head back up, then bent down to check on the newling again. His breath stirred Tebah's hair, and Palon wrinkled her nose—she still needed to teach the girl how to braid her hair properly. While the newling looked uncertain in the face of High Flight's welcome, at least her features were softer, not filled with the scorn Palon had feared.

Tsían approached, and she lowered her head, tugging on Tebah when she failed to imitate her. High Flight loomed over top of them, tilting his head to one side.

Tsían stopped before them, his features stern. "Follow me."

"Am I in trouble?" The girl froze, huge eyes on Tsían's face.

The ridiculousness was too much, and Palon laughed. "Of course. We both are."

Gesturing toward the tunnel, Tsían stalked ahead of them, clearly expecting them to follow. "There may be room for lenience, as you two were coming back home. We were afraid for a moment, Palon, that you had run away too."

"That's not fair," Tebah shouted.

Palon glanced at Tsían as he stiffened, but he continued walking. Dragging Tebah with her, she hurried to explain. "It is completely fair. We both broke the rules. We put the nest at risk."

"But they left too, to get me!"

"Their retrieval of you was sanctioned. That's the difference."

Tebah tossed her hair back, straightening. "That's foolish. You convinced me to come back. That should be the end of it."

While part of her was pleasantly surprised that Tebah would bother arguing for her at all, it wasn't going to do any good. It would only bring down more trouble. Palon growled. "Remember what I've told you about submissive posture and trouble."

Lifting her chin, the newling only puffed herself up further. "Well, they can't banish me, can they? That'd risk the nest because my bond can't fail. So there's nothing they can really do."

So much for the truce they'd somehow struck. Palon bared her teeth, but the girl seemed blind to the threat. "How about not flying? How about not seeing the sun, feeling the wind? No freedom, no cache?"

Tebah stuck her lip out again, and Palon glared at her as if to impress her words upon her. Finally, Tebah looked down at the floor and nodded, falling in beside Palon as she followed their impatient leader. Palon's mind whirled, overcome by the remnants of hunger, thirst, and exhaustion, making the future feel almost immaterial.

A howl rose up, as if the very rocks of the cave system were wailing. Palon stumbled. "No," she whispered. "No."

Chapter Thirteen

She was running. Tsían and Tebah's feet pounded beside hers as she sprinted full-tilt through the tunnels. The dragon howls surrounded them, raising their lamentation up to the emptiness of the sky. Around them, other bonded appeared, all racing in the same direction. No one gave Palon a second glance. She wasn't worth it right now—there were bigger concerns.

A dragon had died.

Palon threw herself up the stairs, stumbled out onto Silver Spine's ledge, and dropped to her knees, barely aware of the lurch as the rock crashed against her bones. Tears fell from her eyes, a keening rising from her throat as the grief poured through her, overflowing her bond, pounding at her from all directions like wind in a gale. Miros lay between one foreleg and Silver Spine's huge head on the other side. Silver Spine's eyes were half open, now dimmed without the spark of life in him. And Miros, rigid and howling, had had his very soul ripped in two.

Palon watched. They all did, breaths held as the dragons cried out their mourning. Any moment now, and it would be clear what was to come. Would Miros go with his dragon, even to the very end?

The howl faded. He drew a deep breath. Another howl. Another breath.

Around her, dragonbonded stirred. Someone shoved her way to Palon's side, clinging to her. Tebah. Palon tightened her arm around the girl as Miros's cries filled the cave, though the numb emptiness inside her wailed that nothing could ever comfort anyone again.

"What's going on?" Tebah trembled, clutching at Palon.

"He's not going," someone said, their voice distant.

She didn't immediately know who had spoken. It didn't matter. She couldn't tear her gaze away from Miros's agony. "When a dragon dies, sometimes the bonded goes too. Sometimes they stay, their mind broken."

"We'll have to take him down the mountain," said someone else, also distant.

"I don't want to die with my dragon!" Tebah shrieked.

Palon glanced at her, surprised to see tears on her face. Well, but her own face was soaked too, she discovered. She squeezed the girl tighter, as if to will her comfort through physical proximity. Around them, the haunting, bone trembling sounds of dragons in mourning rose, quelling any chance of easy communication.

Stepping out of the fray, she sank down with her back to the wall, sliding to crouch with Tebah crumpled at her side. Windward's grief rose within her and she gave voice to the misery of all the cave. Aturadin appeared, suddenly beside them, wrapping his arms around her and Tebah, his voice raised in lament as well. The wailing rose and fell, moving in an age-old song that made time meaningless.

And finally, there were no more voices.

Palon stirred, swimming to consciousness from grief-drugged sleep. Beside her, Aturadin gave a muted groan and sat up, rubbing his eyes with one hand, but Tebah slumbered on, her head pillowed on Palon's shoulder. She brushed the hair away from the newling's face and decided not to rise, instead just holding her. She'd been through a lot, and Palon hadn't prepared her for the intensity of the grief. Across the cave, Salann and Tsían fidgeted in their sleep. The other bonded were gone.

"I'll get us breakfast," Aturadin said, extricating himself from her side. His voice was hoarse—they'd all be hoarse for a few days, while their voices recovered. She nodded.

He smiled, pausing for a moment at the entrance. "You got her back. Great job."

She smiled, but her expression froze as she really looked at him. One eye was swollen, black and purple all around it, and his nose was puffed up and reddened. He had cuts on his chin and the other eyebrow, and as he walked away, she saw his gait was the careful gait of the injured who is trying to conceal that fact.

Of course, he wouldn't have been free from retribution. She breathed out in a great gust, forcing her hands to unclench, beating down the anger that had flared in her. Aturadin was not helpless. He had survived. They all had for another day.

Miros.

She looked for him, shifting carefully so as not to disturb Tebah too much. A boot stuck out from under Silver Spine's muzzle. She leaned the other way, catching a glimpse of Miros's sandy hair. He must be sleeping under his dragon's head. Swallowing hard, she let her gaze drift over the other dragons, visible past the ledge of the Sequestering Cave, scattered despondently on the various ledges and basking sites. Windward hung half off his basking ledge, his neck lowered, his tail twined around the column of rock beside him.

She reached for him, sagging with relief when he allowed the barest connection. Windward was cold and stiff and exhausted and grieving, but otherwise, he was glad her ill-advised mission had worked out. He gave her a brief surge of affection, his musky scent surrounding her. Still, it felt like their bond was strained to fraying, the stresses of the nest eroding it relentlessly like a river eating at its banks. Shadow Soars gaped in bad temper at Windward, and Windward slunk lower on the basking ledges. He would be in trouble until they proved that Palon and Aturadin did not steal from dragons, especially now, when no one would be thinking clearly.

Her heart ached for him and she wished for a quick resolution, but the dragons could not mull over Dragon Law, not now while each was consumed with mourning.

Now was not the time to worry about that, not in the aftermath of a dragon's death. And with that, Windward shoved her away and blocked her out once more, regardless of how she shouted at him through the bond.

She felt adrift, lost without her dragon. Annoyance pricked at her, quickly morphing to anger that he would push her away when she needed him. Even if he had to, so as not to share his pains with her. She'd rather share those pains than be cut off from him for yet another day, especially now.

Tsían stood and stretched, and Palon lowered her gaze. They were probably still in trouble. But Tsían only glanced at her before nudging Salann awake and working with her to drag Miros out from under Silver Spine's head.

Aturadin returned, balancing two overloaded trays. Palon winced again at his battered face and scraped up knuckles. She tried to scoot out from under Tebah, but the girl woke up, yawning and stretching before sort of... crumpling.

"Come on, there's food," Palon encouraged her, scooting over to the tray.

Aturadin tossed the girl some fruit. "It appears we have a respite for a bit. I got nothing more than one or two glares when I got us breakfast."

"Good. Looks like you got the worst of it while I was gone. Who did that to you?" She almost successfully kept the edge from her voice.

"Laetiran tried to make some trouble. I discouraged him."

"Did you find anything?"

"Why do you think he tried to make trouble?" Aturadin grinned.

It was a wonder, how easily a grin from Aturadin could lighten the weight on her heart. Palon smiled back at him, brushing his injured knuckles with her thumb. "Well, I hope you gave as good as you got."

Aturadin's grin faded. He cleared his throat and nodded toward Tebah. "Newling."

Palon turned. Tebah huddled behind her bit of fruit, her eyes huge. "Hey," Palon said.

Tebah trembled, fear and anger warring in her expression. "This is my home? A place where people will attack me? Where my family will hurt me?"

"No, Tebah. No, they won't." Aturadin crouched in front of her. "Look, Tebah. You have the bad fortune to be just bonding and just learning during a very tumultuous time. Usually things are easier here, more peaceful. Less strange."

"What, so people only half-heartedly attack you?" Tebah shot back. "They don't seem very family-like to me."

Aturadin shook his head. "The dragons don't handle change well. Days are much like each other here, rhythms following rhythms. But right now, the dragons as a community are vulnerable and their bonded are feeling that and lashing out as a reaction. Just as you have, I think." He smiled at the girl, and Palon twisted her lips at the twinge of jealousy that stung her, that he so easily saw what she had only just discovered.

"Normally, there's some jostling for position, maybe a few traps or pranks, but nothing really dangerous or serious." Palon looked down at her hands. "We test each other, keep our wits about us, keep ourselves ready for that moment in dragonflight when it all changes and no more plans will keep you alive. It's all down to skill and fitness, instinct and communication. Yes, we might lash out at each other when emotions get high, but it all works out in the end, because we're family. We need each other."

Beside the dragon's body, Tsían and Salann finally dragged Miros to his feet, the formerly bonded fighting them every bit of the way.

"He left me!" screamed Miros, staggering to the dead dragon's snout. He bent his head, peering into Silver Spine's nostril, then blew into it, shoving himself away and spinning around again.

Tears pricked Palon's eyes and she willed them away fiercely. She was dragonbonded, and she was strong. She still had the freedom of the dragons, at least for now. But how long would that last, if her arm never healed, if something happened to Windward? Everything could be taken from her in a blink of an eye, leaving her like Miros, cut off forever from her dragon, captive of one small limited body, and then a prisoner of the Monks. Helpless.

No wonder he went insane.

Gritting her teeth, she suppressed the shiver that tried to run up her spine. She dragged in a deep ragged breath, swallowing her tears, refusing to let her pain and grief be made known. Miros deserved better than for Palon to let the disturbing scene drive her away. She owed it to him to face it, and more so, she was no coward.

Tsían and Salann wrestled Miros away from Silver Spine's body finally, while Miros collapsed, weeping.

Tebah stared at them, as if Miros was some sort of spectacle. "But they can just… turn on you."

Palon shrugged. It bothered her, though she tried not to let it show. Tebah was right, and she hated it, wished she could just ignore the fragility of their way of life. She'd never seen this level of violence in the cave. She'd never feared for her life from the bonded of her nest. Of course, she'd never witnessed a dragon's death, but still it felt like everyone was too much on edge. There was a vague sense of unease at the back of her mind, like an itch she couldn't scratch. It was probably just her missing cache. Or possibly the fact that she hadn't been able to go flying in several days. She scratched her nose, as if she could scratch at the confinement that nagged at her.

Tsían set the tray of food in front of Miros. "Come eat, Miros. Drink."

Palon gestured to them. "See? It's not all bad. We do take care of each other too."

Tsían gave Palon a stern look. "You should have been here. You should have been with him, not making more trouble just before Silver Spine died."

Palon lowered her head, accepting the rebuke, but Tebah bristled beside her. "It's not our fault he died. He was old!"

Wincing, Palon shoved food in the girl's hands. "We made more chaos at an already tumultuous time."

"You did," Salann agreed. "You should stay away from the others for a while. You've made one bad decision on top of another lately."

With a raspy hiss, Miros picked up a handful of pebbles, flinging them one by one against the far wall. Salann grimaced, swiping for his hands. He dodged her, even while Tsían tried to tempt him with food.

Tebah huddled up in a tight ball, glancing in Miros's direction. "He went insane," Tebah whispered.

"Some people look down on those bonded who don't die with their dragon," Palon said. "That they have less honor, or no honor at all, since they didn't go with their dragon."

"I don't think it's a choice, Palon." There was a hard edge to Aturadin's voice, and she bumped him lightly with her shoulder.

"I know, Aturadin. But she needs to know to understand."

Salann glanced over at them, eyebrows raised, but her mouth tightened, and she shook her head instead of saying anything. Palon lowered her head anyway—everyone would be especially touchy in the coming days. Her bond couldn't be the only one that felt frayed.

Tebah nodded, uncoiling a bit. "I know. The insane bonded goes to the Monks of Annularei. Everyone knows about the Monks, that they take care of old knowledge."

"Well, we are why they exist," Palon explained. "We give our formerly bonded to them for care-taking. The Monks keep them safe and healthy, talking to them and writing everything down that they can."

"The dragons allow it, so long as they don't share any secrets." Tebah's voice and gaze became distant. "And the formerly bonded are kept here until they are stable enough and have forgotten enough to be safe to go to the Monks."

A rush of relief filled her, and Palon grinned with sudden hope at Aturadin, who grinned back. High Flight's bond with Tebah must be growing, if he was able to send her that much information along their bond. She nodded to Tebah. "Sometimes they get better, and the Monks let them go wandering. Most of the time, they live the rest of their days doted on by the Monks as an honored guest."

"But you said they have no honor," Tebah protested.

"That's what some think," Palon said. She winced as Miros threw a mostly empty bowl at Tsían. "But Miros loved Silver Spine. I think he would have followed him anywhere, even into death, if it was a choice."

Salann's brow furrowed and she cocked her head to the side. "Don't you think you'd be nothing without your dragons?"

"Of course I do," Palon said.

Aturadin shook his head. "Honor has to do with choices. I don't think one can lose honor for a misfortune that has nothing to do with choice."

"Life's not that simple. Not that easy," Salann said.

Palon lowered her head, resolved not to argue. Salann was the second highest ranking bonded, and they were still in trouble. She tried to focus on eating instead.

"The bond," Tebah said. "It's scary. There's so much change."

Aturadin patted her shoulder. "You're already changing, in how you think and how you act, even how you talk. You haven't realized it yet, but it's happening. It's natural. Don't be scared. As you bond, your dragon will teach you things. High Flight is a younger dragon, obviously, but he's still old."

"He's 120 years old," Tebah said.

Palon grinned. High Flight must be talking to her more. She didn't want to disturb the girl—this was the moment they'd all been anxiously waiting for. This and even further growth.

Tebah looked up, tentatively chewing her lip. "High Flight said he'll try to help my great-mother. But I'll need your help also. Would you... Would you help me?"

Aturadin nodded, his expression earnest. "I've already been looking into it."

Palon glanced at him, eyebrows raised. Of course he had been. She rested her good shoulder against his.

The girl frowned, her gaze still far away. "Is it really so good to fly?" She gasped suddenly, smiling. "It looks beautiful."

Grinning, Palon nodded. "See? It's not so bad at all, being bonded."

"Die, fiend!" Miros leaped up, nearly tipping the tray over. Salann caught it, and Tsían grabbed Miros's arm as he lunged for a knife. Miros snatched a piece of bread, instead and began pressing it into his eyes.

"When will he be taken?" Tebah asked in a small voice, her wide eyes fixed on the scuffle between Tsían and Miros.

"In a few days," Palon said, her eyes flickering to the dragon's body, which lay unaffected by the chaos around it. "First, we put Silver Spine to rest."

Chapter Fourteen

They gathered, the bonded riding on their dragons, winding single file down the rocky slope. The light mist retreated from them, leaving behind droplets to adorn hair and scales as the morning sun burned the last of it away with gentle heat. Claws scraped on the rocky soil, and the sweeping rasp of scaled tails filled the heavy air like a funeral song. The rocks rose, bald domes jutting up from forested crowns around which the slight breeze toyed, carrying the scent of fresh soil, damp mosses, and sawdust. Ragged stumps thinned the trees, evidence of the bonded's activities over the past several months, once it became apparent that Silver Spine's death was near. Once he began ignoring his cache. The raft had been completed and waiting for its morbid duty since about the time Tebah came to the nest.

Silence blanketed the mountainside. No one spoke. The forest was eerily still as its inhabitants fell mute in response to the powerful predators passing by. Tebah, perched above High Flight's shoulders, looked about her with a pensive expression, her face pale and sharp under her freshly washed and braided hair. A bit of pride stirred in Palon: Tebah looked the part of a dragonbonded, for once. Four wide safety straps held her securely in place, since she hadn't had a chance to fly yet. Palon had checked the girl's harness thoroughly before helping her into it. The first flight was always one to remember, but Tebah's would be even more so.

Palon idly stroked Windward's gleaming scales as she rocked with the complex side to side sway of his gait. She had spent all her spare time yesterday cleaning and polishing him, making up for those days when they'd been apart. He kept their bond dampened still, but touching him, being near him, helped. It made her feel whole again, and so much at peace that she was only mildly annoyed when he questioned her about the crystal she'd mentioned. Her missing crystal. As if to remind her of it, the sun glinted sharply off the snow-capped peaks high above them, the runoff combining and forming the raging river that ran nearby.

Dusks Dive, Shadow Soars, Forest Blaze, Stone Eyes, Skyward, and Providence Eye burst into the sky from behind them, the wind from their wings bending the tall trees. The six dragons clutched Silver Spine's body in their claws, laboring hard as they headed for the river. Below them, the winding line of dragons maintained their sedate pace down the slope, the older ones in front solemn regardless of the awe-inspiring sight.

The river whispered to itself as it passed by, heard before it could be seen, and Palon's thoughts turned to poor Miros. They'd had to lock him away, for he'd tried to fight them off when they came to prepare for Silver Spine's funeral, baring his teeth and spraying them with spittle while his white-rimmed eyes rolled in his head. Part of his heart, soul, and mind had gone with his dragon in death, leaving him beyond reason.

The dragons came to a halt, standing side by side along the wide riverbank, which the dragonbonded had stripped of trees completely. They'd spent a month working on the wide, flat bottomed raft that tugged at its moorings, obscuring much of the fast flowing river itself. Palon raised her head, squinting in the sunlight to watch as the six dragons in flight wheeled, coming around. They lined up with the river, swooping in low. Silver Spine's limp wings fluttered in the breeze as the dragons carried him.

Now that the dragons were still, silence blanketed the mountainside. Palon held her breath, watching with a reverence that made physical notions fade. The flying dragons coordinated their movements with telepathy, their voices absent for the hallowed moment. As one, they released Silver Spine. He crashed onto the raft, submerging the vessel to the rocky bottom and snapping the rope that moored it. The river rose out of its banks, washing the dragons' claws. Then the raft lifted, bearing Silver Spine's body back to the surface of the water, and Windward turned, climbing the slope along with several of the other younger dragons.

Palon watched Laetiran and Fired Sand warily. Laetiran's blackened eye and split lip bore proof of his encounter with Aturadin while she'd been away. But Windward wasn't concerned, and his confidence filled her. No dragon would attack another during a funeral. Fired Sand and Laetiran would bide their time.

As they reached the top of the hill, the young dragons turned, spread their wings, and galloped for the bluff that overlooked the river. The sharp drop off was perfect to launch into flight, Windward shared, remembering the last dragon funeral several decades ago.

Windward's wings snapped open, the wind caught at them, and the dragon leaped into the embrace of the sky. He turned, gliding around in circles to avoid the others also launching themselves into flight. The six dragons who had borne Silver Spine's body were looping around in a great circle, coming back for another pass. Filled with anticipation, Palon tightened her hold on his neck spine.

First came the six dragons of the funeral procession, down, down, toward the floating raft, its broken rope trailing behind. The older dragons on the river's edge trumpeted as Stone Eyes unleashed his fire. As soon as he was clear, Forest Blaze belched flames so the raft was bathed continually in fire. Then it was Dusks Dive, and Fired Sand, and Scorch Frost, and then Windward, each new dragon's passing flames lighting the pyre just as the previous dragon's flames ended.

Palon shouted her own farewell to the old dragon as Windward passed overhead. The roaring of the flames drowned out the sound of her voice, but Windward caressed her with fond appreciation.

She twisted in her seat to glance back at Tebah. She looked tiny, terrified, and elated. Then High Flight folded his wings and dove for the river. Palon imagined she could hear Tebah's scream through the roar of High Flight's fire, the sticky dragon flames by now a mighty blaze consuming Silver Spine's body as well as the top of the raft. Just before the stream of fire ended, Silver Spine and the raft went over the great waterfall.

It was a fitting end for a dragon. A life of flight and flame, ending with one last flight, one last flame.

Circling lazily, the young dragons flew back to the main basin of the caves. There, they mixed in complex patterns in the air as they waited for the older, land bound dragons to walk back up the slope. The older dragons would re-enter the Basking Basin first, Windward showed her. Palon leaned forward, resting her cheek against the blade of the neck spine before her. She was glad to fly again, grateful for the tiny undercurrent of Windward. He still had the bond mostly dampened, but at least he wasn't completely shutting her out any longer.

Palon caught Aturadin pointing her toward Tebah and checked on her again. The newling wore a huge smile on her face, her hands white as she clutched her dragon's neck spine. Palon smiled. What a first flight.

And finally, with the older dragons claiming their basking platforms, the younger dragons set down one by one in order of rank. Palon urged Windward to stay far from Fired Sand, just in case. The dragon's mental snort blew at her, musky and warm. He didn't need reminding.

After landing, Palon slid down Windward's scales, immediately running to help Tebah. The girl was laughing and crying at the same time, trembling as she sat on her dragon.

"Unhook the lines, Tebah, and come down," Palon called, standing just beside High Flight's leg. She thought for a moment about climbing up to help her, but the very idea caused her to recoil. High Flight was not her dragon.

Windward rumbled. Mine. The possession and affirmation rumbled through her like a warm wind. She smiled, agreeing.

It took Tebah some time, her hands were so shaky, but the newling finally unfastened the straps and slid down, clinging to the safety line. Palon grabbed her hand once she was in reach.

"You'll get better at that with time." She wrinkled her nose, taking a good look at the girl. "Oh, you need to change. And let's get some bandages on those hands."

"That was amazing!" Tebah's voice was breathy and her legs quivered beneath her.

Palon beamed at her. "Yeah, it is, isn't it? Most people don't get their first flight and first dragonfire experience all in one go."

Hands full of illness-warding salve and a small roll of bandages, Aturadin jogged over. Palon smiled fondly. Aturadin was always prepared. She turned to strip the harness from Windward's back as Aturadin went to work on Tebah's hands. They'd have to help the girl take High Flight's harness off and stow it properly. She grabbed Aturadin's harness and dragged it and her own out of the way, over toward the bluff that the tunnel entrances were cut into. Collecting the wide straps and rolling them into their bundles, she kept half an eye on Windward as he climbed up to a ledge to bask. Someone slammed into her shoulder, and she narrowly avoided crushing her injured arm against the rock wall as she stumbled. A chill ran though her.

She turned to meet Laetiran's eyes. He reached out as if to help her, his expression concerned, but she turned away before he could touch her. His hand snaked out, grasping her upper arm. "You want to be careful. You don't want to injure that arm further. It might never heal."

"Yes, wouldn't want to tempt you to shed any tears for me," she said. Irritation with him rose in her. She'd chosen this spot to be out of the way, to avoid trouble, so of course trouble had come seeking her out.

Laetiran smiled. "It's a wonder they let such disgraced bonded as you take place in the ceremony."

She matched him smile for smile, false-friendliness for false-friendliness. "Now then, Laetiran, be careful. Your bitterness is showing."

He squeezed her arm, and she shoved him away, glaring at him. Tripping over a rock, he tumbled to the ground with a crash. He flashed a brief smile up at her, so quickly gone it might have been her imagination.

"If you don't want help, you only have to say so," he said, sounding wounded. "You don't need to be so violent about it."

Palon scowled. Stupid. So stupid! Windward rumbled in her mind, but not audibly, his head low. She glanced around, though she knew what she'd find. The others had paused in their chores around them, staring at them with expressions of shock, anger, and disappointment. The last was Aturadin, of course. Tebah stood beside him, her eyes wide.

Laetiran picked himself up with lithe grace. Doubts bloomed in her mind. Was it more than an overreaction on his part? Had he intended for her to be seen as the aggressor? Or was she imagining the smile and he actually wanted to reach a sort of truce with her. How insolent did he have to be, to pick a fight just after a funeral? Surely not even Laetiran would dream of such a thing. Was she seeing fault where none existed? Were Tsían and Salann right, and she mistrusted him too much, carried their rivalry too far?

Hands raised in exaggerated care, he stepped around her, making his way toward Tebah, though he stopped when Aturadin stepped in front of her. He looked around at the others, pitching his voice to carry. "One wonders if they are so needlessly violent with the newling. At such a time, we must take care to protect all our bonds."

"I was the one who brought Tebah back," Palon growled.

"Yes. I wonder, what did you threaten her with, when the reason and kindness of all the rest of us failed to make her move?"

"Oh, Tebah knows all too well of your kindness." Aturadin's voice was soft and low, the tone that made Palon's skin prickle with wariness. He took one measured step forward, hands curled into fists.

"What, are you poisoning her against me?"

Palon had to credit Laetiran, he really threw himself into his role. Such wide-eyed innocence would be comical, if he didn't seem to actually believe it.

He was still talking. "Your antagonism truly has reached unknown bounds. I have waited patiently for you to come to your senses, to realize that the last thing we need right now is in-fighting. But I cannot stand by and watch as you continue to tear these caves apart, even to the next generation. Tell me, what good will all this do? What is your goal?"

Aturadin folded his arms, not rising to the bait. Palon glanced around at the fence of unforgiving, unfriendly faces around them. Tsían's and Salann's hard expressions especially hurt her to see. How could she have been so stupid as to step into Laetiran's trap?

Laetiran leaned forward, eyes on Tebah. "Tell us, little one. Are they hurting you? We can find better tutors for you, I am certain. Can't we, Tsían? Salann?"

Neither spoke—they just watched with stern expressions. So they hadn't made up their minds yet, then.

Tebah glowered at Laetiran. "Go away."

"Do they not allow you to speak?" Laetiran turned to his crowd. "Maybe she's reluctant to tell the truth with them so nearby, afraid of repercussions."

Palon couldn't help but watch Tebah, her heart beating against her ribs for escape. If the girl wanted, she could get her revenge right now, and there was nothing Palon could do. Laetiran had set this up neatly.

"Look!" crowed Laetiran, pointing at her. "Look how she tries to control the girl with her glare. How can we expect such a youngster to stand up to that gaze?"

Palon's lip curled, and her hands fisted, but she managed to reign in her temper. "You're talking nonsense, Laetiran."

"Of course you would say so, but look how your first reaction is violence. Your very actions betray your words."

"You started all this," she snarled. "Everyone will realize sooner or later that you're just trying to make yourself look better. They're smarter than you think."

"Perhaps they're smarter than you think, Palon, smart enough to see through all your lies. Of course you'd be so angry. It all makes sense."

Laetiran reached for Tebah, who scuttled behind Aturadin. Extending an arm out to shield her, Aturadin readied his stance.

His gaze flickering over Aturadin's face, Laetiran recoiled. Palon suppressed a grin. Aturadin surely had given as good as he'd gotten, to make Laetiran think twice about taking him on. Even so, Laetiran quickly rebounded. "Poor, traumatized thing. See how she hides? How she fears a friendly hand?"

"I don't want to talk to you!" Tebah screeched from behind Aturadin.

"Of course not. I understand. Not with this sort of people around. Come with me and tell me all about it. Tsían and Salann can listen, if you wish."

"Leave me alone!"

"She doesn't want to talk to you, Laetiran," Palon warned.

"Yes, I see. Everyone here can see what's going on."

"I hope they can," she snapped.

"Enough!" Tsían shouted. "Have the three of you no shame at all? Palon, Aturadin, take Tebah. Stop flaring wings at each other."

"Let's go. We need to check on Miros." Aturadin kept one arm around Tebah, who all but clung to him.

"We're here for you. We can protect you from them," Laetiran called.

Trying to push down her unease, Palon joined Aturadin in hustling Tebah down the corridor and out of sight. Palon sneered as behind them Tsían scolded Laetiran. She couldn't quite accept what had just happened. "Is he insane? We know he isn't who he's pretending he is. Everyone knows Laetiran's antics," Palon hissed to Aturadin. "He won't be protecting anyone."

Aturadin nodded, but said nothing, his expression so tense that Palon's flow of words stopped. Behind them, did she hear footsteps? Laetiran's easy charisma gave him many friends, and she wouldn't put it past them to do his dirty work for him. She turned to look, but saw nothing. Even so, her scalp prickled with warning, though Tebah seemed oblivious. As they got further from Laetiran, the trembling girl burst with emotion.

"I hate him! He scares me. Do I have to talk to him? Will that cause more trouble?" Tebah looked so vulnerable, and Palon hesitated, not wanting to make things worse by saying the wrong thing.

Aturadin seemed to know what to do, rubbing her back as they continued walking. "No, Tebah. You don't have to talk to anyone you don't want to."

With renewed confidence, the girl nodded. "I won't forget that he tied me up and gagged me. I won't forget, no matter how he tries to seem otherwise. It happened. It happened, and I won't ever be caught helpless like that again!"

"We know, Tebah, we know," Palon said.

"Come on." Aturadin beckoned to them as they turned down the short tunnel to the chamber where they had left Miros. Palon wrestled with the lock, hyper-aware of Aturadin peeking out into the tunnel behind them, his posture wary. Finally, the lock gave, and Palon hurried Tebah into the room.

His back turned to them, Miros was rubbing his side against the rock wall, his sleeve torn and ragged from the motions. Aturadin frowned, going over to him. As he took him by the shoulder, Miros turned, and Palon gasped. His arm was rubbed raw and bloody.

"Miros! What have you done?" she said, running over to him.

"Scales damaged. Won't shed. Itchy."

"Miros, you aren't a dragon!" Aturadin said.

Miros squinted at him. "Blind."

Palon exchanged a worried look with Aturadin.

Crossing her arms, Tebah said from the middle of the room, "It's like we're some crazy family of rejects."

"Does that make you feel better?" Aturadin asked as Palon grabbed the bandages from the shelf.

"A little," Tebah said.

Palon slathered on the salve that Aturadin handed her, then tossed the container back to him. As gently as she could, she began to wind the bandage around Miros's arm. Miros slapped her hand away in an odd movement, his fingers curled. He shook off the bandage, which Palon snatched up before it hit the floor.

"Miros, you need bandages," she said, beginning to wrap his arm again. It was a struggle, since he was waving it around.

"Suffocating, suffocating, can't feel!" Miros swiped at her again. This time she realized, his curled fingers were like dragon claws. Tightness squeezed her chest, grief rising. This was her mentor, reduced to... this.

"You aren't a dragon, Miros! You're dragonbonded!" she shouted.

He slammed his hands over his ears. "Can't hear, can't hear, no dragons speaking in my head!"

She swallowed hard. She'd had a taste of that recently, with Windward shutting her out so completely. She never wanted to feel that alone ever again. "I know, I know. It's hard." She took the opportunity to wind several more loops of bandaging around his arm as he pushed his hands against his head, swaying slowly from side to side.

With a scathing glare, he dropped his arms and pulled the bandaging off with his other hand. "I'm not dead, you know!"

Frustration was easier. She embraced it. "Of course you're not dead. Stop it, Miros!"

"Help me hold him," Aturadin said.

They wrestled with the formerly bonded, until finally she and Aturadin held an arm each, while Miros thrashed and kicked between them. Struggling to avoid the flying feet, Tebah did a passable job wrapping up his injured arm. As soon as the final knot was tied, Palon instructed her to tuck the knot out of sight under the bandaging, and then she tugged Miros's sleeve straight over top.

In moments, he settled down. His lips moved as he muttered to himself, eyes staring at nothing while he weaved slightly. Palon raised a hand to pat him on the shoulder, but paused, afraid that even a touch might set him off again.

"Good work," Aturadin said to Tebah.

"If High Flight dies, this is my fate?" Tebah sounded subdued.

Palon nodded, suppressing a wince. She really didn't want to go in circles with the girl yet again. Tebah had said she'd put all that behind her, but then again, she'd tried to go back on her word before too. "But in between, there's so much to know, amazing sights to see, and there's flying. You can't beat flying."

"How long until I stop missing home? How long before you two thought of here as home, of this as your family?"

Palon shrugged, glancing at Aturadin, who was standing near the entrance as if on guard. What was he doing there? "It depends. Usually within the first year. I don't remember how long it was for me."

"Nearly instantaneous," Aturadin said. He smiled at them, adding for Tebah's benefit, "I was here about two years before she came."

A smile came to her lips as she thought back to that time. "When Windward told me his name, I knew."

"What do you mean?" Tebah asked.

"I chose him as much as he chose me. Windward. That's where I am at my best. Lots of people take shelter when it gets windy, in the lee of rocks or whatnot. Windward and me, though, we're out there, in the wind. Riding it, facing it down." Palon grinned. "I hated being told what I could and could not do. Kinda like you, I guess, Tebah."

"Was your family so bad?"

Turning her back on the girl as if she could so easily turn her back on her past, Palon crouched by the food and water they'd left for Miros, which lay on a shelf untouched. She took the cup to Miros, coaxing him to drink. "No," she said. "They weren't bad."

"My family had just died," Aturadin said. "My village burned, but I was out hunting. I was lucky. After, I ran away. And then Scorch Frost flew overhead and I knew that's where I wanted to be. Running was too slow. He took me home, and I was able to heal."

"Home, home in the sky. Wind carrying you. Can't run from the wind, boy!" Miros cackled, water leaking from the corner of his mouth.

Palon wrinkled her nose, dabbing up the liquid with a cloth. "Drink, Miros." It was easier to focus on Miros than this useless reminiscing.

"But what about your village?" Tebah protested.

Aturadin shook his head. "What would happen to them if I had died instead? They carry on. And you are dead to them, Tebah. That's the way of things."

That seemed too harsh. They weren't dead, and to say such a thing so close to a funeral, so close to Miros, felt wrong. "But it's an honor, too. Don't forget that."

Tebah nodded. "I wanted that. Honor. Fame." She smiled, then hid her face by looking down.

"What?" Aturadin prompted her.

Tebah shook her head. "You'll laugh at me."

"Then make us laugh," Palon said. There'd been far too much anger and grief and tears lately.

Tebah peered at them for a bit, then grimaced. "I wanted to gain honor, to be famous. As famous as Taunos, the hero of Torkae."

Miros barked a laugh. A groan escaped Palon, and she turned her back as her whole face heated.

"What is it?" Tebah asked. Laughing again, Miros grabbed a hunk of bread, stuffing the whole thing into his mouth.

"Yes, what is it?" Aturadin echoed. She could hear the amused grin in his voice. He knew exactly what. She turned around to glare at him, and there it was, that knowing grin, his eyes sparkling with mirth.

She sighed, defeated. If she didn't spill her secret, Aturadin would, just to enjoy Tebah's inevitable reaction. For whatever reason, he thought it was hilarious to make her uncomfortable in this one area, watching her deal with the hero worship of other people. It'd be annoying if he wasn't so cute about it, so good-hearted in every other situation.

Pursing her lips a bit, she faced Tebah. "Taunos is my older brother."

"No way!"

"Ok," Palon said, shrugging. If it was that easy, she'd take it. She glanced at Miros as he wheezed around his mouthful of food.

"Really?"

So it wasn't going to be that easy, after all. Of course not. Palon sighed again. "Really."

"What's he like? Really?" Tebah gushed. Palon rolled her eyes. People always asked the same questions.

Aturadin was still grinning like a fool. "You weren't the only one hoping to gain honor for yourself, Tebah, and I wasn't the only one running from things I couldn't control."

Tebah frowned, and Palon shook her head. "No, he's fine, for a brother," she assured her. "But I wanted to go my own way. I don't want to just be Taunos's sister. And I'm not. I'm Palon, dragonbonded of Windward. It's much more fulfilling to be me, rather than just someone famous's sister."

Tebah nodded. "I can understand that."

Miros swallowed hard, and Palon relaxed a bit, offering him the cup again. "Can we stop talking about family now? Can we just accept being dragonbonded and all that goes with it? The good is waiting to be enjoyed."

She startled as Aturadin threw his arms around both of their shoulders, pulling them close. His voice was low and hurried, and even Miros seemed to catch some of his tension, leaning in silently with his mad eyes fixed on Aturadin's face.

"Ok, really quickly while it seems like the hallway is clear. We need to assume we're being watched and listened to at all times, got it? No conversation is private. I don't want to give away what we're doing to Laetiran, and that means we have to be a bit stealthy and a lot suspicious. While the dragons are mourning, we should take advantage of the imbalance we're presented with and continue to collect evidence to prove our innocence."

This was something she could do. Action. Something she was good at. She jumped at the change in topic. "Yes, what did you uncover while I was getting Tebah? You said you made Laetiran nervous."

"I don't have enough to tell Tsían or anything. Laetiran is definitely guilty, though," Aturadin said. "We just have to prove it."

Palon nodded. "And Dragon Law will be delayed in coming down, with the grieving. They won't discuss anything for several more days, which delays any sort of resolution, which gives us some extra time to put together evidence and arguments."

Aturadin nodded. "We just have to be careful in the meantime."

Palon nodded, looking at Tebah. "That includes you."

Eyes wide, Tebah nodded, her expression excited. Hopefully the newling understood this wasn't a game.

"Nothing private in a dragon warren. Dragons share, except what they don't." Miros dissolved into giggles, tears leaking from the corners of his eyes.

Chapter Fifteen

With a grunt, Palon drove the cleaver into the ribcage of the herdbeast carcass. Her arm was exhausted, since she could only use the one, and sweat poured down her face. She was nearly through. She gave a guttural yell as she slammed the cleaver into the gap once more, though the knife stuck in the rib meat, slipping from her weary grasp. She grabbed hold of one massive rib bone and kicked the other. It shuddered, and she kicked again.

She should be in the sky with Windward, free to hunt their own meals, not being delivered food like an invalid. The nest shouldn't even have doubts about her, much less be siding with Laetiran. Except Tsían, who was keeping silent, waiting for Dragon Law.

Venting her frustrations, she pulled back and slammed her boot into the bone. The remaining sinew gave, and she let the rib fall, wiping her brow with the back of her wrist and walking around to get to work on the other side. The rib alone was about her height—herdbeasts were massive. Even dragons relied on the momentum of their dive to carry them off.

Without her collection, with her crystal potentially lost and no way to look for it without seeming suspicious or drawing unwanted attention to it, she kept her mind off things by annoying Windward. She grimaced, hacking into the connective tissue and prodding Windward with her musings, enjoying his growing irritation. Keeping her mind busy during the boring task helped keep her temper in check, and irritating Windward proved to herself she wasn't completely powerless. It proved her bond wasn't as far gone as it seemed.

Her arm needed a rest. It throbbed with heat, and she took a moment to pour her cup of cool water over it. Drawing in deep breaths not just from pain, but from exertion, too, she looked over at Miros to check on him. He was still calm, curled up in the corner with a chunk of meat. Her heart stung with pain, and she grabbed her cleaver once more, setting her body on the carcass and her mind on annoying Windward. She was kept far from him doing chores, but nothing could separate them mentally. Not truly. He was stable as the mountain, someone she could always depend on. She just wished their bond didn't feel like grass in a wild wind right now, ready to collapse at any moment.

She devoted herself to her math problem. About sixty dragons in the caves, and Windward said there were six more caves scattered throughout the mountain range. That made something like 400 dragons eating, though they only ate two or three times a week. Older dragons might eat once a week, or once every other week, while the younger, faster growing dragons ate more often. Of course, in winter, their appetites diminished almost to nothing as they spent most of their time sleeping.

In a sudden surge, she reached for Windward. He seemed so far away, his presence muted. When he went into torpor and couldn't spend the energy to keep up their bond, would it deteriorate like a newling's bond? Was it that weakened? Might it even break?

She drew in a ragged gasp of air, pushing away the sudden panic crashing down on her. They would be fine. They had to be.

Windward rumbled at her, and she felt him shifting on his basking ledge in her mind's eye, staring at the blue sky that was forbidden to them. He was her wings, always her wings, and they would go hunting again soon, he promised her. He pushed at her along the bond, and his musk enveloped her. Closing her eyes, she drew in a deep breath, letting his calm soothe her. Together, by reaching for one another in this way, they could strengthen their bond again.

He couldn't hear her, but she was tired of the silence, so she spoke aloud, returning to trivial matters since the important things hurt too much to consider. "Do only dragons from our cave cull the herds I've seen? Are there other herds for other caves? Had you dragons considered the possibility of attracting others with your herdbeasts? Or had you even considered that other large, sentient predators would exist?" Palon had been shocked when she'd first met the walavaim, though later she decided it made sense for them to exist. "The walavaim are built just like you: four legs and a pair of wings. Is there a reason for that?"

Windward scoffed at her, pushing away her questions. He sent her an image of her as a small rodent, scurrying and nibbling, and never sitting still, never letting others have peace.

She sighed. She missed patrolling the herds and keeping the walavaim thieving down. It felt like it had been forever, waiting. Patrolling, flying, even fighting walavaim—those were simple things, things she could control. All she and Windward had to do was be better than the packs, and they were. They didn't need anyone else. There was none of this negotiating and betrayal as those she thought of as family turned on them, swayed by Laetiran's charisma as he set her up time and time again while she repeatedly fell into his traps.

With a grunt, she heaved at the carcass. "How's Dragon Law going?"

His irritation filled her as he rumbled. The dragons had begun mulling over their case, inspecting dragon memories and thoughts piece by piece, dragon by dragon. Stone Eyes was being thorough and taking his time, even after Windward had confirmed that Fired Sand had targeted Palon during their fight.

Stone Eyes had noted that Windward shared Palon's rage at Fired Sand, not the other way around. It was normal for emotions to travel from dragon to bonded. Since dragons were so much bigger and more powerful, it took much more for emotions to travel the other way, from bonded to dragon. This had apparently impressed Stone Eyes.

Even so, Dragon Law took time. They wouldn't question bonded for days, at this rate. They'd already been waiting several days as the dragons mourned Silver Spine, while Aturadin poked around and Palon tried not to get them in more trouble. Several days, while Tebah's bond strengthened, and they waited for Miros to lose enough memories, even as he devolved further and further into insanity.

"Miros is eating the meat raw," Salann said, pausing in the entrance.

Palon glanced over her shoulder at the former bonded. He was so far from his normal, well-kept self. If he'd been himself, he'd have been disgusted, but Palon couldn't keep him so clean and composed as he used to keep himself. His face and hands were all bloody, and Aturadin had helped her hold him down while he instructed Tebah in bandaging his forehead that morning. He'd been convinced he could walk through a wall.

Palon turned back to Salann. "It's keeping him quiet. I had to throw the meat over there to keep him from trying to grab the knife from me."

"He's not doing well, is he," Salann observed.

Palon shook her head, gritting her teeth as she ripped another rib free of the carcass. Using her injured arm sent lancing pain through her, but it was becoming increasingly hard to hold the knife in her good hand.

"It's a shame he didn't die with his dragon."

"Don't you say that." Palon spun, turning on her with the knife raised. She lowered it belatedly, but stuck to her words. "Don't say that."

Salann raised her eyebrows, her expression full of disdain. "You really want to threaten me? My dragon is one of the ones stolen from. By all accounts, I'm being far too lenient giving you the benefit of the doubt."

"That's not—" Palon groaned, feeling trapped. She wanted to confront someone, anyone. Everyone. She also wanted to give Aturadin the best chance to gain information, which meant *not* confronting people.

"Tell me about Laetiran and Tebah."

Palon turned to look at Salann, eyebrows raised. Was this some sort of trap? If she told of what happened, would she find her words twisted around and used against them later? The last thing she wanted was to be accused, yet again, of allowing her rivalry to get out of control. That particular accusation was really getting under her skin. If it came from Salann, here, she wasn't sure she could handle it. The idea of being thought so petty by someone she so much respected dried up the words in her mouth and stilled her tongue.

Folding her arms, Salann returned stare for stare. Then she came further into the cave, picking up a knife and carving off a slab of meat. With a graceful movement, she tossed the meat into Palon's pile. Palon stared at it. This task was not just necessary, as Windward would eat this meat, but it was also, in part, a punishment. And Salann was helping her? She wasn't sure if she could believe it, and she hated the newfound uncertainty dogging her thoughts and actions these days.

Another slice of meat slapped into the pile, and Palon returned to her work, thinking quickly. Laetiran or anyone could be outside the walls, listening. She had to be conservative. And yet, desperation filled her not to lose Salann.

"What do you want me to tell you?" Palon asked.

Salann scowled at her. "I want you to tell me the truth. I want you to stop making it so hard to help you."

"I'm not the one making it hard," Palon muttered, tearing off another chunk of meat.

Salann tossed another slab of meat on the pile. "You aren't making it easy, either."

Her temper flared. "I can't even count on you all to use your brains rather than listening to Laetiran," she growled.

The knife slapped down on the table beside her and Palon peeked up. Salann's stormy expression made her wilt. "Sorry."

She couldn't seem to stop lashing out. Every time she found some relief from the near constant stress, something else happened to destroy it, and she found herself getting snappier and snappier. It didn't help that everyone had been temperamental these days. Trying to watch her words and not cause offense only made her more stressed out, and it seemed each time, Laetiran or one of his friends was there to take offense and make her seem like the issue.

Out of the corner of her eye, she caught sight of Miros coming toward them. "Watch out," Palon warned.

"Why's Miros so battered?"

Palon sighed, wincing inwardly. It did look like they were mistreating him, she had to admit. Except they'd been careful to stay in earshot and eyeshot of others, to reduce suspicions as much as they could. Too many of the bonded didn't care to watch Miros, sharing Salann's sentiment, and those who would watch him quickly lost their patience with him. Palon found herself caring for him more and more. It was ridiculous—the only one she could manage not to offend was completely out of his mind.

Under the guise of cleaning, Aturadin and Tebah planned to do some snooping, something impossible with Miros around, so Palon had brought Miros along with her today, though there'd be no extra eyes. Perhaps it was good that Salann had come, then, to witness that she wasn't mistreating Miros.

"He sometimes thinks he's a dragon," Palon told her. Miros moved to grab the knife, and Palon blocked him. "He tried to walk through walls too."

Miros reached around her other side and Palon shifted, switching hands to keep the knife away from him. "Sometimes he's suddenly, tearfully happy, and the next second might be violently angry. Or sometimes it's fear or sadness."

Shoulders suddenly slumping, Miros turned, apparently giving up on the knife, and wandered around the carcass, blowing on it. Palon began cutting free a slab of meat while he was occupied.

"What's he doing?"

"Breathing fire," Palon said, barely glancing up.

"What? I'm not a dragon!" Miros shouted.

"That's right, Miros. You're not a dragon. You're Miros," Palon said, not missing a beat. Soon enough, handling Miros would be second nature to her. The thought made her feel guilty again. Miros shouldn't need "handling". Was she doing right enough by him? Should it ever be second nature? She wrinkled her nose at her doubts.

"My brain, they think, broke," Miros said. "See? See, it's all one piece!"

Salann watched him, her stance wary.

Miros slammed his fists on the table. "Do I show you? Do I show you, is what you want? I will! I will! It's not broken, it's all in one piece!"

Lunging forward, he grabbed for Salann's knife, but she dodged him. He kept after her, though, his hands swiping in single-minded concentration, driving her backward as she tried to keep him away.

"Don't—" Palon shouted, too late.

As he scrambled for her knife, Salann rammed him in the stomach with her elbow. Miros hit the ground, then bit her boot near the ankle, trapping her foot in his arms. He rolled toward her, and Salann crashed to the ground with a squawk of outrage and fear, knife raised out of his reach.

"No!" Palon grabbed Salann's knife arm, hauling her upright. She crouched over Miros, fending off his clawing, shouting frenzy. Miros wasn't in his right mind, and sometimes he hurt people, but she couldn't let him be hurt in return. Even if he'd otherwise deserve retaliation. Even if he was sometimes dangerous.

"Think I'm not whole. Can't think, can't think! Darkness so bright. So noisy, so alone. Nothing here!"

In moments, he had dissolved into sobs, and Palon held him, smoothing back his greasy, bloody mess of hair. Salann's ragged breathing filled the space, until the higher ranked bonded got herself back under control.

Salann's voice was even when she spoke, though there was a tension to the undertones. "Palon, you have to give me something. The things you and Laetiran are accusing each other of are just insane."

"Then why side with Laetiran against Aturadin and I?" Palon shook her head. "You treat us like we actually did these things."

"I know you and Aturadin are close, but teaming up against Laetiran is not exactly fair."

Palon bit her tongue, desperate to keep her temper this time. "This isn't about rivalry. He attacked us, smeared our names. And you all accept it!" She cut herself off. Someone might be listening. She wasn't quite sure what damage could be done from talking, but she trusted Aturadin's sudden paranoia. Just because she didn't see Laetiran didn't mean that he or one of his allies wasn't listening. Laetiran spun every argument back against them, as if he anticipated it.

She glanced at Miros, guilty again. He'd told her not to think of it as us and them. It was one of the last things he'd told her, when he was still him. And here she was, still constantly forgetting his advice.

Salann shook her head. "Funny, that's what Laetiran says about you. He points fingers at you, you point fingers at him, and the rest of us just want this chaos to stop. But you have to admit the evidence is largely on Laetiran's side. Everyone's heard you threaten people when your temper rises, and I keep hearing about you picking fights with him."

"He's been starting the fights! You just—" She cut herself off again, her chest heaving. There was an edge to her voice as she inclined her head toward Miros, "*I* didn't hit him."

"He was dangerous. I needed to get him under control."

Palon stared at her. "Yet there can be no reasonable explanations for Laetiran's so-called evidence against us? What about Laetiran spilling his soup the other day? If I hadn't been watching him, he'd have scalded me!"

"Mistakes happen. You can't blame every misfortune on Laetiran." Salann sighed. "What a mess."

Palon frowned, looking down. Was that what she was doing? Had she begun using Laetiran as a scapegoat, no longer allowing for innocent accidents? Was she automatically assuming the worst of him now, no longer able to see fairly? When Tsían had set the three of them to deep cleaning tunnels and caves as punishment, Laetiran had told her the wrong cave to clean, but he'd said she'd misunderstood him. Was that possible, that she'd actually misunderstood? Her stomach churned and she chewed on her lip.

"How's Miros been today overall?"

Palon looked at Salann from over the top of Miros's head, happy to change the subject. "We need to shave him, but it's too dangerous. He thrashes around too much and we don't want to cut him."

"Is he dangerous?"

"We can handle him," Palon said. "He was calm when you came in, remember."

"Sitting in the corner with handfuls of raw meat."

She shrugged, uncomfortable with the sudden rush of self doubt. "Yeah, but he wasn't hurting anyone. He remembers a lot sometimes, and nothing at all other times."

Salann grimaced. "So we have to keep him here a little longer."

"When it's time, I want to bring him to the Monks of Annularei."

"Why?"

She looked at Miros as he wiggled out of her grasp and wandered around the room again. At least he was still calm. "He trusts me. And I owe him from… from before, when he was still bonded."

"You can't leave the caves, Palon. The dragons still haven't decided what to do with you."

No. Nothing would keep her from seeing this through. She wouldn't allow it. Miros deserved this final honor from someone who thought it an honor. She clenched her fists, speaking through gritted teeth. "Others will be there too. It's not like I'll be alone—it'll be like Silver Spine's funeral. And I give my word I'll come right back. I'm not trying to escape Dragon Law."

"Keep Dragon Law!" Miros's fingers dug into Palon's shoulder with a force that made her gasp, her wrath dissipating. His wide, white, wild eyes looked around frantically. "Keep Dragon Law! Don't break it! Not broken, not broken. Seventeen, they were, not twenty. Not twenty. Seventeen. Then they said twelve. But no. Seventeen should be. Seven, then ten. Five, then twelve."

His voice faded to mutters and he shook his head fiercely a couple times, but calmed as Palon rubbed his shoulders. She wished she was snooping with Aturadin and Tebah, rather than here alone, doing chores. They didn't have much—some pine needles by Laetiran's cache, some rocks that could be anyone's, or no one's.

"If you wanted to leave the cave, you shouldn't have stolen from the dragons," Salann said. "You should have kept Dragon Law."

It wasn't fair, and she wouldn't stand for it. "You can't think I did that. I'm not that stupid, and neither are you!"

"Right. Not stupid." Shaking her head, Salann stalked out.

Shoulders slumping, Palon frowned at the entrance. She'd messed up, again. Salann had come to help, and she'd insulted her. They didn't have enough allies as it was. Dragonfire, she was an idiot.

Chapter Sixteen

Once she had cleaned the carcass, she packed all the meat on a two-wheeled cart. Palon had carried a pair of safety lines earlier in the day, and these she attached to the cart, crisscrossing the lines in front of her as a makeshift harness to save her arm from having to pull. She leaned into it, hauling the laden cart down the tunnels behind her. Miros, in a rare lucid moment but for the constant blinking, pushed the cart from behind, lightening the load. As they approached the gentle slope up to the basking platform, Palon strained forward, focused on her goal. Windward's hunger lighted along their bond, but she assured him she was close.

Her foot slipped, and she caught a glimpse of a greasy clear substance as she hit the ground. The weight of the cart pulled her backward, and she shouted, fearing for Miros. But he grabbed her, apparently having dodged around the cart, and hauled on her harness until the cart's momentum stopped.

"Come on, no time to waste," he said, pulling her forward.

Palon risked a glance backward. Some of the meat had fallen, and she wanted to go back for it, but Miros was right. The cart was still mostly full, and she needed to get it to Windward, even though other bonded would likely scoop up the fallen food while she was gone. She peeked down at the slick substance on her boot.

"It was herdbeast oil," Palon gasped.

"Pull!" Miros responded.

"Miros, it was oil I slipped in. From the lamps." She blinked as she pulled on the harness. Was she paranoid to suspect that Laetiran had put the oil there just for her? But she did. She did suspect. Was she wrong to do so? Was the current strife truly her fault?

Windward roared in her mind, and she shook her head, her self doubt fleeing just as quickly as prey scampering from any powerful predator. Eyes crinkling, Miros was laughing at her. She smiled, though her heart sank. Already, his lucid period had ended.

"Dragon says No, no, no!" he crowed. "Food for the hungry!"

"Thanks, Miros," she said, though the Miros she knew had already gone. Maybe a part of him would hear it.

"Thanks, Palon!" he grinned back at her, too broad, his eyes too fierce.

After they crested the top of the slope, the wagon rolled easily into the basking area. Palon grabbed the smaller wooden chest of meat she'd set aside for Aturadin, Tebah, Miros, and her and pulled it out of the way. They'd need more meat in another couple days, though they'd probably still be grounded by then. Dragon Law took an agonizingly long time to decide.

She looked up, wishing they could just have a dragon drop some herdbeasts onto the basking platform, as that would be easier, but then any dragon who was hungry would eat. Dragons wouldn't respect the kill of another dragon if they were angry at that dragon, even if the anger was because of lies.

Trumpeting with possession and hunger, Windward bounded toward them from the nearest basking site. He flared his wings around them, his great head lowering to the wagon, which suddenly didn't seem so big anymore compared to the dragon's head. The sun was blotted out as suddenly they stood in a shelter made entirely of dragon and rock.

Miros screamed. Windward rolled his near eye downward, looking at them, as he gulped down the meat. Miros backed up, still screaming, his eyes frantic as his back hit the wall behind him. Palon hurried to his side to try to soothe him.

"Dragon!" he screamed, panting in terror.

"Yes, Miros, it's Windward," Palon shouted back at him, trying to top his volume with her own so that he could hear her.

"No wind!"

"No, that's Windward. You know him."

Abruptly, Miros stopped screaming and started laughing, tears running down his face. "Do you know why the teeth are cryst—ah, crys, crys…. see through? They—" He groaned, grabbing his head and falling to his knees. She'd given up trying to determine if there was any reason to his ramblings during the worst of his incoherent times.

But at least he wasn't screaming anymore.

A blur of red scales thrust Windward to the side. His wings flapped, tail lashing as he was shoved off balance. The wind of the commotion threw Palon off her feet as well, and she fell to the ground. A cry ripped from her as she landed on her wounded arm. Miros was still kneeling there, in the way. She struggled to get to him through the flurry of pounding feet and claws and tails. Belatedly, she realized they were in grave danger. So many dragons stomping around, so much chaos. Again.

Dragons roared and people shouted, but she couldn't make out any words, her eardrums so abused by the volume of dragon voices. She had to get to Miros. He was in no condition to realize the danger. She didn't know what was going on, or why, but she had to get him out of there, into the tunnel where it would be safer. At least it was close by.

She dodged pieces of the splintered cart and was immediately buffeted into the wall by something—maybe a dragon wing—clipping her back. Knocked off balance, she fell again. She picked herself up, only to be slammed into by something else, so that by the time she staggered to Miros's side, she was bruised and out of breath. She didn't even know who the blows were from, there was so much tumult. Miros sat quietly, staring into the distance. He looked like he had gone dormant somehow with his eyes still open. Or like he'd died.

There was no time to think about it. Palon grabbed his shoulder and shoved him toward the tunnel, just as something large hit her back, bearing her to the ground on top of Miros. She struggled, shoving him forward, trying to get out from under the weight. But instead, someone grabbed her arms, and white hot pain flashed through her, blinding her for a moment with agony as her injured arm was twisted behind her back.

When she could see again, gasping for breath through the pain, all was still. Miros! She looked around, dreading to see him hurt, and a rush of relief made her sag when she saw Tsían holding him up. Windward lay pinned under several larger dragons. He assured her he was not injured, although he'd very much like it if Black Cloud weren't stepping on his leg. With a hiss, serrated teeth displayed right in front of his face, Stone Eyes took one step back from Windward, and the other dragons stepped back as well. Windward rolled carefully to his belly, keeping his long neck stretched low and his head on the floor of the basin, while Stone Eyes flared his wings and trumpeted.

Reassured that Windward was physically unharmed and trusting the dragons to sort it out amongst themselves, Palon strained to see who was holding her, wincing as another stab of pain took her breath away. She was laying on her stomach, her arms trapped behind her, a knee grinding into the small of her back, but she got enough of a peek to recognize her captor.

"Yiyin, let me go!"

"What were you doing to him?" thundered Tsían.

"What? Who?"

"Don't play innocent, we all saw you! Dragons attacking bonded now? What are we coming to?" Salann said. "Yiyin, keep hold of her!"

"Dragons don't attack bonded, we all know this!" Laetiran shouted. Palon's head spun. It didn't make sense. Why would he help her? He knew as well as she that his dragon had attacked her. But she couldn't say that, not now, not without placing suspicion on Windward.

She looked around, trying to find some metaphorical solid footing. "He's not hurt. Windward didn't hurt him."

"Thank goodness we got here in time," said Eltavae. Her words were nearly drowned out by the roaring from the dragons as they shifted positions and negotiated space.

"Why would Windward hurt him?" Palon shouted as soon as the dragon noise quieted.

"Why were you attacking him?" Tsían asked.

"I wasn't!"

"We saw you pushing him!"

"I was trying to get him out of the way of the commotion." What was going on here?

"A likely story." Laetiran smirked.

"Why was he screaming?" Eltavae asked.

"I don't know! He... it was like he forgot about dragons."

A wing stretched out over her head, then retreated. Scales whispered over rocks, tails moving out of her field of vision. The enormous reptiles were moving again, adjusting their wings and neck spines.

Laetiran leaned over to Eltavae and whispered, but Palon heard his words. When he smiled at her, she realized she was intended to. "It's fortunate she's not an evil genius—she has everything set up to portray herself in a positive light if anything were to happen to Miros. After all, everyone knows he's crazy."

"I'd never hurt him!"

"Oh yes," Laetiran said, nodding. "You being so nonviolent and stable."

"That's enough!" Tsían snapped. Laetiran had the grace to look abashed for a moment.

"Check him. Is he hurt?" Desperate terror filled her voice.

Her heart pounded in her ears as Tsían checked Miros over. He couldn't be hurt, he couldn't be. Not only because of the trouble it would place her in, but just the thought of him hurt in the ruckus made her feel sick. The former bonded simply stood there blinking and occasionally swaying. Out of the corner of her eyes, she saw Tebah come running from High Flight's ledge, while the dragon poked his head over the rocks. Palon blinked rapidly, beginning to feel lightheaded, whether from the stress or the pulsing pain in her arm, she wasn't sure.

Finally, Tsían shrugged. "He seems fine, apart from some scrapes and bruises."

"Don't you think if Windward was trying to hurt him he'd be injured?" Palon snarled. Aturadin came running up, but at her words he stopped in his tracks and put his hand over his eyes. Trying not to panic, her thoughts ran over and over her words, looking for the problem. What had she said that Laetiran could use against her? Anything?

"It's clear we need to lay some questions to rest right now, whether or not the dragons are ready to confer on Dragon Law," Tsían said. "This is tearing us up, and I won't have it anymore."

She was trapped and on display and wounded. Desperation boiled in her. "Yiyin, let me go!" Palon tried to twist her good arm free, but only ended up bumping her injured arm. The pain drove everything else far away, and the floor slapped her in the face. Windward whistled, shrill and anxious, his scales rustling on the stone as he shifted restlessly. He couldn't take her pain.

She shoved at him mentally. He was injured too, from the fight with Fired Sand. Of course he couldn't, and she didn't expect him to.

"Let her go," Tsían's voice said from far away.

Aturadin was there and relief flooded her as the rushing in her ears faded, even as he gingerly pushed back her sleeve. Her arm had swollen noticeably larger than her good arm, red and angry. She closed her eyes a moment, seeing the look on Aturadin's face.

"That doesn't look good," murmured Tebah, crouching nearby.

"Did I do that?" Yiyin sounded stricken.

"No," Palon snapped. Yiyin was a good bonded, but she knew if she didn't cut him off, he'd spiral into a cycle of self-beratement and anxiety.

Laetiran's voice murmured low as he passed behind her. "You're weak, Palon. Weak and unworthy—"

Snarling, she turned on him, punching him right in the face with her good arm. He fell backward, covering his nose, while his friends rushed forward.

"Palon!" Salann and Aturadin shouted.

She winced. That hadn't looked good, she supposed. Her temper was still up, her blood pounding in her ears, though a chill went up her back when she caught a hint of a smile from Laetiran. Fired Sand roared, lunging toward Windward, but Stone Eyes got between them, wings flaring. Palon glanced at Windward, disoriented by how far away he felt.

"Keep them away from each other, but stay in the Basin. No one's going anywhere for a while," Tsían said. "So get comfortable. I want everyone visible. You too, Eltavae. Now, Palon, what happened? I won't ask again."

"Where do you want me to start?" Her voice was harsh with tension. She hissed as Aturadin's fingers, gently prodding her arm, hit a tender spot. "Can you not do that now?"

"I think it's broken," he said. She took a deep breath and nodded. She'd figure it out. She always did. She'd fly again, and when the flight ban was lifted, she'd be on the wind, broken arm or not.

"You might as well start at the beginning," Tsían sighed. "Keep in mind, everyone, we are not inserting ourselves into Dragon Law. We are not initiating our own version of it. We are not subverting it. We are not rushing it. We are only clearing the air so we can function once more as a proper nest. The dragons will lay down Dragon Law when they have finished their discussions."

Her nest was broken, like the remnants of a dragon egg after hatching. Who would have thought their way of life was so fragile? But with everyone's emotions raging, the ugly side of dragon life was showing. Tebah's bonding had shone a light on broken aspects, and still more were glittering. It needed to be fixed. Surely, once everything was aired, reason would return to the nest and they could address these problems, make safeguards for future newlings.

Drawing in a deep breath, Palon told her story along with Aturadin. Around them, the others formed a solemn ring, save for when Miros began trying to eat rocks and then to bash Laros over the head with them when he tried to stop him. Tsían's gaze hardly wavered, his face impassive even when Palon relayed the story of Fired Sand targeting her, aiming to maim her. She peeked behind her at Fired Sand, only to grimace at Laetiran's perfectly composed expression of innocent horror.

"Who could believe that a dragon would target a bonded?" Eltavae scoffed. "Has such a thing ever happened before in the history of dragonbonded?"

"You all believed just moments ago that Windward was attacking Miros," Palon pointed out.

"That's different." Eltavae shook her head, apparently consulting her dragon. "No. Such a thing has never happened."

"When did you break your arm, Palon?" Laetiran asked. If Palon hadn't known him, she'd have sworn he was sincere.

"I just told you."

"No, I mean, did you break your arm after our dragons had their spat, so you could blame it on Fired Sand, or before? I want to know how far in advance you planned this. You know, if you were trying to disgrace Fired Sand with this ploy so Windward could stretch out over his basking space, I think you and your dragon sorely misestimated us —and the others too."

Palon gaped. No one would believe such a wild story, surely! Yes, they'd had their spats, but it was due to Laetiran's ambition. And now he was saying it was her ambition instead, and heads around the circle nodded as if it made sense. Emotions would be running high, with everyone's bond's pinched and crippled, but surely they could still reason!

"Her arm was probably broken when I wrapped the bandage," Aturadin said, his tone as hard as the rocks around them. His patience was fraying. "Maea was there—she can tell you."

Maea stammered. "She said this all there in the Wounds Cave, yes. But I don't know about her arm. She wouldn't let me look at it. Only Aturadin saw it. But, you know, that's not really unusual. I never thought much about it."

"And then you two ran to the Sequestering Cave, where none of us would follow," Salann said.

Palon took a breath. That move had probably done more to help Laetiran than anything else—aside from her punching him just now.

"Away from eyes to witness what you did to yourself," Eltavae said, her tone filled with suspicion.

"And the lone witness to your attempt to set me up as the villain is completely out of his mind." Laetiran shook his head. "What have I ever done to deserve such treatment? Though I do applaud you on your commitment, to break your own arm. But then, we all know you are good with the follow through, don't we, Palon?"

Palon shook her head in denial. How could they be so blind, to ignore the truth right in front of them?

"I saw no signs of self harm while they were there, including when I looked in on them," Tsían said. "Though I cannot say for sure. I did see Palon rubbing her arm a lot, as if it was tender and she was trying to hide it. But surely Windward would have signaled about the pain in some way if she broke it there."

"But Windward and Scorch Frost were trying to avoid the other dragons. We might have missed such a sign," Salann reminded him.

"I didn't do it. Why would I break my own arm? My arm!" Palon pressed her fist to her forehead, fed up with the fabrications and lies.

"Bonded can't fly with one arm," Tsían cut in, raising his eyebrows at her as if he knew she planned to disregard that rule, too, as soon as she could. Provided they were cleared of all this trouble, of course. She gritted her teeth, staring defiance at him. She would not be a burden, useless.

"You didn't have a choice, did you?" Laetiran said. "If anyone saw Fired Sand when he accidentally maybe bumped your arm a little, and then you claimed a broken, I don't know, foot or something, people would know you were lying. You wanted your lie to be believable, at least on first glance."

Palon snarled at Laetiran, the urge to tell him what a despicable piece of garbage he was surging, but Aturadin's warning look stopped her. With Windward rumbling in her ears, she glanced over to see Tsían watching her as well, and struggled to settled herself back down. She'd already helped Laetiran too much. She let out her breath slowly, fixing her eyes on Tsían instead. At least he was showing a somewhat rational mind.

"Maea," Tsían said abruptly, causing the meek dragonbonded to jump. "If Palon here had indeed broken her own arm, perhaps after you saw her, would there be sign of it on her skin? Abrasions or something?"

Maea shrugged. "Maybe, if she did it by hitting it on the rocks or something. It depends on how she did it, though. If she had someone step on her arm hard, or kick her arm or something, there might not be anything more than bruises, and her arm was already bruised. It might not show up, but I don't know for sure, Tsían."

Tsían nodded, and Maea rushed to say more. "And I have to say, I doubt Aturadin would have done such a thing to her, even on request."

Mouth agape, Palon shook her head, her voice trembling with the temper and disbelief she tried to control. "You can't believe I'd ask someone to break my arm for me? On purpose!?" Windward rumbled, low and threatening.

"We were there during the Childless Ceremony. You didn't even cry out when Maea cut you," Laros said.

Fired Sand gaped in an open-mouth threat display. Windward rose up, bristling, and Stone Eyes snapped at them both.

"I was drunk, lying on Windward's leg, and he was taking all my pain!" That was completely different. "The Ceremony isn't meant to be painful, regardless of the surgery."

"What?" Tebah squeaked.

"A dragon nest is no place for children," Aturadin said. "There's a ceremony—a completely optional ceremony—that Palon took part in to make sure she would not be able to bear children."

"But that's different than breaking my arm!" Her stomach twisted. All she wanted was Windward. Windward whistled, and she wished he hadn't dampened the bond, that she could feel him.

Maea shrugged, ducking her head. She scuffed at the stone lightly with one boot. "I don't know. I don't think so, but... Well, it takes a certain kind of person to do the things you do when flying with Windward. I've seen you two fight walavaim. And not many of us actually go through with the Childless Ceremony."

"And Palon's always pushing the boundaries, keeping her harness straps too long, breaking every rule she thinks she can get away with. We shouldn't have been surprised when she went to the Sequestering Cave, after all," Eltavae said.

"What does that have to do with anything?" Aturadin's voice was so tense, he would have shouted had he been anyone else.

Tsían drew in a breath. "You're referring to Palon's style of fighting walavaim. I agree she's more hands on than most of us. Even reckless at times."

"So focused on her goal she doesn't consider the cost to herself physically?" Salann suggested.

Palon blinked. That was one of her strengths. Her fearlessness was not a liability. It made her and Windward a near seamless team. They couldn't be insinuating... couldn't be thinking... She refused to finish the thought, bile rising. This was all wrong.

Tsían nodded. "Yes, even that. This though... this accusation goes far beyond the realm of walavai fighting."

"I know, it's really unfair that she relentlessly attacks me. The two of them—" Laetiran started.

Tsían cut him off with a sharp look. "I was referring to your accusation against her, of course, Laetiran. Yes, the two of you have accused each other. And both are serious accusations. Dragonflight, I hope the two of you understand whoever is lying is going to wish to walk through dragonfire before I'm done with them."

Palon nodded, inwardly relieved to see the worry that flashed across Laetiran's face.

Tsían sighed, rubbing his forehead for a moment before he dropped his arm. "Alright. Palon, you accuse Laetiran of framing you and Aturadin for theft and further, of Fired Sand specifically intending to injure you. Correct?"

Palon nodded again, unable to trust her voice.

"And Laetiran, you accuse Palon of blaming you and breaking her own arm in an effort to ruin your reputation and standing. Correct?"

Laetiran nodded, his expression resolute. "That's what's happening, as everyone can see."

"Dragonfire, I want to drop both of you off a cliff right now, so shut your mouths. Don't either of you say a word," Tsían growled. "I'm thinking."

Palon stood silent, watching Tsían, feeling the presence of the others around her. Everyone seemed somewhat subdued, even Laetiran.

After a few moments, Aturadin spoke. "Can I at least set her arm?"

Tsían waved them away. "Stay in the basking area, but get out of my sight for now. Go to your dragons."

Keeping her gaze straight ahead, Palon walked over to Windward, checking him over reflexively. He watched her, his golden eye amused as she went over his scales and spines and wings, looking for injuries. It helped her relax, the closeness with Windward, the familiar task. It made her feel less like she was going to jump out of her skin. She could see Aturadin waiting with folded arms and a similar bemused expression, a little way away, and Tebah stood beside him, half turned toward High Flight as if she'd paused in her way to him.

"What's she doing?"

"Checking over Windward, obviously."

"But her arm is broken! He can wait."

"Palon takes being dragonbonded very seriously. She always has."

"Can't the dragon take your pain through the bond?" Tebah asked. "He's bigger. He should be able to take more pain."

"They aren't jugs, Tebah," Palon said. "Anyway, Windward's still got the bond dampened, which I don't appreciate." She gave her dragon a fierce poke, scowling when he didn't react.

"So?"

"So, in order to take more of Palon's pain from her arm, Windward would need to open the bond up more than it is. It's a poor example, but I hope you understand. And if he does that, she'd share his pain too. A dragon is bigger and can take more, as you said. He can only hold that back for a short time."

"I'd rather stay conscious, thank you very much," Palon added. "Besides, Windward doesn't want me doing anything stupid with my arm."

"Me too," Aturadin said dryly.

Palon gave him a sharp look.

"What, your dragon and I can't agree?"

"No. You can't."

"Why would..." Tebah trailed off, watching them.

"Bonded whose dragons take all their pain tend never to fully recover, or take longer to heal, because they re-injure themselves. Pain is the body's warning sign."

Finished with her cursory examination of Windward, Palon stroked the scales of his shoulder, considering where she wanted to be while Aturadin set her arm. She felt most comfortable up on his back, her common perch between his neck spines, but Aturadin would never consent to climbing up so he could reach.

Windward rumbled, rolling one eye back to look at her. She patted him. Ok, so Windward might not consent either. She caught Tsían staring at her, his arms crossed and his eyes like daggers, and lowered her head in submission.

"Come on, Palon, stop dawdling." Impatience filled Aturadin's voice.

"Fine, fine," she grumbled, walking the length of Windward's foreleg. She climbed up, sitting on his foot, and he lowered his head like a wall next to her. Smiling, she leaned against the smooth flat scales of his face, as safe and comfortable as she'd ever be.

Aturadin reached up, and she extended her red and swollen arm toward him, placing her other hand flat against Windward's face, basking in the glow of her dragon's protective gaze. Tebah watched, sidling toward High Flight with her hands clasped tightly together so her knuckles were as white as her face. Palon smiled at her, overwhelmed by close feelings with Windward. She knew Aturadin was doing something, but she could barely feel anything and for the moment, didn't care.

"It's ok," she called out to Tebah. "Windward can hold back his own pain for a short time so as not to overwhelm me. Are you done yet, Aturadin?"

"And here I was hoping you'd be less crotchety," Aturadin said with a grin, tying the last knot of a new bandage.

Chapter Seventeen

Palon squinted at the scale in front of her, tapping it with her fingernail. It was on the leading edge of the gash the walavaim had left in Windward's side, but the scoring on it would probably fade once he shed. Dipping her fingers in the bag at her side, she polished the scale with some salve. His wounds were healing nicely.

She stepped back, looking at Windward critically, causing the dragon to preen. She couldn't help but laugh as his head bobbed around. At least she was with him, and the brisk wind reminded her of flying. She was happy to push her anxieties to the side for a moment and simply concentrate on her dragon.

"Not quite back to full strength, but you're getting there," she said in response to his surge of pride.

He puffed up. Clearly, he didn't need to be back to full strength to be glorious.

She laughed again. "Yeah, you're glorious alright."

His head swooped down low to confront her, giant eye to eye. Tilting his head a bit, he sent her a query.

"Yes, I was joking!" Palon responded. "You're not too terrible to look at."

He drew his head back, muzzle pointed straight at her, and sneezed, throwing salt flecks all over her. Raising her good arm and turning her back, she made sounds of disgust, trying to hide further laughter. Shaking her head to clear it of the salt particles, she brushed down her clothes and shook her finger at the dragon.

"Gross!"

He drew his head back, his laughter ringing along their bond.

She grinned up at the sun, relishing the warmth of the sunlight on her scales, especially with the cold wind. Skin. She meant skin. She shook herself, glaring at Windward, but it was hard to hold a glare when he gleamed so nicely in the sunlight. With a sigh, she leaned against Windward's claw, delighting in the bond being open again. It was one good thing about waiting for the dragons' slow timetable—it was giving them time to heal.

From one of the nearby basking ledges, Tebah squeaked, hopping down off High Flight. The girl stumbled, catching herself with her hands, and her dragon curled his neck around her. Palon smiled. The newling needed more practice—a lot more practice—but she was trying, and that by itself was improvement.

Still, she couldn't pretend everything was normal, not for long. She glanced about, noting the various dragons and their bonded. Laetiran was not in sight, she saw, though Fired Sand was. She didn't think about that too much until she realized she couldn't see Aturadin either.

Scorch Frost bugled. Heart suddenly pounding, Palon raced for the tunnel entrance, only to run straight into Tsían's chest. She scrambled back to her feet, adrenaline surging through her.

"Where are you going?" Tsían asked, dusting himself off as he, too, regained his feet.

"Aturadin! Where is he?"

"I told you to stay in sight, Palon, do you remember?"

"But Laetiran is also missing," she shouted.

She held her breath, waiting for the awful excuse for a garbage bonded to poke his head out of nowhere and prove her wrong. He didn't, and she felt a bit confused. Relief filled her, that he didn't prove her wrong, and also worry that she was missing something somehow. He had had everything under control and all lined up so that he came out looking squeaky clean. She was irritated at herself for even thinking that—he was only bonded. He wasn't perfect. He would make mistakes.

And she would catch him in those mistakes, regardless of what he wanted anyone else to think.

Tsían looked troubled too. "Stay here," he said, pointing at her. "Go back to Windward."

"But Aturadin—"

"I will find him. And if he and Laetiran are fighting, may the dragons help them both."

Tsían stalked down the tunnel while Palon stood there, trying to control her breathing. She looked around again as she slunk back toward Windward. Tebah was watching her, one hand on her dragon's shoulder. Miros was nowhere in sight. Aturadin had been watching him near Scorch Frost, keeping him safe—and keeping the others safe from him. It wouldn't be long before they would have to take him to the Monks of Annularei. Part of her wanted to put off that day for as long as possible, while another part of her, traitorously, was looking forward to the relief it would bring, no longer having to worry about what Miros might do next.

Scorch Frost paced back and forth, wings half flaring, trumpeting. Windward watched with wariness in every line of his body. Palon looked toward Fired Sand, who stood, turning in a circle and flaring his wings, his back arching.

Anger filling her, Palon stopped still in the middle of the open space. Why should she be confined? Why did she need to stay in view of everyone else just because they couldn't manage to look at the evidence objectively? Of course she hadn't stolen anything from the dragons, and anyone thinking so wasn't actually thinking, obviously.

It was stupidity for her to be down there in the basin, especially if Fired Sand and Scorch Frost fought. It was suicide. Surviving one dragon battle on her own two feet was lucky. Same with the chaos of the "misunderstanding" a few days ago. Her luck was surely all used up now.

And yet, she stayed in the open, turning in a circle as her rage erupted. "Do you see what's going on? Laetiran is getting rid of anyone who will oppose him. Sure, you think you're fine right now, but once Aturadin and I are gone, you think he's going to be happy? You think he won't want more?"

Arms folded, Salann stared down at her from in front of her dragon. Palon met her stare for stare. This had to end. They couldn't continue on like this. "Laetiran has always wanted more. Why do you suddenly find it hard to believe he does? He's struggled for more since his very bonding. More glory, more food, more light. It never ends with him. Aturadin and I won't bend to him, though, and Scorch Frost and Windward won't let Fired Sand trample all over them."

Met with only impassive faces, Palon turned, appealing to specifics. "Maea, do you remember when Fired Sand and Lake Bolt got into a fight? Lake Bolt tried to run. Females don't take part in dominance battles. But Fired Sand wanted the treasure she'd found. How did he make her fight? Laetiran went after you to force Lake Bolt to fight.

"High Flight's last bonded, remember? Fired Sand fought High Flight in the air while their bonded were on the dragons, and Laetiran nearly made him fall off his dragon. These things don't just happen by themselves. This is a pattern."

Stone Eyes dropped from his high ledge, catching the air in his wings just before he landed with a ground-shaking thump that staggered Palon. As she recovered her balance, she realized the dragon had hit the ground in between Fired Sand and Scorch Frost—right in front of Fired Sand, in fact.

She quailed in front of the enormous gold dragon, Windward's own submission surging through their bond. But her rage and irritation had hold of her too. She was tired of taking the blows, of being doubted. She was tired of being grounded, blocked off from the joy of flight.

Gritting her teeth, trembling in every limb, Palon stood her ground as Stone Eyes thumped forward, one step at a time, closer and closer to her. And then, he lowered his head, staring at her close up with one brown eye. Her legs trembled so much she was afraid she'd fall down and all this would be for nothing, while part of her—the rational part—screamed at her that there was no "all this", only stupidity and insanity, and she needed to get out of there right now.

Dragons were not meant for speech. Their mouths and teeth and tongue were not mobile enough to accommodate what Palon knew as speech. But they were strong telepaths.

We have heard your complaints, little bonded. The words reverberated in her head, accompanied by a fearsome hissing and groaning from the dragon as his mouth tried to make the sounds. Her ears rang. Her head rang. A sort of clanging ricocheted along her bond with Windward, and she looked at him, gulping down sudden nausea. Windward never spoke in words. Why was Stone Eyes?

Because you will not listen. You will not wait. You run like a rodent, scurry, scurry, scurry, and will not know patience. You try to keep dragons to your own timetable.

Palon gasped for breath, struggling to think under the onslaught of the dragon's speech. Under the weight of his disapproval. She could feel how worthless she was. How slight. How small. A noisy creature trying to bully her larger predators.

She struggled back to her feet, digging down deep for further stupidity, and glared right back at the dragon. She was not a bully. She was small, yes, and noisy, yes, but she wasn't trying to bully the dragons. All she wanted was Dragon Law.

Dragon Law on your timetable.

"Dragon Law on any reasonable timetable! You live for so long, you may forget that we have shorter lives. We need things to move more quickly. This is destroying our nest, because we bonded need Dragon Law. We need justice. You have to give that."

Bonded police their own.

"You know I accuse a dragon!" Palon screamed. No more could she stand for everyone to pass the responsibility on to the next person.

Stone Eyes roared, blasting her off her feet, and she curled into a ball, clutching her ears, trying to shrink down into herself as the world spun.

The ground bounced around her, and Palon curled tighter, eyes squeezed shut. She'd dared too much, flown too dangerously. No safety lines here—she'd fallen to her death. Well, if you had to go out, doing so by taunting a dragon was at least a way to go out with style.

Slowly, she became aware of the rumblings in the air around and through her. Vibrations. She opened her eyes, hardly daring to believe she was somehow still alive. Her abused ears had shut down, and the world still spun if she moved too quickly.

Windward stood over her, his head low as he looked up at a puffed up Stone Eyes. He'd been unwilling to let her confront a dragon on her own, even if that dragon was the highest-ranked in the nest and confronting him was the epitome of foolishness. He'd stand with her anyway, always. A well of love rose up in her, tears pricking at her eyes though she refused to let them fall.

Behind her, Scorch Frost stood with his wings tucked, tail flicking with worry. She looked at the other dragons, expecting satisfaction on Fired Sand's face, but his head was low too, hanging off the side of his ledge and pointed toward the ground. Everyone cowered before Stone Eyes' wrath.

And then, Stone Eyes stepped backward.

Palon blinked, questioning what she'd seen, but Windward confirmed. Dragons never moved backward if they could help it. But Stone Eyes had taken one deliberate step backward, and now he was lowering his head again, this time a graceful bow.

A hard nose pushed at her, and Palon looked at Windward, bewildered. The dragon pushed her forward again, filling her in as she took step after hesitant step.

Stone Eyes had decided that she was right, and had commended their courage and their loyalty to each other, both daring to confront him, to support each other, even with such a shocking testimony.

Palon stepped out in front of her dragon, meeting Stone Eyes's gaze with her own level stare—or as level as she could make it when she felt like the last leaf on a tree in autumn and her knees seemed as weak as if they were made of water.

"It's true, our testimony. We only await your timing, Stone Eyes," she said.

Fired Sand growled, sliding down to the bottom of the open space, and Palon reacted in a moment, turning to leap onto Windward's foot, from there to his elbow, and then flinging herself upward to catch hold of his spine one handed. As she pulled herself into her seat with her good arm, Windward raised his head.

"You've got no harness! No safety lines!" Salann's voice was filled with alarm.

Nervous muttering rose from the others, shifting in an agitated huddle. Palon patted Windward's neck scales. No harness, no safety lines, and only one arm, should it come to it. But she had her dragon, and what's more, she had the attention of Stone Eyes, as Windward lifted her level with the dragon's eyes, keeping his own neck arched so his head was lower. Palon patted him again, smiling. Of course Stone Eyes would know Windward wasn't challenging him.

Windward continued to translate for her, something Palon was infinitely grateful for as she held tightly with her good arm wrapped around the neck spine in front of her. She'd be happy if she lived the rest of her life never hearing another dragon in her head.

Fired Sand hissed, saying once again how no one had seen him commit such an atrocity, to target a bonded. It would have crossed a line there was no coming back from. But no one had seen it because it hadn't happened: Palon had damaged herself to support her accusations, another thing that was despicable and surely had crossed a line of its own.

The rage built up in her, and she could feel it building up in Windward again, exploding with a roar. Windward would not be called a liar, and neither would Palon.

"Behave as befits a dragon!" Palon shouted at Fired Sand. "This is shameful behavior coming from one who should be respected!"

Stone Eyes rumbled, and Palon clung tighter as Windward's head dropped. He admonished her to be careful. Stone Eyes had warned that being cute and plucky would not save her from overstepping herself. Hubris affected all, even dragonbonded. Maybe especially bonded.

Palon pressed her lips together, railing inwardly about being called "cute". Even "plucky" was bad enough, but "cute" was just demeaning.

Windward sent her another warning. She dropped her gaze to Windward's spines.

"Palon!" Aturadin shouted.

Forest Blaze began to move—Tsían must be back too. Laetiran's voice rose, yammering on about something, and she leaned over to look for them. Stalking toward the Basin, Tsían had a hand on each of the backs of Laetiran and Aturadin's shirts. Laetiran's disgruntled expression caused her blood to roar in her ears, but the anger and fear on Aturadin's face made her heart pound, ready for a fight. He had one arm around Miros, holding him up, and Miros's face was puffy, with crusted lines where the blood had scabbed and dried, his eyes already beginning to swell closed. He grinned though, stumbling as Aturadin drew him around a pothole he'd otherwise have tripped on.

"Dragon Law!" Miros shouted.

Laetiran had messed with her loved ones again. She'd need to teach him a lesson he wouldn't forget. Palon was moving before she'd fully perceived everything, jumping up to step through the spines and then off, sliding down Windward's neck as the dragon flexed, trying to keep her safe while obeying the laws of gravity and physics in general. His worry thrummed against her, but she couldn't spare a care for him, not at the moment. Aturadin and Laetiran had been missing, and Miros had clearly been beaten. The story wrote itself.

"Laetiran, what did you do to him?" Her feet hit Windward's arm and she ran up to his elbow as he moved forward, elbow rising with his gait. Then she leaped, into the palm of her dragon's hand as he extended it behind him. Bounding again, she landed as Windward's claws hit the ground once more, just behind her.

"Why do you think it was me?" growled Laetiran. "Don't you think you're showing your prejudice, to instantly leap to the conclusion that I'm at fault?"

"No, I'm showing my intelligence, to base my conclusion on your past actions, you scum."

"Palon, stop there. *Right there!*" Tsían thundered.

Palon slid to a halt, breathing heavily. Her eyes went from Laetiran's sullen gaze, to Tsían's ferocious glare, to Aturadin's dark eyes, full of too many emotions for her to pay attention to just now, to

Miros's mad ones.

"Now *that* is a dragonbonded," Miros cackled, rubbing his hands together. "In my day, dragonbonded would sprout wings themselves and fly."

"No they didn't," Aturadin said, sounding tired. "We were there in your day."

"Not a bad idea though," Palon said. If she could sprout wings and fly, she'd be unstoppable. She and Windward would be unstoppable.

"What is going on here?" Tsían asked.

Stone Eyes rumbled, and Forest Blaze responded, his eyes on his bonded. Tsían bowed his head for a moment. He released Laetiran and pointed at Fired Sand, then released Aturadin and pointed at Scorch Frost.

She was moving before she thought about it, heading toward them. Miros needed somewhere to go, and if he wasn't given direction, he'd find his own way—and the rest of them would probably not like it. "Miros!"

"Take him with you back to Windward!" Tsían shouted. "All dragonbonded, back to your dragons!"

Palon ran forward, taking Miros's hand when she got to him and Aturadin. Her eyes, however, were on Aturadin. Again, he was beaten, both of them were, and knowing he was tough and could take care of himself didn't stop the twisting in her gut and the pounding of her heart when she saw his injuries. "Are you ok?"

"I'll live," he said tersely. "This will all be over shortly."

"Is Miros ok?" Palon asked. "What happened?"

"I'll tell you later, I promise."

"Palon, get to Windward! Now!" Tsían thundered.

Ducking her head in appeasement to avoid further trouble, she slipped her arm around Miros, taking his weight. Aturadin gave her a grim smile as he stalked away, one arm clamped tightly to his side. Palon stared at Miros, afraid that if she saw Laetiran's face, he would be smirking, and if he was smirking, she would do something really stupid.

"Miros, are you ok?" she murmured.

"Wrong dragon, wrong dragon!" Miros balked. "Where's Silver Spine?"

"Shh, shh! Silver Spine's dead, remember? He's dead."

"Dead. All dead. Dead and cold, washed away by the river. Washed away. Not dirt, not ever the dirt!"

"Miros, listen to me. The dragons are convening. They will lay down Dragon Law. We have to be quiet now. Come with me, over by Windward. I know he's not Silver Spine, but he's not so bad, is he?"

She winced at the mental huff Windward gave her for that comment, assuring him that of course she thought highly of him, lovable buffoon though he was. Slowly, she hauled Miros toward Windward.

A disturbance spread through the dragons, hissing and growling and clacking filling the air. Palon paused, the hairs on the back of her neck prickling. Not again, not again! They couldn't handle another crisis. Windward hissed, a clacking sound reverberating deep in his throat. Hatred emanated from him. She turned, Miros's arm slipping from her shoulder as he staggered away. The dragons were sliding off their basking ledges, converging on something that lay in the dust of the basin. Laetiran smirked at her, continuing toward Fired Sand.

Her crystal lay in the middle of the basin.

Windward was going to take it from her. She couldn't let that happen. Laetiran had already taken it. It was the only thing she had left of her cache—if she could grab it first. She raced forward. It was her rock. Hers!

Alarm twanged along their bond, but Palon pushed Windward away, scooping up the crystal. In a flash, it was cradled in both hands, pressed to her chest, as she turned on the dragons.

"Palon, what is that?" Tsían barked, striding swiftly toward her.

She tucked it behind her back. "Mine!" she snarled reflexively.

Windward hissed, and she flinched at the heat of the alarm and denial and hatred he sent her. He hated that rock, with a passion she'd never felt before. Her hands spasmed on reflex, tossing it to the floor.

"What is it?" Laetiran asked, and Palon jumped, pivoting to face him. She hadn't realized he was so close. He was holding her crystal.

Conflicting, confusing emotions roiled in her, possession warring with revulsion, fear warring with rage. She hissed. "It's mine—I found it. You took it from me, from my cache!"

"I'm not the one who had it in my hands," Laetiran said, offering it to her.

Windward bugled, but she couldn't help it. She grabbed for it, but Laetiran whisked it out of her range just in time. She clenched her fists, annoyed at being toyed with, the need to get her crystal back beating through her. Why had she dropped it, anyway? She couldn't remember, could only remember being shocked at the force of

Windward's hatred.

The dragons were bellowing and trumpeting, and she couldn't take her eyes from her rock. Windward's snarling broke through her own rage, naming that crystal a tool of the enemy of dragons.

"A tool of the enemy?" Laetiran crowed, holding the crystal up so it caught the light. "And Palon says it's hers?"

Palon snarled wordlessly. She'd made a huge mistake. And yet, she needed that stone!

"We have a bonded working for the enemy of dragons!" Glee filled Laetiran's voice.

"It's not true."

"Yes, of course you would say that."

She couldn't do it. She couldn't stay calm any longer. The stone was hers. She tackled him, grabbing for the crystal. They crashed to the basin floor, rolling. She fought for the crystal, hampered by her injured arm. Windward roared a warning in her head, and she stopped, trying to pull back, but Laetiran was on top of her. Quick as a blink, he dug the rock into her ribcage. Her skin tore and she hissed as he stood up.

Windward's alarm resounded in Palon's mind. She froze. And then, half of her mind was ripped away.

Chapter Eighteen

A voice rose around her, wailing, howling, screaming. It cracked, going hoarse. Nothing existed, only the one fact that made her blood run cold: she couldn't feel Windward.

The bond was severed.

No, no, nonono. It couldn't be. She refused to accept it, reaching for Windward, willing the bond to be there, as it had every moment for ten years. She could not accept being cut off from him. How could anyone live this way, bound to one tiny, horrifyingly limited body, unable to fly? Cold spread through her, chattering her teeth.

Vaguely, she felt someone shake her, but it didn't matter. Someone was screaming at her, someone besides whoever was keening. That was going to get annoying. Who was it? Oh, it was her. And she couldn't stop. Her loss was so great, so horrifying, it had to be given sound.

A hand cracked hard across her face, whipping her head to the side, and then again on the other side, pain exploding inside her head as her bruises protested the rough treatment.

For a moment, everything went white, and then the abyss surrounded her again and she was alone, so very, very alone. She was maimed, horribly injured, and she didn't know how she could survive. The whimpering cries continued, joined by the wild whistling of a dragon. She knew that voice, and desperation rose in her in response.

"Windward! Windward!" she screamed.

Her awareness slowly expanded. Her face was wet with tears, hot with pain. Her throat was raw, and still she couldn't stop the high-pitched whine of a horribly mutilated animal. Tsían gripped her shoulders with fingers like talons. Coppery gold scales formed a wall on one side, not the beautiful purple grey of her Windward. Where was he? She had to get back to him. She looked for him, glimpsing the wide eyed, pale face of Tebah, her mouth open in horror.

"Coming back to us now?" Tsían asked her.

"Windward!" She crumpled under the weight of the grief, pain, and terror engulfing her. How had this happened? She was weeping, and Palon hardly ever wept, not even when she'd been a newling. Windward would be disgusted with her.

"What happened?" Tebah's voice was sharp with hysteria.

"The bond is gone! My bond is broken. Windward!"

Scales loomed close in front of her face as Stone Eyes whipped his head around, staring at her with gold eyes. She shrank from him, shuddering. He was the wrong dragon and she was so raw and broken.

Tsían spoke for Stone Eyes. "Your bond with Windward was severed? How?"

"I don't know. Help me. Please, Tsían!" Terror was climbing her as inexorably as the sun climbed the sky, and several times faster. She couldn't breathe, couldn't move. She was going to vomit.

Dragons were bugling, trumpeting, shaking the ground. Forest Blaze flared his wings, trapping her between him and Stone Eyes. Trapped, trapped, trapped! She'd never felt so powerless, so weak. Where was Windward?

Aturadin's voice, shouting her name, broke above the fray. Tsían whirled around. "Get him out of here. Get everyone out of here! Salann, where's that rock?"

Stone Eyes remained by her side, but he was the *wrong dragon* and all she wanted was Windward. She sobbed as Stone Eyes hissed at her, spines flaring in frustration. She curled in on herself when he dipped his wing over her, covering her. She didn't want him to touch her. He was not Windward.

Tsían returned, his expression tight with that tension that came from communicating with a dragon that was not one's own. "Stone Eyes can't reach you, he says. Neither can Forest Blaze."

Palon shuddered. She fought back nausea, but her stomach couldn't stop turning. There was a gaping hole in the middle of her, a mortal wound where Windward had been. She was going to die without him. The further mystery of other dragons also not being able to reach her seemed small and insignificant next to that.

"Palon, where did you find that rock?"

"Where is it?" she asked, fear gripping her.

"You're not getting anywhere near it," Tsían snapped.

"Laetiran cut me with it," she said, showing him the wound. It was only a small scratch, only a little blood soaked into her shirt. And yet, it was the worst wound she'd ever received.

"Where did you find it?" Tsían asked again.

"In Stonefield."

Miros's gruff voice snatched her attention. "This is not something that should ever be in a dragon nest."

Her head snapped up. Miros stood there, the only one who could possibly come close to understanding what happened. "Miros!"

He embraced her, rubbing her back as she wept and clung to him, disgustingly weak and needy. Above her head, time slipped by and Tsían and Miros murmured meaningless things to each other, as if she couldn't hear.

"What is it? It's not like any rock I've ever seen."

"But it's familiar, right?"

"Miros, I'm not in the mood for guessing games."

"You see this every time you see your dragon's mouth."

"It's a dragon's tooth?"

"Part of one. Cut down, harnessed, and tuned to snap the very things it came from."

"But it only scratched her a little bit."

"It's not meant to cut physically. It's meant to cut psychically."

"Can it be fixed?" she interrupted them. "I can't live without Windward. Where is Windward?"

Miros continued to rub her back. "I know. I know how it hurts."

"I'm going to die without him."

"I know. Like someone took a big chomp out of you, right?"

She nodded. His understanding calmed her, but still didn't make her feel better. Nothing could make her feel better again—nothing but Windward. "Like there's only pieces of me left, loosely connected."

He nodded too. "Not enough to function. Not enough to call you."

"Every movement is agony. Every motion makes me want to get sick all over the rocks."

"It's the worst pain you'll ever feel, my girl."

"Miros, what's going to happen? I wanted to send you to the Monks of Annularei, to say goodbye. Am I going to have to go too? *Where is my dragon?*"

Roaring shook her, trembling in her head. She blinked. Was she going insane, like Miros? "How are you managing to stay lucid?" she asked.

Tsían snorted. "Oh Palon, he's been far from lucid. But then, you haven't been sane either."

"I have the tooth," Miros said. "Well, I don't. I gave it to Tsían."

"No one else is getting hurt today," Tsían said. "We'll figure this out. But what are we going to do with the two of you? What am I going to do with Laetiran?"

Windward burst into view in a flurry of purple grey scales, and Palon wept, for in all the years they'd been bonded, he'd never been able to sneak up on her. Stone Eyes whirled to confront him, scales hissing on the stone. Snaking low and skidding, Windward threw himself to the side, diving under Stone Eyes' wing. The bronze dragon twitched as if to block Windward with a tail swipe, but the movement knocked all three bonded to the ground.

Stone Eyes struck Windward several times, nipping his neck, shoulder, and side. Whistling, Windward stubbornly slithered forward, his belly scraping the floor as Stone Eyes roared. Someone was whimpering again, the crying and roaring and whistling all combining to form a truly awful sound. Someone was sitting on her too, and she couldn't shove them off, especially with her bad arm.

The weight left. She didn't know why, didn't care. All she could see was Windward galloping to her. Then, scales all around her. Wonderful, warm, musky scales, smooth and hard and soft and beautiful in their purplish grey color. Windward's tail coiled around her in great loops and his body curled around that, his neck completing the loops. His head was right next to her, staring at her with his massive, intelligent, beautiful eye, wide with stress and agitation. His wings were extended over top as a canopy so that she was in a cocoon made of Windward, the best place in all the worlds to be.

And still she got little comfort. Agony filled her, though all her senses seemed dulled to the outside world. She felt so mangled, ripped to pieces. And the keening continued. She couldn't stop it. Windward thrummed anxiously deep in his throat, and the whole world was full of mourning and despair. And the question remained: How had this happened?

She couldn't stop shaking, and she went from wall to wall in her dragon cocoon, stroking the scales and hugging the coils and wetting everything with her tears and the snot dribbling from her running nose. She couldn't stop moving, and moving hurt so much. She couldn't hear Windward, not truly hear him, only the audible thrumming she'd never heard before from a dragon voice. It sounded like a hoarse scream, with elements of a wounded whine. Not unlike her pathetic whimpers, really.

Words drifted into her cocoon. They swam around her without touching her and she didn't care. She had Windward, but she was separate from him. Hideously separate. It was like having her legs chopped off and hugging those disembodied limbs. Except that would probably hurt a lot less. She didn't pay attention to the words that made it to her ears, because they had nothing to do with her. All that mattered was reattaching her limbs. Reconnecting with her dragon.

"...feed her."

"He won't let anyone near them."

"Miros, don't eat the rocks."

"...can't blame him..."

"...really terrible timing..."

"...Scorch Frost be able to fly again?"

"...better than Aturadin."

Palon closed her eyes and pressed her cheek against Windward's scales. It hurt less than she expected. She must be getting used to the pain. Her cocoon shifted, and Windward roared, and Palon shouted her rage at whoever dared hurt her dragon.

Her cocoon shook. It squeezed her. Her world exploded. She screamed.

Sunlight blinded her, far too bright. Cold wind blasted against her, driving her into the ground. The world was full of sound, far too full. Dragons roared and trumpeted, and bonded shouted. None of that mattered.

Where was Windward?

Behind her. He screeched, twisting to escape the clutches of two larger dragons. Palon ran at them, roaring her challenge. All around her dragons were bugling and blasting out challenges, drowning out hers. Windward dropped, galloping through the chaos to her, and all she wanted to do was be surrounded in his embrace once again. She needed her dragon cocoon, needed to merge with him to be whole.

But she did not recognize those dragons.

Windward skidded around her as the dragons galloped by, veering to avoid them. Palon blinked, suddenly aware of how much danger she'd been in. She hadn't even thought about it.

Five unfamiliar dragons faced off against the dragons and bonded of her nest. Palon leaped up, clutching Windward's elbow and pulling herself up further, climbing her way to her seat. She didn't have a harness, nor instant communication with her dragon, but she was not going to lie down and wait while this storm passed by. She needed to know what was going on.

Windward lashed his tail, rising and stalking forward with his neck spines bristling. He held his wings awkwardly, half out and stretched forward, and Palon realized belatedly that he intended to catch her if she fell. She smiled, patting his scales and sniffing as sudden tears sprang to her eyes again. So many tears in such a short span. She needed to get a hold of herself.

The strange dragons had bonded astride them. She hadn't noticed that before—what was wrong with her? More and more bonded from her nest were harnessing up and climbing onto their dragons to confront them. She looked around, but didn't see Aturadin and Scorch Frost, nor Laetiran and Fired Sand. She shivered, hoping nothing was going on between them. Her chest ached, knowing she couldn't protect Aturadin should he need it. She was too wounded.

She forced herself to focus on the issues directly in front of her, glaring at the strange bonded and their strange dragons framed between Windward's horns. They were far away—the whole world was, even the dragon she rode.

Tsían was shouting. Forest Blaze stood in front of Windward, and Tsían perched behind his dragon's horns, his back straight and head high. "Why have you invaded our territory? This nest is *mine!*"

"*MINE!*" Palon shouted with the others. Even maimed as she was, the territoriality still pounded within her, though it was dead now, no longer thrumming between her and Windward.

The dragons rumbled, their own conversation an undertone to that of the bonded.

The bonded who sat astride the foreign dragon closest to them leaned forward, face stern. "You have something that endangers all dragonkind. We felt it—the enemy of dragons! We come to kill it."

Her crystal. Revulsion filled her. She didn't want it now. How could she have been so stupid? She had brought this on her nest, and her nest was far too weak right now to defend itself. Humiliation and guilt burned within her, eating her from the inside. She should have listened to Aturadin's warning. Now, she had to find a way to fix it before her mistake doomed everyone she loved.

"We felt it too, when it...activated. We are dealing with it," Tsían replied, and Palon bowed her head against the rush of relief that he did not implicate her.

Even so, the other leader's dragon stepped forward, his gaze on Windward. The other nest's leader also focused on her, and she shivered. Windward rumbled beneath her, and she stroked his scales, wishing she could feel what he felt, wishing they could comfort themselves by comforting each other again.

The stranger snapped his gaze back to Tsían. "What is this abomination? Surely your dragons can sense the broken bond between these two as well as ours can!"

"We just learned of the enemy of dragons. This is the result. Can the bond between them be reformed?" Tsían asked.

The leading dragon took another step forward, and Palon fought the urge to cower.

Windward crouched, but flared his wings too, rumbling a warning. His pose was conflicted, part submission, part aggression. She'd rather be the aggressor. Palon pulled herself up, climbing further up from neck spine to neck spine, hating the way Windward tensed as she moved. It was terrifying, how he no longer could predict her motions, to move in sync with her. Reaching his head, she clung with one arm to a horn.

"Is she insane, as when a dragon dies? Not only is she riding a dragon, but without a harness?"

The stranger's derision made her bristle. "Windward won't let me fall!"

"Palon, get down from there," Tsían snapped.

She wrinkled her nose. If her bond was broken, was she really Tsían's responsibility anymore? She didn't like the idea of meekly giving in in front of the foreign dragons. And yet, the nest was for dragons and their bonded. If she wasn't Tsían's responsibility, she no longer belonged.

A sob broke from her at the thought, and she crouched down, hugging Windward's horn tightly. Her arm blazed with pain at the pressure. The air rushed past as Windward lowered his head further.

"So, that answers that question then," mused the foreign leader.

Palon bristled.

"We're handling it," Tsían said again.

"Not well enough."

Tsían puffed up, a rattling challenge emanating from Forest Blaze as well as from Stone Eyes. They stepped forward with wings flared and neck spines bristling, Forest Blaze only a step behind Stone Eyes. The strange dragon retreated, reluctance in every movement, and Palon bared her teeth at the success of their nest.

"Destroy the enemy of dragons," the leader snapped. "We'll fly back through in a few days. If we sense it, we'll come in force."

"Stay out of our air," Tsían snarled. The air burst with the sound of Stone Eyes and Forest Blaze trumpeting and roaring their territoriality.

As the leader and his dragon retreated further, back to their little group of invaders, he pointed at Palon and Windward. "And put those two out of their misery."

Palon hissed, while Windward rumbled a threat she felt in her bones. The foreign five turned, galloping off the ledge and launching themselves into the air. Stone Eyes and Forest Blaze advanced as they retreated, bugling. The foreign dragons circled, belching flames before winging away.

Hiding her discomfort and vulnerability behind a sneer, Palon watched them go. Forest Blaze walked back toward his basking place, pausing by Windward. Tsían looked up at the sky, following Palon's gaze. "Rude," he grumbled.

Then he looked at her. "Get down."

Palon's arms tightened on the horn beside her. She didn't want to go. Her arm shot blinding pain through her as she clung to Windward, and her head spun.

"Palon!"

The horn dipped, Windward's head falling away. The world moved around her, and she was caught in something broad and flat, both hard and soft at the same time. It crinkled around her, squeezing her against purple grey scales. She was enveloped in Windward's wing, and she pressed her face to him, smoothing her hands down his scales. There was a commotion outside, but she didn't care. It had nothing to do with her.

"You're not supposed to be in here." Tebah's high, shrill voice jolted Palon awake. "I've told High Flight! Salann and Tsían will be coming."

Palon opened her eyes, squinting. The harsh glare of a lamp approached. That didn't matter though—not next to the knowledge that her dragon cocoon no longer surrounded her. She needed to get back. She tried to sit up, unsuccessful.

Thick leather straps bound her to a board under the mats she was laying on. She thrashed against them, fighting the restraints. They held tight, biting into her wrists, elbows, across her chest and waist, just above her knees, and again at her ankles. She was blocked from her cocoon. Where was Windward? Lips curling back from bared teeth, she looked around wildly, rage and frustration building in her. She was in the Wounds Cave. Why had they removed her? What right did they have to keep her from Windward?

Hot oil dripped on her shoulder and she hissed, pain snatching her back to the moment. Bound, helpless, immobile. The lamp swung away, splattering more oil nearby. Palon blinked as Tebah shoved Laetiran, standing between him and Palon.

This was wrong. Palon should be stronger, shouldn't need help, especially not that of the newling. Needing Windward was one thing —he never let her down, and he needed her just as much. But leaning on others, especially a newling? That was weakness. Tebah didn't deserve this, to have to try to protect Palon when Laetiran terrified her.

"Oh, no," Laetiran said. "My apologies. These lamps are quite dangerous, you know. And in this room, full of flammable cloth... quite a fire hazard. Why, should one tip over, Palon and Aturadin would be trapped."

"Get out!" Tebah screeched, her words cut off as Laetiran pushed her. She careened into a wall and crumpled, the sound of her panicked breathing filling the air.

"Laetiran," Palon growled, gritting her teeth against the agony of her shoulder. She wouldn't let him see how much he'd hurt her. But she knew he already knew. Sweat had broken out on her face, and she trembled, covering it by thrashing against her bonds.

"Oh, careful now. You could upset the lantern. As we've already seen, that would be most unfortunate, especially at such a time." Laetiran set the lantern down beside her foot.

She stilled, breathing hard, fighting to keep calm. There was a way out of this. She just had to find it. She glanced around more carefully, really looking this time, and her blood ran cold. Aturadin lay on the next mat over, eyes closed, a sheet pulled up to his neck. Tebah curled into a ball, sobbing. Fury raged, and Palon gritted her teeth.

"Leave her alone." The lantern's heat quickly became uncomfortable, but she tried not to think about it.

"I'll leave you all alone if you stop fighting me. None of this would have happened if you had just been reasonable. Fired Sand and I deserve the better basking ledges." Laetiran sauntered to Aturadin's bed.

"You deserve a broken nose," she growled, even though the threat was clearly empty.

"So much misery. Your accident, Aturadin's accident—you two are very unlucky, you know. And Miros soon to be released to the Monks. And then that Tebah." He smirked. "The nest teeters on the brink."

She understood in a flash of clarity. The only thing holding him back would be his tenuous appreciation of how that might destroy the nest. It would just matter which he decided to care about more. Palon gritted her teeth, blinking sweat from her eyes and struggling to focus on anything but the pain of her shirt melted into her shoulder and the intense heat next to her foot. She kept her gaze locked on Laetiran. She had always faced her future with eyes wide open, and that would not change now.

Her stomach turned. There was no roar. That scared her more than anything, that reminder of how very alone she was. Windward should have felt her pain, her worry. And yet, no dragon roar echoed in the caverns. Her bond was still broken. She could not feel Windward.

Laetiran jabbed his fist into her sleeping mate's side. Aturadin hissed, eyes snapping open, growing wide and wild with pain. One eye was bloodshot, and the sheet covering him slipped as he lurched upward, revealing numerous purple and black bruises mottling his brown skin. Aturadin's beautiful face with its open features was swollen, his lips split, his fine fingered hands puffed up and useless. Bandages bound his ribs tightly—had Laetiran punched him in an already broken rib?

Tebah screamed.

Rage grew in Palon, along with a desperation to protect what was hers, especially while Aturadin was so clearly injured and Tebah was frightened nearly out of her mind. With a hiss, she slammed her wrists against their bonds, and then abruptly went still as the lantern rocked. Her vision darkened as her arm protested, and she turned, vomiting onto the ground.

Aturadin's wheezing echoed in her head.

"No!" Tebah lunged forward. Laetiran spun toward her, and she ducked under his arm, tripping and tumbling into the lantern. Oil spilled everywhere and Palon gritted her teeth, struggling to keep conscious through the pain.

Tebah sobbed, pushing at Laetiran as she stomped out the blooming flames near the bed where Palon was tied.

"Tebah, let me out! Put out the lantern!" Tears of frustration pricked her eyes as Palon slammed at her restraints, sickened to think this might be her end. Laetiran had been right after all—she was weak, unworthy of being dragonbonded. She couldn't even protect herself, much less those she cared for. She didn't even have a bond anymore.

"What is going on here?"

At the sound of Salann's voice, Laetiran hurried to help put out the flames and right the lantern, though Tebah pounded at him with her fists, tears streaming down her face.

"Tebah had an accident with the lantern, but they've clearly turned her against me. I'm just trying to help," Laetiran explained as Salann entered the cave.

"You were not supposed to be anywhere near here, Laetiran. Get out, now!" Salann snapped. Shoulders slumping, Laetiran left with a wounded expression. Palon shook her head, emotions raging inside her like the winds of the Airstream.

"You should never have left her here alone," Palon shouted. More civil words stuck in her throat, all sense of manners ripped away by the burning in her shoulder and ankle and the great hole in her heart, drowned by the terror and wrath of being defenseless.

Tebah froze, shoulders hunching and lip quivering. "I tried!"

She was doing it again, driving the girl away. She had to be better. "Tebah, it's not your fault. No one could expect you to stand up to Laetiran."

By the anger and hurt on Tebah's face, that hadn't been right either. Frustrated, Palon redirected her focus. "Salann, let me out! I need to check on Aturadin."

"You'll run back to Windward. Calm down." Salann turned, rummaging among the medical supplies, too slow.

Palon glared at the newling. "Tebah! Let me out!"

She shook her head. "I have to follow the hierarchy. You told me that."

Dragonfire, of all the lessons for the girl to learn. Aturadin was hurt, and she couldn't check on him, and she needed to do *something*. "Tebah!"

She fought her bonds until nausea rose and pain blazed through her body, especially in her arm and her ribs.

"Palon, if you don't calm down, I'll sedate you," Salann said sternly. "Let me look at your burns. Tebah, put that lantern away."

It was too much, them fussing over her while she was tied down, unable to do anything. She turned to look at her mate instead, but his eyes were shut once again.

"Aturadin," she said, her voice thick.

His eyes fluttered open.

She smiled brokenly. "Aturadin, what happened?"

Salann rubbed the salve in, ignoring Palon's hiss of pain, and wrapped her ankle in a bandage. "Laetiran was supposed to be raking out the Nesting Cave. I had to run to another dispute before it turned into a fight. We've had enough of those."

Palon glared at her. "You should have been more careful. Laetiran could have killed Aturadin! You all should have been more careful not to let him in here."

Moving to her shoulder, Salann smiled. "Still lashing out when angry?"

She was messing it all up again. She struggled to beat back tears.

Aturadin's voice was hoarse, even after sipping from a cup Tebah gave him. "I confronted Laetiran. The nest is divided. Some saw him drop the crystal, and if he had your crystal, he'd raided our stash and could easily have planted the stolen items. But others are further against us because of the crystal. What it is."

More mistakes. She bit her lip. "This isn't how you planned to confront him."

He winced. "Not exactly."

"I'm sorry, Aturadin. He beat you?"

Aturadin grimaced and nodded. "Everyone was distracted by you and Windward, by Tsían and Stone Eyes and Forest Blaze. He was on me before I knew it. Fired Sand attacked Scorch Frost at the same time."

"You've been here since?"

There was betrayal and accusation to his tone, and it stabbed Palon through the heart. "You didn't come to see me."

"My bond with Windward. It's broken." She turned back to Salann, hissing as she tied off a bandage. "How is Windward?"

Salann sighed. "Better than he could be. He's tethered to the ground, to keep him from doing something stupid."

Aturadin glared at her. "I would have come to you."

"You don't know what this is like." Tears spilled from her eyes, and she thrashed her head angrily, unable to even wipe the evidence away. "I feel chopped to pieces, only fragments of myself."

Aturadin narrowed his eyes at her. "Yeah, clearly I know nothing about pain."

Gasping for breath, she stared at the cave's ceiling. She hated the restraints, loathed being trapped. How they must look down on her, to have fallen so far. And she despised herself, for lashing out at Aturadin. She blinked hard to clear the tears. "I'm sorry. Everything happened so fast. I don't remember... Windward was holding me. And then I was here."

Aturadin's lips twitched, even as his eyelids fluttered. He was barely clinging to consciousness.

She sighed, facing Salann and Tebah again. Her skin crawled, that her weakness was being viewed by Tebah, who should respect her, and Salann, whom she admired so. Humiliated, degraded, she pulled at the restraints again, searching for a way out. "Let us go! We need to renew the bond. Bring Aturadin with me. I'm not taking anymore chances with Laetiran."

Salann's black eyes stabbed at her like daggers. "Windward nearly killed you, did you know that, Palon?"

"Ridiculous."

"You're both unreasonable. We had to forcibly separate you, and in the struggle Windward cracked two of your ribs. It could have been much worse."

Palon opened her mouth to retort, but Salann shook her head, her braids flying out behind her. "You are staying in these restraints until we know you will not run right back to Windward."

"You have no right to keep me from him. He'd never injure me on purpose."

"That doesn't mean you won't die, Palon," Salann shouted. "And the nest can't handle losing another bonded, not right now. Scorch Frost and Fired Sand are both gravely injured, Windward is battered, and Stone Eyes is furious with everyone. You thought Tebah's bond was under a lot of scrutiny and pressure? Yours is under so much, hers looks normal."

"I don't have a bond anymore."

Salann shook her head, ignoring her comment.

"Please. Can I have one arm loose?" Palon pleaded.

Salann glared at her. "One arm. But don't push it."

Palon took a deep breath and let it out slowly, shakily. She felt like she was going to jump out of her skin as Salann loosened the restraints, let her draw out her good arm, and then tightened the straps again. "When is Miros's farewell?"

"Three days."

"I want to be there."

Salann raised her eyebrows. "Then you'd better behave yourself."

Aturadin groaned, half conscious, as Salann adjusted him on the bed, and Palon stroked his arm lightly, covering him with the blanket. She rubbed the material between her fingers. Blankets. They felt so strange, now. She rarely needed one, sleeping in a heap with the others. If she got hot, she moved to the edges. If she got cold, she wiggled her way toward the middle. But Aturadin and she were separated from the others now. They had been since Tebah had come, yet she didn't resent the girl for it.

She caught the newling's eye as she hovered near the beds and forced a tight smile. Warmth lit in her heart when the girl responded with a trembling twitch of the lips.

Swallowing hard, she turned to Salann. "Is there any hope for our bond?"

Salann shook her head. "I don't know, Palon. Maybe not. And if there is any hope, it could be a long while."

Palon nodded, playing with the fringe of the blanket. She focused on her breathing, demanding that it be smooth and even. She was dependent on Tebah and Salann for now, however much she hated it. She was weak, and apparently she wasn't completely lucid. Everything she'd worked so hard for was slipping through her fingers, and she couldn't do anything about it.

She distracted herself by staring at her mate. He'd told her to bring the crystal to the dragons, way back when she'd first found it. She should have listened to him. It had broken her bond, and she hadn't been there for Aturadin.

What had Tsían done with the crystal? Could it be destroyed? If the foreign dragons came back and still sensed it, they had implied they'd attack. She believed it. After all, they'd also sensed her, and said she and Windward should be put out of their misery. "Abomination", they'd called her. A broken bond was a small portion of the punishment due her if her fears were true. She wouldn't let the nest suffer for her foolishness. She had to figure out what to do about the crystal, how to destroy it. She had to say goodbye to Miros. And somehow protect Aturadin and Tebah from Laetiran.

And she had to fix her bond, or somehow manage all this while insane, crippled without her dragon.

Laetiran was winning. But she found she hardly cared. Instead, her thoughts were consumed with her weakness, her dependence on others. Her stomach turned that she was reduced to this. How far could she trust Salann? She'd only completely trusted Aturadin before, and look where that had got them.

She stroked the back of Aturadin's hand. "Is Aturadin going to heal?" The words broke from her of their own accord. She felt so alone, so cut off from the world.

"I don't see why not. Laetiran gave him quite a beating, but Aturadin should bounce back. Don't worry, Palon. Tsían's got a whole force organized to investigate your broken bond, and the dragons are even more invested. They will figure it out," Salann said, turning and walking away.

Palon couldn't help but watch with mounting fear, but Salann didn't leave them alone. She stopped in the entrance, leaning against the wall there. Guarding them. She was grateful, and at the same time, she hated it.

Chapter Nineteen

Palon slipped, skidding down the sandy trail for several paces. The wind whipped past her, jostling her. She hissed. Her ribs ached, her arm pulsed with agony, and she couldn't remember why. All she knew was they were going to the Monks. She was going to the Monks, to never again fly. She might as well die.

Salann pulled her back to her feet, and as she caught her balance, her eyes locked with Aturadin's. His drawn expression spoke of pain and weariness, and he supported Miros, half falling at his side. Her stomach knotted. That's right. They were going to the Monks, but not for her. For Miros. She would come back. She would fix her bond with Windward and fly again. Somehow.

The send off for Miros should have been a more splendid thing, but the nest was sullen and suspicious. No one else had wanted to go. Hopefully, Tebah wouldn't make too much trouble for Tsían while they were gone, but she needed to stay close to High Flight for her bond to grow. Blinking to clear her head, Palon drew Miros's free arm across her shoulders, helping to hold him up. A shell of a person holding a shell of a person, but she refused to let go, despite how the journey jumped and jolted, disorienting her. She hadn't been able to cling to his mind, to keep him sane. Thankfully, with her and Aturadin out of the nest under Salann's watchful eye, they would be safe from any ill-advised retribution, at least for a couple days.

The path to the Monks of Annularei was overgrown, being rarely used. Even Salann had trouble finding it sometimes, and they had to backtrack far more than Palon would have liked, especially once the rain began to fall. It wasn't at all as simple as seeing their way from above. They rested far more than should have been necessary. None of them spoke through the humiliation, and they were mostly silent while walking, too focused on keeping their feet and finding their way. She was grateful when the rain stopped, though the cold seemed to seep into her bones. The dragons would curl up and enter torpor soon, and she shuddered. If she couldn't find a way to rebond Windward before then, how could she make it all winter without his presence? This solitude was nightmarish.

Next thing she knew, she was sitting on a boulder, shivering as the pelting rain trickled icy fingers under the lining of her jacket and down her back. Aturadin's face was drawn with exhaustion. Then they were walking again, Miros hanging on her, barely supporting half his weight. She hadn't heard him speak for days. He was thoroughly gone. As gone as her dragon. The abyss inside her yawned and swallowed her.

The sharp rocks stabbed her through her boots or rolled beneath her feet treacherously. It should be easy for a dragonbonded to keep her balance regardless, but Miros was unresponsive even to sudden jolts, and his blind movement forward often ruined her coordination so that she slipped and slid. Even more awkward was balancing his weight with Aturadin or Salann, who was sometimes ahead of her, sometimes behind her, sometimes beside her, depending on the width of the trail at the moment. Weariness soon dragged at her, and sweat slicked her braids and ran down her back. Stubbornly, she refused to show her fatigue, even when blinking sweat out of her eyes, and she was ashamed and grateful when Salann called for another halt.

The sky was growing dark, the horizon a blaze of colors to their right, when the trail opened up suddenly before them. Numerous torches and campfires lit the darkness, surrounding several dark mounds with more firelight glowing along paths between the mounds. Salann let out a sigh of relief, and Palon shared the sentiment. She wasn't sure she'd have been able to make it much longer, though she'd never admit it. Chewing on her lip, Palon looked at Aturadin. He staggered onward with one arm clasped to his side, his eyes fixed on their goal. Palon tightened her lips at his clear fatigue, suppressing the desire to help him. His pride wouldn't stand it, nor would she shame him so. Miros simply walked on, staring blankly ahead. There was no sign he'd even seen the torches.

Their pace quickened as they descended the final slope and finally stepped onto the torch-lit path. From the shadows, soundless Monks materialized around them, hands outstretched to lead them onward.

Palon shook her head fiercely when two of the Monks beckoned her to let them take Miros. She had brought him this far. She couldn't just dump him and run. She'd let him go soon enough, but only when the time was right.

Ever silent, ever placid, the Monks led them onward to the center of the mounds. A circle of flames blazed much higher than they should and cast more light than expected, given the size of the wood pile that was its fuel. But then, these were the Monks of Annularei, and they would have access to dragon knowledge from generations past. A tower loomed over the circle to pierce the sky, its stone base lit with torches. It drew her eye, as always.

It was from that tower that the head monk came to greet them. She struggled to remember his title.

"Dragon's Scale," Salann greeted him with a bow, which he returned. "We have brought to you a former bonded."

That was right. Dragon's Scale. A thing left over from dragons, to care for those left behind by dragons.

"Former bonded, step forward." The Dragon's Scale's voice was harsh and rusty, and his words came forth so muddied they were nearly unintelligible. Fortunately, his slow speech gave Palon some time to process. It would have been easier with Windward working to decipher it too. She drew in a long slow breath, though the calming effect was immediately ruined by a violent shiver.

Miros remained staring into the distance as if he didn't hear, and the seconds stretched on. Aturadin gently took Miros by one arm, and Palon quickly followed his lead, guiding Miros forward to stand in front of the small, hunched figure. He shivered in the cold air. They were all soaked and needed to get warm and dry, but the ritual needed to be observed properly first. She wouldn't disrespect Miros by rushing this.

"What is your name, former bonded?"

Again, Miros didn't answer. Palon swallowed hard around a sudden lump in her throat as Aturadin answered for him. "His name is Miros."

"Former bonded Miros," the monk began, and then his voice softened abruptly. "What was your dragon's name?"

A sob broke from Miros's throat, and his face crumpled. "Silver Spine."

An ache in Palon's chest nearly brought her to her knees, as if something within her broke in response to Miros's pain. In response to his breaking.

The monk's voice remained gentle, barely above a whisper. "Silver Spine's bonded, Miros. Would you like us to help you rest? Would you like to take part in our peace?"

Miros swayed silently, and Palon thought that he wasn't going to answer again. But then he took an awkward step forward, tears making tracks down his cheeks. His hands groped forward almost blindly as he tottered. "Yes."

Two Monks walked forward, catching Miros's hands in theirs, and led him into the shadows. Palon watched until the darkness swallowed him, and then remained there, searching the shadows for any sign of him. Beside her, Salann finished the ritual with the Dragon's Scale, their voices washing over the edges of her consciousness.

Miros needed to go, and she needed to let him go. Even if she hated the finality of it, knowing that she would never see him again. But then, that had been true for as long as Silver Spine had been dead— he'd never truly been back, not since then. She'd never again hear his sage advice on matters of dragons.

"Come on," Aturadin said, pulling her from her thoughts. "He'll be fine."

Palon nodded, turning to offer her arm to Aturadin for support. He smiled at her. "I'm not an invalid, Palon. And that's your bad arm."

She winced, a broken laugh bursting from her. Her gaze drifted back to the shadows where Miros had disappeared. "I'm going to miss him."

"Yeah." Aturadin kissed her forehead and took her hand as they followed Salann and the Dragon's Scale to one of the larger mounds.

"I miss Windward."

"I know. I miss Scorch Frost."

She shot a look at him, stomach knotted. "Your bond..."

He shook his head, but she read worry in his expression. "It's still here. But barely. I can't always hear him, can barely feel he's there. It's been bad since Silver Spine died, but even worse now, with the distance."

She squeezed his hand, suddenly able to completely empathize with how awful that would feel. Everything needed to stabilize back at the nest, but Laetiran was only making more tension, putting the bonds under even more strain. And she was insane, and couldn't do anything about it. He and Fired Sand would move up in rank, past her, and likely pick on Scorch Frost to secure a higher rank than Aturadin. She gritted her teeth, imagining it.

He couldn't get away with it, but what could she do, crippled as she was? She wasn't even bonded anymore.

The inside of the mound was open, the space filled with fires on one side, where the ceiling had a slit to allow the smoke to escape. Benches filled the rest of the area, some laden with food, some with Monks seated on them, eating. Delicious warmth filled the room, and Palon fought the urge to huddle next to the fires.

"Please, share our meal with us," the Monk said.

Salann graciously inclined her head. Palon filled her plate with meat, vegetables, and fruit, then perched beside Aturadin on the edge of a bench close to the fires. A monk set a steaming cup of some sort of drink in front of her and she held it close, sipping slowly. She didn't care what it was—it was warm.

Across the open space, two Monks sat coaching another man on table manners and the uses of knives, and she smiled. The Monks of Annularei took care of all former bonded, either easing their minds among the company of those who understood their pain and madness, or helping them to remember who they were as men and women, not as dragons. Most of them would die here, though some would stay and become Monks themselves to help others. A few would regain the ability to function normally enough to go back out into the land. They would never go back to their old villages, the ones they had left to live with dragons, for there was no space there for them. They might visit, but never to stay. Instead, they would wander, most of their dragon knowledge faded, but dispensing what wisdom remained to them as they could.

It was all an act, though. There was no being normal—no being whole—after losing your dragon. Palon knew this like she knew she needed air to breathe. This place was the graveyard for bonded who had died, because that's what really happened when you lost your dragon. As a dead person herself, she knew. She shivered, not ready to be dead, not ready to be left here to rot in this graveyard. Some way, she'd find out how to renew her bond with Windward and come back to life. There was no other option.

She ate absently, her eyes drawn to the strange supports of the mound. They were massive curved arches, interlacing overhead and then diving back down unbroken into the ground again on the opposite side of the structure. Had the elves made the trees for the supports, bending them as they grew in the way the elves were said to do? But then, how did the Monks come to be here? The supports were dark, with a very smooth bark pattern and striations. On the outside, a patchwork of hides weatherproofed the room. Torches jutted periodically from the supports, though Palon wondered that the Monks felt comfortable with fire so close to the wood. Well, it was their problem, not hers, and given the age of this structure—or at least how old it looked—they had the potential danger well in hand.

"Will you be leaving us in the morning?" one of the Monks asked.

Salann answered, while Palon leaned lightly against Aturadin's shoulder. "Aturadin and Palon need medical attention. We would also like to replenish our medical supplies while we are here, if you can spare some."

"I have a message too, for Faralir in Dragonmoor," Aturadin said, taking a rolled piece of parchment from his coat. A hint of a smile came to her lips. They must have figured out a cure for Tebah's great-mother.

The Monk accepted it with a bow. "We are happy to extend our care to you. Only be warned, we are expecting another former bonded from a different nest as well."

"We will not cause trouble."

"Even so, we would prefer to host bonded of only one nest at a time."

Salann nodded. "We will leave within a few days and be ready at a moment's notice should you need us to return home."

"We thank you for your understanding."

"We thank you for caring for our former bonded."

Palon shivered. So formal, words drawn out, dancing around meanings. She had to get back to Windward. She'd go mad for sure, stuck in a place like this for too long.

The former bonded weighed on her mind. Palon thought about them all through breakfast the next morning and while she helped Salann and Aturadin fill a bag with bandages and salves and another bag with pouches of wine from the Monks. Aturadin moved slowly and carefully, and she was grateful they had some time to rest before returning. They were warm now, and yet she jealously craved more heat, as if some part of her wished to stoke dragonfire deep within her heart.

She couldn't help but watch the former bonded. She was no longer bonded herself. Did that mean she belonged here? But Windward was alive. She belonged with him. She needed him. And yet the muttering, fumbling shadows of their former selves around her loomed like a specter of her future. She scowled and shook her head. She and Windward would go out together, or he would outlive her. That had always been her plan. She would not end up here.

Her gaze kept being drawn to the tower. It called her every time she saw it, each time she had brought a formerly bonded to the Monks of Annularei. With a deep breath, Palon finally decided to answer that call.

"Want to go to the tower with me?" she whispered to Aturadin as they shared a lunch of bread and cheese.

Aturadin furrowed his brow. "You never go into the tower."

"I know. But maybe it would help."

Aturadin raised his eyebrows.

Palon sighed, scowling down at the table. "You knew my crystal was dangerous. I should have listened to you. Maybe we can find out more about it, to destroy it. Those other dragons will be coming back to check. And maybe..." Her throat closed up, and she stuttered to a stop.

"Maybe we can find a way to restore your bond with Windward."

Palon nodded. She was adrift without him, like a sudden breeze might blow her away. It terrified her.

He smiled at her. "Sure."

She threw her arms around him, immediately regretting it as she wrenched her ribs, her arm, and his bruises. Even worse, Aturadin grunted in pain. Wrinkling her nose at herself, she retreated, apologizing. He waved her off. "You promised me books, remember? Let's go."

Her steps were quick, her heart beating with nervous anticipation as they left the mound and crossed outside. In the light of day, mounds spread out in all directions around the solitary tower, some smaller, some larger, all with the same overturned-bowl shape covered by hides. Reaching the plain wooden door at the tower's base, she pulled it open and slipped inside after Aturadin. The dimly lit space was not large, only big enough to hold maybe thirty people. A wooden staircase spiraled upward, disappearing from sight. The walls, floor, and ceiling were plain stone, and simple lanterns hung on crude hooks spaced around the walls.

Palon smirked. Here they worried about fire, forgoing torches for lanterns. She paused, inspecting it. Dragonglass, gifted to the Monks by the nests and formed into something beautiful and functional.

Taking a lantern in hand, Palon followed the staircase, the wood creaking unnaturally beneath her feet. She was glad Aturadin was with her, for unease grew in her as she climbed. Stone never groaned like this. Stone was steady, constant, dependable, like dragons. She continued, her shadow dancing in the light of the lantern, swaying from its ring.

The stairs continued upward, the walls cut at rare intervals with narrow windows, through which the afternoon sky spread above, blue decorated with puffy clouds. A cool autumn breeze passed playfully by. The windows were not big enough or numerous enough to light the tower, though, possibly to limit damage from weather. She paused as she poked her head above the level of the ceiling. Books, sheaves of paper, and boxes of scrolls lined the curved walls on shelves of wood. This place would go up in flames in a moment, given a spark. It was all tinder, contained in a tower of stone.

She shuddered. Fire had never scared her before. She'd never given it a second thought. But then, she'd been bonded to a dragon. Dragonfire was just another thing she had access to, that she could control. Now, she was nothing, a speck of dust to be blown away in passing. She was vulnerable. Palon gritted her teeth.

"Another flight up." Wincing, Aturadin pressed a hand to his side.

Palon frowned. "We can pause here for a while."

"No, this is all boring stuff. Up another level," Aturadin grunted.

Glancing at him repeatedly out of the corner of her eye, Palon resumed the climb, the lantern lighting their path. The next level was much the same, though dustier, and the third level was where the stairs ended, even more dusty than the second level. The stone arched above her in a ceiling, each piece fitting neatly in its place.

"Here we go." Aturadin grinned. "Here's the good stuff."

Palon sneezed as she set the lantern down in a clear space and picked up a pile of papers stacked haphazardly on the floor. A few books, some parchment and loose paper, and some boxes of scrolls were scattered chaotically.

But why hold all this tinder here? Why keep it around?

Again, she shook her head. She was a dragonbonded, or she would be again. Why should she care about the dangers of fire?

Palon looked down at the papers in her hand, staring at the ink brushed so carefully on it by some neat hand. It took her a moment to remember the characters, for dragonbonded had little need of reading or writing. She angled the papers toward the slash of daylight coming in the narrow window.

Aturadin sat down heavily on a box, wincing as he held his side. Palon pretended not to notice, mindful of his pride, even though they were alone here. To take her mind off her worries for him, she threw herself into the task, staring at the writing in front of her. Slowly, she pieced together what someone had apparently felt it necessary to write down for another unknown person to later read. She hadn't read in years and had to read the paper multiple times before accepting that it said what she thought it did.

She hurled the papers away from her. "The supports of the round buildings are made of dragon bones! Ribcages!"

"Hey!" Aturadin groaned, levering himself up to gather the papers.

"Sorry," she said, going to her knees to help him. She shuddered, thinking of the hide-covered mounds.

"It makes sense, though," Aturadin said.

"Why?"

"Well, they're former bonded. The dragons don't need their bones anymore, anyway. Besides, the river runs past here."

"It does?"

"Yeah, see this map?"

Palon peered over his shoulder as he pointed it out. She glanced briefly over the map and then focused on his fingers, smiling as she noted that his hands seemed less swollen than they had been. Luckily, he hadn't broken any fingers.

The wind gusted past and the lantern light flickered. She blinked, the room swaying slightly around her. The rock was solid underneath her, she reminded herself. Rock was solid, like dragons. And yet, ever since losing Windward, nothing seemed quite real.

"Palon?" Aturadin glanced up at her with concern. "Are you ok?"

She wrinkled her nose, dismissing his question. "The idea of living inside the carcass of a dragon... I mean, they must long to be near what they could no longer be close to, but..."

Aturadin smiled. "It's weird, isn't it. Fascinating and creepy."

"Anything about the crystal? Or bonding?" Palon was eager to put the morbid pages out of sight. She cast around for something else.

"Let's see... I believe it was in a book." Aturadin picked up a book bound with a blue cover and flipped through it.

Palon turned away to sneeze, the dust clogging her nose and throat. "Why do they keep all this here? Clearly no one reads it."

"What would you do if you had the knowledge of dragons weighing on your mind?"

"Ok. It's not what I would do, but *you* would write it down. I see."

"The Monks believe all the knowledge they can remember, or that any former bonded can remember, should be preserved. So they write it all down and keep it here."

"They're all former bonded too, right?"

Aturadin nodded.

Palon sighed. "That's... really sad."

What was worse was that this would be her fate if she couldn't prove she was sane. Former bonded went insane and came to the Monks, and some of them recovered enough to become Monks themselves. She shuddered at the thought. She had to be lucid enough to help Aturadin prove their innocence, though Laetiran's claims were growing more outrageous. It was probably the high emotion in the nest, with every bond strained, that distracted the others so they didn't see the truth. At least that's what she told herself.

She pushed the thoughts away, rubbing her eyes and picking up another book. A smile came to her face as she slowly deciphered the words. This was what Aturadin had told her of, way back when they'd been in their cache. An obscure section of Dragon Law. If a dragon harms a bonded, the bonded had the right to retribution. Because of the difference in size and strength, that retribution took the form of trial by combat between each pair: the accused dragon and their bonded against the accusing bonded and their dragon.

Shaking her head, she smoothed the page. How much was lost, that even the dragons had forgotten about? And yet they all held to Dragon Law—at least what they remembered of it. This was the way to beat Laetiran and Fired Sand. But she could only use this if she was bonded again. Shivers overtook her, and her throat closed up. She would never have gotten this far without Aturadin.

They searched a little while longer before Palon reached out and took Aturadin's hand. "Aturadin. I just want to say I'm sorry for... everything."

He smiled at her, taking her face gently in his hands. "Palon, listen to me. I love you for you, and for who you are not. I knew when we decided to be together that I would have someone who would fiercely guard my back, someone who would run into danger at the slightest hint of trouble. You are insane, and you have a death wish, and I worry every time you do a stupid stunt like face off with a dragon that this will be the day I see you die, but I'd never have it any other way. I'm happy to be mated to a woman who will run into dragonfire, even if it also exasperates me."

Palon sniffed, blinking as tears ran down her cheeks, dripping off her chin. "Ok, you're making me leak."

"Ew," he said, kissing her tears. "Gross."

Laughter made her shoulders shake, and she embraced him, holding him a long while. For as long as she held him, it felt like the world was stable around her once more.

"Ok, what's your plan?" she asked once she released him, turning back to the books. "I know you have one."

"Oh yes, I have it all figured out." Aturadin picked up another book, grinning at her. "I asked Tsían to send me and you with Miros to the Monks. It got us out of the way."

"We are not in the way!"

"The trial is putting enormous pressure on Laetiran, and he's cracking."

"I've seen it."

"Laetiran will want to solidify his position as the victim, unfairly targeted by us. With us gone, it gives him a huge opening to do so."

The book dropped from her hands as she stared at him. "Aturadin, that's terrible! He can say anything. We can't defend ourselves!"

"I know," Aturadin chuckled. "I asked Tsían to watch our cache—wherever he hid our collections, as well as the cave we had stashed our stuff in. Yes, don't worry, he's also keeping a sharp eye on Tebah to make sure she doesn't do anything stupid and to make sure Laetiran doesn't target her. She's as safe as she can be with High Flight. Don't worry, Palon."

"I'm not," she grumbled. "Why did you have Tsían watch our cache?"

"I'm pretty sure Laetiran is going to set us up."

"What?!"

"Calm down. Tsían will be watching, right? So if Laetiran sets us up, like I think he will, Tsían will catch him. It'll prove what we've been saying. He's been framing us. There's nothing like letting Laetiran prove our story."

Palon shivered. "Aturadin, you are an evil genius, and I love you."

She grinned as he threw his head back and laughed.

Aturadin returned his gaze to his book, and Palon tried to concentrate on the papers. Pages on dragon anatomy were shelved beside books describing other realms, which in turn were next to a tattered scroll discussing Dragon Law. That scroll she read with interest, though fatigue crept up on her.

The room was warm from the sun spilling along the stonework through the slit window, and before long, Palon just curled up next to Aturadin, watching him read. He was better at this anyway. The angle of light seemed to jump forward now and again, but she dismissed it, focusing instead on Aturadin's shoulder, solid beneath her cheek.

"Now you're creeping me out," he said. "I can feel you watching me."

"Good. Hurry up."

"Here," he said, turning to show her the book. She scooted forward, wrapping an arm loosely around him. He pointed at the page. There was a picture of a crystal much like hers, just as he had remembered. She furrowed her brow, reading the page.

"This doesn't make sense," she said. "A dragon's tooth, like Miros said. Cut and tuned to sever bonds, because of something called technomancy? No wonder the dragons call it the Enemy of Dragons. It's a thing of nightmares!"

"Yeah, I don't know what that is, but see here it says these were left in the care of the fae. That'd be why you found it in Stonefield."

"Ok, but how do we destroy it? How did it break the bond? How do we stop it?"

"Oh..."

"Oh what, Aturadin? Don't 'oh' me!"

"We have to get back."

"Why?"

"Look, see? If they destroy it before we undo it, you won't be able to rebond to Windward!"

"But how do we undo it?"

"I found it. Windward's blood needs to touch it next. Your bond will transfer to whoever's blood touches that crystal next."

Palon shuddered, nausea rising at the very thought of bonding anyone else. "Let's go."

They placed the book back where it had been, and Palon picked up the lantern. As they descended the stairs with brisk steps, she resisted the impulse to run, not just toward Windward, but away from the things she'd read. All this knowledge, locked away. Palon replaced the lantern on its hook and suppressed another shudder as she stepped out of the tower and into the late afternoon, pulling the door shut behind them.

Stomach turning, nerves taut, she grabbed Aturadin's hand as they headed back to the mound where they'd eaten. She peeked inside, but it was empty except for a few Monks cleaning up.

If she looked around the landscape, would she see Silver Spine's carcass somewhere out here? Windward would say she was being silly, and she missed hearing him. Even so, she kept her head low, except for when she caught a glimpse of a Monk leading Miros, currently calm and peaceful, into the mound where food was. She smiled. Though she'd miss him, it was still good to see him one last time. He'd be well taken care of here, with people who understood. Former bonded, able to function and help others facing the same difficulty. And based on the tower, the Monks had already accumulated a lot of dragon knowledge over the years. Over the generations, really.

They prowled the area, searching the other mounds for Salann. Palon breathed a sigh of relief when she heard Salann's voice, and she hurried into that mound. She shuddered with distaste, her eyes drawn to the dragon bones that formed the supports. They were obvious now, in hindsight. How could they have ever been anything other than dragon rib bones? And it made sense, it did. She just couldn't help but recoil a bit from them, drawn as they were from a dragon's carcass.

It was almost like stepping inside the body of Windward, and felt morbid. She'd never be able to sleep there. Not with what she now knew.

Salann was checking their supplies as they entered. "Are you two alright?"

"We have to go back right now." Palon bounced on her feet, skin crawling to get away from here, to get back to Windward. Before it was too late.

"What, has the other nest arrived?" Salann frowned.

Aturadin stooped to pick up a pack. "It's about the crystal. We can restore Palon's bond, but only if we get back before Tsían destroys it."

"Do you know how to do that?"

"Of course," Aturadin scoffed.

"He read a book," Palon said, smiling at him.

"Remember, Dragon Law is coming down. We won't have time for mucking around when we get back home," Salann said.

"There will be though," Aturadin said, explaining what he'd told Palon.

"You think Laetiran will plant stolen items in your cache while you're gone?" Salann asked. "We don't have time for your petty games."

Palon shook her head. "We have everything we need now. We know about the crystal. Laetiran has had time to set us up. And we can settle the score with Laetiran once Windward and I are bonded again." Bonded with Windward, as she should be. She could do anything, then.

Aturadin shook his head, his eyes worried. "But Scorch Frost can-"

Palon cut him off. "Scorch Frost is wounded."

"So is Windward."

"Less than Scorch Frost. And I'm less wounded than you. Windward and I are ready for this."

Aturadin shook his head, his lips a flat line. "What if the rebonding doesn't work as we think it will? What about—"

"I trust you. You trust me now." She didn't have time for worries and what-ifs. They needed to get home. She needed Windward. The decision was made, and dithering would only increase the risk that they would all be too late.

Aturadin paused, then nodded.

Salann sighed. "Fine. Let's get all this over with. We're already packed, and if we hurry, we can make it back before dark."

Chapter Twenty

Dark shapes circled in the sky as they neared their nest. Salann hissed and broke into a run up the final two slopes. Bristling, Palon stared at the circling dragons, trying to determine if they were familiar. She hated not knowing immediately. Still maimed, still broken, but soon no longer. She would be whole again. The world would make sense again. Urgency sped her steps, until she realized Aturadin had dropped behind. She started back to him where he leaned with one hand against a boulder, holding his ribs.

He shook his head at her, voice tight. "Go, hurry. The dragons, not ours!"

They were out of time then. The other nest had promised to come back. Even so, she couldn't leave him behind. "Not without you. You'll tell them about the crystal. You'll help me rebond to Windward."

He grimaced. "Give me a hand then."

She squeezed his hand as she hauled him along, her own injuries protesting as she panted her way up the hill. The nest entrance opened before them, and they paused for breath. Above them, the sky was empty of dragons. That couldn't be a good sign. She took a deep breath, focusing. Deal with the other dragons, rebond Windward, destroy the crystal, deal with Laetiran.

It sounded almost neat when she laid it out like that. Almost like it could work.

Palon's shoulders were tense, her every nerve taut as she tried to stop herself from second guessing all her decisions. She sorely missed her extra senses—dragon senses—and despised how vulnerable she and Aturadin were.

"There they are!" someone shouted as they stepped into the tunnels.

Palon froze, half crouching as adrenaline flooded her body. She couldn't see yet with her sun dazzled eyes.

"Secure them!"

That was Laetiran's voice, and Palon bared her teeth, widening her stance and finding Aturadin's boot right next to her own. She shifted to step in front of him and blinked rapidly, trying to help her eyes adjust. They would not have another chance to hurt Aturadin, not without going through her first. He'd suffered enough for her.

"What's going on here?" That was Salann's voice.

Palon held her breath and strained her ears, trying to pinpoint her location.

"They are thieves—they stole from Fired Sand. We won't accept it," Laetiran protested. "They will face justice."

There was a pause before Salann spoke, her tone careful. "Did they really? They've been with me the last days."

"It must have been before they left," someone said.

"Have you told Tsían? This is very serious," Salann said.

Laetiran's voice was tense with anger. "We'll tell him as we bring in the thieves for justice. He can't deny us. They clearly won't stop until they are made to."

"There are other dragons here, Laetiran. This is not the time," Salann said.

The interior of the cave was becoming clearer as her eyes adjusted to the lower light levels. Laetiran and two others stood confronting them, all brandishing knives, little more than an arm's length away. Palon hissed.

"Get them!" Laetiran's eyes went wide. He must have realized his edge was diminishing as their vision adjusted.

"Stop! Put down your knives!" Salann's voice echoed off the rocks. To Palon's surprise, everyone stumbled to a halt.

Laetiran's voice took on a pleading note. "We have to keep them contained."

"We will go to Tsían, all together," Salann said firmly. "Right now."

There was a wariness to Laetiran's expression, but he nodded. "Good," he said. "Let's go then. Make sure those two don't flee."

Salann glared at the other two. "Don't hurt them. We are certainly not going to squabble amongst ourselves while foreign dragons threaten."

Palon kept close to Aturadin as they walked. The hair on the back of her neck prickled, and she glanced at the others, their expressions nervous and determined. Laetiran's friends were not bad bonded, just those who tended toward dissatisfaction. She'd never considered them a danger before, but they'd never been friends, either. Laetiran must have been hard at work gathering support while they were gone. And yet their capture hadn't quite gone as Laetiran would have expected: they hadn't had a chance to rough them up. A small win.

She glanced at Aturadin. His expression was calm as he hurried along beside her, but there was a tension around the edges. It did not help her feel more optimistic.

She didn't say anything, not wanting to provoke Laetiran or the other two who'd fallen to his foolishness. Even so, as they walked, Laetiran appeared to feel more confident, at one point turning to sneer back at them.

"Time for reckoning is coming. You won't get away with this, I promise," Laetiran growled.

Palon almost laughed. They wouldn't get away with it? There was nothing to get away with. Laetiran was the one lying and misleading everyone and provoking normally sensible people to violence. She refused to be baited though, lifting her chin as she caught Aturadin's lightning fast glance at her. She'd decided to trust his way, and so far everything was going as he'd said it would. She'd messed his plan up enough—from now on, no more mistakes.

"Everyone is meeting in here." Laetiran gestured, stopping beside the entrance to the Meal Cave. Almost immediately, one of Laetiran's allies shoved her hard in the back, sending her stumbling forward. She turned to catch Aturadin, worrying for his ribs.

"No need for violence." Salann's expression was stern. Regardless of where she stood on the thefts, she would insist on decorum around the other nest. In that, she and Tsían were very similar.

Laetiran's face darkened with anger when he caught Palon's eye. He shoved his way forward, and she pulled Aturadin out of his path as he stomped past. Looking around, Palon's stomach turned to see that everyone was looking at them. The open space was filled, with a clear simmering tension as most of her fellow bonded kept careful eyes on the foreign bonded, who clustered together with ready postures. Meals were laid out on the benches, and more bonded were eating at one time than Palon could ever recall seeing before. Eltavae paused from scouring pots to watch, her eyes flickering back and forth between them.

"What is that abomination still doing here?" the leader of the foreign dragons spat, standing up and pointing at her. Palon pressed her lips together to avoid baring her teeth at him.

"What's going on?" Tsían asked, pushing himself up from the table where his meal lay half-eaten. He wore his riding jacket, but the closures at the top were unhooked. He must have been giving a nod to informality.

"Did you completely disregard my warnings, Tsían?" the foreign leader asked.

Tsían stilled, looking at the other man. "You lead your nest as you and your dragon wish, Kessan, and I will do the same with mine. Your bluster was noted."

The foreign leader stepped back from the bench, eyes narrowing. There was a rustle as the other foreign bonded followed, gaining a clear space around them. Space to fight in. No dragonbonded would let a challenge like that go from a bonded from another nest. Especially not leader to leader.

"They stole from my dragon this time!" Laetiran's face was red with rage, and his finger shook as he jabbed it at Palon and Aturadin. "I won't tolerate it, Tsían! Fired Sand and I demand justice."

"It's justice you want?" Tsían asked.

Palon disregarded them, focusing most of her attention on the foreign bonded, those who'd threatened her nest. She longed to be able to talk to Windward, to know what the foreign dragons were doing while the standoff simmered among them. And Laetiran was only heightening the tension, his tantrum surely embarrassing Tsían. Her eyes flickered to their leader, the hair on the back of her neck prickling at the stony expression on his face.

"Of course!" Laetiran exploded. "They've been harassing me, smearing my good name, and now stealing from my dragon? What outrage do they need to commit before you finally do something about it?"

Palon fought to keep her expression still. Dragging Tsían's name through the mud, insinuating he was unable or unwilling to do his job, in front of a group of other bonded? This could not end well.

"Oh, I'll do something about it, never fear." Tsían walked forward, his eyes fixing on their packs. "Gifts from the Monks?"

Salann nodded. "Here, Palon, give me your pack."

Palon shrugged her way out of her pack and handed it over, then took Aturadin's pack from him. Salann opened each pack and gave them to Tsían, who looked through the packs thoroughly, emptying them item by item onto the nearest table. She gritted her teeth at the show of distrust, at being regarded as suspect even for a moment longer. Aturadin gave her a glance, and she pressed her lips together, determined not to make her thoughts audible. She took his hand, hoping he could read her actions, to know she was with him.

"Nothing stolen in there," Tsían declared, handing them to Yiyin, who scurried to put them away. Tsían looked around, too slow, too at ease, and Palon's tension mounted. Why the show?

"Of course not, do you think they're stupid?" Laetiran spat.

Palon crooked an eyebrow at him. Did *he* think *they* were stupid?

The foreign leader pounded the table with his fist. "That abomination has no place here. She should have been left with the Monks. A dragon nest is exclusively for dragons and their bonded."

Palon glanced at Aturadin again, but his gaze was fixed on the scene before them. Surely this was more chaos than he'd planned for. She held herself still, refusing to give in to her impulses. She had to trust in the system, rather than trying to fix it by herself. Doing things alone, her way, had only made things worse.

"Tsían, we discovered something about the crystal. Did you manage to destroy it?" Aturadin asked. Laetiran glowered at him, and Palon stepped between them, staring a warning at Laetiran.

Tsían spoke slowly, his tone careful and touched with suspicion. "Not yet. Forest Blaze was about to blast it with fire."

"No!" Palon and Aturadin shouted at the same time. Her heart leaped to her throat, strangling her. She couldn't lose her one chance to repair her bond with Windward. Not when she was so close.

"Not yet," Palon added, seeing the fierce look the foreign bonded, Kessan, gave them. "We can fix my bond, but only if the crystal is intact."

Tsían raised his eyebrows, then looked back at Kessan. "Care to witness this?"

The other leader crossed his arms. "I'll witness your folly. And then I will take the crystal and root out the dragon traitors."

Tsían smiled broadly. "Brilliant."

The way Kessan's mouth opened and he hesitated was amusing, but laughing would only make things worse. She smothered the impulse and hurried after Tsían into the tunnels, giddy with hope. It was difficult to remain at Aturadin's side, helping him along, for all she wanted to do was run to Windward. But she refused to leave Aturadin when he looked so exhausted—not with Laetiran there, even if there were witnesses. So she reined in her jumping nerves and her eagerness to see her dragon, and wrapped an arm around her mate, pulling him forward step by excruciatingly slow step.

"Don't worry," she told him. "We can do this while you stand next to Scorch Frost, ok?"

"I'd rather not be close by, just in case," he said. "No offense, but I really don't want you accidentally bonding my dragon. It's not like we've done this before."

She shuddered. "No thanks. Ugh. Aturadin, make sure it's Windward, please!"

He grinned. "I think it'll be best for you two to be in the middle of the basin and everyone else watching from around the edges, as far away as possible. This is between you and Windward. You'll have to hold the crystal. Remember, you just need a little blood."

"What are you two plotting now?" Laetiran grumbled.

Palon kicked Laetiran's foot away before he had a chance to stumble into them, and swallowed hard, pushing down the fear that flared inside her. She strove for the outer confidence Tsían wore.

Tsían looked over at them. "I informed Forest Blaze of your intentions to clear a space. He isn't sure the crystal will work to reinstate your bond, Palon. You might need to temper your expectations. Even if it could work, he wants nothing to do with the crystal—none of the dragons want it near them. I would not be surprised if Windward is unwilling to risk this, and Forest Blaze will not force him."

Palon flashed a smile at him. "Don't worry. Kessan will have a story to bring back to his nest."

They couldn't fail. If Windward wouldn't even try... Her stomach knotted tighter at the thought.

The foreign leader grumbled under his breath, moving away from her. Tsían cautioned her with a wave of his hand. "Don't provoke him, please."

Trembling despite herself, Palon walked out into the basking basin under the watchful eyes of every dragon in the nest. Not just familiar faces, but also several unfamiliar dragons from Kessan's nest. She dismissed them all, her breath taken away by Windward standing in the middle of the basin, empty space extending all around him. He trumpeted, seeing her.

Letting go of Aturadin, she ran to him, and in a flash he had curled around her, tail, neck, and wings, folding her up in a cocoon once again while she clutched his foreleg.

"Windward, we can bond again!"

He whistled, and she could hear his hope and fear. She grinned, patting him. "I know! But let me go so we can do this. Then we'll be together again, whole again."

Slowly, his scales slid past as he uncoiled, and Aturadin was standing there, looking bemused. Brow creased with worry, Tsían pulled the crystal out from a pocket in his jacket.

Windward hissed at it, flaring his wings and lashing his tail. Palon leaped onto his forefoot, patting his leg. "You have to cut yourself with it, Windward!"

He hissed again, backing up a step, and she tumbled to the ground when he moved from underneath her. Palon picked herself back up, grabbing the crystal from Tsían. Her stomach turned as he and Aturadin hurried away, while Windward gave a low rattling hiss. She didn't need the bond to know he hated the crystal, hated it and was terrified of it.

"Enemy of Dragons!" Kessan shouted. "No dragon will have anything to do with that thing. It is foul, belonging to those who would dare torture us, steal from us."

"Like Palon?" Laetiran asked, and Palon shot him a look.

"No, this is much worse," Tsían said. He started forward abruptly, shaking his head. "No, this was a mistake. We must destroy it."

"As I have told you," Kessan crowed.

Palon looked at Windward. "Windward, this is our chance. Aturadin believes this is how it works. You have to cut yourself with it."

Windward bellowed, and his lashing tail sent pebbles flying through the air. Palon glanced at Tsían as he took cover, her heart pounding. She kicked the crystal to her dragon, her hands curling into fists. "Don't run from the fear, Windward! Don't leave me!"

Windward whistled, the shrill, high pitched noise piercing straight through her. Palon's nails bit into her palms as her fists clenched. It was now or never. If Tsían grabbed the crystal again, he'd destroy it and she'd be separated from Windward forever.

She snarled. She refused to accept that fate. She needed him, because together, they were stronger. Just as together, Aturadin and she had discovered how to set the nest to rights.

Palon snatched up the crystal, her fingers cramping and fighting her demands. Windward backed up, lowering his head, snaking his neck back and forth, his jaws partially open. She stalked right up to him.

"Are we going to do this? Are we going to bond again, or are you happy to be apart?"

He hissed, his breath blowing past her, and she shut her eyes, leaning into it. When he stopped his exhalation, she stumbled forward, caught off guard. She held up the crystal, trying to ignore the buzzing in her head, the clenching of her fingers.

"I know it's scary. I hate it too. But I hate the idea of continuing this broken existence more. I want to be whole again, Windward. We can make the other nest go, make our nest strong again so they never come back. Together."

He lowered his head all the way to her level, gently butting against her. She laid her cheek on his nose scales, stroking them with one hand while keeping the other extended with the crystal, as far away from him as she could reach. Tears leaked from her eyes, wetting his scales.

"Please. Please, Windward. I need you. I can't do this alone."

He bumped her with his nose, snorting a blast of salty air.

"Are you ready?" she asked him. He blinked at her.

"Palon!" Tsían strode toward them. If he reached them he would give up on the bonding and destroy the crystal, and they would be separated forever.

She stared at her dragon, eye to eye. "Windward," she whispered.

Gritting her teeth, she slammed the crystal into his foreleg, scraping downward before she could think better of it.

The world exploded around her, fire and ice breaking her bones, devouring her. She was screaming, and something bigger was bellowing, and there was shouting and trumpeting all around.

Her pain faded, Windward's beautiful musk blooming in her mind. The smell of home, the way it felt when all was as it should be. She was whole once again, the enormous emptiness inside of her gone. She sobbed in relief, letting go of all her fears and insecurities like the tears streaming down her cheeks. Her arms clutched Windward's face while the dragon hummed against her, his own relief filling her to overflowing.

Finally, she turned to the circle of watching dragons, laughing. "It worked. I'm dragonbonded again!"

Windward lifted his head and trumpeted, flaring his wings. And as it should be, she not only heard it with her ears, but along her bond, and her legs felt weak, her body trembling with relief.

Tsían grimaced at her, starting toward her again from where he'd paused several feet away. He reached for the crystal, then winced, drawing his hand back. Palon understood—she wanted nothing more to do with it either.

Tsían drew in a deep breath. "Alright then. Dragonfire?"

Palon looked over at Aturadin, who nodded. She grinned at Tsían, holding out the crystal.

Tsían looked over at the visiting leader. "Ready to see how we handle things in our nest?"

Kessan merely crossed his arms, frowning. Tsían nodded, and Palon chucked the crystal into the air as high as she could, immediately racing out of the center of the circle with Windward and Tsían. Around them, dragons belched flame in huge plumes.

The crystal never landed, incinerated by dragonfire. Laughing and crying, Palon hugged Aturadin tightly, then released him to go back to Windward, squeezing his foreleg as if she'd never let him go. She stretched toward him along their bond, thrilled and delighted to discover him stretching toward her too. The bond was weak and distant, but it was there, and Windward had hope that it would strengthen back to how they'd been before. His fears for her, his resolution that nothing should ever tear them apart again, wrapped around her like the warmest embrace.

He also lectured like rolling thunder surrounding her about hiding dangerous—and delightfully shiny—things from him, but Palon didn't mind. She beamed, reveling in the bond regardless of Windward's ranting and the looks on the faces of the foreign dragonbonded.

Chapter Twenty-one

"Look how smug she is," Laetiran screeched, jabbing his finger in her face. She blinked, having been unaware of his approach, and stared at the offending finger. The urge to bite it welled up in her, and it must have shown, for he snatched his hand back, curling his lip at her. "You cannot let her get away with theft, bond or no bond."

"We'll check their cache, as I said," Tsían said, sounding a bit exasperated. "Can't we have just a little time before putting out the next fire?"

"Why exactly does your nest have so many fires, Tsían? Do you need a stronger leader?" Kessan stood beside his dragon, his clear voice carrying across the Basin as he lingered.

Tsían breathed deeply, but otherwise didn't react to the nettling. "Thank you for all your assistance, Kessan. Please, never come back."

Turning on his heel, the leader scaled his dragon. "Tsían, I leave you to your nest." Kessan paused, as if about to say more, but then shook his head and the foreign dragons took off, trumpeting as if to protest.

Palon let out a breath. Finally, her nest was free from that threat for now. Once they were strong again, no foreign nest would come to pester them.

One last threat remained: Laetiran and Fired Sand.

It was hard to remain calm. Palon's instincts roared at her that those she loved were in danger. She stroked Windward's scales. She wouldn't go to Aturadin or take his hand for fear of him being a target again as well, but she couldn't help but peek at him. By his clenched fists, she guessed he was denying himself the same impulse.

Tsían raised his eyebrows at Laetiran. "We've been over this. I don't want another spectacle. Aturadin and Laetiran, come with me.

Everyone else stay here. We'll tell you what we find."

The three left quickly, anger in every movement of Laetiran's stride. She drew a breath. Surely Tsían wouldn't let Laetiran take his anger out on Aturadin while they were gone, right? Pressing her lips together again and patting Windward's snout, Palon tried to calm herself. She wasn't ready to be apart from Windward yet anyway, but now she was fully relying on Tsían and Aturadin. Her fingers twitched and her skin crawled. It was easier when she was risking her life on some stupid stunt.

Fired Sand flared his wings, staring at them. Her skin prickled. Windward shifted, readying his stance, and Fired Sand tossed his head, prodding Windward toward a fight. Windward's readiness for battle filled her, and Palon couldn't help but smile. She'd missed being connected to him so much, even this felt joyous. And this promise of a fight, this physical risk—finally, this was something she intuitively understood. Something she was good at. Stroking his leg, she asked Windward to send a message through Scorch Frost to Aturadin to ask him to bring her harness.

Manic giggles poured out of her. Once again, she could communicate with her mate from a distance, provided their dragons helped. She kissed Windward's scales, unable to stop petting him.

She would do as Miros asked her to: stick to Dragon Law, especially as she'd read it at the Monks' tower.

Windward responded that he had sent the message. He hoped Aturadin would return soon, for Fired Sand was intent on fighting.

Palon sent him her understanding, glee once more filling her as she worked the bond. She needed her harness before bringing the challenge, and Tsían and Laetiran would have to be present. If Fired Sand started a dominance battle before she could bring her challenge, Windward would lose. He couldn't handle two battles back to back.

She clenched her hands, opened them, and clenched them again, nearly jumping out of her skin with anxiety and impatience. Fired Sand bugled at Windward, spreading his wings and stalking toward them. Of course he would try to force Windward to respond prematurely. Tapping her foot, she ran her fingers obsessively along Windward's scales.

Running footsteps in the tunnel. Laetiran burst out of it, holding a large white tooth high above his head. "This is his favorite! And there were more teeth, newer pieces, all in their cache! Do you deny it?" he rounded on Aturadin as he and Tsían stepped into the basin.

Palon breathed a sigh of relief as Aturadin ran to her, carrying her harness. She held the harness as Windward stepped into it, and then tossed the loops over his neck spines. Leaping to his elbow, she pulled herself up as she fastened the buckles.

"Why such a rush?" Laetiran asked. "What did you do to my dragon to rile him up so much?"

Straightening the safety lines, she scowled down at him, irritation filling her. "Fired Sand started it." Too late, she caught Aturadin's grimace and the slight shake of his head.

"He's getting retribution for your acts," Laetiran crowed. "Your dragons are responsible for your thefts, you know."

"And Fired Sand is responsible for you—and his own actions." Palon hauled the harness straps taut, fastening the last buckle.

"Stop." Tsían stepped between them. He looked at Laetiran, gesturing to the bones he held. "I have no doubt those are Fired Sand's."

"See? Stealing again!"

Tsían held up a hand, his face stern as mutters rose from the bonded around them. Palon checked all the buckles, hooking the safety lines to her jacket. She was free now, she and her dragon. They would take on the world if they had to, to clear her name and her mate's. She'd settle this, for the sake of Aturadin and Tebah as well as the nest at large.

Tsían's voice was sharp, his eyes on Laetiran. "What I wonder is how these items, your dragon's, ended up in Palon and Aturadin's cache."

"They stole them," Eltavae shouted from the ring of dragons and bonded. "That's how!"

Laetiran nodded, his lips pulled tight in a fierce grin. Palon glanced at Aturadin, taking a deep breath. This was what he'd set up. Now it had to go as he planned. She could take on Laetiran and Fired Sand, but not the whole nest.

Tsían shook his head. "I have held Aturadin and Palon's collections this whole time. And Aturadin asked me to come to their cache site before they left, to be certain it was still empty. And it was."

The murmuring grew around them, some sounding confused, some outraged.

"So they stole it later!"

Palon looked for the source of the shout, but couldn't tell who it was. Were they still so blind?

"They were in public, either in view of Tsían or myself the entire time after that," Salann said.

Laetiran sputtered, looking around as if for help or escape. "But then—"

"Are you going to accuse Salann or myself of being in league with them next, Laetiran?" Tsían asked, his voice going low and dangerous.

Laetiran paused, his face red.

Palon winced as her bond thrummed with warning. Fired Sand body checked Windward, sending him lurching into Aturadin. Palon leaped over the side, her safety line catching her and swinging her toward her mate. Reaching out, she threw Aturadin out of harm's way, though her bad arm snagged in the line. Black spots danced in her vision, and she sucked in cool air, nearly sagging with relief as the pain drained away.

Windward growled along their bond, lashing his tail as Fired Sand stepped back. Taking advantage of the moment, Aturadin grabbed her at the end of her swinging arc, reaching up on tiptoes, and kissed her. It was one perfect moment in the chaos, and Palon's heart soared, even after he stepped away, back to his own dragon. She smiled even more broadly, catching sight of Tebah safe under High Flight's wing.

As Fired Sand snapped and postured, she climbed back to her perch, careful of her injured arm. It was now or never. She didn't know if this was Aturadin's "right time", but at this point, it had to be.

She lifted her chin and glared at Laetiran. "You stole from dragons. You set Aturadin and me up. You turned the others against us, and furthermore and most obscenely, your dragon Fired Sand targeted me, injuring my arm when he tried to kill me." Palon bit off the words, clutching self control by the fingertips and losing the battle. "I demand retribution. I demand Dragon Law."

"We'll go up to the basking ledges." Tsían's voice was calm, as if they were going to discuss it with the dragons yet again.

Palon shook her head. "I found it at the Monks', and Aturadin knows. Aturadin told you. Ask your dragons. I, a dragonbonded, am asking for retribution against a dragon."

Tsían stilled for a moment, and then his eyes widened. "Are you sure?"

"I accept," Laetiran snapped. "Fired Sand and I will teach you and Windward a lesson."

Palon drew in a breath as Fired Sand charged Windward. That was wrong. The challenge was ritualized for a reason. Laetiran had to be mounted on Fired Sand, since the challenge pitted pair against pair.

The impact shook her, and Windward's claws slipped on the rock as he flapped his wings to keep his balance. Fired Sand reared back, his chest expanding.

"Not before the challenge," Palon shouted. There was a prescribed ritual for such things, to prevent them from being common occurrences. She would hold to that ritual. She would not be the cause for undoing her nest.

Stone Eyes bellowed, and Fired Sand stopped, lowering to his feet. Windward passed the message on to her: If Fired Sand persisted or if Windward responded before the ritual's beginning, that dragon would lose and Stone Eyes would punish him. Such a challenge had not been issued in many generations of bonded, and the dragons were taking it deathly seriously.

There was a moment of relief, though it didn't really make sense. The challenge would still occur, and she wanted it to happen. They needed to settle this. Still, she let out a breath as Fired Sand stepped slowly backward.

Windward lumbered to the center of the Basin, and her body rocked reflexively with his gait. She caught sight of Tebah, clinging to Aturadin's waist in front of their dragons. Such fear and concern! Most of these challenges ended in death, she remembered reading. Often a bonded, sometimes a dragon, occasionally a pair. She didn't mind facing death. She only minded that those she loved feared it so much. There were worse things than death, and she'd come through that too.

She gave them a smile and lifted a hand. If she was going to go out, she didn't want it to be a solemn affair. It should be with a crash like thunder.

An odd calm filled her as Aturadin returned the gesture. With a grin, she made a show of checking the safety lines one more time, tugging on them to be sure they were secure. All was right in her world as he shook his head at her, even if his smile was sad. There was nothing else to fret about. She had brought her challenge, and it had been accepted. One way or another, they would never fight again.

The dragons roared, encasing Windward and Fired Sand in a ring of sound. Windward and Fired Sand rose up and bellowed, the vibrations of Windward's challenge coursing through her whole body as she yelled along with him. Fired Sand flared his wings. Crouched between his neck spines, Laetiran shouted, his eyes locked on her.

Claws scraping, feet crashing onto the ground, dragons roaring all around them, Fired Sand charged.

But this was not a fight for the ground. She knew it instinctively, such that Windward's intentions didn't need to come through their muted and crippled bond. Palon leaned with her dragon as Windward turned, tail lashing behind him. He lurched into a gallop away from Fired Sand. Behind them, Laetiran laughed and shouted, and she flushed at the thought they might think her a coward.

Windward rumbled low. It didn't matter what they thought—what mattered was what was. His thoughts were muted, as if coming from far away during a high wind, but at least some came through.

Palon drew in a slow breath. She would need to pay close attention, even more than normal, to compensate for the weakened bond.

Windward leaped off the landing ledge, opening his wings to catch the wind. They circled almost lazily, gaining height, and Palon grinned as Fired Sand faltered, losing momentum in his surprise, causing his takeoff to be cumbersome.

This was not a fight for *this* sky, either, Palon realized, pressing the idea upon Windward.

"Run away, you coward!" Laetiran's screeching came faintly to her ears through the wind.

She shook her head at him. "I'm not running. You hunted me and *mine*. The most suitable place for this to end is the hunting grounds."

Windward Shifted, and the world lurched around her dizzyingly. Nausea clawed up her throat and she spat out the foul taste in her mouth. She hadn't been ready for that. She should have been ready for that. Windward's concern filled her mind.

Fired Sand and Laetiran appeared below, and Windward folded his wings, diving. This was no time for a fair fight—this was life or death. The bond thrummed with Windward's resolution: Fired Sand would not get another chance to hurt Palon. He aimed for just behind Laetiran, avoiding Fired Sand's horns, using his tail to make minute course corrections as they approached.

Fired Sand rolled to the side, and they plummeted past him, almost within arm's reach. As they went, Laetiran's hand flicked forward. A knife. Palon instinctively ducked behind one of Windward's spines and felt the thunk as something hit it. Her eyes narrowed as she caught sight of the knife falling to the ground below. She'd never found knives very useful in flight, except in coordination with Windward. Was their bond strong enough for such teamwork?

Windward caught the wind and began to rise, only to have to roll to dodge as Fired Sand dove at him, heedless of their low altitude. Their opponent immediately veered around and Palon shouted a warning. Windward turned a moment later than Palon expected, jostling her as he lashed out with his claws.

Laetiran held another knife. The sun shone on it, or she might have missed it, concealed in his hand. Palon gritted her teeth. She wasn't going to let him hurt Windward, especially not when she'd just gotten him back. Swallowing hard, she thought of the last time they'd been able to practice. The maneuver had worked, but not so well as they had hoped against Laetiran and Fired Sand. She had to do something truly unexpected.

Palon unclipped her safety straps. Windward sent her a flood of worry, and she grinned, elated that he had gleaned her purpose from her mind. "Don't worry. You keep Fired Sand busy."

Windward's negative was emphatic as Fired Sand barreled toward him, ready to ram him. She had no safety straps. Either she committed, or the collision would fling her off her dragon's back anyway. He was close, so close she could see the sweat on Laetiran's face.

She jumped.

Her stomach surged into her throat as she fell, with Windward clutching at her along their bond, his whistle of fear something she heard mentally as well as with her ears. His wing reached for her, throwing him off balance, but he missed her, corrected, and grabbed Fired Sand, biting him with a fury she'd never seen before.

And then she crashed against Laetiran. Fired Sand's scales scraped the leather of her riding jacket as she held tightly to her rival to avoid skidding right off the dragon's back. Tears blurred her vision, every nerve instantly screaming at her. This was the wrong dragon, and she hated being on his back, hated touching him. It was wrong, wrong, wrong!

Laetiran slashed at her. Adrenaline thrummed through her, along with urgency. She needed to end this now, so she could go back to Windward, so she didn't have to touch the wrong dragon! She blocked the knife with her forearm, hammering her fist into his ribs. He gasped, his hand opening and the knife slipping away, down Fired Sand's side as the dragon bucked and roared. Windward was fighting him, she remembered, and she lost her grip on Laetiran as Fired Sand twisted and writhed. No safety straps.

Only air surrounded her, and she fell.

Scales approached at blinding speed. She bounced off them and immediately, instinctively, embraced his neck spine, though pain shot through her bad arm. Windward, she knew even before seeing him. Windward had caught her.

The dragon's scolding was loud in her mind, but she couldn't help laughing, even as she rehooked a strap to her harness, then collected the other safety line and hooked that on as well. They needed to end it.

Approval caressing her, Windward turned for the spires of rocks marking the edge of the closest pasture to recreate the move they'd devised for the walavaim. Except now, they would use it on another dragon from their nest, because they'd been pushed too hard. Sometimes a person had to take a stand and say, "No more."

Hopefully they wouldn't bite off more than they could chew. If walavaim attacked as well, they could be in trouble.

Taking a deep breath, she nodded to herself. She had to be as attuned to her dragon as she ever had been if they were going to make it through this. Behind them, Fired Sand gave chase, and above them, dragons circled. Their nest, giving witness to the challenge. Below, the valleys spread, broad and peaceful, undisturbed by the turmoil of the skies.

The spire loomed. Fired Sand was gaining on them from behind. Palon tugged hard on her safety straps. This would test their skill.

Windward hit the spire and turned, switching directions. The rock cracked and fell, but Palon's eyes were on Fired Sand. He was too close! He rolled, presenting his back to Windward's, and Laetiran jumped. He'd released his safety straps, she realized, but then he was on her, clutching at her, slashing at her. Her vision narrowed to blocking that flashing knife, grappling with him as he tried to tangle her in her own lines. She was at a disadvantage, seated with him over top of her, that knife always seeking her blood.

Something hit Windward hard. Her dragon screeched, rage flaring in her. Losing his footing, Laetiran fell, knife aimed to plunge into Windward's side. Releasing a roar she lunged for him, twisting his hand to keep him from harming her dragon. She crashed against the end of her safety straps. He grabbed for her, fingers snatching air a hands-breadth away. Fear shone in his eyes and he grasped futilely for a hold in the empty sky as he fell.

Her stomach turned and bile clawed up her throat. Guilt drowned out the tiny spark of relief that bloomed, for even after everything, he had still been of her nest. He had still been family.

Too late to catch him, Fired Sand screamed, his loss pounding against Palon and Windward's vulnerable bond like a gale against a spiderweb. Palon shrieked in response, clinging to Windward with desperate strength, her world wrapped up in the telepathic chaos. She had killed a bonded of her own nest. She didn't know what she deserved for this, whether it was the wound that would allow the infection to drain, or a fatal blow to her nest. All she knew was that she couldn't lose Windward. Not again.

Fur flashed by her, screams and roars filling the air. Fur. She scrambled up the safety lines as Windward's side curved and bucked. He was caught in a fight, something more than the challenge. The walavaim had attacked.

Two walavaim badgered Windward, while another flew alongside Fired Sand, slashing at his flanks as the dragon sped straight toward Windward. His chest expanded, and Palon gaped. Was he still focused on Windward, despite the walavaim? Despite the loss of his bonded?

Windward dropped, yanking Palon down with him. The spout of flame went over their heads, the burning stickiness falling, chasing them toward the ground. Windward angled, turning again so that he could direct his fall toward Fired Sand, and therefore out of the fiery goop faster. He twisted his neck, shooting flame toward the walavaim that had been after him, rather than at Fired Sand. Palon gritted her teeth and pulled as Windward leveled out, taking her chance to swing herself between his neck spines and onto Windward's back once more.

Fired Sand was on them again, ignoring the singed and enraged walavaim. Palon took a deep breath. They had known this was a possibility. They were skilled at this, they trained for this. Four opponents against the two of them.

Palon grinned. A couple more walavaim and it might be fair, she sent to Windward.

A roar burst from him, his laughter echoing along their bond, and she could feel him regain focus and confidence. Patting his scales, she leaned forward. "Let's finish this and go home."

Tucking his wings, Fired Sand dove toward them, trailing the three walavaim. Gripping the harness, Palon leaned with Windward as he banked, ready for the shudder as one of the felids peeled off to crash against them. He bit at it, and she threw a knife, striking the broad muzzle as the walavai dodged. The impact didn't do much to hurt it, but it did surprise it enough to let Windward blast fire at it.

One down. Palon turned her attention on Fired Sand, where he battled the other two.

Guilt tinged her, though she knew he would pounce on them were the roles reversed. Attending to the bond, she could feel the beginning of Windward's fatigue. Dragons weren't meant for so much flapping, and Fired Sand must be getting tired too. He was struggling against the walavaim, finally resorting to blasting flame at them until they sped away. Fired Sand ignored the fleeing felids, and roaring his challenge, winged his way straight toward Windward rather than rising in a thermal as was normal.

Windward roared in return, banking as Fired Sand reached them. But the other dragon grabbed at them, his talons reaching, reaching. Reaching for the harness. Her blood ran cold. They tumbled through the sky, all semblance of control lost, the two dragons' wingbeats hampered by each other. Fired Sand's fatigue was evident in his clumsy motions, and if they hadn't fought the walaviam, they might have been able to stay in the sky. But as it was, the ground was rushing up at them.

Fired Sand was going for her.

Palon grimaced, unhooking her safety straps again. Windward shrieked at her, his neck reeling back, but she cautioned him to hold on a moment. To time it right. Clinging to his neck spines, she waited.

Scoring a long line in Windward's scales, Fired Sand's talons grabbed Palon's harness. The leather broke. She hopped over it as it rushed past, swept away by gravity and Fired Sand, nearly catching in her boots as it went. Mentally, she screamed at Windward to go upward, picturing the switchback maneuver, hoping the bond could carry her plan.

He surged upward, catching her firmly as he rose, lifting her into the sky. Propelled by Windward's leap, tangled in Palon's harness, Fired Sand fell away. Palon wrapped her arms around a neck spine, shaking with relief. Such an insane maneuver, she could hardly believe it had worked.

It had worked.

Windward wheeled around, relief and exhaustion and the remnants of his panic for her surrounding him. Resting her cheek on his neck spine, she let it all wash over her, sharing the sentiment. Below them, Fired Sand lay where he'd hit the ground. Guilt filled her like an overflowing cup. She'd lost the nest another pair, added to the tension of a nest already walking the edge. Hopefully, she hadn't shattered her home. But they had destabilized the nest with their accusations over and over, and she didn't know which caused more damage.

Her dragon came to a rest on top of a cliff, folding his wings and twisting his neck to look at her. She closed her eyes, just holding onto his neck spine. She didn't really want this moment to end, wanted to delay the reality of the challenge, of the effects on the nest. Wingbeats stirred the air around her, but she didn't move, couldn't face the others yet.

"Palon?" Aturadin's voice was full of panic.

She and Windward had come through. A team, as always.

And they would face anything together, as a team, Windward sent to her. Buoyed by his confidence, she raised her head. Aturadin stood by Windward's foreleg, practically hopping up and down in his anxiety, while Tebah stood nearby, her hands covering her mouth, her eyes huge.

Tebah. Tebah had Shifted for the first time to watch her. Palon closed her eyes for a moment. The girl was trending toward extraordinary firsts.

"Palon, are you ok?" Aturadin asked.

Palon slid down Windward's side. Her legs buckled when she landed, but Aturadin caught her. She winced, her arms and hands burning. Several slashes and scrapes marked her hands, and her jacket was scored with slices where Laetiran's knife had made it past her defenses. She trembled with exhaustion and the remnants of adrenaline. Windward whistled in concern, and she looked at him, wrinkling her nose at the gashes in his scales.

"The challenge is done," Tsían said solemnly, closing the ceremony as she suddenly knew he must. "Windward and Palon are cleared of wrongdoing, and by extension, Scorch Frost and Aturadin."

Palon groaned. It was as eloquent as she could be at the moment.

Tebah grabbed her hand, and she had to stop herself from reflexively shaking her off. "High Flight says it was a good challenge," she said. "He's proud of my flight here, too. This is a whole other world?" The girl smiled at her and Palon was amazed to see awe and pride in her eyes.

"Are you alright?" Tsían asked.

"I'll survive," she growled, demanding strength to her legs. She leaned against Aturadin, glad of his arms around her holding her up, the same way she and Windward mentally held onto each other, holding each other together.

Tsían beckoned to the newling. "Tebah, come here. Salann will teach you while Palon recovers."

"No," Palon said. "She stays with Aturadin and I." She smiled at

Tebah's open-mouthed surprise. "We're family, right?"

"It was a bit of a punishment, tasking you with this," Tsían confessed.

"I know," Palon said. "She stays anyway."

"She may be as irritating as scale fleas, and trouble besides, but we'll overlook that somehow," Aturadin agreed, and Palon had to laugh at the mortified embarrassment on Tebah's face. She tugged the girl closer and slung her arm over her shoulder.

"You sure?" Tebah's face was filled with uncertainty.

"Sure," Palon said.

Slowly, Tebah beamed.

Windward snorted at Palon, asking if the fight had made her soft, and she shoved at him mentally, and then immediately reached for him. Depending on others was how they had finally won.

The wind whipped past, toying with her braids. She drew a deep breath and sighed. She was alive, and she was bonded once again. She couldn't ask for more than that.

Epilogue

Palon grinned as she leaped up onto Windward's side, scaling the harness to gain her perch.

Below her, Tsían's shout chased her. "Palon, be careful! You're still not fully healed."

She waved at him, laughing as his expression soured further. It had already been a month since the foreign dragons came, since she rebonded Windward. Since they challenged Fired Sand and Laetiran. She patted Windward's scales, stretching out along the bond, reveling in the feel of it. It still wasn't as strong as it had once been, much like her broken arm, but both were getting stronger every day.

Eagerness for flight coursed through her veins, rebounding along her bond, echoing Windward's own eagerness, but Tebah was still fumbling with her harness. "Hurry up," she called, laughing.

Aturadin shook his head at her as he tugged on Tebah's safety straps. They still made a point of double checking her riding equipment to minimize the risk. The girl sat with pride, the hooks of her oversized leather riding jacket gleaming. Earlier that morning, she'd worked on polishing her jacket of her own accord while Palon braided her hair for her.

Finally, Aturadin hopped down and moved away, and Tebah shouted something, too far away to hear. She wasn't using the hand signals Palon had taught her. Shaking her head, Palon raised her arm, circling it wide in the air, and waited. She grinned as the girl ducked her head with embarrassment and returned the ready signal.

Windward turned, galloping toward the ledge. Palon whooped, too overwhelmed with joy to hold it in. This was her first flight since the contest, and it was a welcome relief from the days of agonizing grounding. Besides, she'd been looking forward to teaching Tebah to fly. With a surge, Windward sprang into the sky, his claws tucked close to his belly. She closed her eyes, teeth bared, relishing in the feel of the wind rushing past her scales. His scales, her skin. She slapped his side lightly in rebuke, his laughter echoing in her head.

She turned to check on Tebah. A grimace of terror and elation froze the girl's face, her hands clutching the harness. Windward circled over High Flight and whistled, and the other dragon whistled in return.

"How close can we get?" Palon asked. Windward's response thrummed through her as her dragon rose to the test of his skills.

He swerved, looping closer to High Flight, chasing the younger dragon down as he tried to move away. Tebah squawked, glancing up at them, and Palon waved at her, shouting with the joy of the challenge. She sent Windward a continuous stream of what she saw, so he could fine tune his distance and approach, and then, her dragon lazily rolled.

Laughing, Palon passed within feet of Tebah, giving the girl another wave upside down as Windward completed the roll. He immediately dove, looping circles vertically around High Flight and Tebah.

"Show off!" the girl shouted.

Palon laughed, Windward's amusement filling her.

They paused in Dragonmoor, allowing Tebah to stretch her legs and the dragons to rest. Palon helped Tebah climb down, grinning as the girl clung to her. "Fun, right?"

"I don't want to go upside down."

"Tell High Flight that."

Palon chuckled as the girl turned and repeated her comment, hands on her hips. She stroked Windward's nose fondly as High Flight nudged Tebah with exaggerated gentleness.

"Check your dragon, Tebah," Palon said, turning to do the same for Windward.

"Why?"

Palon rubbed her forehead and shot the girl a look. "You don't want the harness to rub, do you? Every chance you get, check your harness. Be aware of every sign of wear, every weakness."

The girl nodded, the joy draining from her face to be replaced by fear. Palon sighed. "Don't be scared, Tebah, be aware. That'll keep you safe, got it?"

Tebah nodded again, her head a smidge higher.

Once Palon had addressed all of Windward's pleas for attention, she nudged Tebah. "Want to go for a walk?"

Tebah paused, looking at High Flight, then nodded. "High Flight says he'll rest for a little while and then we'll go home."

Glee filled her, hearing that word from Tebah's lips. Home. She didn't want to spook the girl by calling attention to it, though, so she just nodded, her strides carrying her quickly over the springy turf of Dragonmoor. The girl caught up to her, and they walked in silence for a while, Palon curving habitually so they would loop around their dragons.

"My village was there," Tebah halted, pointing at a smudge on the horizon.

Palon froze, her breath catching, before forcing herself onward. "Do you want to go back?"

There was only a moment's pause before Tebah shook her head. "No. It's not home anymore. My great-mother got better, but the messenger didn't like me or High Flight. He couldn't wait to leave."

She nodded.

"I'm not leaving High Flight," Tebah grinned, then bumped her shoulder. "Besides, what could beat flying?"

"Nothing." Palon smiled at the girl. "Do you regret it? Bonding?"

Tebah shook her head. "No."

"Truly?"

The girl laughed. "Truly! Tsían told me your plan. I like the idea—imagine me, talking to newlings before they bond, making sure they know what they're promising."

"This should always be an honor. No one should feel trapped into this way of life ever again."

"The other nests might make fun of us, but it'll be worth it."

They continued on, boots stepping lightly over the grass. "Anyway, I can do more here. Learn more. And I want to fly like you one day. The way you were one with Windward, the way you flew!"

Palon laughed. "You still want to be a hero."

Tebah bared her teeth at her before smiling. "Yeah. What of it?"

Chuckling, they went on, past their resting dragons who were sprawled on the large flat stones typical of the region. Tebah leaped off of one of the slabs and stopped, tilting her head.

"What is it?" Palon asked.

"I found something." Tebah crouched, her fingers closing around something obscured by a thick patch of mossy greenery.

Palon's heart thudded in her ears. Surely not another crystal, another Enemy of Dragons? She never wanted to touch another crystal as long as she lived.

Windward whistled, raising his head to look in their direction, and Palon found her palms sweaty. She wiped them on her pants.

"Can I see?"

Tebah cradled the thing close and hissed at her.

Suppressing a smile, Palon crouched low to alleviate the territoriality that held the newling in its grip. "I just want to make sure it's not another Enemy of Dragons."

Slowly, her hand shaking, Tebah extended her arm. A piece of horn, polished by weathering to a gleam, lay in her hand. Palon breathed a sigh of relief.

Tebah's lip quivered, inching upward, and Palon stepped back, smiling. "It's yours. I don't want it."

Clutching it to her again, the girl's expression flickered to worry. "Is it safe?"

Palon chuckled, nodding. "Should be. I'm going to head back to Windward. Put that in one of your pockets for the flight back—I find the inner pockets to be more secure."

She made it several strides before Tebah caught up to her, her hands empty. "Did you set up your cache yet?"

The girl shook her head. "I've been distracted."

"Want help with that?"

Tebah grinned.

Her spirits high, Palon watched Tebah clamber into her seat, snapping on the safety hooks and tugging the straps to check their strength. She nodded in approval, warmth filling her heart at the pride that bloomed in the girl's face, and swung herself into position on Windward. Windward rose to his feet, bugling as he charged toward a ledge and flung himself out into the emptiness again, wings beating the air into submission beneath them.

The sky was theirs, once again.

Thank you for reading!

If you have a spare moment, please leave an honest review. Reviews are the best way to help other readers find books they'll enjoy, and they make an enormous difference for independent authors especially! Even just a sentence or two about what you liked and didn't like is wonderful.

If you want to help support your favorite authors, telling others about them and asking your local library to stock their books are among the best ways to do so. Thank you so much!

Don't forget to stay in touch to get free books like Palon, a Windward prequel, as well as more exclusive content, including bonus short stories not available anywhere else. Simply go to skaeth.com and subscribe to the newsletter!

Acknowledgements

There are so many people who have supported me in this writing adventure. I truly stand on the shoulders of giants and I am so grateful for the advice, support, and encouragement from family, friends, and fellow writers.

To my lovey, thank you for all you do. A more consistently, deeply supportive partner I could never hope to find. From reading everything I write multiple times, as the best alpha reader ever and then again out loud to help put on final polishes, to troubleshooting and helping to design swag, you are there every step of the way. And through it all, you handle my waffling and nerves and stubbornness with grace and humor. You are the dragonfire in my heart.

To my children, thank you for your support too. Understanding while I take time to write, pitching in around the house, and even giving me your feedback in places—all of this has been extremely helpful to the end product. I hope watching me work hard to achieve this encourages you to reach for your own dreams, regardless of the limits others may place on you.

Thank you to my family, for encouraging a love of the written word. Especially my father, for introducing me to the amazing varied worlds of speculative fiction, and the late night talks discussing everything from comparing works of fiction to the basics of quantum mechanics. For my mother and siblings, for your support in my dreams.

* * *

To my absolutely phenomenal critique partners—how did I ever luck out to get the best CPs I could ask for? R. Lee Fryar and Ariana Townsend, you drive me every day to be better, to go deeper. You see what my stories could become and consistently ask questions to help uncover deeper motivations, never letting me rest until the words on the page are the best I can make them. My writing wouldn't be nearly as solid and polished without your insights and passion and tremendous help, and I can't wait to hold your books in my hands as well!

To my writing groups, for the community you provide and the encouragement and critiques: you have made my writing so much better. So thank you, to you Inklings, and the Parliament of Pens, and yes, you in the Eagle and Child. You all are amazing. So much gratitude goes to my Writer In Motion friends, for endless support and camaraderie, through high times and low. You are the most amazing community of inspiration and information and spirit-inflation!

To my fantastic beta and gamma readers, for picking through the crud and helping me polish this to a shine: Kyndall, John Vaughan, Jonathan Lamb, CharlieXóots, Lachlan Hawkins, and also Timothy, Agnes S., Timothy Currey, Thuy M. Nguyen, Camilla Lynn, and Sam Hammond. Thank you!

To Jeni Chapelle for your genius editing advice so generously given after RevPit! The beauty of your advice is it's so deceptively simple and yet so very powerful.

* * *

To KJ Harrowick and Melissa Koberlein for your launching advice and pointers, and to Misti Wolanski for your grammar tutorials: an enormous thank you from the bottom of my heart!

To my amazing cover artist, Dave Brasgalla. You took my idea and you made it visible, and I can't tell you what an amazing gift that is. You've been amazing to work with and I hope my readers can get lost in my words as fully as I can get lost staring at the art you made for me.

To Michael J Sullivan, for your writing and marketing advice. I'm amazed and humbled by your generosity and hope to pay it forward.

And to you, dear reader: Thank you for reading and giving me a chance to entertain you for a few hours. Without you, I would not be able to continue.

Dragons and Bonded

Palon - bonded to **Windward**, a younger male dragon of lower-middle rank. Aturadin's mate.

Aturadin - Palon's mate. Bonded to **Scorch Frost**, a younger male dragon of lower-middle rank comparable to Windward.

Tebah - a fiesty newly bonded, bonded to **High Flight**, a young male dragon of low rank.

Laetiran - bonded to **Fired Sand**, a younger male dragon of lower-middle rank comparable to Windward and Scorch Frost. A long-time rival of Palon's.

Miros - a middle-aged bonded, bonded to **Silver Spine**, the oldest of all the dragons in the nest. Silver Spine is too old and large to fly, and is dying of old age at the beginning of the book.

Tsían - the highest ranked bonded, bonded to **Forest Blaze**, the second highest ranked dragon in the nest.

Salann - the second highest ranked amongst the bonded, mainly due to her organizational skills, as she is bonded to **Dusks Dive**, a female dragon, and female dragons do not normally participate in the hierarchy structure.

Eltavae - another bonded in the nest, bonded to **Shadow Soars**, a female dragon

Yiyin - another bonded in the nest, bonded to the female dragon **Night Hunter**

Maea - bonded to the female dragon **Lake Bolt**

Laros - bonded to the female dragon **Sand Snout**

Stone Eyes - a recently unbonded dragon, the highest ranking dragon in the nest. His bonded died of old age a few months before the beginning of the book.

Black Cloud - a female unbonded dragon

Cave Song - a female unbonded dragon, the second oldest dragon in the nest.

Sea Rim - a dragon in the nest.

Skyward - a dragon in the nest.

Providence Eye - a dragon in the nest.

About the Author

Ever since a college professor told S. Kaeth she'd have to eventually focus on just one thing, she's been dead set on proving him wrong.

From charging through the wilderness, wrangling alligators and snapping turtles, trapping and counting moles, or supervising prairie burns for college credits to doing research and training frogs, lizards, and a lungfish, she treats life as an adventure. She traded hikes, natural history interpretation boating tours, and creature encounters for the slightly-less-exotic-but-no-less-fun mammal training about the same time she began to get serious about her writing craft.

You can find her teaching herself languages and lesser-known fiber crafts, hiking, or playing Capoeira when she's not practicing the fine art of weaving a tale.

Other books by S. Kaeth:

Children of the Nexus series

Between Starfalls (Book One of Children of the Nexus)

Never leave the path.
It's sacred law, punishable by exile.
When her son goes missing in the perilous mountains, Kaemada defies the law to search for him. She enlists the help of her hero brother, a priestess berserker, and a fire-wielding friend.
But the law exists for a reason.
When the search party is captured by the mythical Kamalti, they learn that Kaemada's son was sent to an ancient prison city. As they battle for freedom, they discover a horrible truth that will change the future of both races forever.
With their world in upheaval, Kaemada must find a way to peace if she's to save her son—but tensions between the two races are leading to war.

Let Loose The Fallen (Book Two of Children of the Nexus)

The priestess searches for her faith.
The fire-wielder wrestles with her past.
The psion dreams of peace.
And the hero is torn between his heart and his duty.

While grief scatters the four protectors to the winds, outside forces write history according to their own whims. The fate of the Rinaryns lies twined with that of the boy, Eian, caught in a tug of war the heroes are unaware of.

But the evidence lies waiting for Taunos and the others to see, if only they can move past their betrayal.

Beneath the Gods' Tree

Amanah knows all-too-well the dangers of catching the attention of the upper class of Arruk. Using her position as a guard to steal secrets of healing and help other lower class people means she must remain unnoticed, working from the shadows.

Fellow guard Taunos is boisterous, laughing, larger than life-and always around. He attracts attention as easily as breathing, which makes being associated with him dangerous. Better to stay far away, regardless of her attraction to him and his easy calm.

But when Amanah inadvertently insults a magistrate, she must flee the city to avoid his vengeance. She takes a last-minute job escorting a pair of noblemen to another town-a job Taunos is also hired for.

As she spends more time with Taunos, his confident charm draws her in, especially when he uncovers her dream of becoming a healer and offers to help make it a reality. Taunos sees her as no one else has, even when she's doing her best to be invisible. But opening herself to romance might be as dangerous as the wildlife and bandits they face in the wilderness.

Yet as the end of her mission looms, she's not sure she can resist the draw of Taunos and of pursuing her dreams, even if it means drawing the ire of those in power.

(This book takes place about three years before Between Starfalls, a little after Prelude Cycle)

www.ingramcontent.com/pod-product-compliance
Lightning Source LLC
Chambersburg PA
CBHW030105260626
47156CB00008B/2536